Comanche Love

Their knees were almost touching; there was no sound save for a wind softly prowling the trees, but for the far song of a bird. The sun was warm, and made his hair a blaze of gold. Tosanna said, "I do not call you Walker Fairbairn. I call you Sunhair, and you are beautiful."

He went pink. "Men are not beautiful; that's a term reserved for women."

"It should not be," she said, then: "How long can we stay from the hunt before someone comes to seek us?"

"A long while." His eyes were skyblue, blue as a mountain lake, his lashes long and redgold.

"Good," Tosanna said, and stood to free herself of the jacket, the long skirt and the white pantaloons beneath it. "I will hang this shirt," she said, reaching to a limb, "for it would dirty itself and make sign for all to see."

"Migod," Walker breathed, a huskiness in his throat. "You just—you simply bare yourself and stand there so—so—"

"Do you not like me, not desire me?"

"Yes, damn it all; of course. What man wouldn't?"

She spread the skirt, making a cloth of it, making a couch for them upon green grass, a couch open to the sun and sky. "Do you wish help with your clothes?"

"N-no; no, of course not. It's just—you startled me so much—my God, but you are the most beautiful woman I've ever seen."

Books by Con Sellers

Last Flower
Marilee
Sweet Caroline

Published by POCKET BOOKS

CON SELLERS

LAST FLOWER

PUBLISHED BY POCKET BOOKS NEW YORK

Another *Original* publication of POCKET BOOKS

POCKET BOOKS, a Simon & Schuster division of
GULF & WESTERN CORPORATION
1230 Avenue of the Americas, New York, N.Y. 10020

ISBN: 0-671-81749-3

First Pocket Books printing December, 1980

10 9 8 7 6 5 4 3 2 1

POCKET and colophon are trademarks of Simon & Schuster.

Printed in the U.S.A.

To Carolyn, Laurie and Jessica—
special ladies in my life

PROLOGUE

Their faces were slashed by funeral black, the color of death. Such master horsemen that rider and mount seemed to share a single heartbeat, they rode far upon the warpath or on lightning raids for loot and the blooding of young, eager warriors.

Each proud fighter trailed a reserve band of swift, magnificently trained horses. By changing mounts often, riders never pushed any one horse to exhaustion. Incredible to their enemies, for them a strike three hundred miles away was not unusual. And these riders had few friends.

It was rare for other horse Indians to travel great distances after dark, but these doted on chill autumn nights, so that when the bright Comanche moon rose, all other men looked to their weapons and cursed the light while their women prayed.

Comanches hit with stunning force and surprise, and were gone in an eyeblink. When dazed and maddened survivors followed for vengeance or in thin hopes of taking back captured loved ones, they lamed and windbroke and burst their horses' hearts. And those who carefully paced more wiry mustangs were likely to blunder into ambushes Comanches set upon their back trails. Worse, men whose wives and children had been taken pushed too fast, and might find the mutilated bodies upon the trail.

The raiders returned to camp with matted and bloody glories dangling from war lances, laden with treasures to be given away in grand gestures. They also brought prisoners, for captives were important. Because war was the only honor and danger was glory, Comanches sought replacements for the fallen.

Women, especially pregnant women, and children were preferred for marriage or adoption into the tribe. They could be Mexicans, White Eyes, and, possibly Texans— *tejanos*. Comanches set Texans apart from other whites, for more than a hundred years of bitter enmity lay between them.

Oddly, the Comanches would also accept Apache women and babes, but any adult Apache male unlucky enough to be captured would die in prolonged and studied agony. Blood war between Comanche "True Human Beings" and Apache *Inde* was ancient and merciless as history, but fed by cultural, not racial, differences.

Now Comanches had driven Apaches from the Great Plains of the Southwest, that vast and mostly uncharted territory early Spaniards once called Apacheria.

Long ago there had been a great battle between the tribes, and now Apache survivors were hemmed into a strip above and below the Rio Grande, the two major bands of Lipans having to share living space—and not peacefully— with Tonkawas and Karankawas, whose own numbers were swiftly dwindling through constant warfare.

For a small taste of revenge, men from these tribes would act as scouts for the white man pushing ever deeper into Indian lands, thus hastening their own destruction.

In the beginning, before defeats caused them to scar their flesh and chop their sacred hair, Comanche never warred upon Comanche. Near the ending, there were murders, perhaps brought on by frustrations and humiliations; maybe the killings of brothers was caused by inherent pride set so hard that no warrior could admit wrongs and, instead of going to the council, went to the knife.

Comanches had not always been rich and powerful. The eastern Rocky Mountains of Wyoming were themselves young when generation after generation struggled for bare existence through cruel winters, poor hunting afoot, and attacks by hereditary foes. Forced southward step by dragging step, they came upon a tribe called Spaniards— strange, pale men who wore iron or black robes.

These wanted the Comanches to give up old gods and swear to serve a single spirit. They asked that Comanches turn into women and scratch the dirt to raise corn and other crops.

But the Spaniards had one great possession which was forever to change Comanche destiny—the horse. The Comanches watched and listened and, when the time was right, stole many horses and rode them away.

Quickly, Comanches turned into fleet cavalry with tactical skills perhaps best in the world. From the moment a warrior breathed his own scent and touch into the nostrils of a newly born foal, through handling so that nothing frightened the animal, to leg training and weight shifting, Comanche and horse became one.

They attacked in swift, sweeping lines, circling when fired upon. Riders bobbed low behind a running horse, one foot hooked into a buckskin loop, firing from beneath the horse's neck. So they came to rule over an area shaped roughly like a human heart, a domain some six hundred miles long and about four hundred miles wide—*Comancheria.*

Through the eighteenth and nineteenth centuries, the casual boundaries of Comancheria axed off a corner of Colorado, bent like a war bow into New Mexico, knifed deep south and east through Texas, and lanced across half of Oklahoma.

Comancheria was lush and beautiful; buffalo came in their millions; antelope, bear, and elk; rabbits and small wild pigs. These provided food and clothing, covered tepees, and gave tools of bone, horn, and sinew. Green banks of the Canadian, Red, the Cimarron, Arkansas, and Colorado rivers gave fruit, berries, and nuts. The bountiful earth took easily to maize planted by women, and certain roots. The desert offered yucca, whose stalks could be stripped of leaves and eaten, or fed to horses if grazing was sparse.

In the dry lands also were cactus berries to eat or ferment, other edible tubers and the mesquite bean, salt licks, and Saguaro cactus, which might nest bees and honey.

The new Comanche empire was swept clean of other Indians—Caddoan and Tonkawa, Cheyenne, Wichita and Pawnee, and, of course, the hated Apache. Only the Kiowas and Kiowa-Apache, with many relatives and customs in common, were to remain their allies.

Slow to recover from murderous raids and sent little

help from home, Spaniards hid behind walls of their forts and missions, and finally deserted them.

Frenchmen were wily traders, probing for possibilities of more than barter. They brought iron war axes, guns, and whiskey to exchange for buffalo robes, and tried to set the tribes against all other whites. But a war in Europe called back many emissaries, and stopped support for those remaining. Grown ever more powerful, their needs catered to by Mexican-Indian Comancheros, The People, as the Comanches referred to themselves, killed or drove out the French also.

Then White Eyes appeared through the land, travelers along the Santa Fe Trail, seeking yellow metal far to the west. Buffalo hunters came, using long guns that reached very far and with great accuracy. These were followed by settlers bringing their women and children, claiming lands to farm and raise cattle. The White Eyes were all fools, but the dirt scratchers more so. The Comanche killed them and took their women and children. Or, depending upon their mood, merely raped and killed them all, not bothering to bring back captives, for The People were great and strong.

Tejanos were a different tribe of White Eyes. They were hard and stubborn, banding together to raid Comanche camps, clinging to the trail as the turtle clamps to his prey. *Tejanos* repaid Comanches in kind, killing any they found—women, children, and old ones. There was never to be peace with them.

Some chiefs, unlucky on the war trail, signed treaties with White Eyes, again proving them fools, for no Comanche could make his mark for another Comanche. These warriors were their own men, and would turn away from a war chief with bad medicine, or from a council chief who gave bad advice. And those who held the Llano Estacado never sat down with White Eyes, until the end. Yet the White Eyes felt one Comanche could speak for all, and were angry when these "treaties" were broken. None of The People argued, for they enjoyed the ceremony of meetings and the tribute of presents.

When winter nights were cold and withered warriors hunched around council fires, they told of the time White Eyes came first into Comancheria. In that dim past, a hundred times of snow or more, White Eye trappers and traders appeared north of the Red River. They brought precious iron hatchets and more iron for arrowheads with which to kill Apaches; their blankets were good, as were their mirrors and beads, sugar, and tobacco.

The People did not kill these men, but soon Blue Soldiers came, and, worse, the *tejanos*. When warriors attacked them, *tejanos* caused much mourning in the tepees, following and slaying and burning food stores. Worse, *tejanos* called Rangers slew horses.

The *Pehnahter-kuh,* True Human Beings, abandoned Texas, not to return until White Eye chiefs in the camp of Washington made their marks on papers and spoke of treaties. Blue Soldiers came to build forts in Comancheria, which was very funny, since the soldiers had no horses and tried to fight on foot. But *tejanos* respected no treaties, those sons of snapping turtles, and went on killing.

Later came Yellowlegs on horses, muscled and sturdy horses that might not be very fast, but could travel until even all a warrior's band of reserves tired. These Yellowlegs had no sense, for they came fighting in the snow, or at night, and they rode lightly. They were named Second Cavalry, and each squadron could be recognized by different colors of their horses, and by subchiefs who wore long feathers in their hats. But something happened back at the camp of Washington, and the Yellowlegs were called back.

Great was the rejoicing in Comanche camps, for now they could rest in winter and raid all other times. But *tejano* Rangers returned, on tough mustangs and carrying many weapons—the long range Sharps rifle that hurled a bullet the size of a man's thumb, breech-loading carbines, double-barreled shotguns for close-in fighting, and a new, deadly short gun—the Colt repeating pistol. The new Yellowlegs, the Long Knife soldiers brought a magic gun, one that spoke with the voice of thunder and spewed great flames and smoke. Where these magic guns spoke, warriors and horses fell in clumps, for that medicine was great and could not be defeated.

Some bands, mumbled the old storytellers, made treaties and went to live on land called reservations, which they could not leave, even to hunt. They were to be fed and clothed by White Eye spirit talkers, but sometimes the chief in Washington broke his word, and The People had to eat their horses and dogs and became less than men.

In the north, the Antelope Band signed no papers and smoked no pipes with White Eyes, raiding as ever and gaining much honor. Then White Eyes to the east began fighting each other, and Comanches saw no more cavalry and Rangers upon the plains. Once again The People could breathe and make war. Ah, how they revenged themselves upon *tejano* dirt scratchers and cow raisers, who did not fight so well without help.

Gray Soldiers appeared, enemies to Blue Soldiers; Comanches stole cows to sell to Blue Soldiers and took payment from Gray Soldiers to scout the Blues. It was a fine time for The People, who killed both kinds of soldiers when they could. Again they became rich and bought better rifles from Comancheros. They returned to the Brazos, the Rio Grande, and rode defiantly to the very gates of manned garrisons.

The old men who had seen these things said the True Human Beings grew once more in strength and pushed back invaders of Comancheria for a hundred miles and more. As the women ate well, more children were born to become warriors and take the place of those fallen in combat—and worse. There had been the time of Spotted Sickness brought by the White Eyes; it killed half of all Comanches, and the children went first.

When Blue Soldiers and Gray Soldiers stopped fighting, the Mexicans warred among themselves, so that their northern lands below the Rio Grande lay open to Comanches, and even the Antelope band came down from its protective mountains to join the raiding.

Legend and historians identified thirteen Comanche bands, but some of these came together or split apart; names changed back and forth, so that some groups were known only to the Comanche themselves. But only six played major roles in recent history, surviving into the late 1800s as warriors and into the next century as pitiful remnants.

These loosely knit, highly independent bands never mounted more than five hundred warriors each, even in the best of times. Yet they blighted Spain's dreams of an American empire and cut off France's tentative incursions. They held Mexico to limits crossed only by fools and grief-stricken survivors.

And for more than sixty years, these few warriors, rarely

gathering under a single leader, blocked American "manifest destiny" overland expansion to the Pacific Ocean.

They were: the *Pehnah-terkuh* (Eaters of Honey), who claimed most of present Texas; the *Nokoni* (Those Who Turn Back), rovers seldom long in one area; the *Kuhtsoo-ehkuh* (Buffalo Eaters); high on the southern plains, the *Yahp-aheenuh* (Yap Root Eaters). Among smaller bands assimilated or disappeared were Burnt Meat, Water Horse, and *Wawah-hees* (Maggots on the Penis), said to have practiced incest.

And there were the *Kwehar-enuh* (Antelopes), sometimes called *Kwahadi* for their carrying of sunshades, parasols of animal hide. Smallest of the major bands, the Antelopes rode the windswept ridges of the Llano Estacado to the west and north. They were the most remote, proud, and fierce, having few contacts with their kinsmen and avoiding White Eyes. They killed the whites, yes—and burned Mexican pueblas, carried off prisoners; but they never swore to peace.

The *Kwehar-enuh* wintered in sheltered canyons of the Llano Estacado, some reached only by secret trails, deep in the Palo Duro and Tules. They held the richest hunting grounds of all, seldom disturbed by even their own kind. Here they thought themselves safe from blizzards and foes, their lodges piled high with prepared food and warm robes.

Along the banks of flowing streams, their huge horse herds gathered to graze or came for maize dried on the cob, for acorns that kept a layer of fat upon them. With buffalo close and easy to down, the Antelopes had no reason for extended hunts, and sat in council around campfires, retelling great deeds of war. Old men nodded and drew upon pipes, while young and untested warriors fretted. Each proven warrior's tepee was centered among those of his wives, connected to them by rawhide strings. A tug upon one summoned the woman he desired for the night.

Cynthia Ann Parker grew to womanhood here, taken as a child when most of her family was slaughtered around her. When she came of age and was renamed *Naduah*, she was wed to *Nocona*, an important warrior who would someday lead his own band.

To them was born *Quanah*—Sweet Odor—who was to become the last and greatest of all Comanche war chiefs. Grudgingly, *tejanos* admired him in a backhanded way while doing their damnedest to kill him. They claimed his white blood made him so brave and cunning and called him Quanah Parker.

He came from the Llano Estacado to fight for Comancheria and retreated to those rocky barriers when forced by hunger and overwhelming odds.

There, beneath the Comanche Moon, might have been born *Tosanna*—the Last Flower.

CHAPTER 1

Her heart leaped to answer the rolling thunder of drums that called forth the dancers. It seemed forever that the great ceremonial fire had been hurling bursts of brightness against the scraped buffalo hides of her father's tepee.

Tosanna struggled with herself so she would not join the celebration of skipping shadow lights. It would not be seemly, and might bring bad medicine to her marriage; Comanche brides did not dance at their own weddings.

"Quiet yourself, my daughter," Wise Woman said. "A lifetime awaits to be shared with your husband."

Tosanna backed from the entrance flap and looked at her mother. "Unless Big Tree tires of me. Never to be called to his lodge—I would rather die."

Wise Woman grunted. "As yet Ado-eeti has no other wife, and always you will be the favored one, First Wife. And when you bear him a son—"

"Oh, I will!" Tosanna said. "Many times will you and the Spirit Talker go forth to tell him: 'You have a friend.' Only after many sons the telling will be: 'You have a daughter.'"

Now Wise Woman smiled. "It is good of you to plan for the spirits, especially since you carry nothing in your belly yet."

Tosanna flushed. Her wedding would be prouder if she were already swollen by seed—Ado-eeti's or another's. The sire made little difference; what counted was visible proof that a woman could bear. To be barren was shameful.

9

"I will grow his first son, and soon," she said. "It has always been hurried between us, and my other lovers were only the boys I was obliged to teach the mysteries."

Rising from the furred couch of her own husband and Tosanna's father, Wise Woman said, "You have been blessed by spirits, given beauty and strength and the gift of tongues; not even a traveler uses handtalk so well. Only a wise Mexican can tell it is not one of his own women speaking their talk. You have learned some White Eye language from Naduah. You are worth your bride price and more. Your medicine will be good; I see this in the fire and hear it whispered by the shadows."

Tosanna held her mother close. Many of Wise Woman's dreams had come true, and her words were good. "I thank you, mother, as I thank the spirits."

Calmer now, although the drums were rolling faster, Tosanna stroked her marriage dress, feeling fringes and beads and feathers that decorated it. The doeskin had been chewed and rolled and thinned, made very soft by Wise Woman's teeth and bleached white by salt and sun. It was beautiful.

"I know I please him upon the couch," she said, "and already Ado-eeti rides to war at the right hand of my father. One day he will be a great chief like Tet-Sainte, and his honors remembered as long as Ten Bears'. "

Wise Woman said, "Men remember wars; women remember husbands and children."

Tosanna whirled; only a single drumbeat now—the marriage drum calling her to the side of Big Tree. First bowing her head for blessings of the spirits, she ducked from the tepee to walk sedately between two lines of gaily dressed women and children.

Unmarried girls looked envious and their mothers pretended they did not care. The boy Small Calf leered and cupped his genitals as Tosanna passed. Then she was beyond the lines and at the fire. Moving around it with dignity, timing her steps to the slow rhythm of the drum, she stopped in her proper place, at the right hand and a step behind Ado-eeti. Although a firestorm raced through her body, she willed herself not to tremble or show anything but a still, quiet pride.

Cactus flowers had been woven into his hair, black and shining hair longer than any woman's of the Antelope band. Coup feathers were placed in it. Being a woman, Tosanna could wear only flowers and certain leaves that gave forth pleasant scents. Big Tree loved her hair; he loved it washed clean and spread like a lover's tepee over his naked body. When they lay upon his couch, bodies joined, the mingling of their hair somehow brought them even closer.

Although custom dictated she keep her face and eyes lowered, Tosanna peeked through her lashes. There was her father, Ten Bears, often named council chief as well as war leader and one of the ten greatest warriors—the fabled Koheet-senko, bravest of the brave.

She glanced at other young women, some who had hoped to snare Big Tree themselves. Tosanna's heart winced as she realized that some of these same women might yet share Ado-eeti's lodge. Sternly, she told herself to think clearly, as befitted First Wife, for what respect was given to a warrior who could afford only one bride?

And had not Big Tree paid a bride price of two hundred horses to her father? Surely that was more than other women could command. The drums rose to a crash of thunder, as if Mother Moon were angry and hurling her lances of white fire. Then they stopped, and across the council fire the spirit talker of the Kwehar-enuh shook his medicine rattles and chanted to the sky, to Mother Moon.

He wore his ceremonial dress—a hairy black helmet with polished buffalo horns, a necklace of bird bones, his best buckskins and quilled chest plate; there was also the bear claw charm with its hawk feather. Truly, old Mook-waruh meant this ritual to please each of the spirits.

It was done. When the spirit talker stopped dancing, everyone else started again, prancing to the drums and willow whistles and bone rattlers, the gourd shakers. Tosanna was not to touch her husband before so many onlookers, and when he nodded she hurried to slice off a succulent piece of young buffalo turning above the cookfire. Calmly, Big Tree ate and wiped his hands upon his breechclout. When he nodded again, she was permitted to eat, and the few bites nearly choked her.

When her husband strode for his tepee, she followed, laughter and ribald jokes rising behind her. A small fire had been laid inside the lodge, and she watched its pale smoke rising, smelled crushed pine needles placed beneath the couch of furs. Stripping himself, Ado-eeti stood beside his bed, his manhood erect and swollen. Tosanna smiled to him and took his throbbing strength into one hand while her other caressed his lower belly and the wrinkled sack that held his seed. From here would come his sons.

Caressing him gently, she knelt upon the couch when he did, and lay beside him as his hands roamed her body. He had done this before, but it was different for her now; she was his wife.

When her nipples were hard against his chest and she was spread wide for his entrance, Tosanna prayed briefly to Mother Moon and Father Sun. Then she gave herself joyfully to the powerful, deep penetration. She reached up to meet his thrusts and crushed her mound into his crotch, sliding almost off his staff only to recapture it with swift movements and little moans of pleasure.

After he burst within her, she stroked his sweaty back and nuzzled his throat, keeping him prisoner within the gripping of her strong thighs.

She felt his shrinking, and his new growth. This time she attacked with sudden surprise, as Comanche warriors fell upon enemies. He was not an enemy, and she would not kill him with the flexing of her well, even if it were possible. Yet she battered his groin and wrapped him tightly with her legs, rolling back and back until only her shoulders were against the couch. When Tosanna felt him convulse and pour more seed, oh, so deep into her, she gasped and cried out and loved him.

When Father Sun creeped drowsy from his bed, his bright face still hidden, Big Tree possessed her once more, or she took him. Identities did not matter, for each was the other and they were one.

A good wife, she rolled a blanket for him and filled a pouch with dried meat and crushed maize. She added mesquite beans he could soak in water or eat as he rode. Carrying water gourds married by a leather thong, bridle and lead ropes looped over one shoulder, Tosanna followed Ado-eeti to a roped-off corral, where his chosen horses had grazed and strengthened themselves with maize. When he picked three horses, she knew the upcoming raid would be long and far away.

Lead horse bridled and eager beneath the hide saddle, her husband swung to his back and tested the sinew loop about his favorite stallion's shoulders. If needed, he could thrust one foot beneath that loop and swing from the sight of enemies, only to fire at them from beneath the horse's neck.

She handed him up the thick hide shield with its centered feathers and medicine markings. On the next horse she loaded supplies, the war lance and bow, and a stock of arrows carefully made by old men and onetime chiefs.

Ado-eeti held his prized trophy rifle across his knees, that far killing and swift firing weapon taken in battle with White Eyes. Across his deerhide jacket's shoulder rode the belt of ammunition, and in the calf-high moccasin of his right leg waited the long-killing knife. His face was stern beneath slashes of black war paint, the color of death. She touched his bare knee and sent love upward through her eyes. Big Tree's smile showed understanding before he trotted his horses for Tet-Sainte's tepee, the gathering place.

Tosanna stared after him praying that Bear spirit might give him strength, Antelope spirit make him fleet; she asked Water and Wind to protect him.

She knew sorrow that her wedding couch was so soon lonely, but she was proud of her husband and her war chief father. Sure that both would return with many honors and thrilling tales to be told and retold around council fires, Tosanna returned to Ado-eeti's tepee, her lodge until he came back. She was no longer a girl of fifteen summers, but a woman grown and wife.

Wives had duties, and tribal chores as well. After a solitary meal in her tepee—she would not return to her father's lodge unless asked—Tosanna put away her beautiful marriage dress and donned an old, worn buckskin, whose every fold knew her body well.

This was not the winter home in the Llano Estacado, but a place far to the south and near an edge of the Great Plains. The Kwehar-enuh came often here, for this camp was within easy reach of Mexicans and their cattle, yet close enough to hunt despised Apaches. Perhaps a few stupid White Eyes lingered nearby, or hated *tejanos,* whose scalps would be welcome atop the camp's victory pole.

Moving among tepees, Tosanna loudly called her helpers for the day, and although the girls hurried to hear of her wedding night, sullen boys hung back, their coming manhood insulted by woman work. Clear air and pungent sagebrush soon excited them into boisterous warrior play, brandishing stick lances and the small bows of young hunters. They had not been blooded nor counted coup upon a living enemy, that touching of danger by hand or the red coup stick.

Tosanna walked ahead into the mesquite. Fat beans became a joy to her fingers, so that sometimes she held them awhile before dropping them into a tightly woven willow basket. The silver gray bushes were heavy with their offerings, a good omen for her marriage, as was the freshly washed and cloudless sky, the plentitude of game near this camp of many blessings. An even better portent would be the victory of the war party and its treasures brought back.

Already known throughout the Five Tribes, her father's name would ring beyond Comancheria, so that even the whisper of "Tet-Sainte" would bring terror to any who heard it. Tosanna lifted her chin and breathed deeply. The spirits willing, Big Tree would soon be as honored.

She stood above the bushes and stretched, memories of the night tingling her body. *Hu!* Big Tree was a mighty lover. When she was a child, she had been shamed by her tallness; now she took pride in the height and litheness of her body, its muscled and secret softnesses. Ado-eeti said she matched him perfectly, that no lesser woman was fit to bear his sons.

Looking south at the haze of blue hills where lay the lands of Mexicans and Apaches, Tosanna heard the song of a bird, and her heart echoed answer. Her body throbbed with song, as if magic bird music had been born to her last night. She was conscious of each ripple of her flesh, every caress of her worn buckskin. Her nipples hardened for Big Tree and her inner thighs quivered. *Aiee!* He was truly a stallion.

She hurried to fill her basket with beans, working off the heat rising inside her. She and her workers were picking in a little arroyo where a hidden spring fed mesquite The People needed to carry them through the time of snows. Girls younger than herself, suddenly younger since she was a wife, were spread chattering through the brush.

The boys—Coyote Droppings and Small Calf and Mudfoot—unwilling to work as mere women, pretended the importance of setting out guard posts, where they stayed awhile, only to break forth into wrestling games or practice with their short bows. Then, remembering manly duties, they would act as sentries again. Tosanna smiled. As if any foe dared to attack a camp of The People!

In the camp itself, only worn-out warriors, women, and children remained. All fighting men rode with Ten Bears, about four hundred Kwehar-enuh; it would be a mighty force. Tosanna smiled at the picture of her husband, so brave and honored. She also saw inside her head the camp routine, which changed only with the seasons.

Old men sat circled around a low fire, where an iron pot hung from green cottonwood sticks. The pot was a wonder from some long-past raid and owned by Wise Woman. Mumbling of ancient wars and retelling great deeds of valor only they remembered, some old ones patiently smoothed and straightened arrow shafts with sandstone and sharp knives. Others carefully dripped the pot's near boiling water onto angular pieces of flint, creating arrowheads. Sometimes the rock flaked perfectly, one shallow bit after another, until the tiny rabbit or squirrel killer was just right, or the bigger, more jagged wild pig slayer was properly shaped. And the big buffalo and bear arrowheads, the war heads—these must be best of all.

Sometimes the drip of water took too big a bite, and the old man had to throw away much of his day's work.

Women went about their daily tasks, gathering firewood, grinding maize in stone bowls with a stone pestle. Perhaps they ground dried mesquite beans to make a paste; it could be sunbaked and stored for the making of stews. Thinned buffalo, deer, or elk meat was salted and drying on racks; smaller animals were opened and dried halved. Hides were scraped of fat, especially that of the bear, useful in so many ways; they were pegged down and stretched.

Because girls had stronger teeth, theirs was the task of chewing skins to make moccasins or ceremonial shirts. Other women sewed with thin bone needles and sinew, or searched out new lodgepoles to be downed, peeled, and dried of sap. All girl babies old enough to walk and speak helped; they learned work which would be theirs through a lifetime.

Young boys played games that would make them someday warriors: wrestling, throwing sharpened sticks as lances, practicing endlessly with bow and arrow. They ran races and stalked sleeping camp dogs or learned horsemanship from some wise old rider, so that boy and animal knew each other. It was a proud day when his father presented a boy his first horses, a major step toward manhood.

Tosanna sighed. It was a beautiful camp, a wondrous camp; she would remember its sights and sounds, its feel and flavors for all time to come. Here she became wife to Ado-eeti. Was it wrong to be happy he had no brothers?

Unmarried brothers slept with a wed brother's wife. She would not mind later, but now Tosanna wanted only Big Tree.

She jumped when a voice spoke lightly at her elbow: "There are no more bags, older sister; all are filled."

Glancing at the sky, Tosanna said, "We will return next sun; there are many beans to be gathered here."

"Aiee," Little Cry agreed, "there will be no flat bellies this winter. All have much dried meat, much corn for the horses, because the hunters and warriors have been lucky. But what of us now, Last Flower? If we return to camp early, the old ones will find work for us to do."

Tosanna smiled. "There is the spring."

Little Cry clapped hands. "And time for a long bath! And the boys—but you do not care for them now, Last Flower. Not since you have become a bride. How I envy you."

Putting down her bag, Tosanna touched the girl's cheek. "It will happen to you, sister—quicker than you know. Let us go to the spring."

When the girls stripped, the boys made noisy comparisons of their bodies, and Small Calf recalled out loud that he had been taught by Last Flower and suggested that if she became dissatisfied with her husband his tepee would always be open to her.

"Small Calf and big fool," she answered. "When will *you* have the horses for a bride price? Unless you grow up quickly, you will not even be able to pay a council judgment, *if* some wife is silly enough to seek your tepee some night."

His companions laughed, and Small Calf said, "I am growing. Do you wish to see how much?"

Stepping into the chill bite of the water, Tosanna said, "Cover yourself, boy. These girls do not want to drown by laughing."

"Ho," said Mudfoot, shaking his bow. "The Last Flower carries a stinging wasp hidden in her petals."

"Big Tree will pull her stinger," Small Calf said, and Coyote Droppings said, "If she does not drag *his* out by the roots."

Amidst the laughter, Tosanna waded deeper into the clear waters of the spring, her skin prickling all over, stretching taut over lifted breasts. Taking a deep breath, she plunged beneath the surface and reveled in the sudden shock. She rose quickly, blowing and tossing back her long black hair, to scrub at her flesh with her hands.

Her last bath had been ritual, aided by several young wives eager to bring her into the full flowering of womanhood. Hair neatly plaited—only to be loosened when the great moment came—body fragrant with oils, she had gone to her husband-lover.

Now she remembered drums thundering through the night, although she had not heard them when Big Tree was buried inside her, and much feasting, dancing, and drinking of fermented cactus berries. Even though the great war party was to leave early in the morning, all warriors had celebrated late, showing honor to the daughter of Tet-Sainte and to Ado-eeti.

Young subchief Quanah had led the festivities, leaping and singing. Blood brother to Big Tree, Quanah was himself an outstanding fighter. If it had not been for Ado-eeti, Tosanna felt that Quanah would have brought presents to her father and named a bride price. Standing hip deep in the cold spring, Tosanna squeezed water from her hair and thought she would not mind if Quanah was true brother to Big Tree and would thus share her.

Tilting her face upward, Tosanna thought the spirits had been good when Quanah's mother had been carried back from a raid upon a White Eye settlement. That was long ago, and if Tosanna asked Naduah for more White Eye words, the woman sometimes had to search her mind for them, so thoroughly Comanche had she become.

Girls splashed laughing about her as Tosanna reached the bank where she stood on short, wiry grass and cupped water from her body, turning this way and that in sunlight. It was good to be alive and young and one of the True Human Beings. She didn't understand how others could bear to live and not be Comanche—to never know the fierce pride and superiority of the Kwehar-enuh. What misery it must be to be despised Apache or cowardly Mexican or stupid White Eyes.

Turning her head, she saw two of the boys lying upon the opposite bank joking with each other as they eyed the naked girls. Small Calf was gone, probably to impress the others with his warrior skills, to prowl the high ground on the watch for enemies. As if any foe would dare invade these tribal grounds. Weaker tribes had invasions to fear, but not the mighty Comanche. They raided, they struck hard and fast for captives and loot and horses, and were such great horsemen that none could follow them for long. *Aiee*, it was a blessing to be born to The People.

Mudfoot and Coyote Droppings stopped playing, their heads lifted and alert; the bathing girls went still in the water, their giggling cut off. Faintly through the brush came a repeated bird call.

"Small Calf," Mudfoot said, leaping to his feet. "He has seen something."

Tosanna continued to wring out her dripping hair. "Or pretends he does."

"No," Mudfoot said. "A sentry does not lie." He jerked his head at the other boy, and they slid off into the brush, fitting arrows to their bowstrings.

Little Cry led the other girls from the water. "Perhaps we should run for the camp, older sister?"

"If you wish," Tosanna said, "but if there is an enemy out there, we would be leading them straight to the old men and women."

"But if we stay here—"

"Yes," Tosanna said. "Dress quickly and go different ways into the brush. Leave the mesquite beans." She moved farther up the bank and stooped for her skinning knife, kept always honed to a fine edge.

The horses were upon them before they could scatter, thundering down at the spring in an echo of gunshots. Snatching at her dress, Tosanna bolted for cover of the bushes, but a horse's plunging shoulder knocked her spinning. On her back, stunned, she peered up at the ugly face of a squat Apache.

When he leveled his rifle at her, Tosanna rolled at his horse's feet, surprising the man, so that his shot went wild. Passing beneath the belly of the plunging animal, she came up on the other side and slashed at the Apache's hamstring.

Squalling, he kicked off the horse and hit the ground on one knee, but Tosanna was already running, splashing through the spring and heading for safety in the far brush. She never reached it. A spinning rope fell over her shoulders and, as she tried to throw it off, circled her waist with a jerk. She was thrown from her feet and dragged back through the roiled water, kicking and gasping.

There was a roaring in her ears, and as she was skidded out upon the bank, Tosanna heard more gunshots, the death scream of a Comanche girl, the hated war cry of a triumphant Apache. She sawed clumsily at the rope and was through it, suddenly. Tosanna leaped to her feet and swung her blade in a glittering arc. Panting, dazed, she was conscious of action swirling around her—men and horses and dust. A shriek, curses, the sharp cracking of a busy pistol—and the horror of seeing Little Cry's smashed body beneath the hoofs of a rearing horse.

Tosanna quickly ducked away from the Mexican who tried to knock her down with his mount, who cut at her with the long rope. Hissing, she bobbed away, but they came at her from behind, and she had to dive to avoid being trampled. Mexicans and Apaches riding together! A raiding party of enemies combined to surprise The People's camp, and while the warriors were gone—this was bad medicine.

Rolling, she saw a bullet kick dirt close beside her head and heard it whine angry upward. She was back in the muddied spring, staring down at the limp body of Small Calf, the top of his scalped head gory and staining the water. An Apache left his horse and came at her with a lance, splashing knee deep into the spring to reach her.

As she parried the thrust with her inadequate knife, Tosanna felt her death chant rising in her throat. Lips peeled back from yellowed teeth, the Apache drove at her again, only to catch a handful of wet sand across his eyes. Yelping, he swung the lance blindly, and she came under it to hack at his bare belly. His medicine was good, for he stumbled backward just as her blade reached out for him, and did not gut him. The steel left a bright line of scarlet behind, and when she leaned to finish the job, a man on horseback numbed her arm with a swinging carbine.

Gasping for air, hands empty, Tosanna stood facing them, her head thrown back and eyes blazing. Proud, as befitted the daughter of a Comanche chief, she sang her death song quietly. She was not afraid.

"Wait!" the man shouted in Spanish. "Wait, damn you! Not that one—do not kill that one!"

Dirty and dripping, her naked breasts heaving up and down, Tosanna glared at him, this chief of raiders who had found no warriors to fight, only fleeing girls and small boys. Had any of the boys gotten away—Mudfoot, Coyote Droppings? As the Apache backed muttering from the water and shook his lance at her, Tosanna saw a fresh scalp at his belt and others being waved by his ugly brothers.

"Inde dog," she spat, "the Mexicano saved your belly."

Eyes slitted, he took a step toward her, sand still marking his slash-painted face, water dripping from fringed leg-
gins. In the bastard Spanish they both used, he growled,
"I will pull out your guts, bitch of the Comanches."

"Back!" the chief bellowed. "Hear me, you—get back
or I blow off your head!"

Face dark, the Apache wiped at his cheeks and Tosanna
made a talk sign with both hands that told him he was only
a weak woman and spread for the mounting.

One-handing his carbine casually at her, the chief said,
"Come here, squaw."

When she hesitated, he said, "If I give you to him, you
will take a long time to die."

"You do not have a long time," she said, striding from
the spring. "The People have heard, and they will come."

Jefe," another Mexican said, "that one is right. We must
be near a large camp. Let us kill her and ride."

The chief's eyes probed every curving of Tosanna's body.
She saw he was richly dressed, but his finery was stained,
as if he had ridden hard and long. He said, "Carlos, bind
that bitch and put her on a horse. We did not come all this
way to revenge ourselves upon only a few Comanche. We
will also strike the camp."

"But Don Joaquin," Carlos began, and paused to point
at the Apaches, bunching now and mumbling gutterally
among themselves. "They are about to desert us, and we
cannot ride against the Comanches alone. Such bravery
would only be suicide."

They seemed busy, so Tosanna tried to escape, to bend
low and dart away before they noticed her. A painful sun-
rise burst behind her eyes as the chief leaned over his
horse's neck and slapped her beside the head with the butt
of his carbine. She staggered and held herself erect only by
clutching at his stirrup.

"Tie her," Don Joaquin repeated. "She goes with us,
wherever that is. Those *bastardos*—do they think I paid
them so much just to take a handful of scalps?"

"*Por favor, conde,*" the man said, taking off his big hat
and turning it in his hands. "We are far from home, and
those *indios*—"

"No better than the Comanche," Don Joaquin said. "I
know, but one uses what one must to pay a blood debt."

His lieutenant swung down, uncoiling a rope. Dully,

Tosanna stared at him as he threw a loop about her ankles, her wrists. "And this one, *jefe?*" he asked. "Why save her?"

Sitting his horse while Apaches mutilated the dead, the chief stared at the naked, muddied girl. Why indeed? Why should she be spared the gutting, the scalping? He felt strangely out of place, and suddenly so. He was the Conde Joaquin de Arredondo, and this savage should mean no more to him than any other poisonous reptile.

Yet there was an odd, alien beauty about her, a compelling defiance, a certain familiar arrogance in her carriage that appealed to him. He frowned; he had been too long on this hard trail, still carrying his pain. There was fever in his brain, else he would not compare this filthy heathen with aristocrats. True, she stood proudly, certain of her impending death but not cringing.

And beneath the smeared grime was a magnificent body —tall and supple, graceful and sleek. His eyes wandered her—the high, pointed breasts, flat belly, smooth flanks, the fluffy black cushion of her womanhood. Her thighs would be strong, he thought; her mouth would be flavored with fire and fury, and he would enjoy the added spice of her hate.

"I save her for myself," Don Joaquin said slowly. "I keep her so she may know the shame of what her kinsmen visited upon my wife. And then—she will be turned over to the rest of you to enjoy as you please."

"Ah, then," his man said. *"Yo comprendo, conde.* She will suffer."

"Never enough," Don Joaquin said. "Never, never enough. Take her then, Carlos. If these Apache dogs will not attack with us, we must be content—for now."

"It is best, *jefe,*" Carlos said. "These *indios* are restless and will turn upon us if we give them the chance. And we are few."

Don Joaquin watched the girl being lifted upon a spare horse, saw her ankles lashed beneath the horse's belly. She would know the sting of animal sweat upon her bare crotch, the rubbing of coarse hide into tender parts. By the time they camped for the night, perhaps she would not be so defiant.

Beyond the reddened spring, Apaches were on horseback, beginning to file south without orders. Don Joaquin stared at them with bloodshot eyes, despising them for what they were, wishing with all his heart they were regular Mexican cavalry. Ah, to strike hard and furiously into the Comanche camp, lance points glittering and flags snapping—to slash through the tents and cut down the squealing animals who scattered in terror, to make the bastards pay and pay again for what they had done to Hacienda de Arredondo.

Turning his horse, stiff in the saddle, he moved out, telling himself there would be other chances, other roving bands of Comanches to punish on the way back to Mexico. *Dios* willing, he would run across them, leave them weltering in their own blood. And this night—he turned in the saddle to eye the captive wench—this night he would rape the woman, ravage her as his beloved wife had been mauled and degraded. Ah, her stoicism would vanish then, and she would beg, writhe, and plead with him.

Young Isabel Arredondo, his daughter, had not begged —of that he was certain. But she had died in the dirt, like any common peon, when the Comanches were finished with her. Then they drove lances through the pale white bodies of his sons and carried the mother off to more dishonor. Don Joaquin rubbed his bristled face. *Madre de Dios!* Could he never remove that terrible picture from his mind?

Not until he had killed every Comanche he could find. Perhaps then Isabel's soul would rest in peace. He would first give her this savage girl, sacrificed upon the altar of vengeance.

CHAPTER 2

Glad for the pain, Tosanna rode with her captors, her horse prisoner on a lead. Because she ached, she did not feel as guilty for being the only one left alive. The others —she struggled to keep their names from coming to mind, for it was bad medicine to speak of or to think of naming the dead. When the tribe remembered them, it would be by description.

Was Big Tree describing her now? And her father— surely they must both know she had not been killed at the spring with the others. A study of the ground, a counting of corpses, and they would piece together exactly what had happened, realize she had been taken prisoner. They would come after her on fast horses, come like the great north wind, furiously.

Tosanna drew a deep breath and tried to ease her naked thighs into a less painful position. It might be a long time before warriors rode after her, if at all. It could be several days before the band returned from its raid, and by then even her bereaved father would know it was far too late to search for his daughter. Perhaps Tet-Sainte would cut his hair in mourning; perhaps Ado-eeti might do the same, and not marry for several moons.

For they would know that a Comanche woman taken by an enemy was not meant to live for long—only until her newness was worn off, only until bodies were sated, or she became a burden to her captors. Then her throat would be cut and her scalp taken, for Comanche scalps were paid for in certain places.

So, she thought, was Apache hair, and she had heard of scalp traders being fooled by Mexican hair also. It was a pride to the Comanches that White Eyes offered rewards for their death.

Dust caked her lips, but she would not show them she suffered from thirst or let them see what pain she felt from sweaty horse hide moving between her legs, the constant chafing of wrists and ankles. She would show them nothing, give them nothing, and when they at last killed her, she would die well. It was her duty as one of the Kwehar-enuh, and she would not shame her people.

Looking ahead, Tosanna saw the Apaches fanned out to both sides and ahead and noted with satisfaction that they looked over their shoulders, fearful that Comanches were after them. The Mexicans were not so alert, five men riding behind their chieftain, slouched tired and drowsy in high-backed saddles. Only the leader rode erect—the one called Don Joaquin. He also turned often to watch the trail behind, but in eagerness, it seemed to her—as if he wished Comanches would suddenly appear.

Tosanna's cracked lips twitched as she pictured The People slashing down upon this fleeing band, and her smile widened at what she saw in her mind's eye—Mexicans and Apaches alike twisting and turning upon lance points like so many snakes with broken backs. *Aiee,* but this killer of children, this Don Joaquin, would know the difference when he faced fully armed warriors.

To the right, the sun was reddening and would soon drop behind mountain ridges to be swallowed by the moon. This war party might camp then, or at least stop for water. Tosanna would welcome a rest, but she would never ask for it, and if the Mexican chieftain thought she would beg for water, he would discover the Comanche were not such weaklings.

Her horse scented water ahead and blew its nostrils anxiously. Like so many coyotes approaching a den, Apaches flitted closer, faster, making for water before the Mexicans knew it was there. Did not this Don Joaquin and his ragged followers know that Apaches were never to be trusted? But then, she thought scornfully, the Mexicans probably could not have come upon the water hole without Apache help.

The sun was eaten, resting now in the belly of the moon, when her horse was led to water by the subchief Carlos. She held her back straight and her eyes fixed upon the hills, ignoring the cold that raced quickly down from them as she had ignored earlier heat. Neither would she look at the man who ran a hand over her thigh until Don Joaquin called out sharply: "Feed the wench, Carlos—but only after she is well bathed. These savages all carry lice, and *Dios* knows what else. Untie her feet so she may walk, but keep thongs secure upon her wrists. As any other wild animal, she will flee if given the opportunity. But since we are civilized men, also give her a blanket."

"*Sí, conde,*" Carlos answered, and roughly dragged To-sanna from the horse after unfastening her ankles. Lower voiced, to her he said: "Comanche bitch—that I should play nursemaid to such a one. But remember, animal, that I will be next in line for you after the don. And I will be neither quick nor merciful."

When he pushed her, she stumbled to her knees in water that still held a little heat of the day. She drank of it first, swallowing hurriedly, feeling the wetness and strength flow into her body. Ducking her head beneath the surface, she used bound hands to cleanse it of the trail's dust, and it seemed as if her very pores drank in welcome liquid.

They were fools, these Mexicans, to allow her water and later, food. The Apaches, those leering *Inde,* would never do that. They would keep her weak and in much pain, so she would have little chance of escape. And the *Inde* would have left her back at the Comanche spring, dead like the others. Worried that a war party would come upon them, they would not have taken time to bind and save her for later rutting. Not that *Inde* did not carry off Comanche girls, but never were those girls found alive, only their stiffened bodies with breasts cut off and perhaps a lance forced up their genitals.

Surely the Mexicans had kept her alive only to degrade, torture, and humiliate her, and therefore her tribe. She would not scream, would not plead, so the dishonor would be upon them, when she died proudly.

A gun, she thought, and if that was too much to ask of the spirits, then a sharp knife, so that she could send an enemy or two ahead to prepare the way for her. The *Inde* would not be careless, but the Mexicans might. She bathed her body as best she could, nostrils widening as they caught tempting odors of cooking food. To avoid thinking of it, she concentrated upon a prayer to the gods. It would be a fine way to die, chanting a death song and flinging herself upon an enemy, forcing him to kill her cleanly and quickly.

Perhaps Big Tree would hear of her manner of death, and be proud; perhaps her father would tell it in the councils and be proud, for a daughter of Ten Bears could do no less. Tosanna lifted from the water and turned to the staring Mexican.

He licked at his lips. "You are a fine-looking *chica,* when the filth is off you. *Vene aquí,* bitch—so that I may dry you before hiding all that with a blanket. Conde Joaquin will not mind, if I—inspect you first."

Eyeing the low-slung holster and its black-handled pistol, noting the position of a skinning knife in its fringed case, Tosanna came to the bank and stood straight, stood quietly, as Carlos ran a hand over her.

"Breasts like young melons," he breathed, standing close to her, "smooth, but firm. Ahh—and a belly so flat, and this mound—"

Tosanna did not flinch as he fumbled between her thighs, although they were raw from riding naked all day. She even spread her feet a bit, so he could cup her womanhood fully, but when Carlos began to finger her, she darted her bound hands for his pistol.

She had it out of the holster before he realized what she was doing and fisted her heavily in the belly. Still, she almost had the muzzle centered upon his body when Carlos slammed it from her hands. Cursing, he struck her again and again, and she rocked silently beneath his blows.

"Comanche *puta!* Murdering whore—you would shoot me, eh? I will beat you to death."

"Carlos." The name was said softly, but it halted the man and froze his fist high in the air. Panting, Carlos slanted angry eyes at his master. "She—she tried to kill me."

"Of course," Don Joaquin said. "Would you not do the same in her place?"

Lowering his arm, Carlos said, *"Jefe.* Surely you are not turning merciful to the Comanches? Your wife and sons—"

"I do not have to be reminded," Don Joaquin said. "But perhaps *mi capataz,* my foreman, has forgotten how to obey orders?"

"I am sorry, Don Joaquin. She provoked me."

"Bring her to me at the fire," Don Joaquin ordered, "within a blanket, so that she will not provoke others before I am ready to have it so."

Carlos touched his broad-brimmed hat, bowed his head. "I obey, *conde*."

The man hissed threats into her ear as he wrapped a blanket about her. She was grateful for its warmth, and for that of the fire, but nothing showed in her carefully schooled face. Tosanna ate greedily, quickly, before her captor could change his mind about giving her food. The stew filled her hollow places with strength, so that she blamed herself for missing the opportunity with Carlos.

Crouched before the fire, huddled within her blanket, she listened to the Mexicans talk, not knowing every word, but piecing together enough to follow them. Beyond, Apaches squatted at their own fire, muttering, lifting a head now and then to search her out. She would have liked to know their tongue also, dog talk though it was. Apaches used a few Spanish words, but for real communication outside their tribe resorted to hand signs, and Comanches were recognized as the best at that.

This graying chief stretching his boots to the fire—did he know the *Inde* might well turn upon him and his men, unsatisfied with the small killing at the spring and surly because they had gotten no loot? She looked more closely at the man and saw that he was well made enough, although past the years for an outstanding warrior. His hair, worn short, was glossy black as any of The People's, but streaked with light snows of gathering age. He was taller than she, taller perhaps than Big Tree, but not nearly so powerful.

Yet he was a war chief, or spirit talker, or both. His men obeyed him more than a free Comanche warrior listened to any chief, and even the *Inde* had not taken his hair—yet.

He saw her watching him and motioned for her to stand up. Carlos brought her hands from in front and retied them behind her back. The blanket fell away from her body, and she heard a concerted intake of breath from Mexicans seated about the fire. Chin lifted, she looked through and beyond them. Were they such children that they had never seen a naked woman?

Don Joaquin, Conde de Arredondo, had seen more than his share of nude women, but his past experiences didn't stop his eyes widening. The savage wench was stunningly

beautiful, a pagan goddess whose golden flesh was enhanced by the leaping caress of firelight. Gleaming midnight hair cascaded past her wondrously modeled hips, and
the arrogant, superior stance of her—an outright challenge
to every man who watched her now.

And every man *was* staring, mouth hung open, eyes
gone fiercely greedy. Don Joaquin came swiftly to his feet
and caught the girl's hair, pulled her from the circle of
firelight into shadows. His blankets had been spread a few
yards away, saddle positioned for a pillow and rifle laid
close to hand. The woman did not resist, and that disappointed him a little; he would have enjoyed dragging her
kicking and screaming by the hair. So he pushed her down
more roughly than was needed, and she fell clumsily,
hands lashed behind her, another thong giving her feet
little room to brace.

At the fire it was silent, save for the quiet popping of
wood; even the Apaches had stilled their grumbling, and
Don Joaquin felt every eye turned toward him, trying to
pierce the darkness. His own men were between him and
the Indians and outposted to the rear, where the threat of
a Comanche attack was still very real.

A weak moon had not risen over the mountains, and
the girl was only a pale blur against his blankets. He remembered how she had tried for Carlos's pistol and, when
he removed his gunbelt, placed it at a distance. Even with
tied hands, one could not trust any spawn of the bloodthirsty raiders who had murdered both male heirs to the
de Arredondo name, who had carried off Ynez de Arredondo to further rape and torture her at their leisure,
who'd pinned his only daughter to earth.

"*Bastardos!*" he grated, going tense at the thought of
Ynez being violated before the eyes of the servants and
her children, for that was what the Comanches had done.
They selected the mistress of the *hacienda* to shame, to
soil, to hurt—

Closing his eyes, Don Joaquin clenched his jaws, his
hands. Such a long and almost fruitless ride, this trail of
vengeance; only a handful of savage pups had fallen. When
he got back, perhaps he could gather more men, brave
men who would not quail at invasion of the Comanche
strongholds. He would ride again and again, until he found
Doña Ynez or her body, until he had shot down every
slinking *indio* who had come to plunder the rancho.

But for now his sole revenge lay helpless at his feet. Don Joaquin opened his eyes and focused upon her shadowy form. Moving slowly and deliberately, he sat down and removed his boots, then the tight-fitting doeskin breeches. A silver concho glinted briefly in stray starlight as he lay his clothing aside. Much colder now, night air sawed at him as a toothed wind sprang up, but he did not care.

Kneeling at her side, he said softly, "Comanche wench, do you understand me?"

"*Comprendo,*" she answered in the voice of a small cricket.

"You are afraid," he said with gratification, "and that is good. Your miserable tribe attacked my *hacienda,* killed and burned and carried off my family. I do not have to explain my actions to such as you, but I wish you to know what you represent."

Putting one hand upon her bared flesh, he found that she did not tremble. He cupped both her fine breasts and, when she still did not flinch, squeezed them brutally, thumbed their nipples. Pulling a blanket over them, he leaned close enough to smell her wildness, the smoky perfume of her hair and skin. She was so slim against him, yet there was a comforting cushioning to her, a warmth that he gathered close.

Taut, shapely, her buttocks were small and solid in his grip, and he might have spanned her trim waist with the spread fingers of only one hand. Her breasts gave way to the pressure of his chest and flattened to him. Don Joaquin's manhood thickened, swelled, and he told himself it was only because of his need to defile this girl-woman as a symbol, not for any true urging of flesh or spirit. To him it would be almost the same as coupling with a beast. The Holy Church forbade both. But where were priests and prayers when his children were killed?

His hands roamed her, searching and discovering, and Don Joaquin thought that she eased her thighs farther apart at first touch. Her mound was downy and just ripening, pulsing under his palm, throbbing damply at the prying of his fingertips. With a shudder, he barely stopped himself from kissing the mouth that panted hot wind into his ear.

Gasping, he swung himself above the bound body and between the girl's knees, spreading them with his bulk and weight. He covered her, prodding savagely until she was centered and trying to writhe away from the insistent thrusting of him. But he penetrated her violently, powerfully, and heard the sharp catch of her breath as he locked himself deeply within her body.

For all that was done to my wife, Don Joaquin thought, hammering at her giving softness—for rape and murder and pillage. This one is for unbearable shame, bitch—does it hurt you?

And that is for what your kind did—are doing—to Doña Ynez. Ahh! You shiver and writhe, but you cannot escape me, cannot avoid me, for I am too strong, and this is a special kind of justice. There, and there—and *there!*

Rocking her to him, Don Joaquin was nearly certain that the Comanche girl was matching his rise and fall, but a haze was in his eyes and a thundering in his chest, so that he was not sure of anything but the mighty, swirling crest he rode. Hissing and bubbling, it spun him helpless along its foaming wave until he moaned between clenched teeth and dug his fingers madly into her tender flesh and was flung gasping upon a far beach, where stars collided and the water boiled.

How long he lay there atop her, he did not know. In the distance, a coyote howled at the moon; wind shook mesquite brush, and a man laughed beside the fire. A horse stamped and stamped again. Pushing with knees and elbows, Don Joaquin lifted from the quiet depths of her and rolled aside.

He was glad she did not speak, glad now that she had made no sound of pain or fear. The silence and no resistance made him feel as if he had not released himself into a real woman, but into some dream thing, some dumb animal. It was better like this.

"Señor?" Carlos came step by slow and warning step through the darkness. "Don Joaquin?"

Don Joaquin eased his head from beneath the blanket, all too conscious of the girl's throbbing heat touching him the length of his body. "*Sí. Qué pasa*, Carlos?"

"I—" Lying with her head pillowed upon the Spanish saddle, Tosanna heard the man shifting his feet upon the earth. "I—" Carlos began. "It is not for me to disturb you, Conde Joaquin; but the men, they grow anxious. And the *indio* leader, he came to our fire and demanded the Comanche woman."

The blanket slid down her shoulders when Don Joaquin

abruptly sat up. Tosanna's ankles ached where the bindings had bitten deeply, but she had managed to keep most weight off her wrists. Don Joaquin said in that deceptively calm tone, "Demand? Who dares *demand* of a de Arredondo? Certainly not a flea bitten savage. He would have shot the girl, but for me."

"*Sí, mi patrón, sí.* But you said—I mean—the woman was to go to all of us, to repay her kind for what was done to—to Doña—"

"*Basta!*" Don Joaquin said. "Enough, *hombre.* I command; I am not commanded."

Listening hard in the blackness, Tosanna's sharp ears picked up the sound of the gunbelt being drawn closer, a faint scratching of leather against sand. She held her breath.

"Of course, Don Joaquin," Carlos mumbled. "A thousand pardons, *patrón.* I will see that—that you are not bothered again."

Don Joaquin said, "I will kill that Apache *hijo de puta,* if he or any of his cowardly kind so much as comes this way. That is my answer to his—demand."

In her imperfect Spanish, Tosanna said breathlessly, "Kill him now, *jefe;* shoot him while you have the chance."

He slapped her, hard. "Quiet, you bitch of darkness, you whore of the devil! I will not tell you again."

Tosanna closed her eyes. So this was not her night to die, and if the spirits were good, some of her captors might kill the others. She did not care which.

CHAPTER 3

He kept her bound to a led horse during the long, dusty days and tied to him through watchful nights, never trusting her for a moment, never relaxing his watch of her or the sullen Apaches. As they moved farther to the south, farther from strongholds of the Comanches and deeper into *Inde* country, Tosanna saw the warriors were becoming more brazen and sure of themselves. The Mexicans rode close, fingering weapons and constantly looking about them.

All but Conde Joaquin de Arredondo, who sat his horse tall and daring as any Comanche war chief, contemptuous of danger and lesser men. He was a proud figure, this *hidalgo,* and Tosanna was beginning to admire him for what he was—but only a little, giving only that grudging respect one of The People presents to a worthwhile enemy. After all, it was better to be used by one man than by all of them in turn.

And lying with an Apache would be like taking a snake between her thighs; if it didn't kill her, she would be poisoned for life. In the tepees, strange tales were told of the *Inde*—how they fed upon small children roasted, how they did it like dogs, forcing the woman to her hands and knees, so that they might enter from behind. Tosanna was glad now that her friends at the spring had died swiftly, without torture and not filthied by Apaches.

If they turned upon the Mexicans, as well they might, she would try for Don Joaquin's knife, to defend herself.

It would not be so bad to die, if a Comanche might take along at least one foe to serve as slave in the world of spirits.

The Mexican *jefe* was not an evil man, she thought; he fed and watered her well, and had given her a blanket to cover her nakedness, slitting a hole in the fold so that she might wear it as the Mexicans carried their serapes. At night—after Don Joaquin had taken his fill of her—she was allowed to use the blanket to keep herself warm.

Thoughts of escape were never far from Tosanna's mind, but Don Joaquin's suspicion of his paid killers kept her effectively at his side. His Mexicans ringed his bedding each night, with two men always awake and alert, the fire kept high to throw a circle of protective light.

If the situation had not been not so touchy, she might have taken every opportunity to taunt the Apache leader, the ugliest of them all, and possibly make him go blind with anger and attack the Mexicans. But Tosanna could not be certain of a way out, of riding far and fast with hands and feet bound. If her horse stumbled once, if it veered suddenly, she would lie helpless upon the desert floor until the fight was over and someone came prowling for her.

She welcomed the nights. At first, it was because she was sore and aching from long hours bareback, grateful for any respite. Later Tosanna looked forward to time beneath the blankets, while the perfume of sage and fire drifted past, when she could look up at uncountable sparkling lights of the spirits blinking in the night sky and feel the man's hands roaming over her bared flesh.

For Don Joaquin was different in his taking than Comanches she had been with. He was not as large as Big Tree, nor swiftly greedy as some of the younger boys, but there was a streak of cruelty in him, a need to hurt that caused her to respond in turn. Tosanna would like nothing more than to be able to conquer him with the tom-tom beating of fierce hips, to drain his strength into herself and absorb him with her depths.

But it was better that she allowed him to be the victor, Tosanna thought, better she responded only so much, for he was a chief and needed to be certain of his power. Long ago, her mother told her this, instructed her in the art of making a man believe in himself.

This Don Joaquin—he did things to her that no Comanche had, and there were times when she did not have to pretend, moments when she was a writhing blaze of passion. And when she came out of it drained and shaken, Tosanna was just a little ashamed that a man not of The People could transport her so. When she returned to the tribe, as she would someday if the spirits kept her alive, Tosanna would have much to teach her husband in turn.

Big Tree—she thought of his smooth, near hairless skin as compared to this bearlike Mexican, of Big Tree's tenderness and lengthy lovemaking against that of Don Joaquin's need to punish her at the same moment he sought release. She turned carefully, so as not to disturb the Mexican, pillowing her head upon his shoulder. Ado-eeti would come for her, leading a band of warriors that would put this mangy group of Apaches to flight—a band that would come howling to strike down the Mexicans and mount their fresh scalps upon triumphant lances.

If there was time. She peered up at a black velvet sky and knew that it was possible for her captors to be far away, to be safe somewhere, before her father and Big Tree even learned of the killing at the spring and her disappearance. The cowardly Apaches had chosen just the right time, when the tribe's fighting men were away. But still they looked over their shoulders, the filthy *Inde,* afraid of retribution, praying to their evil spirits that the Comanche moon would not arise full and round. For the Apaches knew The People rode at night, rode hard and fast upon a trail of vengeance, by the light of the moon.

Eyes slitted, she watched the low fire for a while, seeing passing shapes of wakeful sentries, of men sleeping where they could guard their chief. Beyond the circle of light, a horse blew through his nostrils and another stirred restlessly. The horses, Tosanna thought—that was where the Apaches would hit first, if they meant to betray Don Joaquin. They were not real horsemen and only clumsy thieves, but even *Inde* were more cunning than Mexicans. Without mounts, they would be helpless in the desert—and perhaps left to await the coming of Comanches.

But no—Apaches were not so patient. Their chief would need to taste blood, to make medicine with more scalps, so he might boast of mighty exploits around another campfire. Tosanna lifted her head a tiny bit and stared beyond the Mexicans to where *Inde* slept with their moccasins turned to the embered glow of a dying fire. She longed to

hear a sudden thunder of hoofs, a keen chorus of war
cries, the bloody yelps of *Inde* as true horsemen slashed
through them. But there was only the crackle of burning
sagewood, only the mourning of wind and the far, lonely
call of a coyote.

Beside her, Don Joaquin moved in restless sleep, and
she felt the tug of rawhide that bound her ankle to his.
When he stilled, Tosanna closed her eyes and willed sleep
to come, willed her ears to stay awake. But her dreams
were bad, filled with strangeness, and she was glad when
dawn broke over the camp, when men lifted from their
blankets and threw wood on banked coals, hawking and
yawning and muttering to each other.

When Tosanna sat up, hunched against morning cold,
she saw Don Joaquin watching her. Eyes steady, she stared
back at him, and he said, "It is odd that a savage can appear so—so lovely, after traveling hard and living in primitive conditions. But then, you are familiar with primitive conditions, *es verdad?*"

She waited until he raised his head from the saddle, until
he lighted a cigarillo with a glowing coal his subchief
brought. Then she said, "Is it permitted to go into the
brush?"

"Ah," Don Joaquin said, "the savage turns delicate. Why
not? The Apaches watch you every moment anyhow—and
how far would you go with that pack at your heels? Remember, little animal, that Chief Mimbres would like
nothing better than to roast you over a slow fire—after he
and his men are done rutting upon you." He loosened the
rawhide from his ankle and passed the end to her.

Tosanna said, "Remember, Mexican, that Mimbres and
his dogs would like you spitted over the same fire."

His face hardened. "To your ablutions, wench, and show
me no more arrogance. I do not yet know why I keep you
alive."

Biting back a reply, Tosanna stood erect and slipped her
blanket over her shoulders. Across the camp the *Inde* leader
glowered at her and she lifted her chin. All Apaches were
ugly, but Mimbres more so; his small eyes glittered like a
snake's, and his pocked face was square and scarred, his
nose flat. Thick lips curled back from brown teeth as he
eyed her and cupped a hand suggestively over his crotch.

She spat and ducked into the bushes. A piece of rag and
brown water dipped from the water hole and Tosanna

moved refreshed to linger at the fire. There she received a plate of beans heavy with grease. Surly Carlos also gave her a tin cup of coffee, which she drank for its sweetness. Eating quickly, she gathered plates from the men and rubbed them with sand, rinsed them with water.

Carlos said to another man, "She is of some other use."

And Don Joaquin said nothing, but the flick of his eyes quieted any more talk and kept them from pinching her buttocks when she passed among them.

When they moved out again, with Apaches riding in front and Mexicans on the flanks and in the rear, Don Joaquin surprised her by coming alongside her horse and matching pace. The sun was climbing its sky ladder and Tosanna could taste cold in the wind against her face, see the mark of coming snows upon bushes and scattered clumps of grass gone brown.

"You have never been so far south," Don Joaquin said, "but Comanche warriors have."

"The People ride where they please," she answered.

"And slaughter whom they please, especially the helpless."

Tosanna rocked to the motion of the plodding horse. "The People conquer the strong as well as the weak."

"There were no strong at my hacienda—only old men, women, and children. Your brave fighters butchered my sons—only children, they were; they raped and killed the women, but for my wife. They carried her off with them, comprende?—to work more of their torture upon her, to— to defile her over and over again."

"There were only children at the spring," Tosanna said.

"Nits that would have grown into bloodsucking lice. I regret there were not more of them to crack, that the Apaches turned tail before I could find the camp." For a while he stared ahead, lips thinned and a muscle twitching in the corner of his unshaven jaw. Then Don Joaquin said, "What of white women Comanches take? Do they—do they—"

"A warrior may do as he wishes with a captive; it is his right."

"Torture," Don Joaquin said.

"Yes. Any of The People expect the same, if they are captured. But sometimes a woman is taken into the tribe, where she bears children."

Don Joaquin's horse slowed and he kicked it with irritation. "Are women ever ransomed?"

Tosanna frowned. "This word I do not know—*ransom*."

"Sold back," Don Joaquin explained. "Is any captive ever sold back to her family?"

"It has not happened in my tribe," she said, "but I have heard of it."

"My wife," he said. "You have seen her?"

Tosanna shook her head. "There is no prisoner in the tepees." She remembered the mother of Quanah and thought the woman was no slave, and had never been. Naduah had been taken long ago, long before Tosanna was born, and Tosanna never thought of her as anything but Comanche. "No prisoner," she repeated.

"Dead, then," Don Joaquin muttered. "May *Dios* have mercy upon her soul, for I will have none upon her murderers."

Adjusting her position on the horse so that her blanket protected her inner thighs, Tosanna said, "My father is Tet-Sainte, war chief of the Antelope band, the Kweharenuh. For three moons he has not led a raid. The tribe has been hunting, preparing food for winter. This will be the last war party until the time of green grass."

Ahead of them, a jackrabbit burst from a clump of sage and a Mexican rider cursed as his horse danced. A Comanche horse would not shy like that, Tosanna thought proudly.

Don Joaquin said, "Do you tell me that your tribe did not attack my *hacienda?*"

"I would know," she answered, the Spanish words coming more easily to her lips as days passed. The Antelope band's spirit talker had said that Tosanna had the gift of tongues, and Big Tree had laughed at that. Women talked too much anyhow, he said, and what was there to answer in different tongues—buffalo hides, the stew pot, deerskin? When she chewed hides for moccasins, her mouth would be too busy for speaking anyhow.

But his blood brother Quanah had said that times changed and even a woman with the gift could be useful in dealing with Comancheros who brought guns to trade, with Mexicans and White Eyes. More and more these others touch our lives, Quanah said. And Big Tree said he would do his talking at the end of a war lance.

"You would also lie," Don Joaquin said.

"The People do not lie," she said.

"Anyone will, to save his life. Not a *hidalgo,* of course, but anyone else—certainly any savage."

She looked at him. "You may kill me at any time—if not you, then the *Inde.* The Kwehar-enuh fought no Mexicans, took no slaves."

His eyes fell away from hers. "No matter," he said. "Comanches murdered my heirs, carried off my wife. Comanches paid."

"It is so—as Mexicans and *Inde* will pay for the attack at the spring. It is the way of life."

Don Joaquin stared hard at her. "Simply that? You surprise me, savage. I do not expect philosophy from a brute in the middle of the desert."

Tosanna said no more, because she did not fully understand him. His language was more complex than Comanche, words shading from one meaning into another—no more than could be expected from those to whom trickery and lies were honorable. She would never understand the Mexicans, and White Eyes were even less trustworthy, it was said. Tosanna had never been close to a White Eye, for Naduah was turned Comanche and so could not be counted.

When Don Joaquin spurred his horse ahead, she looked around at the far mountains again, at the flatlands, and marked them well in her mind. There might be trouble finding water in a land she did not know, but she would manage. Even though she could not cover ground like a horse, still she would put mountains between herself and any pursuers, given only a little chance.

Perhaps she could steal a horse—a good one with endurance to carry her far. If ever Don Joaquin relaxed his vigil, Last Flower would vanish. Maybe someday, when the signs were right, she might be allowed to ride with the war party to extract vengeance from him and his tribe.

CHAPTER 4

It was difficult not to show surprise, for Tosanna to keep her face without expression, for the camp of the Mexicans was huge. It was all fences and small huts and the grand tepee of the chief centered in it, towering over all. Tosanna thought that her captor must be an important war chief in his own tribe to have so grand a dwelling.

But as the group neared the *hacienda,* she also saw marks of a Comanche raid—smaller homes with thatch roofs burned away, fences skewed, a broken wagon tipped over, apprehensive brown faces of survivors, most of them children, peeking frightened from wreckage. Scarred from the fighting, the big house kept its roof of red clay tiles, but fire had blackened one side. Tosanna, straight backed and aloof, thought The People must have gotten many horses here, and much treasure.

An old man limped from the stables to take the reins of Joaquin's horse, white hair bristling gaunt cheeks, tired eyes lighting with hate as he looked up at Tosanna. He spat as one of the other men unbound her legs and she slid from her mount to stand defiant before them all.

When she glanced at Joaquin, his face was dark, brow knitted and mouth gone thin as he saw again the scene of his tragedy. She did not understand, for today's defeat could be tomorrow's victory. To live too long with sorrow was to lose heart. Among The People, mourning was intense, but not dragged on for many moons. Wives of warriors killed in battle scarred themselves with knives, cut off

39

their hair and sometimes fingers or even a hand, and wailing at the campfires was terrible. But a death hurt was not held closely to the breast and suckled as a baby.

Life went on. If the dead warrior had a brother, that one took the widows to wife and adopted the children. Even an old wife or worn-out mother was not abandoned, as among the uncaring *Inde*. The People protected their own, paid swift homage to death, and went their way, for was not dying a part of living, and would not brave warriors ride again with the spirits?

"That way," Don Joaquin said sharply, pushing her toward a low stone wall where flowers had grown in profusion before the cold breath of winter blew upon them. Now they were browned, bare stalks rattling in the wind, much like the rancho itself. "Look around you, wench; see what the Comanche *bastardos* have done. My family is buried over there, my cattle and best horses stolen, vaqueros, women, and children murdered. Ah, if only all my own men were with me in the north; there would be no camp of yours, none alive to boast."

Saying nothing, Tosanna walked ahead of him to the great doors, one battered and sagging from iron hinges. Rawhide thongs chafed her wrists, pulled tight by the vicious Apache Mimbres, who pretended to be checking them. It had been just before the *Inde* left them, glancing longingly at Mexican horses and Don Joaquin's silvered saddle.

Mimbres had hissed to her: "I will not forget where you are, Comanche bitch."

And had Tosanna answered, "A pack of Comanche curs would not allow the Mexicans to leave, but then Apaches are not as brave as Comanche camp dogs."

His eyes had been like the black desert stones polished and used for making jewelry, but glazed with frost. Mimbres had wanted to kill her then, wanted it very much, but there were the Mexicans, rifles in hand, all watchful. He said in that whispery snake's voice, "There will come a time, bitch," and whirled away to leap upon his horse, to lead his band yipping and racing back into the hills.

So Tosanna failed to turn her enemies against each other and escape in the resulting confusion. And now she had made a lifetime foe in Mimbres, but *Inde* and The People had been born to do battle with each other. For some reason, the spirits put Apaches on the earth as fleas and lice had been loosed, to irritate The People and to be crushed by them.

Inside the house was a shambles, although some attempt at order had been made. But no straightening up could hide lance rips and dried bloodstains or repair broken woods. She stood uncertainly in the shadows, letting her eyes drift here and there. It was amazing how much room a Mexican *jefe* needed; half Tosanna's tribe could be sheltered in this great house. Yet even its adobe walls and thick doors had not been strong enough to keep out raiders. Her heart swelled with pride at the striking power of The People.

"Barbarians," Don Joaquin muttered. "What they had no use for, they destroyed. So much gone, so much not replaceable—"

His voice trailed off when an older woman came from the back of the house to take his sombrero and serape, her eyes flicking Tosanna like paired, sharp whips. "Your bath will be ready in a moment, *conde*. And what do you wish done with—this?" She indicated Tosanna with a sniff and nod of the head.

"To the root cellar," he answered, untying his bandana and slapping dust from his clothing. "She is to be watched constantly, *comprende?* Constantly. I will assign vaqueros to the task when they are rested, but until then, Luisa—"

The woman was wide and thick, all heavy arms and juglike breasts. She said, "Do not fear, *conde*. She will be here when you want her. Is it permitted to punish her if she tries to escape, to kill her if I must?"

Don Joaquin lifted sagging shoulders and eyed Tosanna. "I would prefer this one kept alive. It is in my mind to use her as—as an exchange for the Doña Ynez."

Luisa crossed herself. "May the good *Dios* guard our lady until then." She snatched Tosanna's bound wrists, yanked her off balance. "Come, savage. I will lock you in your den."

"Scrub her first," Don Joaquin said, "and find her some clothing—if her countrymen didn't burn it all."

Filled with strange smells, the kitchen was also large and hung about with many odd instruments of cooking. That's what Tosanna presumed they were, although some looked as if they could be shiny weapons. Pushed and pulled by Luisa, she was tied to a ringbolt in a heavy door while the Mexican woman shouted rapid Spanish for help that was soon coming.

Another woman came, breathless, younger, eyes going wide in fright as she saw Tosanna. Her hands flew to her cheeks. "A—a Comanche! Oh, *Tía* Luisa—"

The cook snorted. "Stay away from her fangs, and this one cannot hurt you. Water, girl—hot water and lye soap and sacking. I will not soil the Don's towels on such as this animal, those that remain to him."

The girl cowered. "I—I do not want to touch her."

Luisa slapped her hands. "Nobody cares what *you* wish, worthless girl. You were fortunate to escape the Comanches when they came, but you will not escape the handle of my broom. And also bring two dresses—old ones, plain ones. The *conde* has a plan for this savage. Hop, Josefina!"

Knives—a rack of them glittered beside a table—knives and short axes that drew Tosanna's eyes, but the cook blocked them from her. Was she one of Don Joaquin's wives, and the young one also? If so, why was he so angered by the capture of just a wife? Surely he could buy another— as many as he wanted. A man might have a favorite wife, to be sure, but Don Joaquin showed himself less a warrior by grieving too long over his loss.

Closing her eyes, Tosanna stood quietly naked while the women scrubbed at her skin, never giving them the slightest indication that the rough brush hurt, that the strong soap burned. She ignored Luisa's sly pinches and nail-raking, too.

Josefina said, "She—she does not look like the others."

"Fool," Luisa snapped, "the others were men, but this one will breed more like them." She glanced at the kitchen entrance, then lowered her voice. "The *conde* has no doubt shown this one the difference already. He will be fortunate if his pizzle does not drop off."

Gasping, Josefina said, *"Madre de Dios*—to speak of him in such manner!"

Roughly, Luisa began to towel Tosanna, using feed sacks cruelly. "To one who changed his baby clothes, the *conde*'s pizzle is not holy, but he should keep it out of such holes." She gave Tosanna's pubic hair a brutal yank. "Put on this dress, *indio*—if you know how—and dry your own hair. It is probably crawling with lice."

Hands unfastened from the door but still bound at the wrists, Tosanna toweled her hair, glad for its clean smell, for the chance to rid herself of trail dust and the grime of a long ride. She said through the black, dangling dampness of her hair, "Then Don Joaquin scratches himself also."

The flat of a meaty hand stung her face, and she rocked silently under the blow. It was nothing; these Mexicans could do nothing to humble her spirit. If they were Apaches now—Tosanna restrained a shudder, seeing a quick scene of herself in an *Inde* camp, possibly turned over to the women after warriors were done using her. In that case, the only hope was to enrage them enough to gain swift death.

Cursing, Luisa hurled her into a lightless room dug into hard clay, its shelves lined with dried foods. Huge earthenware pots held meats covered with melted animal fat that had jelled over them. There were dried peas and beans, corn and cornmeal, a white powder that tasted of nothing, sugar, and a very sweet liquid that Tosanna drank until she thought she might be sick. There were smoked meats hanging, and smoked fish. She made a face at the last, for Comanches never ate things that came from the water, no more than they would cook a bird—unless bellies were flat in the time of snows. Then they would eat anything— willow bark, cactus leaves peeled of their spines, even carefully culled horses.

With strong white teeth, Tosanna worried loose the rawhide thong that bound her hands; in a while, the *natsakerna* gave way, and she stretched her arms. It was strange that The People's raiding party had not discovered this hoard of food. Perhaps they already had loads of booty, or Mexican *soldados* appeared too soon; something caused them to ride north again before their raid was completed, else Luisa, the girl, and all this food would have been put to use. And where was the don while his hacienda was under attack, where the vaqueros that remained to him? He did not seem a coward, this man, but he would allow the taking of his wife and killing of his sons to become a sickness, eating away at him until it caused his death.

Nibbling at a raw vegetable with crunchy white insides and a brown skin, Tosanna looked about her prison. It was cold here, and the worn dress given her did not keep out the chill. No windows, only the massive door; could she somehow dig her way through a wall? She tapped it with knuckles, scratched with a short fingernail and found the surface flint hard.

Tearing off a piece of meat, she chewed it slowly. There was nothing here to use as a weapon, unless she chanced breaking one of the big pots for a knifelike shard, but brittle clay would shatter at the first stroke. And first she should find where the horses were kept, see if she could choose the best one, for surely Don Joaquin would do his best to run her to earth, if that meant following her all the way through Comancheria.

He meant to exchange her for his wife—if ever that woman might be found. Tosanna shrugged, hoping that he had other trading material—rifles and ammunition, a herd of cows for whichever roaming band of The People held the woman, *if* they yet kept her alive. For Comanches, and rightly so, looked upon such an offer as a sign of weakness, the foe trying to buy back one that could not be retaken by war. They would demand more than a simple trade.

Beyond the door she could hear noises made by cooking, and wondered if the strange metal pots were better than clay and gourds. They should last longer, but must be difficult to pack on a march, and heavy. Tosanna ate more meat; she would not starve here, and enjoyed tasting foods she had never known. Some she liked, some she didn't.

When the door creaked back, she came awake suddenly, fully alert to her surroundings. It was the way Tosanna always woke up, from the time she rode her mother's back in a willow basket covered with doeskin; it was how all Comanches left the land of dreams—very quickly.

"Get up, animal," Luisa said. "He wants you. Hurry now, or I will—" She tried to kick, but Tosanna flowed lithely up and away.

"You are his wife?" she asked.

Luisa's eyebrows crawled up. "His *wife?* No! Your kind carried off his wife, the Doña Ynez."

"Then you are only a slave," Tosanna said. "I am the daughter of Tet-Sainte, great war chief of the Comanches. Do not touch me again, slave. I will rip out your throat with my teeth."

The big woman paused, capable hands fisted. "There—there are no slaves here, and—and you had better hurry. The *conde* does not like to be kept waiting." Luisa's eyes went big. "The—your hands; they are free."

"More free than you have ever been, servant." Tosanna took a step forward, and Luisa ran from the root cellar screaming that the savage was loose, the murdering Comanche would escape.

In the kitchen a vaquero let her run past. He lounged against the big table, lean left hip propped there, right one kept open with the big pistol showing his gloved hand upon the butt.

"*Hola,* girl. What have you done to scare the fat one so?"

Tosanna searched for his name and remembered: he was called Carlos, a subchief. He was the one who had wanted her left dead or given to the Apaches, one frightened of Comanche retaliation. But he did not appear so now; he wore clean clothing, a black sombrero with silver concho, tight pants flared at the bottom over polished boot tips, a shirt open at the throat and showing curled black chest hairs. Were they all furry as belly-up coyotes?

"Carlos," she said, and watched the effect mouthing his name had upon him, the way his black eyes gleamed. "Carlos, the old cow bellows because she trips over her own teats. Where would I go without a horse and weapons— through Apache country?"

His eyes licked over her and she could see he recalled the nights his chief had spent in the blankets with her, could see him wondering if she was different from Mexican women. Carlos said slowly, "You look different in a dress, with your hair clean and loose. You look almost—human, and I know now what the don saw in you."

She lifted her breasts and pushed them out, thrust one hip forward. "But it is not a woman who seems one of yours that interests you, Carlos. It is the savage."

Drawing a heavy breath, he said, "I heard you with him in the night—moaning, hissing. Yes, a wild beast in heat, growling and heaving."

Hot-eyed, he stared at her, the fingers of one hand digging into his thigh. Tosanna stared impudently, challengingly back. Perhaps she might find a use for this one.

He said, "You were forced, *raped,* yet you loved it, loved what the don was doing to you. Do Comanche women come in season like mares, to stand ready for any stallion that has unsheathed himself?"

"For certain stallions," she answered softly, running the tip of her tongue across her lower lip. "But you cannot hope to challenge for control of the herd. It is true that the fat cow, Luisa, the other woman who runs like a rabbit—all the women here are Don Joaquin's?"

"Not all of them," Carlos muttered, then flinched as the door swung open behind his back and Don Joaquin said harshly, "What keeps the wench? I sent Luisa for her."

Hastily, Carlos swept off his hat. *"Jefe,* the cook ran screaming and I came to see the cause. This— I did not know you sent for her, but here she is, washed and dressed."

Don Joaquin strode into the room, a quirt slapping the side of a well-shined boot. "And with her hands untied."

"Don, I swear I did not—"

"The rawhide was weak," Tosanna said, "weak as some men, and no trouble to chew through."

Lifting one dark eyebrow, Don Joaquin looked at her. "Maybe you are wise enough to realize there is no escape from here. All is guarded—the house, the stables, everything."

Tosanna said nothing, knowing she could pass through his sentries unseen as a night wind. Carlos did not lift his head, but she watched him bite his lip and marked him down as one who carried his wisdom between his legs.

"Come then," Don Joaquin said. "You have lessons to learn, wench."

CHAPTER 5

He gave her something to drink, a liquid dark as wild grapes and sweetly sour. It made her head buzz and a warm place grew in her belly. It also cried warning inside her head, for this that Don Joaquin called wine was stronger than drink made from cactus berries, and therefore dangerous. Tosanna thought she would swallow no more of the stuff, obviously bad medicine for Comanches. In the tribe, sometimes the spirit talker drank something to bring his visions quicker, but that was different than warriors made maddened and reeling sick upon their horses because of throat-burning water captured from the White Eyes.

"I wonder," Don Joaquin said, lounging in his big chair, "if you could be taught civilized ways, dressed properly, hair fixed—if you could be instructed in courtesy and language."

Cross-legged on the multicolored floor mat, she put her hands in her lap and watched the man through thick, lowered lashes. He wore black trousers and a dazzling white ruffled shirt open at the throat. Don Joaquin's hair was combed loosely back and lay in waves. There was a ring sparkling upon one hand, and the braided quirt dangled from his wrist.

"No matter," he said, "for you will never walk among civilized people." Sipping from a glass he said, "What are you called?"

"Tosanna," she told him.

"Not as mouth-filling as most primitive names, and

sounding almost gentle. But I have seen you with steel in your hand, my lady *cuchilla*, and there is naught tender about you. Well, Tosanna, how would I go about reaching the Comanches that may have my wife?"

Tosanna considered. "I do not know which band, but all are going into winter camps, and there are *comancheros*, those of your people who trade with mine. They travel everywhere and are only killed if they attempt to cheat The People with broken guns or bad bullets."

His smile was bitter. "Mexicans selling guns with which to kill Mexicans. I suppose one might reach such a traitor to his own kind at one of the lowly cantinas in the town." Don Joaquin turned the ring upon his finger. "I have little left with which to bargain. Doña Ynez's jewelry was taken with her—and the fat cattle, the fine blooded horses— *Madre de Dios!* When we were not fighting off Apaches and Comanches, when we did not do battle with common *bandidos,* there were the soldiers. So far from Mexico City and the French emperor, I thought—but he was an aristocrat, and Benito Juarez a peasant. I gave money to the royalists, and my men spent more time beating off Juaristas than caring for cattle. Most so-called revolutionaries were only thieves. They shot my vaqueros from ambush, and drove off herds of cattle, stole my horses. Then you damned Comanches—"

He looked at her hard. "Beyond exchanging you for my wife, I do not know why I kept you alive. It is a slim chance, but one I must take. Yet when I look at you, I see also fresh graves in the de Arredondo cemetery, and do not know why you still live."

She murmured, "Because you desire me."

"Puta!" he snapped. "Whore and bitch wolf—I do not desire you, only use you, degrade you as my Ynez is being soiled even now—if some animal that walks on two legs has not taken her scalp."

Saying nothing because she did not want to enrage him further, Tosanna simply waited, standing erect and readying herself for any kind of torture this man could devise. But he only jerked his head at the stairway and followed her closely when she moved to it. It was like climbing a little hill, Tosanna thought, but one with footholds cut into the side to make it easier. She had a swift image of *all* the hills with their sides cut into and did not like it. It would be like putting a great tepee over the spirits to imprison them so they might never again see the sky.

At the top of the stairs, he dug fingers into her elbow and guided her on past closed doors. "Not that room," he said, "for it was Ynez's."

This was the first time Tosanna saw how Mexican chiefs slept. No piles of soft furs here, but a frame on wooden legs and covered with blankets that were thicker and more colorful than any at her camp. Thin white blankets lay beneath these, and puffy pads high up, covered with the same whiteness. She glanced around. No fires, no weapons, but mats upon the floor, and a smoke-blackened hole that possibly could be used for cooking.

"Wine," he said, and she saw a bottle near the sleeping frame and went to pour some into a container for him. "You, also," he said, and when she shook her head, he frowned at her. So Tosanna splashed a little purple stuff into another gourd she could see through and drank it quickly.

"The dress," he said, his eyes boring into her as he came out of his own clothing. Naked and waiting, Tosanna thought: Not now. There was too much unknown about the hacienda and its guards, the availability of horses, the best time to flee. And there was Carlos, who might help her if she gave him the right reason.

Coming toward her, Don Joaquin moved tall and sturdy, his manhood full and ready. He lied, Tosanna thought, when he said he did not desire her. Calling it anything else—vengeance or punishment—was trying to hide the truth. The hot light was in his eyes and his hands trembled as he reached for her. Was this not desire?

Roughly, he bore her backward to the blankets and down upon them, crushing his mouth into hers, his tongue searching, probing. Hands at her breasts, her thighs and buttocks, Don Joaquin mauled, his teeth cruel at her lips, breath gushing hotly into her gasping mouth.

Oddly, he did not mount her at once, but lay beside her, caressing. Tosanna was beginning to like the meeting of mouths that he called kissing. He took away his lips and slid upward. She felt him moving over her body, all the way up to her breasts, which were mashed over him. And then she suddenly knew what he wanted of her, what he was demanding.

Among The People, sometimes there was a boy born who walked a different way, a boy who was not interested in hunting, war, or girls. In time he dressed and acted as a woman, even to taking a man as lover. This was a change the spirits put upon him, said the spirit talker, and no fault of the boy, so nobody laughed at him or teased him for what he was not.

But this was not the same; she was a woman and Don Joaquin a man, a chief among his own people. He should not be doing—but then it was too late, and his powerful hands locked into her hair to hold her in place. Eyes closed, mind whirling, Tosanna could do no more than accept.

Or kill him, and this was not the time.

With an arching of his body and a shudder that raked him, it was done. Don Joaquin lay upon his back, breathing hard, his flesh gone slack. Tosanna turned her head upon the pillow, staring through the window where the sun was getting ready to be eaten by the moon. Was it anything like what she had done with this man? No love, no tenderness, only mastery.

But the flames still roared in Don Joaquin and he was not yet finished. Putting a hand lightly upon her breast, he said, "Do the Comanche men do that to you?"

"No," Tosanna answered.

"Then they do not know the other," he said, "the way to bind a woman to you without ropes or chains."

"The People are bound by their words."

His mouth was at her nipples, then her rib cage and belly. Tosanna felt her backbone tighten, and she gnawed her lip, finding the taste of him still there. Surprise broke through her, raced up her back and went off inside her head like rifle fire. Twisting and heaving, she tried to escape him, but there was no breaking free of his strong hands. Then she did not want to be free.

The very stars went crazy, up high where she could not see them, but feel the searing of their rushes. The bed rattled, rocked, and she clung to it frantically, fearful that she might fall off the world. It grew and grew inside her, brightly darting tips of wet fire that reached every tiny corner of her being. She burst against him, exploded madly against him, and small, aching bits of her were thrown moaning throughout the land of the spirits.

She came drifting slowly back, dreamily back, every bone in her body gone soft and her flesh singing. It had not even been like this with the man she married, Big Tree. She was weak, drained of her strength, and wished she had a medi-

cine bag like Big Tree, though women were not allowed
them. She needed something to protect herself, and now.

Biting the inside of her thigh, Don Joaquin made her
flinch. It seemed she was all feeling, every inch of her
skin alert, and without defense for any of his attacks.
Tosanna could not allow this and continue as her own
woman, remain one of The People, proud and defiant.

"There," Don Joaquin said, and for a moment she
thought his eyes had softened. "There, wench—you have
been given one of the greatest gifts a woman can receive."

She was not expected to answer, and she did not. Watching his broad, naked back as he turned again to the wine
bottle, Tosanna knew a little stirring of fear. Maybe his
medicine was strong, his spirits watchful, and there would
be no escape from him. Hands tightening into fists, she set
her chin and refused to believe that, to give way to her
woman's heart. She was a woman, yes, but also daughter
to a great war chief, and here she had more than her father's
honor to guard; she stood for the Kwehar-enuh band, and
for the entire Comanche nation. Last Flower, daughter of
Ten Bears, she must remember who she was, what she was.

Curling her legs beneath her and struggling to ignore the
leftover tingles that coursed her thighs, her belly, Tosanna
sat up. When she crossed arms over her breasts, there was
sensation left wild in them also. She said, "If your man finds
a *comanchero*, I will tell him where some bands might be.
The time of snows is near, and some Comanches use the
same campgrounds until it is done. But your *comanchero*
must be known, and careful to ride openly, or he will never
live to pass along your words."

Unconcerned with his nakedness, puffing at a dark cigarillo and drinking wine, Don Joaquin said, "You are eager
to leave here."

"Would you not be eager to leave a camp of The People?"

He stared unwinking into his wine cup. "As my poor
Ynez is. May the hand of *Dios* stop her from killing herself."

Slowly, Tosanna's hand crept to find her dress. "I have
heard that few prisoners do."

"Those animals have never before taken the wife of a
hidalgo. The Doña Ynez is an aristocrat who thinks of her
honor and my own."

Tosanna worked out that the word must mean highborn,

proud. But life was sweet to all who lived it, and it was beyond her understanding to understand a captive killing herself simply because men had coupled with her. Wisdom counseled patience, a waiting that might even last many snows; then, when her captors were lulled by time and obedience, *then* was the time to strike hard and escape. And capture by The People sometimes was not bad; many women and all children chose to remain with the tribe, be adopted into it. Look at the Parker woman, who had borne Quanah, blood brother to Big Tree. She was Comanche, not White Eyes, and Quanah would take his knife to any who hinted he might be.

But being with The People was one thing, being slave to Mexicans another. Were not all tribes inferior to the Comanches, afraid of their prowess in war, envious of their skill with horses, their success at hunting? Comanches were The People, chosen above all others to be blessed by the spirits.

It was true it took time to learn Comanche ways, to have old and angry women stop picking and beating. That also was the way of life, for wives who had lost husbands and sons to the enemy were not kind.

Striding to the window, his buttocks flexing, Don Joaquin looked down, and Tosanna could hear the pounding of a horse's hoofs across the great yard. Don Joaquin said, "They go to search for a *comanchero;* my vaqueros will bring one back, if they must bind him, then travel north with him.

"Then all will die," she said. "One man may journey where many cannot."

He whirled on her. So much hair, she thought, a matting of it as if he was brother to the bear. He said, "Will the Comanches trade my wife for you?"

Looking at her hands, Tosanna said, "I do not know. If my father searches far for me and offers enough horses and guns, then the band that has your wife will trade. Perhaps if *you* offer guns and bullets, whiskey and gold."

"They took everything," Don Joaquin said, and for the first time his voice was tired. "Before them, the Juaristas and those who fought for Maximilian; they made my lands a battleground. War, always a war that robs and burns and brings sorrows, even to those who do not fight. I have little left to me, but offer all I have to bring back my Ynez. You—you are my prize, for your father will pay whoever has you—if not some other tribe of wolves, then me directly."

Sliding the dress over her head and pulling it down, Tosanna said, "It is possible," because that was what he wanted to hear. It could be that her father had already given her up as dead, and the rites held, the spirit talker asked safe journey for her into the other place. It would not be so for many women, but Last Flower was daughter to a great man and was to have passed his blood on to her own sons. She was a loss to the tribe then.

But she would not dwell on that. Tosanna would rather think of Big Tree, and perhaps Quanah, riding with Ten Bears to track her here. Ado-eeti would not accept the death of his wife until he had seen her body. Furious at her being taken from him, he would come alone if he must, riding by night and hiding by day until he reached this rancho. With eyes of an eagle, he would see each place she had left sign for him—the broken bough pointing south, the clear print of her bare foot in sand beside a spring, rocks piled to tell a story where she had slept. Ah, yes, Big Tree would come for her, and only if his medicine was very good would Don Joaquin de Arredondo escape his wrath. Otherwise, his hidalgo scalp would ride dripping back upon Ado-eeti's lance.

"There is nothing to do but wait," Don Joaquin said, his mouth twisted. "*Wait,* unable to do more myself, only to pray her bones are not left somewhere in those harsh mountains." He looked at her. "Wait, and take my pleasure of you, as they do of Ynez. It will not please them to get you back soiled."

"Soiled?" Tosanna asked, lowering her feet to the pelts beside the bed.

Frowning, he said, "*Sí.* I will see that your father knows you have been raped by me, that you probably carry my seed within your body, where it waits to swell."

She shrugged. "I will remain his daughter. What is this word, this *rape?* I do not understand; *no comprendo.*"

"What? It—it is—" Don Joaquin spread his hands. "It is what they have done to my wife, coupling with her like so many animals, one after the other. It is what I have done to you, taking you against your will."

Touching the end of her tongue to her lips, Tosanna said, "But I had no choice; your wife had no choice. Therefore we are not to be blamed. My father, the man who is my husband—both will accept me as I am. Am I not the same woman?"

Shaking his head, Don Joaquin said, "It is my turn not to understand, perhaps because your Spanish is still clumsy, although much improved. A woman who has had another man is soiled, never the same, whether it is her fault or not. When I get Ynez back—*if* she is returned to me—of course, she will not expect to share my bed again."

"This is strange," Tosanna said. "Did not your wife sleep with others before you?"

Don Joaquin flushed. "Never! She was a virgin, pure and shy, a true daughter of the church. She prayed every day, and said confession to our priests."

"A pity," Tosanna said. "She had no experience and knew nothing—a great disappointment on your wedding night. I have heard of priests, the Black Robes; long ago they tried to force The People to accept only one spirit."

He came back to the bedside and took a great gulp of wine. "Savages, primitives with no more morals than rutting animals. Who can expect more of them? The world will be cleaner when you are all stamped out."

Stroking her hair, Tosanna said, "And you—you had no experience either before bedding your wife?"

Don Joaquin's white teeth clamped hard upon his cigarillo. "Of course. I had my first woman when I was fourteen, a housemaid. Many others after her."

"Then you are also soiled. Does not your church say this?"

He made a chopping gesture with one hand. "It is different for a man, much different."

"I see none," Tosanna said.

He drank again and spoke as if to the bottle: "Why do I argue ethics with an *indio*? One might as well discuss morals with a dog. Be silent, wench! When you are with me, your mouth is only for my gratification, and because I am kind to you, do not mistake that for weakness. If my Ynez is not found, if in some fashion you cannot be exchanged for her—then I will have you killed."

CHAPTER 6

Don Joaquin slapped the table viciously with his leather quirt. "Three of them! Three comancheros partially paid and set out upon the search, and not one of them heard from again. Could it be that our Comanche wench misguided them, sent them into ambush?"

Carlos Lopez, twisting his sombrero nervously in his hands, said, "I do not think so, *conde*. It would be to her advantage to be exchanged, would it not?"

Drawing the quirt through his fingers, Don Joaquin said, "It is possible she has an easy life of it here, among civilized people."

"You have been very good to her, *jefe*. If one did not know better, it would be easy to think she is—has been turned into—a true Mexican. But if the *conde* will pardon me, it is best never to trust one of them. There is a certain wild look in her eye, a watchful waiting—"

Outside the door, Tosanna blended with corridor shadows, quiet against a wall, listening. She wore breeches like a vaquero, a shirt and vest and boots. Don Joaquin had given them to her, unable to part with any of his wife's clothing and somehow disturbed by her coarse peasant dresses. Three moons had passed, and although a few chances for escape had presented themselves, she had hesitated.

There in the mountain passes, snow would be too deep for even a strong horse to travel, and deadly ravines would be hidden by whiteness; there would be steep hillsides ready

55

to come hurtling down upon a traveler, sometimes at the slightest noise. When the ice thawed, when the passes were again clear, hunting parties, war bands of The People, would be ranging afar. Then Tosanna would catch up a good horse—she already had her eye upon a strong stallion with heart—and she would outrace the don's men until she could reach her own kind. She had managed to steal cornmeal and dried meat, a gourd for water, a bit of rope, and an old blanket; they were secreted now in the stables. She had placed her hoard where the barn cats prowled, so it would be safe from mice.

"No matter how she looks," Don Joaquin said, "she is a Comanche beneath. Because I keep her close by me and treat her well, dress her so that she does not pain my eyes, all this does not mean I forget what she is."

Tosanna heard him stride across the room, and prepared to run, but the sound of his boots stopped and he said, "She is not living as an honored guest, Carlos. Luisa works her hard in the kitchen, and she acts as a maid in the house. At the barns, old José takes out his spite on her as she cleans stalls."

Smiling, Tosanna thought that if what she did was considered work, they should know what it was like for women in an everyday Comanche camp. This was almost no work at all, especially since Luisa was afraid of her. Old José was something else, since his only son had been killed in the raid and he tried to punish her for it. But she suffered his insults in silence, with a patience that did not suggest she could easily drive the hay fork tines right through his wrinkled old belly.

Carlos said something she could not make out, and Don Joaquin said sharply, "Then nobody else will act as go-between? Not even for land, for good land I will give them from the Hacienda de Arredondo?"

"*Mil pardones, conde,*" Carlos answered, "but the dogs say they cannot spend the land, and even if they could sell it for gold, of what use is gold to a dead man? In the spring perhaps we can find a *comanchero* starting out upon his trading trip. The Comanches will be less touchy then."

"And Doña Ynez may well be dead by spring." Tosanna heard the impatient boots again, stamping up and back, up and back. Don Joaquin said then, "Or already. There is nothing more we can do for the moment, *verdad?* And it will give me a chance to visit Don Escobar and Don

Ugalde. Perhaps they have not been hit as hard and can spare—never mind, Carlos. When I am gone, and two riders with me, you are in charge. Be especially careful of the *indio*, for if *Dios* is good, she may help bring back Doña Ynez."

"*Sí, mi jefe*," Carlos said, and Tosanna moved quickly down the hall to the kitchen.

"Hah," Luisa said, fat arms encrusted with flour, "so you are not lady of the house then? You honor my kitchen with your presence."

Picking up leftover crust, Tosanna nibbled it. Already she was heavier than when they brought her here, filling out the dresses or breeches, feeling the weight of her breasts more. All through the time of snows, there would be enough to eat here, and she wondered if any on the hacienda had ever gone without, belly flat and ready to fight a wolf over an old bone.

Giving thanks for her gift of tongues, Tosanna said in her now almost fluent Spanish, "You are a fat sow, a peasant. In my own place, I stand high as your Don Joaquin."

Luisa made a noise with her lips. "*Indio* posturing; all savages. The lowest peon here knows more of life's goodness."

"You are only slaves," Tosanna said. "Is there pride among slaves?"

Luisa stopped kneading dough in a wooden bowl. "We are not slaves; we can leave any time we wish. It is just that Conde Joaquin is—is our *patrón*, our, our—"

"Master," Tosanna murmured.

"It is the way of things, but we can leave."

"And go where—to another master?"

Slamming at the dough, Luisa said, "You are an evil women, godless and evil. You—you confuse me. Do you not serve a master among the *indios?*"

"Only so long as we wish it, only so long as a chief proves himself. There are war chiefs and civil chiefs and spirit talkers; all are served in some way, but if a war chief fails in battle, he is no longer a leader. If a civil chief is foolish, he is barred from the council fire. If a spirit talker reads too many omens wrong, his position is taken from him. Among the Comanche, there is no law that binds a man to *any* chief. Any warrior may disagree at any time and do as he pleases, ride his own path."

Staring for a long moment, Luisa said, "That is foolishness. If there were no *patrones,* no peons, there would be no order of things."

Leaving behind the frowning woman, Tosanna moved across the patio beneath planted trees and beside bare flower stems that would soon be springing to new life. In the lodges, The People would be restless, eager for fresh meat and the joy of battle. Perhaps they would strike the Mexicans once more, or the detested Apache, or the White Eyes scattered on the edges of Comancheria.

Wherever there might be horses, loot, and honor, there would The People raid, for there was no place they dared not ride.

When she stopped to stare longingly north, there were footsteps behind her. Tosanna turned to face Carlos Lopez. "The don prepares to take a journey," he said. "While he is gone, I will stay close to you at all times."

Dropping her midnight lashes, she said, "Even in the nights?"

Carlos knuckled at his mustache. Tosanna could never understand why these people cultivated facial hair, but did not care for the hair of their heads, did not grow it long and thick like the Comanches. Face hair was ugly and unwanted; a warrior's head of hair was pride and honor.

He said, "You have eyes that would destroy a man's heart, and a body to steal his soul. But Don Joaquin is my *jefe,* and to betray him—"

"Takes courage," Tosanna said, and brushed past him, but so that her breast touched his arm, her thigh slid across his. She heard a sharp intake of breath behind her and smiled. The trap was baited. With Don Joaquin gone and his subchief off guard, she might catch up the strong, fast stallion and ride him into the mountains, ride him swiftly to Big Tree and again become the wife she was meant to be.

At the doorway, Carlos caught up to her. "Wench, that you flaunt your hips that way, beckoning every man who watches."

"How could only an ignorant savage tempt civilized Mexicans?" She did not look around, but felt him close behind her.

Carlos said, thick voiced, "Perhaps it is that special wildness that tempts me. There is some dark magic in you,

Tosanna, else Don Joaquin would have cut out your heart and hung your body at the river, to be a lesson to other Comanches."

She laughed low in her throat and walked from him, certain his eyes clung to the way breeches molded her legs and wondering how long it would take him to come to her room. For some time she had been living on the upper floor, in a small room next to that of Don Joaquin. It could have been for one of his children, but Don Joaquin never mentioned that, and the room had been stripped of all its former decorations. It was bare and unfriendly, but warmed by its own fireplace, and Tosanna seldom tired of going to the window and looking out.

There was much to see on a rancho like this, much to remember about time and habits and arms. The few men left here walked guard now day and night, but were becoming careless and sullen at the extra work. A few old men and self-important children also carried weapons, but the hacienda was vulnerable. If Big Tree watched from a hilltop, he would know where to come slashing in, where to strike suddenly and overwhelmingly. She would be gone with him and on the powerful stallion before any sort of real defense could be mounted. *If* he came.

The don made no special point of telling her goodbye, saying only that he would return soon and that if she tried to run away she would be beaten. Saddlebags over one shoulder, dressed in a full *charro* suit of gray buckskin with silver conchos down the legs, he looked every inch a prosperous chief, down to the *pistola* slung upon one hip, the big knife sheathed upon the other. He hesitated a moment in the doorway, as if he might say something more, as if he might take her hand or kiss her cheek. Instead, he clapped on his broad hat and stalked down the hallway to the stairs without a word, his tall heels banging hard upon inlaid tiled floors.

She went about her chores quietly, knowing that she was closely watched, that every pair of eyes on the rancho followed her from one to the other. Bringing in water from the well, forking out the stables, whenever she lifted her head, somewhere close by lounged a vaquero with a rifle casually over one arm.

Since the don was gone, Luisa was careful to stay beyond range of a sudden slash and spoke nicely to Tosanna. The maid Josefina moved furtively around her, saying little. Tosanna took time to wash herself, to thoroughly soap and rinse her hair. On a whim, she slipped down the corridor and entered the forbidden room, where Doña Ynez de Arredondo had slept.

It was feminine, spread with softness and light, and the bed was large and silken looking. Behind another door was a marvel of dresses, many colored, lacy, and flowing. Tosanna had a difficult time choosing which to try on first, but at last picked one red as a sunset, a wondrous thing that fitted tightly to her breasts and the tops of her hips, then spread flared to touch the floor in whispering ruffles and flounces.

The woman who peered back at her from the reflecting glass was a stranger, a highborn and brilliantly dressed Mexican. When she found the comb made of a carved white bone she did not recognize, and tucked it into her hair, the image was complete.

Turning and posing before the mirror, Tosanna pretended she was someone else, but soon tired of the play, for nobody was good as a Comanche, nobody so proud and triumphant. She was taking the comb from her long hair when the glass showed her someone behind her shoulder—Carlos.

He came slowly into the room, sombrero tilted on the back of his head. *"Por Dios,* but you could be a fine lady, if one did not know better."

Eyes boldly upon his, she said, "Did you worry that I might have run away? Then Don Joaquin would put you to the lash."

Rough hand upon her bare shoulder, Carlos spun her around. "No man whips Carlos Lopez. I owe *el conde* loyalty by my oath, but I am not his dog." He stopped talking to catch one end of his mustache between even teeth; he did not take his hand from her shoulder, but lifted the other one. "Damn," he said, "but you are beautiful. I have always seen it, but never before like this. What are you, to send a man's blood racing and cloud his mind—a sorceress, a witch—what are you?"

"Only a woman," she said quietly, breathing her answer through softly opened lips.

Something very like a moan broke from him as he pulled her close, crushing her slim, supple body to his and seeking her mouth with hunger. Tosanna tasted the need in him, the fiery demand that shook him as a strong pine tree rocks in a stronger wind. She gave him her lips, her darting tongue, the yielding pressure of her body and, despite a part of herself that stood aside as if in council, knew the stiffening of her nipples and a thundering in her ears. Carlos's hands slid over her back, across the moundings of her buttocks, where the fingers clenched as if they would drill their tips deeply into her flesh like so many war lances pinning her solidly to him.

Tosanna's teeth clashed with his, and her panting breath mixed with his. She knew the swift rising of his manhood against her and, with an effort, put her hands against his chest and pushed, fighting free of his devouring mouth.

"N-no," she gasped. "Oh, no, Carlos! He—Don Joaquin would kill you."

As she backed away, he came after her, stiff-legged, moving as a spirit in a dream. *"Mi corazón*—my darling—"

Hands out, almost caught up in the passion that racked him, Tosanna said, "Please—think of Don Joaquin, of your future—your life. Carlos, please—"

Swiftly, both his hands clutched at her breasts, and the bright gown ripped, fell away from her upper body so that she stood bared to him. He cupped the mounds, flattened them so that their points trembled against his hard palms.

"Her dress," she panted. "The dress is torn and Don Joaquin will know—"

Straining her ears, she heard the sound she had been waiting for—the clumsy step of Luisa upon the stairs, the woman's clattering tongue beating at Josefina the maid. They came up at about the same time each day.

"Quick!" she said. "The women come; they will see us and tell him—quickly, Carlos!"

He moved stiffly as she shoved at him, guided him into the closet of colored dresses. In a wink, she was across and behind the great bed, whipping off the red gown and snatching up her own plain dress. Crouched there, she named Carlos a fool for leaving the outer door ajar.

Bulky, suspicious, Luisa paused before the open door, and Tosanna ducked her head. *"Mira, mira,"* Luisa grunted. "See what the sneaky *indio* does when no one is about. She prowls to see what she can steal, although *Dios* himself knows her kind left little here. I shudder to think of what would have happened if the Comanches had broken through up here, if they fired the house—I shudder to think of our lady, Doña Ynez, caught helpless in the patio with the children—so pitiful—"

"I see no one here," Josefina mumbled. "Shall I close the door, *Tía?*"

"Of course, little fool. And keep your eye out for that savage. If the men do not watch her closely, she will cut both our throats."

The footsteps faded down the hallway, and Tosanna sat up, holding the torn dress close. Tonight she would find needle and a narrow thread, that woolen wrapping of a lacing so fine no Comanche had ever seen its like. If Tosanna was very careful, no rip would be seen.

Coming from the closet Carlos whispered, "I do not know whether to thank you or twist your neck."

"It is best to thank me," she said. "Don Joaquin would not like his trade goods damaged. The Comanches will not trade for a dead woman."

"Dead for dead," he said. "Does he really believe his wife still lives? Or is he using her ransom as an excuse to keep you his whore? He goes now to seek money and help from his friends, from other hidalgos whose land has also been overrun by war, and if one of them gives his gold, he will not exchange you—I feel it."

Putting a hand upon his arm, Tosanna said, "I—I desired you as much, Carlos. You are *muy macho*, more the man than your don. And when I can—" She hesitated, looking up at him with dark, liquid eyes. "When I may, I want to know the strength of you within me, moving within me—"

His arm quivered beneath her hand. "You work a black spell upon me, woman. From the time I saw you standing in the spring, your body shining—from the times I listened in the nights to you and him together—"

Leading him toward the door, she said, "I know, Carlos, I know. And soon—I promise you that soon I will find a way. If only the fat Luisa did not sleep so lightly, and if she did not make Josefina lie across my door, with a guard below."

Face flushed and eyes glittering, he said, "The guard can be me. A rope lowered from the window—"

"*Sí,*" she said, "yes, yes. But now—hurry away before those gossips see us together and carry tales."

"Do not toy with me, woman," he said. "I am no *niño* to be teased by smiles and kisses."

"You are a man," she agreed, and eased him into the hall. Door closed again and her back put to it, Tosanna smiled. There was a weakness in the enemy camp, and she had found it.

CHAPTER 7

Joaquin rode in a steely rage, alternating between utter fury and, what was worse, an unfamiliar humiliation. Beneath him, responding to his mood, the black mare danced nervously, tossing her head and rattling the bit. He rammed spur rowels into her flanks and jerked her mouth.

His *friends*—men he had known for so long, men of breeding and stature—turning him down like some tattered beggar come whining to their gates. Oh, they had done it with style and grace, as if the very concept of saying no had torn out their hearts, but the answers were the same.

They had also suffered losses, Don Escobar and Don Ugalde; no, *indio* raids had not been so harmful to them, living so far from the border as they did. But the revolution, you know—looting by *soldados* of both armies, thefts by deserters and camp followers, so many cattle butchered for food and paid for by worthless pieces of paper signed by this officer or that.

Why, Don Escobar had said sadly, toying thin fingers into a trimmed white beard, why—the only horses left to him were those his vaqueros managed to hide. And Don Ugalde thought perhaps, just perhaps, he might lend a helping hand by driving a few of the spring calf crop to Hacienda de Arredondo, but as for gold or silver—those accursed Juaristas had forced him to contribute to the cause until there was nothing left to give. Ah, who would have thought that those bands of ragged peons would overcome royal troops?

Spurring the mare into a short lope, Joaquin moved ahead of the others. A man like the *capitán* who followed, a foreigner, a sly vulture come to fatten upon the lifeblood of a nation: there was gold in the man's saddlebags, much gold. Joaquin had seen it, and the sight angered him even more. That a gringo should benefit from the war, while an aristocrat suffered. Where had these hired *pistoleros* been, such mercenaries, when his rancho was under attack? Looting, killing, and burning—no better than Comanches, any of them.

Now they would further offend his pride by insisting upon "escorting" him back to his casa, in the name of protecting him from ranging bands of Juaristas who might mistake his loyalties to the new government. What this *capitán* gringo probably had in mind was more booty for the grinning wolves who rode at his back. Although the gringo claimed a title, the four with him were certainly *bandidos*, rough and common men who knew nothing of courtesy and cared less. They might even be *comancheros*, Joaquin thought, filling their time between trading missions with the *indios*. But they would find nothing of value at the rancho.

He looked at the sky. Ynez—where are you now? Have you taken the path of honor and destroyed yourself rather than live with the shame of rape? It is what the wife of a hidalgo would do, to save her husband's name.

But Joaquin hoped not. Despite what happened, he would take her back, and if one tiny whisper reached other ears about her captivity, he would flay the hide and have the tongue from the peon who dared speak so. Of course, he would not bed with her again, but to those beyond the bedroom door, Doña Ynez would remain the same respectable woman she had always been, revered for her wifely chastity and impeccable blood lines.

Behind him, he heard the quickening beat of a loping horse. The gringo wasn't going to let him get very far ahead. Frowning, Joaquin immediately slowed his horse and pretended great interest in the sky, in the low ridge of far blue mountains. The other horse changed gaits also, and Joaquin gritted his teeth. Audacity piled upon impertinence by this foreign *pistolero;* it would not have been thus in the old days. Such men would have swung high as an example to others, with vultures circling, eager to get at staring dead eyes.

His mare's ears pricked forward and his hand tightened

upon the carbine across his knees. A jackrabbit zigzagged from the sagebrush and dipped behind a dune. Wild things, Joaquin thought, and the image of Tosanna rose behind his eyes. He tried to shake her away, but with no more success than usual. She clung to his mind and swam in his blood, and when he breathed deeply, she became the memory of sweet wild scents quivering, the woman musk of her compelling, powerful.

The Comanche woman was a sleek animal, mysterious and fascinating, but still an animal, for all her beauty. A serpent possessed a certain kind of beauty also. Always, when desire struck at his belly and clogged his throat, always he had that first moment of guilt, as if he was about to commit a mortal sin, about to couple with a lower form of life. But then, the flashing of those black, exotically slanted eyes, the dampness of a ripe mouth gone soft and redly waiting—and all else was swept from his head, leaving only his savage, driven need for her body.

He could see her face in the sky—high cheekbones, the proud way she held her head, defiance in every line of her, a challenge to any male to prove his manhood. Joaquin forced her image from his mind by turning in the saddle and looking back at the five *pistoleros* following. There was the *capitán* in the lead, four lean wolves at his back, hungry and alert; two more gringos and a pair of bandoliered *bandidos*.

Turning again, he saw his red-topped hacienda in the distance, heritage of his father's father that might pass from his hands. Officials in Mexico City had to be reached, given presents, closer bureaucrats seen to, bribed not to tax the hacienda away from him. Money; it all came down to money—even the unconquered look in the Comanche woman's eyes after he had taken his rioting fill of her honeyed mouth and grasping thighs, after sweat dried upon their joined bellies.

Don Joaquin de Arredondo was not certain as he might have been, with the family lands secure, cattle herds fat and safe, the strong box full. *Dios!* That it should come to this. His family had not been *mestizos,* no blood crossed with *indios* to be called Mexicans, but pure Spaniards, descended directly from the *conquistadores*. Ten thousand acres had been granted the de Arredondos for services to the Crown, and for more than a hundred years his family had improved the land, crossed imported bulls upon scrawny longhorns to grow better beef. They had brought in Andalusian stallions to infuse hot blood into mustang mares.

Once, near a hundred vaqueros patrolled the land, their wives and children living safe and happy in small, whitewashed huts that added another wall of protection around the *casa grande*. The women served as maids, cooks, and seamstresses, as weavers and cleaners, washing and ironing clothes for all. *Muchachos* helped about the stables, girls in the fields; older lads learned blacksmithing and the making of adobe blocks.

The *hacienda* was a city unto itself—no, a small nation, whose *patrón* ruled with a kind but firm hand. It had its own army, before some ungrateful peons slipped away to join the Juaristas, before so many were lost to *indios* and *bandidos*. It had once been self-supporting, with many days of *fiestas*, all newborn, even the lowliest, blessed by the hacienda's own padre in the beautiful chapel built by Don Joaquin's ancestors and only recently enriched by Doña Ynez.

He controlled himself in time and did not rowel his horse savagely. The *indio* sons of animal whores had taken the gold candlesticks and velvet brocades from the altar; they smashed statues of the Holy Virgin and the Christ Child; in a final desecration, they pissed the walls and lovingly carved pews. Even the baptismal font had not been spared.

Now, always the doubt, the worry crept in, and he could not wholly dedicate himself to draining the fiery lust from Tosanna. But he would, he promised himself; sooner or later the wench would beg, cry out, enough, enough!

And by then, *Dios* willing, some arrangement might have been made to exchange her for Doña Ynez. This Tosanna, this Last Flower of the Comanches, would be gone, and good riddance. Another young mistress, perhaps two of them chosen from the remaining peons, and all would be as it had been, with Joaquin in complete control of himself and of his destiny.

There was a horse beside him, and Joaquin glanced at its rider from the corners of his eyes. A big man and raffish, battle and travel stained to be sure, but with a certain carriage about him and his shabby finery. Perhaps it was as this gringo claimed—that he carried a title from another country—and perhaps not; these days, even ludicrous peasants in Mexico City were giving high titles to themselves: El Presidente, General of the Armies, Protector of the Poor.

In execrable Spanish, the man said, "Your home, señor? A magnificent rancho."

"It was once," Joaquin said, "before the so-called liberation by Juarez, before *pistoleros* and Comanches."

"Hardly the same," Colonel Sir John Stafford said, "but I can appreciate your viewpoint."

Joaquin reined in his mare. *"Está bien;* I am at home, and therefore do not require an escort."

Lifting a reddish eyebrow, Stafford said, "Don Escobar feared for your safety as I fear the discomfort of my men —if they are forced to travel on without food and rest."

A cunning one, Joaquin realized, a man who knew just where to strike—at a hidalgo's pride for his hospitality. "Come then," Joaquin said, and legged his horse toward the hacienda, his eyes swiftly checking the outpost guards, seeing the man upon the roof beside a chimney. Sunlight winked from a gun barrel near the stables, and Joaquin thought the *capitán* riding beside him would approve of such security. Angrily, he told himself he did not give a damn.

Carlos came from the front of the house, pistol in hand, and old José hobbled from the barn to take Joaquin's horse. Stiffly, Joaquin dismounted, aching from long days in the saddle and his disappointments, resentful at his foreman for using the front door of the house, as if he were a member of the family or an honored guest.

Two quick strides and he was facing Carlos as the man slid his pistol back into its holster. "She is here?"

Blinking, Carlos asked, "The Comanche?" and stared at the other men climbing from their saddles.

"Who else, fool? If you have allowed her to escape—"

"No, no, *conde,*" Carlos said hastily. "The woman is here and safe, just as you left her." Lowering his voice, he asked, *"Patrón,* are these *bandidos—*"

"Merely an escort provided by Don Escobar," Joaquin snapped. He could not see Tosanna's face at any of the windows. "See to their wants, their horses. The *capitán*— guide him into the house, but by the kitchen door. The kitchen door, Carlos."

The man's eyes shifted and fell. Mumbling apologies, he moved to the *pistoleros,* but as Joaquin walked toward his shaded *galería,* he glanced back and caught a calculating set to Carlos's mouth. So? Was he to also expect treachery now, piled atop everything else?

Slapping dust from his clothing, he went through the *sala grande*, nodding in response to Luisa's excited greeting, to Josefina's shy welcome. Up the stairs then, removing his jacket and touching the buckle of his gun belt, but not removing it yet. Where was the wench?

He turned at the landing and shouted instructions for hot water and clean clothing; Tosanna still had not appeared. Was she deliberately taunting him, or was it something else—some betrayal with one of the riders? With Carlos? Not Carlos; the man might desert for greener fields, but he had not the courage to trifle with Don Joaquin's mistress.

She stood inside the doorway to his room, trim and lithe in breeches and shirt, the special boots she had finally learned to wear. Chin high, sloe eyes steady, Tosanna faced him with the hint of a smile upon her rich lips. Fighting down the tacit admission of how much he had missed her body against his, Joaquin curtly ordered her to ready his tub and stand by with towels, to bring cigarillos and wine.

Without a word, she did his bidding, and for some reason he carried his gun belt with him into the bath, placing it on tiles beside the high wooden tub. Did Tosanna's eyes linger upon his bared body? Despite himself, Joaquin felt a surging of desire in his loins and covered it by shouting at Josefina for more hot water.

Tosanna spoke, after he had lathered himself from head to foot. "You bring White Eyes."

"As I please. Do gringos bother you, woman? You are right, for these are not to be trusted, these *pistoleros* for hire."

"Three White Eyes," she said quietly, "and two *comancheros.*"

Wiping soap from his face Joaquin said sharply, *"Comancheros?* You know this for certain?"

"I think I have seen one of them before—the man who slinks like a coyote. He has traded with my people, but not for two, three winters."

Joaquin grunted. "He has been too busy feeding off the supine body of Mexico with the other jackals. But now, *por Dios*—this may be my opportunity. To send him north, where he may search the tribes—"

Tosanna said, "This will anger you, but it should be

said. Your wife—if she has not been taken into a tribe, she is long dead."

He reached up to strike her with a wet palm. She did not flinch, but her eyes stabbed down at him. "This is so, whether you wish it or not."

Standing up, lifted dripping from the tub, he took a towel from her. "But it is possible she has been adopted, that—that she will soon bear"—he swallowed and forced out the words—"bear some savage's child?"

"It is possible," Tosanna admitted, handing him another towel and ignoring the sting of her cheek. "But this coyote *comanchero,* can he be hired to risk his life? His saddlebags are full, and it will take much gold to tempt him. Even so—"

"There are ways to keep him faithful," Joaquin said harshly. "But you concern yourself overmuch with my family, wench."

"So that I may be returned to my own people," she said.

Damn her, Joaquin thought—so cold and logical and considering herself equal to any man. Yet in bed such a bundle of blazing fury, a sorceress who would conquer a strong man and bind him with the fires of her belly.

"The forbidden room," he said. "Go there and choose a gown, combs. Only cheap jewelry is left, but rouge your lips—just slightly, mind you. This night you shall sit at table with me—and the gringo *capitán.* See that you attempt to act as if you are indeed a lady, and perhaps—just perhaps—I may tempt the gringo into assisting me. Call Josefina, so she may tend your hair and instruct you how to dress."

Tosanna stared at him, wondering what was in his head, wondering what use she would be to him in his plan for the *comanchero* and the gringo chief. His back was to her, muscled and glowing from his bath; strong thighed he was and lean. If only there wasn't so much hair.

Hurrying to Doña Ynez's bedroom, she lifted a window to clear musty air. A tepee never smelled and felt closed in like this; good air always came fingering through a tepee even in deepest winter. She went to the rack of dresses; her fingers stroking, lingering especially upon the gown she had worn before, in secret. Its rip hardly showed, and she remembered Carlos that day when he tore its top from her body, when he cupped her breasts and strained her body to his.

Only with the help of the spirits had she kept Carlos from her—the spirits and Luisa hovering jealously near, a *dueña* of her own appointing. When it was not suspicious Luisa slipping about, quick eyes missing nothing, it was Josefina—if not the girl, then the hard-faced old stableman, José. All seemed eager to carry a tale to their *patrón,* to rid themselves of the savage in their midst.

Tosanna's hand paused at a shining gray-black dress, then passed on; it was too like the color of mourning ash and the black eye slashes of war. A white one then, made of some magical cloth that sparkled like a thousand tiny stars.

When she slid it over her head, her upper body filled out the dress with its added flesh, and the shimmering flow clung all the way to her hips before dropping in a spectacular flare around her ankles. Turning before the full-length mirror, Tosanna noticed an opening on the left, a sly parting that allowed her leg to peek out.

"Madre mía!" gasped Josefina, dropping comb and brush in a clatter at the doorway. "You seem—you look like a highborn señora, in truth. I—I cannot believe what I see. I—"

"Get in here, girl," Tosanna commanded. "Don Joaquin wishes my hair done Mexican fashion, and quickly."

"Sí," the girl whispered, *"sí,* but who would have thought—"

Snatching the comb from her, Tosanna ran it furiously through her hair. She had bathed this morning and used the flower soap upon her hair; it floated like storm clouds about her bared shoulders, but not angrily as those rain clouds which gathered over the flinty mountains of Comancheria. No—it drifted, glistened so that a raven wheeling against the sun might be ashamed of its own plumage.

"This," she said to the mirror, to the maid. "Is this the manner?"

Almost whimpering, Josefina said, "Sometimes Doña Ynez—may the good *Dios* rest her soul—she piled it atop her head."

Tosanna swept her hair up, stared at its picture in the glass, and let it fall again. "I do not like it so. The combs, the white combs—how are they worn?"

Hand trembling, Josefina found ivory combs and placed them. "You—if you were not a Comanche devil, one would say you are—are beautiful."

"Ah," Tosanna said, and no more. Stirring in the dressing table, she discovered bright and shining things—neck pieces, rings like captured moonlight, other decorations in pairs which she weighed in her hands, frowning.

"*Pendientes*," Josefina murmured, "earrings. But you—your ear lobes are not pierced. You cannot wear them."

Tosanna looked up at the girl, holding the gleaming baubles at her ears. "There must be small holes here for them?"

"*Sí, sen*—yes."

"Then pierce them," Tosanna said. "Make the holes."

Josefina's breath gusted out. "But—but it is never done so. No woman ever wears earrings just after her lobes are pierced. There are little sticks to be worn, and the pain. *Verdad*, Comanche—in truth, no woman does this."

"No *Mexican* woman," Tosanna answered. "This needle —if you show me how—"

Crossing herself, Josefina took the needle from her and passed it through the flame of a candle. "*Madre de Dios*, forgive me. Señora, if the pain is too much, cry out and I will—"

Tosanna smiled whitely, and held the smile while the girl's shaking hand pressed the needle point through one lobe, then the other. Josefina hurried away then, only to return with cold water and cloths.

"For the blood," she said, and blinked at the easy smile yet riding Tosanna's lips. "When the loops are passed through, it will hurt even more."

"I am of the Kwehar-enuh," Tosanna said. "Pain does not control us; we control pain. And this—flea bites, Josefina; no more."

She looked into the girl's eyes, really looked into them, and for the first time found respect there, and perhaps something more; perhaps there was also the beginning of friendship. Tosanna patted Josefina's hands. "*Gracias*. Without your help and knowledge, I would not be as your *patrón* wishes me to be. The *pendientes* are beautiful. One of these neck pieces or two?"

Josefina held a necklace against Tosanna's throat. "Only one; this one I think. It calls more attention to your—your breasts."

"So," Tosanna murmured, "you are no girl, but a woman. Again I thank you."

Reddening, the maid scurried to look for shoes and

found an older pair that would fit Tosanna's feet, but tightly. "You cannot wear the boots," she said. "The first backward swing of that skirt would show them. These will be uncomfortable, but if you do not walk much, do not dance—" Josefina put a hand to her mouth. *"Pardone;* I forget myself, but it is so much like readying Doña Ynez for a fiesta—"

Eyes filling with sudden tears, the girl turned away and Tosanna touched her shoulder. "I understand, Josefina. I also have lost loved ones to war. My mother, a brother, many friends."

"La guerra," Josefina said bitterly. "It is the same for you then? This thing of men and cruelty—this war? Mexican and Apache and Comanche?"

"A thing of men," Tosanna agreed, "but sometimes the women must be stronger, *sí?"*

Walking carefully in the strange shoes, ignoring the drag of earrings in fresh wounds, she made her way down the great stairs to learn what sly plan Don Joaquin had in mind for her.

CHAPTER 8

Colonel Sir John Stafford lolled at ease in a chair whose intricately carved arms had been splintered and patched back together. Idly, his eyes roamed the great room, picking out dimples in adobe walls which were daubed-over bullet tracks, and over there stains yet showed, despite obvious efforts to wash them out.

He was used to such markings, for he dealt in broken things: armies and horses and men. Helping himself to more unoffered wine, Stafford rubbed his unshaven chin and grinned. This had been his first time to lead unmitigated rabble against royalty, though. Always before, he'd been for one sort of prince or pretender against another of the same type. Lose or win, and overturned thrones were never real changes for a mercenary, except that defeated leaders had best hie themselves swiftly from the country. Even if your side won, no half-bright new king or emperor felt easy with foreign mercenaries, if he could hire them, so could the next would be ruler.

Looking into his wine glass, Stafford considered his new position. Of course, it was always nice to be on the winning side, since the loot was so much better. But his peers in England would no doubt frown upon his assistance, small though it had been, in displacing Maximilian from the throne of Mexico.

"Damme," Stafford muttered. "Word is certain to reach the court. Too many flapping tongues in any part of the world, yes." And the old duke would be furious, bristling his mustaches and stamping about as if the unpardonable sin had been committed. One Sir John Stafford would be about as popular as the black plague.

Oh, well. He sipped the good wine and stretched booted legs. There would be another war somewhere; there usually was. If he could offer his services to some pasha or sheik, or whatever it was Wog aristocrats called themselves, may-hap the duke and those at court privy to the Queen's ear would forget a bygone peccadillo.

Then Stafford remembered Viscount Palmerston, and knew damned well that frozen-faced prig would *never* forget. The wine tasted sour in Stafford's mouth. If he ever expected to go home, it had to be high on a crest of pub-lic—and royal—acclaim. The booty in his saddlebags was nowhere near enough to make a contribution to the Crown; a decidedly healthy reward for his services, to be sure, but it would not make a ripple in the Thames.

Turning his head, he sniffed at delicious odors wafting from the kitchen he'd been led through. The slight had not been lost upon him, but Stafford only shrugged. Mayhap he had better become used to snubs, if some miracle didn't come his way, and he was no believer in the occult. A well-balanced pistol and a sturdy blade—there the Staffords al-ways put their trust—never in the fortunes of man, the lips of a woman, or the gratitude of a queen.

"Please," Don Joaquin's cold voice said from the stair-way, "help yourself to more wine. *Los indios* did not reach my cellars."

Lazily, Stafford watched the man come strutting into the room. Even over here, bankrupt aristocrats had learned to put on a good face and pretend they could scatter golden sovereigns like seeds if they but wished. This Mexican's purse was empty, his coffers bottomed out, but he walked as if he owned the world.

Stafford said, "An excellent wine, equal to any found in the courts of Europe; I congratulate your vintner."

Don Joaquin blinked. Despite his nasal mispronuncia-tions, this foreigner had a way with words. "And you have been to many courts of Europe?"

"Most of them," Stafford nodded, "small and large."

"Visiting as a"—Joaquin's lip curled— "a *pistolero?*"

Comfortably, Stafford said, "Yes—or mercenary, if you please. An honorable profession, Don. Englishmen, Dutchmen, French, and—ah, yes—even Spaniards have hired their swords."

Joaquin poured wine into a cracked goblet. "You speak of honor, Englishman, but do those riding with you know the word?"

Stafford laughed. "Probably not; they are better acquainted with fear and retribution. But fighting men they are, señor; have no doubt of that."

"Who share in what plunder there may be?"

"But of course; a smaller share, to be certain. And if there be no plunder, why then I am not out wages."

Joaquin considered the wine in his glass. "They are faithful, these men?"

Stafford found a tattered cigar in his clothing and lighted it. This Don was up to something, but what? He nodded and watched the man's eyes. "So long as I keep them so."

With an effort, Don Joaquin smiled and rose from his chair. "I forget my duties as host. This war has done many things. We will eat, and after dinner I have a business proposition to discuss with you."

Following the man into a formal dining room that had seen better days, Stafford wondered what this Mexican aristocrat had in mind, and wondered more if the man could pay for it. The signs of bankruptcy were all about them, but if Don Arredondo had some cache of gold hidden away, why then—

Stafford stood rigid in surprise, looking at the balustraded stairway, for a vision of pure loveliness was descending them. The Mexican gown caressed high, full breasts and a flat stomach; it held to sensuous hips and hinted at wondrous legs, with a tantalizing glimpse of ivory flesh beneath the lifted skirt.

Her long hair floated behind, black and gleaming, a dark halo for her stunning beauty. High cheekbones angling a dusky-cream face, eyes that fair ate into your soul, and a redripe mouth so rich that a man might strangle upon its precious juices.

"This is—Tosanna," Don Joaquin said, hesitating as he didn't put a title before the girl's name. "Tosanna, our guest—Colonel Sir John Stafford, from England."

She came—nay, floated—toward them, dark eyes probing, chin held high. A prize beauty, Stafford thought, local blood without a doubt; those cheekbones gave her away.

But never in his travels in this country had he come across such an aura of direct and uninhibited sensual promise.

"I do not know this—England," she said, and the voice of her was an intimate caress that skipped up and down Stafford's back, so low and husky. Poised, seemingly unaware of her effect upon him, Tosanna waited for his reply.

No courtly chitchat for this one, Stafford thought; no, bigod—she was too open and straightforward for inane pleasantries. He said, "Madame, I envy Don Joaquin his closeness to you."

Cutting his eyes toward Arredondo, he saw the flickering of anger upon the don's face, an anger swiftly hidden, and wondered again.

"England," Tosanna repeated. "It has a strange sound."

"And strange are those who people the island," Stafford said, offering her his arm, certain now that this breathtaking girl was somehow part of some plan Don was cooking up. So be it; there were other things rare as gold—not many, but a few.

Don Joaquin carefully maneuvered them so that they sat closer than the long table called for, close enough so that Stafford could draw in the woman's musky scent and delight in the flashing of her earrings. Not real, he thought, but a good paste that sent back the candlelight in only a few less refractions than if the jewels had been diamonds. Tosanna made them rich with the tilt of her head, made her necklace invaluable against the throbbing of her throat.

Mygod, Stafford thought; if the wench leaned forward just a bit more, at least one of those delicious melons would spring unadorned from the cupping of her exceptionally low-cut dress. These Mexicans knew how to display their women, but were damned touchy about them also. Never had he been practically offered one of their lovelies. What the hell did Don Joaquin want—a swoop down upon one of his neighbors, a man who had refused him a loan? And what part did this delectable girl-woman play in his conspiracy?

The food was excellent, skillfully prepared by some unseen cook and served by a bashful maid. True, there were no outstanding delicacies upon the platters, but anything hot without being burned was welcome to Stafford, he was so close upon memories of campfires and hungry nights. Eating heartily, he told Tosanna about England—its towering castles and crowded streets, its royalty and peasantry; he spoke glowingly of shops where any woman might purchase gowns of much beauty, and hats and purses, and shoes fitted exactly to dainty feet. There were perfumeries owned by Parisians, wine shops and food. And there was the court.

"Ah, the court," Don Joaquin said around his cigar. "Tell us of the court, señor."

Brandy, by all that was holy, honest brandy served with coffee and a sweetcake. Appreciatively, Stafford rolled the golden stuff inside his mouth before swallowing and saw Tosanna attempting to follow suit, blowing out her cheeks.

His laugh was gentle. "The court is nothing to what it once was; it has been too damned democratized—House of Commoners against the House of Lords indeed. But times change, and royalty must change with them. The Queen, bless her avaricious soul, has expanded the British Empire, to near unimaginable bounds. Safe behind the strength of our navy, we send out expeditionary forces and bring back riches. Merchants are damned near powerful as the lords, but still a dash of royal blood can help along a career."

Eyes steady beneath lowered black brows, Don Joaquin said, "You are known at court?"

"I was," Stafford said with a hidden wink at Tosanna. "Tomorrow, who knows?"

"Then you are not anxious to return immediately?"

Ah, Stafford thought, now we get down to the meat of it. "That depends," he said, watching the girl eat like a savage despite Don Joaquin's frowning. No trained courtesan then; but what was she?

"Tosanna," Don Joaquin said abruptly, "leave us."

She glanced at him. "I do not wish to."

"Wench! Do as I say, or the skin will be taken off your back."

Mouth set, she stood up and smoothed her hands over her hips. She looked at Don Joaquin and at Stafford. Then she swung out of the dining room, her hips drumbeating beneath the dress, trailing a scent of wild promise.

"I should hate to see that," Stafford murmured into his brandy glass. "The skin peeled from her, I mean. It is beautiful skin. I take it the lass is not your wife."

Don Joaquin's face flushed. In a choked voice he said, "Times change, señor, as you have said. Once it would have been necessary to call you out for such careless remarks.

But now—I have a use for you and your men. And Tosanna —she is part of the bargain."

"Besides the gold," Stafford said quietly.

The Mexican's flush deepened; he quickly finished his brandy. "There is no gold or silver. I have been robbed over and over again. But I have something else to offer, señor—land—good land that someday will be worth many times its value now."

"Ah, yes," Stafford said, "someday."

Clenching his fist upon his glass, Don Joaquin said, "A hundred measures to each man, more riches than they have ever known. And there may be plunder, horses, scalps. Perhaps those cursed *indios* still have some of my treasure; that also goes to the men who revenge me upon the bloody Comanche, to those who return my wife to me."

Stafford whistled softly. "Your wife, eh? A sad blow to know she's taken by Comanches. I have heard much of them, but luckily have only seen them once, and that at a distance, also fortunate. Don Joaquin, I must be frank: these *pistoleros* of mine, these soldiers of fortune—they fight only for gold, never for vengeance—and *never* do they gamble their lives unless they are assured of a chance to win. Logical men, one must admit; so against the Comanches—"

"Cowards!" Don Joaquin spat.

Calmly, Stafford said, "No—sensible men. As for myself, I am possibly romantic enough to add the beautiful Tosanna to the balances, but my men—I think not. Rapists they are, and murderers, very good at their professions, but such loveliness would be lost upon them. Any woman will do them, señor."

"The land," Don Joaquin said desperately, "the good land of my father and grandfather, and of his father before him. Not an inch of it would I give up in other circumstances."

"My men would trade it for a bottle and whore," Stafford said. "And as I soon return home, I have no use for it either. I am sorry, Don."

Joaquin fisted the tabletop. "Not for honor, nor glory, nor the duty of white men to protect their women. But for my misfortunes, for the arrant cowardice all about me— for this, for this!—I saved the life of that Comanche bitch!"

Stafford lifted an eyebrow. "Comanche bitch?"

Rising suddenly, Don Joaquin shattered his glass into the fireplace. "Wearing the clothing of my dishonored wife, while the sons and daughter of a true woman have only now turned chill in their graves. The whore, the wench, I will—"

Calmly, Stafford said, "Don, don—I beg you. Is it true that this woman whom I took for your mistress, this vision of pride and such startling beauty, is a Comanche, a savage?"

"A dead woman." Don Joaquin raised the brandy bottle to his mouth and drank from it, caught his breath and drank again. "Medicine woman, enchantress, witch, *bruja*—I hoped to exchange her for my wife, but if that is not to be, I will kill her, as is my right."

"Of course," Stafford said, "it is your right. But will it assist the release of your poor wife? Sit, Don Arredondo, and let us speak as logical men."

Logical, hell, Stafford thought; what logic was this that came racing like wildfire through his veins? The very idea of holding such a savage prize, of savoring all the wild sweetness bound to be contained in that captivating body— it was enough to make a man's blood boil.

Rubbing his chin, he thought again: it might also be possible to turn this marvelous find more to the advantage of his career than that of simply slaking the burgeoning hungers of his body. Tosanna, redskin trophy brought to England as oddity of the decade. How many elite gentlemen would fawn upon her, how many ladies hate her for her beauty? What a stir she would cause at court.

"Daughter of chiefs," Don Joaquin said bitterly. "Misbegotten offspring of *el diablo,* say I. I should have left her to the Apaches."

Of course she would be a princess, Stafford knew—if not in real life, then sprung fully titled from his fertile imagination. Princess Tosanna, feral, intriguing, all the more intoxicating because there might very well be blood on her hands. Stafford came more erect in his chair.

"Don Arredondo," he said, "I sympathize with you in your great loss and offer my humble apologies that I am not able to muster more than the *pistoleros* at my back. But I see a possibility of assistance. There are two among my fighters who would trail the devil himself, if they thought he carried a purse. One is Mexican and familiar with the country, the other a Yankee."

Tight lipped, Joaquin said, "I have already spoken of my enforced poverty."

Leaning forward, hands upon his knees, Stafford went

on. "That need not be a permanent condition, sir. For purposes of my own, I am prepared to make you an offer for the Indian girl."

"*Sell* Tosanna?" Don Joaquin's dark brows knitted.

"She is your property, a prize of war; you were willing to—ah, offer her services—if that would aid you in finding your wife. This is a better way, far more certain. You can hire the skills of my *bandidos* and have enough left over for trade goods, rifles perhaps, ammunition. The Comanches value these things more than gold, I understand."

Don Joaquin's eyes widened. "These *pistoleros*—would they undertake to—but what would I exchange with the Comanche, when my Ynez is found?"

"Rifles and ammunition," Stafford repeated. "What is a woman to the Indians? Nothing, I say, though she be daughter to a chief. Weapons with which to kill *tejanos*—ah, what primitive would not trade *all* his children for such?"

Staring at the brandy bottle his whitened fingers clenched, Don Joaquin muttered, "Sell her like the animal she is and use the money to buy back Ynez—or wreak vengeance upon her murderers. It is just; it is appropriate that she pay."

"Indeed," Stafford said, "indeed. And as to the matter of terms—"

Stiffly, Don Joaquin said, "Haggling is for peasants. A fair price, colonel, one—gentleman to another."

"Very well then: a thousand Yankee dollars in gold to be divided between Felipe Cruz and Will Largo, and five hundred more for the buying of guns." Stafford watched Don Joaquin's face.

"Done, *por Dios!* And may the witch sink her claws into a hundred gringos before someone finally kills her." Stalking to a cabinet. Don Joaquin found another glass and poured it brimming, came to refill Stafford's glass with brandy. "*Salud*, señor. May Tosanna bring you more luck than she has me."

"Your health," Stafford answered. "I will arrange things with my men."

"This Cruz and the gringo—they are trustworthy?"

"To a point, señor. Pay them only a portion, an advance, so they will return for the rest. They could desire to remain in your service, since mercenaries are not welcomed by the new government they helped establish."

Don Joaquin thumbed his mustache. "The girl—Tosanna —she will accompany you when?"

"Tomorrow, by your leave. It is a long trip to Vera Cruz and a ship for home."

"She sleeps in the kitchen tonight then. You understand, señor—under my roof."

"Perfectly," Stafford replied.

"Watch her closely," Don Joaquin warned. "Very closely, for she is an animal that longs for its den."

"I just happen," Stafford said, "to have acquired a length of golden chain. It will serve to remind her what she is and to whom she belongs."

"Yes," Don Joaquin murmured, and his face was dark.

CHAPTER 9

Tosanna glided from her listening station behind dusty drapes, went like a quick shadow down a dark hallway, and carefully twisted a cold brass knob. Outside in the night, she looked toward the stables, then to a fire before the house of old José, where the strangers were gathered. Carlos Lopez—where would he be?

Holding the long dress high to clear her ankles, she flitted to the barns, peered in the window of an abandoned hut. Down there then, at the long house, the bunkhouse where riders slept. Cracking the door, she called softly: "Carlos, Carlos?"

As if he had been awaiting the sound of her voice, the foreman came hurrying, left hand trailing his serape, right hand upon the black butt of his pistol. "Tosanna?" He heeled the door closed behind him; his spur jingled. "This is mad, woman. If *el patrón* misses you—"

She caught his hand and pulled him toward safer darkness, the shadows of the stables. "Don Joaquin is busy with the man from England, making final arrangements to sell me to him."

Carlos tightened his hand upon her. *"Madre de Dios! Sell* you?"

Pressing the length of her body against his, Tosanna lifted her mouth close, knowing the pressure of her thighs on his, the flattening of her breasts upon his chest. "Do not let them take me, Carlos. Do not let the gringo carry me away from you."

A shudder moved through him and his arms closed fiercely about her. "If *el conde* no longer owns you, if this damned *pistolero* becomes your master, then it is no act of treason—"

"The horses," Tosanna breathed, loosening herself from his grasp. "The red stallion, your fine black mare; I have been hiding food and water in the grain bins. There is also men's clothing and boots. But you have kept weapons from me."

"Where would we go?" he asked in a hoarse whisper. "To the cities, but, no—I am a horseman and so long *teniente* to Don Joaquin—where would I find work in a city? If we go north, there are the damned *tejanos* and *los indios*—"

"The Comanche will not harm us," Tosanna promised. "If we reach my tribe, I will make you rich with many horses. But we must hurry; I felt the *inglés capitán's* eyes on me all through dinner, and perhaps he will share me with his *soldados*."

"Never!" Carlos swore. "*Un momento, querida,* while I collect some things. Inside the stables, quickly. And if old José comes poking about, here."

She felt the leathered haft of a knife slip into her hand and closed her fingers gratefully upon its chill comfort. Armed at last, she felt stronger, and excitement scampered through her like small rabbits. Her fingers shook as she tore away the gown and dug in dried corn for her cache. Dressed again, she shivered.

The stables were black, smelling of green hay and horse droppings. Unerringly, Tosanna made her way to the tie stall of the big red stallion, cooing softly to him, to other horses that chuffed in half-fear through their nostrils.

The saddle was high front and back, not like the flat rawhide ones of the Comanche, but she had little trouble cinching it on the stallion, and he took the bit easily. Her fingers told his warm soft hide that all was well. Tosanna's heart thundered like dance drums, and she was eager to be gone, to taste night wind upon her lips, to fly through the desert, back, back to the Kwehar-enuh.

Dried meat, salt and meal, water, a pair of stolen blankets, and she led the big horse to the back door. If she did not have to depend upon Carlos to guide her through the thin ring of sentries, she would go now, now! Ado-eeti, she called in her mind. Big Tree, I come to you.

Ears straining, eyes searching the darkness beyond the stables, she thought of Apache country they had to pass through, of desert and mountains that would also be enemies. But at least now she had a chance to return home, to find Comancheria and her own tribe. Taken still farther away by the Englishman, chained to him, her opportunities to be free would grow smaller as the road lengthened.

"Hola."

"Here, Carlos," she whispered back. "I have my horse ready."

He came close to touch her in the blackness. "And I will saddle mine."

The stallion wanted to whinny when she moved him through the door, but she felt it coming and clamped fingers into his nostrils. Behind her, Carlos led his mare at a soft clipclop. When he came beside her, he murmured, "Mount and follow just behind me; do not speak."

"A rifle?" she asked. "At least a *pistola?*"

"Those are my friends," he said. "I will not have you kill them."

All other horses should have been stampeded, she knew, so that pursuit would be difficult. But they were in too many places—barn, stables, tied outside José's shack, behind the big house. Anyway, Carlos would probably not allow it.

Carlos—what would she do with him when they crossed the river to the north? Slip off in the night, she thought. He would be on his own in Apache country or Comancheria, but better so than meeting death at the hands of her own people. The Kwehar-enuh would not have forgotten the killings at the spring. She owed him for that, too, but now the debt for her own life was greater.

Of course, she had told him Comanches would not harm him. She would say anything, do anything, to return to her people, to Ten Bears and Ado-eeti. Tosanna only wished she could bring back Don Joaquin as a trophy. How the women would celebrate their knives upon him, but they would be angered, she thought; Don Joaquin would not give the satisfaction of screaming. There was a hardness in him like desert rock, and in that he was somewhat like the Comanche.

In a fashion, she would miss him and the things learned at his hacienda, the beautiful clothing and strange foods, the easy work.

Up ahead, a horse stamped and Carlos stopped. Reining up her own horse, Tosanna waited for the silence of the night to return. Leaning low in her saddle and staring up at lighter sky, she was able to make out the form of a loafing horse and hatted rider, and her ears followed them slowly to the right until they blurred and vanished.

Carefully, Carlos edged his mount ahead and she followed breathlessly, wishing she could have somehow gotten hold of a gun, but those were things closely watched at Hacienda de Arredondo. Looking back over her shoulder and seeing the house lamps fade, Tosanna wondered how long they had before Don Joaquin's men came roaring after. And the gringos, too, the *pistoleros;* they would be dangerous ones, hard men used to the night and saddles, their guns as much part of them as hands or feet.

A whisper from Carlos floated back to her. "A little farther, and we will be able to go faster. There is a canyon ahead."

He led them down, down into a narrow cut in the sandy earth, and rock walls rose around as light left them. She could barely see him and the horse, though they were close. Tosanna smelled old, tired dirt and sometimes sage. She was glad when the path rose beneath them and they were once more in the open.

Carlos moved them into a jog then, and soon to a long, ground-covering lope. But the horses—these fat Mexican horses—could not hold such a gait for long, and soon they were walking again. The creaking of saddle leather, slow rhythm of hoofs, the sweat scent of the horses—all these things were so well known to Tosanna, and she lifted her eyes skyward to thank the spirits for them, for this familiar, yearned-for sense of freedom.

"A spring up here," Carlos murmured as the ground dipped again, and Tosanna caught the fresh odors of grass. "We will water the horses."

Sliding down, she loosened the stallion's cinch and led him to water. He snorted twice, then lowered his head and began to swallow. Holding the reins, she leaned against his muscled side and thought of the tepees, woodsmoke, how happy her father and husband would be to see her once again. She would be more valuable to them when they traded with *comancheros,* since she had learned the Mexican tongue better.

She came erect when Carlos reached around to take the

reins from her hand. Wordlessly, she followed as he led the stallion and tied him to a bush. "We are far enough away," he said. "There has been no outcry, and I can wait no longer."

Tosanna put her palms flat against his chest and felt the beating of his heart. "We are very close to the rancho. After dawn, perhaps we can stop and—"

"No," Carlos grated, "by all that is holy, the moment is *now*. I have betrayed my *patrón* for you, woman. I will have you."

It would have been better upon a furred couch, or the soft bed of Mexican dons, Tosanna thought, but this was more natural, this soft sinking to the blanketed earth while an open sky smiled upon them. It would have been better if she cared for this man, if there were some feeling in her heart for him. His hands were rough, his mouth hot and eager. Beneath him, Tosanna spread herself, knowing full well she could cut his throat with the sharp knife she was carrying, yet knowing also that she would not.

"Gently," she whispered, "gently."

But Carlos would not take the time. Brutally, gasping deep in his throat, he thrust himself at her, grinding a hard belly against her own, fumbling at her hips, her thighs. Tosanna held back a grunt of pain that built within her and arched to make it easier for him and for herself. He penetrated and her fingers dug into his shoulders as Carlos drove deep.

Against her ear he hissed that she was a devil woman, a bitch with black magics to tempt a man. Pounding at her giving flesh, sledging and panting, Carlos took from her what he thought he needed. But Tosanna of the Comanches gave him nothing of her true self, not by word or action.

When he moaned and shuddered in completion, she gazed up at the stars and at the edge of her eye saw orange-silver of the rising moon. It was only a moment before she realized that the thudding she heard was not only his heart. Pushing at him, Tosanna pivoted her hips, and snapped him from within her.

"They're coming!"

Groggy, hesitating, he lifted from her and Tosanna rolled swiftly away, snatching up her knife, the blanket they'd used. Carlos was fumbling with his breeches and gunbelt when horsemen came over the hilltop. Windblown

torches they carried high flickered over hard faces and reflected upon ready gun barrels.

Don Joaquin sat astride his black mare, and beside him
the *inglés* lolled upon a rangy beast. Only the *pistoleros*
were with them—no riders from the hacienda; these fanned
to right and left, rifle muzzles casually pointed at Carlos.
The torches blew and danced. When a horse tossed its head,
a bit jingled.

Into a silence that spread thin and tight, Don Joaquin
said down to them: "You would run away, wench? Carlos,
you would betray your *patrón*?"

Feet wide to balance his taut body, Carlos said, "She
was yours no longer, *conde*."

"Still," Don Joaquin began, and Tosanna could see he
was not anxious to punish his lieutenant.

But the Englishman, the one called Stafford, hooked one
knee over his saddle horn and said, "One who steals only
from guests is yet a thief, eh?"

Carefully, Carlos kept his hands away from his sides,
away from his holstered pistol. He spoke to Don Joaquin.
"I—the woman is a *bruja* who cast an evil spell upon me."

Tosanna sidled to her right, seeking to move deeper into
shadows, but a lean horseman walked his mount that way
and held a torch over her. She stared at him and wondered
if she could possibly outrace them, if her stallion might stay
ahead until she reached the mountains. But the wolfish look
of the *pistoleros* told her she would be shot from the saddle.

Don Joaquin lifted his reins. "You dishonor the house
of de Arredondo." He turned the mare and jogged her
toward the lip of the hill again.

"Wait!" Carlos yelled. "*Conde—por favor*, wait!"

Instead, the Englishman and his soldiers waited. The
pistoleros were of a type, not a handful of fat between
them—leathery, hard men who wore well-used weapons and
merciless eyes. Two had on sombreros, two the wide hats
favored by White Eyes.

"Well, now," Stafford said, both hands upon his saddle
horn, and Carlos sucked in a deep breath.

That's when Tosanna moved. Snake quick, she reached
up to cut at a man's thigh, cut again when his hand grasped
at the first wound. He roared and his torch fell spitting to
the earth. She ran for the stallion, ducking beneath a horse
and slapping his genitals so that he reared and almost lost
his rider. Reins in her teeth, she leaped atop the spooked

stallion and hunched over his neck, fingers of one hand twisted into his mane.

A wild cry keening between locked teeth, she threw the horse forward and slashed at a white face, chopped at an outstretched arm and clung with all the strength of knees and one hand as her horse slammed into another.

Behind her guns went off—the slap of pistols, louder thunderclaps of long rifles; a man bellowed in pain, another cursed hoarsely. She clung to her stallion's mane, and when he threw up his head in fright, his heavy neck caught her on the cheek. Lights flashed behind Tosanna's eyes and she struggled to hang on, but something else slapped hard between her shoulders and hurled her off the plunging horse.

Knife firm in her hand, she rolled over and over, somehow avoiding hoofs that pounded near her head, tasting dust, gunsmoke, and torn grass. When she came to one knee, a rider clawed down for her. She caught his wrist and threw herself backward, hacking at him as he was jerked from the saddle and almost upon her.

His pistol exploded at her ear and hot powder stung her face. Tosanna scuttled along the ground, running for brush beyond the spring. She saw Carlos Lopez swaying at its edge, a dark stain spreading on his chest. Mouth open and jaw gone slack, he stared at her as his gun slipped from his hand. He fell backward, splashing into the water; a torch still held circled broken light over the rippled surface.

Tosanna stood still when the Englishman rode over to her, and when he commanded her to mount her horse, she slid the wet knife back into her boot top and did so. There was a time to fight to the death, but this was not the night. They were too many for her and she could not escape. She looked once toward the foothills, a great longing within her.

"*Capitán*," a bearded *pistolero* said. He squeezed a dripping wrist. "Do you mean to keep that she-wolf alive?"

Stafford said, "I paid good money for her, *compañero*. Now, if one of you will catch up the dead man's horse—"

The bearded man said, "I will pay a certain amount to kill her."

Torchlight jumped over Stafford's face, his heavy body. He was smiling and nodding. "*Amigo*, I am afraid she cost more than you can afford."

"*Por Dios*, then," the bearded man grated, "I will kill

her for free. No *indio* bitch puts her blade to me without—"

Smiling yet, Stafford fired twice, and Tosanna saw that he had been holding a pistol beside his leg, out of the light. The bearded man rocked back in his saddle, then fell sideways from the horse. Stafford shook his head, but Tosanna noticed that his unsmiling eyes swept back and forth across the other men.

"*Amigo*," he said, "*amigo*, one would think you had learned something by riding to war with me. It seems you did not. Too bad, eh? Too bad."

In the White Eye language, one of the others said, "Reckon we get to divvy his loot."

And another added, "Hell, I'll drag both horses along."

Stafford's booted calf touched her own, and she heard the rattle of metal. She sat quietly as he leaned to flip the golden chain around her waist and drew it tight. Tosanna heard something click then, and Stafford tipped back. "A precaution, my dear—at least until we get to know each other better."

They did not bury the dead men, but left Carlos Lopez to poison the waters of the spring, abandoned the other with his beard hard against the earth and blackening the sand beneath his twisted body.

Riding slowly, held fast by the chain reaching from her to the man's saddle horn, Tosanna sat erect. He had not taken away her knife, but she did not doubt this one knew exactly where it was. The *inglés* was cold as the belly of a snake, and his fangs just as deadly. She would not try to escape from this man without killing him.

And she would carefully choose the time and place.

Carlos, she said to the darkness behind her eyes, I would mourn your death, but I am Comanche and you—you were my enemy. You did not understand that.

CHAPTER 10

It was worse to wear a chain, to be tied like a camp dog being fattened for a special feast. Every clink of metal reminded Tosanna of what she was now, and of what she once had been.

She eyed him with care, this man who had killed one of his own kind so casually. He did not look like a war chief, for he wore no finery—only a dusty jacket and buckskin breeches, a plain shirt, and droopy hat. This Stafford was not clean either; there was trail dust upon him, thick and clinging to his unshaven cheeks, the gray hair at his temples. He was heavy across the shoulders and slightly thick in the middle, but he sat his saddle well as anyone not a Comanche.

The chain rattled against Stafford's saddle horn, and Tosanna checked out the positions of other *pistoleros*—the squat and hairy gringo called Willie, the coyote-thin man known as Latigo, the Mexican Pietro nodding under the shade of his big sombrero. Marks of the warrior rode with them: scars, eyes that squinted at far distances and remained ever suspicious, carefully cared-for weapons, good horses beneath them. And the coldest was Sir John Stafford, who traveled watchful as any renegade war leader, watchful for his own back as well as the trail ahead.

Not an ugly man, Tosanna thought, and wise enough to have grown older. His eyes bothered her; she had never seen eyes that color, like that of a pale sky in early winter, an icy blue. His mouth was hard beneath a smile, and some men might be disarmed by how often, how white and wide Stafford smiled. But she had seen the same curving of his mouth when he pistoled one of his own men. To protect her? No, to guard the money spent buying her.

She had known a great disappointment in Don Joaquin. Over the time since he had captured her at the spring, he had seemed to grow more tender—except for the moments when he flew into a dark and sudden rage. Perhaps she should have tried escape earlier, before this *inglés* came along, but Carlos Lopez always had been hovering near, always fearful his promised prize might vanish into the hills and be forever lost to him. Carlos—dead now at another bloodstained spring. Tosanna shook her head; Mexicans attached so much significance to getting between a woman's legs. And perhaps the White Eyes were the same. It was foolish and a vital weakness, one she might yet exploit.

She felt sorry for Carlos Lopez, but only a bit. He was Mexican and enemy to the Antelope band, to all Comanches; his gun had chopped at boy sentries, at girls fleeing that other spring. If he died, it was his medicine to do so.

But Don Joaquin de Arredondo—she remembered his face when Stafford made Don Joaquin a present of the riderless horses. Blood had darkened the Mexican's face and his mouth went vicious. Stiffly, he ordered Josefina, the maid, to bring her clothing and, without a word, accepted a small doeskin bag that clinked dully.

But his eyes fiercely hated Tosanna as she waited upon the horse she had stolen from his stables. Yet she felt that some of his hatred was directed inward at himself, and some at the *inglés*. Still, he had sold her to the man, and she hoped her price was that of many horses. It would not do for the daughter of a Comanche chief to sell cheaply.

Don Joaquin had moved to her stirrup and looked up, hardness crumbling from his face until it looked almost the way she had sometime seen it—human and hurting, even tender when he did not know it.

"I have sold you like an animal," he said.

"It is your right."

His hand clenched the stirrup fender, then eased over to the calf of her leg. "I have hated you, woman. That also was my right." She sensed he wanted to say more, but was holding back.

Tosanna said, almost in a whisper, "I do not thank you

for my life, *hombre*. But I do say *gracias* for all you taught me, for kindness when you might have been cruel."

Hand tightening upon her leg, he said, "If your kind had not—if you were not—"

"We are what the spirits make of us, then what we make of ourselves. *Adios*, Don Joaquin; may your wife be returned to you."

He had spun and walked quickly away. He had not looked back.

Now she rode easily upon the big stallion she called Ado-tua, Great Son, for Stafford had left her hands free. The golden chain reaching from her waist to his saddle was enough to keep her close—that, and the *pistoleros* watching.

They were going south, ever farther from the land of the Kwehar-enuh, putting more distances of flat, burning deserts and rolling, sandy hills between Tosanna and her tribe. She glanced swiftly at the sun, down at a tall and twisted cactus. By such landmarks she could find her way home, if she was free. It was possible she might not make it through stretches where Apaches roamed, but that was in the lap of the spirits. She wanted desperately to try.

With a tug of the chain, Stafford drew her closer to him. "You know this country, Tosanna?"

"No," she said.

"And no other language but Spanish?"

She said, "Comanche."

He laughed. "Oh, yes, Comanche. Your Don Joaquin—he said you were with him only a few months. You learn quickly then?"

"I have the gift of tongues," Tosanna answered. She would tell him nothing he did not ask directly, speak to him only when commanded.

"You will begin to learn a civilized tongue," he said. "English. We will speak it on the journey. And Tosanna—do not try to escape. If you do, I will make it very painful for you, *comprende*?"

"I understand," she said.

The smile that was not a smile flicked at her. "The knife in your boot—I purposely allowed you to keep it. You will need it around camps we make, and for no other reason. I should dislike losing an investment such as you, my dear. But if I must—well, let us speak of more pleasant things, and I will give you words in English."

The girl rode well, Stafford admitted, with a rhythm that showed rapport with the horse. And she had chosen wisely when she stole her mount from the Mexican; the stallion was powerfully muscled and full of fire, but she held him easily in check. Don Joaquin had parted with a pair of fine mounts, all tight-faced when offered a price for them, but taking the money anyway.

Smiling, Stafford fondled the golden chain; bad luck, his Mexican *pistoleros* said, bad luck to rob the church, to lift treasures from statues of the saints themselves. Yet look what the chain now held for him—such fiery beauty, an exotic spectacle that would ingratiate him again at court. If only the Widow at Windsor were a man; Stafford could then make an outright present of this wild woman. But Victoria's juices, if not dried up, were dedicated to making the world hers, not to sex. Pity, he thought.

The sky reddened now, and the horses scented water ahead, chuffing through their nostrils. So they were on time and the correct route. Pietro's sense of direction was sharp as ever, and his good common sense had held him back from leading their little party astray. A cutthroat greedy as any of his kind, Pietro envied the laden saddlebags carried by Stafford's horse, but the lesson of yesterday was still with him. The sight of his *compadre* spilling backward with bullets punched through him—that remained bright within his cunning mind.

It was always so, Stafford thought, no weakness must be shown, and examples must be made. The Americans with him understood that, and because his cold discipline impressed them, they had followed him throughout the revolution. Discipline and fair distribution of loot—that was the answer. It did not mean he trusted them, only that the Americans did not have to be watched as closely.

The "army" of peons he'd left behind, now that the war was temporarily over—those men were another species. Ragged, hungry, and badly armed, some with only machetes, they had helped bring down the professional soldiers of Maximilian. Now they wandered around damaged villages, hunted down remnants of enemy troops, and waited for the paradise promised by the glorious revolution.

Give him mercenaries every time, Stafford thought, and rattled the golden chain just to catch an angered flash of stormy black eyes. Men who fought for pay were far more practical than patriots, and knew that wars changed nothing but the names.

He came alert swiftly as Pietro rode back to him. *"Jefe,"* the man said, "the spring is clear and the water good. We make camp?"

"Yes," Stafford answered, and knew a quick thrill of anticipation. After they had eaten, after the men had been posted beyond the circle of firelight, he would sample the flavors of his purchase and discover why the bankrupt Don had been so loath to let her go.

At the water hole, he watched her dismount and slipped the chain from his wrist so that she might move about freely. The breeches she wore caressed smooth haunches and clung to sleek, firm thighs; her breasts stood high and rounded, tip-tilted beneath the man's shirt that hugged them.

Other eyes followed the woman, but glanced away when he looked at them. There would be no trouble from the men over a single woman, not when a hundred whores waited them in the cities. They were looking forward to a long carouse, until their gold was gone, or until someone cut their throats.

Though the woman soaked the beans and boiled them for a long time, they were still hard, and jerky was ever the same. Only the bread she made was truly palatable and went well with savory coffee. Across the fire, Latigo and Willie talked of what they would do when they reached Mexico City, of women and wine and high old times. Not far from where Stafford sat, Pietro ate silently and sullenly; from time to time he spat a pebble-hard bean into the fire.

Wiping bread into the juices on his tin plate, Stafford said, "Divide the watch between you, and set the usual ambush beyond the light."

Latigo grunted, Willie nodded, and the Mexican gave no sign he heard, just rose and carried his bedroll into the night. Stafford wondered if he was going to have to kill Pietro before the journey was done.

For now, he placed the Spencer carbine within easy reach of spread blankets and pillowing saddles, placed one .36 caliber Navy pistol beneath his saddle, the other under a blanket. With a glance around at fed, watered, and picketed horses, he sank to his bed. On his knees, smelling the sagebrush that sheltered his nest from the wind, Stafford motioned to the girl to join him.

When she did not hesitate, but came gracefully and calmly to the blankets, Stafford knew a moment of dissatisfaction. Was then her lordly attitude false, and she but a passive peon after all? Firelight flickered upon the heavy wealth of hair Tosanna let down as she kneeled close. "The chain," she murmured.

Bringing the key from his pocket, Stafford clicked the lock. Her eyes holding his with a suggestion of scorn, she slid from the shirt and boldly wriggled from boots and breeches, her smooth body alluring and voluptuous, her lack of shyness intoxicating. When she slowly lifted the blanket, Stafford's hand darted down with a loop of chain, and the lock snapped into place. Tosanna was held by the ankle, her foot close to his.

"Now," Stafford said, "now missy. You'll not slip off into the desert and waste all you've shown me. 'Twould be a mighty shame, were such a body staked on an anthill or thrown away upon men who cannot appreciate its wonders—if indeed, wonders there be."

Blankly, she stared at him, and Stafford realized he had spoken in English. Switching languages, he said, "Never mind," and removed most of his own clothing as she slid beneath the blankets, the soft warmth of her reaching out at him.

He had been long without a woman and quickly caught her close, pressing the throbbing length of her nakedness against himself, his hands running freely over her back, her hips, the moundings of her buttocks. Stafford felt the crushing of melon breasts into his chest, the awakening tremble of her as swiftly her passions rose to match his own. Mouth covering hers, his tongue searched and found violent answer, a curling, seething response that shook him to the soles of his feet.

Gasping, his teeth clashing with hers, Stafford knew the shock of her own deft and agile hands, the rhythmed stroking of her eager belly, the cushioning of a richly furred mound. It was a struggle for him not to mount her without further delay, to rut blindly upon this magnificent body. But he had always counted himself a ladies' man, a proficient and sought-after lover in England, and now he throttled the raw impulses that might make him premature.

He held her close, but tenderly, caressing the slim but lush body, drinking of her honeyed mouth while his fingers sought to delight her. Tosanna moaned and arched, and he saluted her breasts with his lips, paid homage to her belly. She turned feral then, scorching him with pure animal hunger, clawing and biting and forcing him into her torrid flesh. It was like being caught up in a maelstrom, whirled and heaved and locked impossibly deep.

Lashed around him, Tosanna's legs were silken bindings, and her arms further entrapped him for the assault of her wildly lustful mouth. Stafford found himself in a battle for possession, for control, and tasted blood from a bitten lip. Lost in the madness, he fought back, clutching her pounding haunches and hammering at her envelopment. The stars exploded and rained blazing fragments around him; the desert quaked and somewhere deep inside his soul, a cry keened echoing throughout the startled corridors of his mind.

Curled about him, Tosanna purred deep in her throat, for a new man was ever exciting, and this man had not been cruel. There was much to share with him, other things to be taught him, perhaps. But in time, that would come. She did not know how many nights they would be on the trail, nor how far they were journeying. If this White Eyes did not suddenly change, the journeying would be pleasant, each night by a campfire gratifying. And it would serve to lull him, make him not so alert, so that he might forget to bind her with the chain.

Each step of the journey, every day that passed, was taking her ever further from her homeland and those people she loved. Her father—aging Ten Bears, standing so proud and wise, always a leader; Ado-eeti, fierce and strong, someday to be a great war chief himself, and destined to father Tosanna's sons; all her people of the Antelope band, her friends from childhood—all these had been taken from her, and never had she felt so alone, even with the Englishman breathing warm against her throat.

Beyond where she lay with her new captor, snug in soft blankets and held in close embrace, the campfire flame-danced, spreading its light. Tosanna listened to its many voices, and to faint sounds of the night—far cry of a night-bird, restless shuffle of a horse's feet, warning clink of muffled metal as one of the *pistoleros* walked guard beyond the circle of firelight. Breathing deeply, she smelled sage and chaparral and the sweet tang of dried horse sweat, knew the flavor of woodsmoke that tugged at her memories.

By now the tribe thought her dead; Tosanna was certain of that. They would mourn her and swear vengeance in a spirit dance around the council fires. For a long time, no one would speak her name aloud, and her belongings would be destroyed. Tosanna flinched as she thought of her marriage dress, beaded and quilled buckskin of softest leathers. She labored long on that beautiful dress, exulting in each careful stitch, every colorful decoration. Now it would be cast into the flames, and perhaps the prized length of Ado-eeti's glossy hair would be cut off and thrown beside it.

Slowly, she turned and stared up at the campfires of the spirits, those faraway lights in the sky; all The People who entered the other world sat there, looking down upon the land left forever behind. Before she joined them, Tosanna meant to make a fight of her life. She was Kwehar-enuh, a Comanche princess; where others would die in the desert, she would find water and food. She would steer her way by the spirit fires in the sky, and find her own camp, no matter how far over the mountains and dry lands it might lie.

A cold wind began to finger against her cheek, so she pulled deeper into the blankets. Beside her, one leg heavily across hers, the Englishman muttered in his sleep. Tosanna touched the interesting hair of his chest—not so thick and wiry as Don Joaquin's, but far more than any Comanche had. She was becoming used to it, even liking the strange caress of it. It would take longer to become used to hair on the faces of these White Eyes, and to the paleness of the eyes themselves.

Tosanna hoped she would not be prisoner long, that she could somehow free herself of the chain that kept her a slave, then walk a horse quietly away, a horse laden with weapons and water, food and blankets. The desert would be friend to her; she had only to fear Apaches and pursuit by this odd man and his *pistoleros*. The *inglés* had paid much for her, Don Joaquin said—the price of many horses —and that was good. It showed he did not value her lightly.

But since she had been so expensive to him, certainly Stafford would watch her closely, or trail her for many days.

Stirring against her, he nuzzled at one breast and then her throat. "Damn, if you aren't the most fiery wench I ever bedded. Worth every shilling, you are."

She listened closely to the White Eye speech, not yet understanding all words, but knowing what he meant, for his hands told her this. Tosanna pushed aside plans for escape and gave herself up to his renewed vigor.

If not tonight, then the next night, or yet the following one. Sometime, the Last Flower of the Comanches would break free—if it meant cutting every throat in her way.

CHAPTER 11

When the campfire was white-ashed coals and the hills had turned gray, the Yaquis struck.

Howling out of misty dawn, they hit the horses first, scattering them from the picket line. Tosanna was left tangled in blankets as Sir John Stafford rolled out firing his pistol. In the rocks, another of his men loosed shot after spaced, aimed shot. The sentry, Tosanna thought, not caught sleeping, but stunned by the sudden rush.

At first her heart leaped at the war cries, and she fought the blankets so she might rise up and run to her rescuers. But these were not Comanches, and when she saw them leaping, saw their paint-slashed faces twisted and ugly, she rolled into the brush. Not Apaches either; she did not recognize the way their headbands held back greasy hair, nor the breechclouts.

Two went down at the campfire's edge; one rolled into the banked coals and flopped for a moment. The sentry was aiming well. Then she heard him grunt and saw the *pistolero* stagger into the open, a short arrow protruding from his back. Stafford stood with legs braced apart, firing coolly until his pistol clicked empty. An Indian crawled broken at his feet, and another reeled aside, fingers clamped into his bleeding belly.

The sentry kept coming, mouth hung open, eyes wide in disbelief. A pistol bobbed at his belt, and the carbine was only now beginning to slip from nerveless fingers. He tried

100

to say something as he went to his knees before Tosanna, but a gush of red stopped him and he fell forward.

But not before she snatched his rifle and yanked the pistol free of leather. A shriek bounced off the rocks, and she saw the Mexican *pistolero* tangled with an Indian whose stabbing knife was wet. Stafford chopped at a running man's head, then calmly held his short gun and worked fresh shells into it.

They were many, Tosanna saw; two rushing the brushy nest where one of the White Eyes had taken cover, two more dashing in to help their tribesman finish the Mexican. Their yelps were hoarse, more the deep-throated grunts of animals than the shrill war cries of The People.

Stafford fired and a Yaqui fell. He raced for the saddle where his carbine had been left, bending low and dodging the deadly flick of a war arrow. But an *indio* beat him to the weapon, caught it up, and triggered it almost in Stafford's face. The Englishman reached out the muzzle of his pistol and fired against the man's naked belly, but the carbine went spinning out of sight in mesquite.

More of them, one man crashing through the brush too close to Tosanna, another stopped to release an arrow. Too much like Apaches, she thought—squat and dirty. She shot the bowman first, then stood up to fire twice at the running man, working the carbine lever as Ado-eeti had taught her. Her eye was not good, but when she knocked his leg from beneath him, Tosanna's throat ripped forth the Comanche war cry.

Turning, Stafford killed the wounded man, and dropped another, who cavorted while waving a dripping scalp. Tosanna yelled triumph again, the powder smoke and blood taste upon her now, and startled Yaquis hesitated only a moment before whirling to flee. In only moments, they were out of sight among the tumbled rocks and brush.

The air seemed to echo violence and swirl with blood, with stinking smoke. Tosanna stood taut, a weapon in each hand, and stared at Stafford. There was a gash across his cheek and a savage curl to his mouth, but the pale eyes were still calm and watchful upon her.

He said, "We may yet need each other."

Touching the golden chain about her waist, she looked all around at threatening hills, at dead men sprawled. "Yes," she said, and set about finding horses.

Perhaps the Yaquis were gone, perhaps only gathering

courage for another attack, so she watched the brush closely, guns at the ready, until Stafford talked down one horse,
then another. Tosanna guarded them back to camp and
waited. Stafford prowled among the extra horse tack, looting bedrolls and saddlebags, and this was right, Tosanna
thought. If it had been up to her, she would have taken
enemy scalps and weapons.

Stafford said then, "Those were Yaquis; do you know
them?"

"No," she said.

"They knew you." His grin was grimed and lopsided.
"That Comanche yelling scared them off, the bloodthirsty
bastards. To get past them, you'd have a long way to go
alone."

"I thought of that," she said.

Looking at her guns, he said, "Yes, I suppose you did.
Well, then, since my mercenaries won't be needing their
booty now—" Stafford clinked little skin pouches into his
own saddlebags, then dragged saddles and blankets into
the fire.

Moving quickly, Tosanna rescued a hat and shell belt, a
handful of bullets for her pistol, too. She was saddling the
stallion when Stafford came up behind her and touched
metal to her neck.

"Your weapons, my dear."

Over her shoulder she said, "I fought beside you."

"True, but you may also decide to fight against me."
He took her carbine and pistol, but followed her to keep
the ammunition belt. "If Yaquis returns, you may have
these back. I have too much invested in your future to
lose you either to other savages or to the hills. Shall we
ride, miss?"

Sullenly, she rode before him, and admitted grudgingly
that this White Eyes was no fool. He fought well and
stayed alert, and there seemed to be no fear in him. A
proper warrior, Stafford, but a Comanche would be leading *all* the horses, each laden with the belongings of dead
Yaquis and White Eyes. And a warrior such as Ado-eeti
would get them all back to camp, too. He would not have
burned anything, much less good saddles and blankets.

Straightening, she thought that Big Tree would be proud
of her for the manner in which she had fought, for she had
brought no shame upon the Kwehar-enuh. How the Yaquis
had fled when they heard Comanche war cries—how they

had fled from a single Comanche woman. The tale would make great telling about the council fire.

She watched for sign and found where Yaquis had ridden upon this trail. The scuff marks were not new, so she gestured them to Stafford and rode erectly on. He did not command her to stop for food when the sun was high, and she would not deign to ask him. She did not touch the metal gourds of water, either. Shadows grew long over the rolling plains before Stafford drew beside her and said here they would camp.

Picketing the horse, she unsaddled and grained him, and made certain he could reach the spring. Only then did she lower herself to earth and drink deeply. Then she made fire tight against a cupped boulder, so flames would not show far, and Stafford approved. The corn cake was good, baked upon a hot stone and filling with the jerky they chewed slowly. When he offered wine from a small earthenware jug, she shook her head and drank spring water instead. With handfuls of dried grass, she rubbed down the stallion and changed his picket so he might find more graze. Then she sat at the fire wrapped in her blanket, back against the warm rock.

Stafford said, using the mixture of Spanish and English words that was becoming habit when he communicated with her, "You did well at the ambush, and perhaps saved our lives. But do not expect gratitude; I have been too long a soldier. Those Yaquis—"

She interrupted. "What tribe are they?"

Shrugging, he said, "Descendents of the Pima, I think, but a separate branch now. They've enjoyed the Mexican war, looting both sides. Juarez's government will have to punish them, or they will get completely out of hand."

Pima Apache, Tosanna thought; so she had been correct in fighting them. They would have shown her no mercy, those dogs, those blood kin to the *Inde*. She said, "Perhaps the Yaqui will do the punishing."

Stafford peered at her and brought out his pipe, tamped it full, lifted a coal to it. Puffing smoke, he said: "As your own tribe attempts to do in the north? That war between whites is done, also; no more Blue Soldiers and Gray Soldiers, only Blue. The army will come back now, and it is only a matter of time until all Indians are conquered— Comanche, Apache, the Pima."

"You lie!" She flared at him. "The Comanche will never be defeated, never."

"A few years at most, my dear. Then you will see your way of life gone, and who is to say a better way will take its place? But fall the Indians will. They cannot stand against the tide."

Clenching fists in her lap, Tosanna said, "I do not understand this *tide*, but you do not understand The People. They are strong and brave, with many horses."

"We whites are many as leaves upon the trees," Stafford went on, pipe stem clenched between white teeth. "No matter how we try to destroy ourselves, we just keep breeding and inventing bigger, more efficient guns. No, my dear, the Comanche cannot win; they can only die."

"Then die we will," she said, "but before we go to the spirits, there will be much mourning in the White Eye lodges."

"Ah, yes," Stafford said, "I suppose so, but in that war there will be little gain for a mercenary. I shall seek a more profitable conflict." He smoked and eyed her. "And you, my beauty, you will set the bloody court on its ear."

"Court?"

He explained it to her, telling of huge meeting lodges where rich chiefs and their women gathered for medicine dances and ceremonies. Tosanna tried to picture court from his words, but it was too vast and confusing. Why did so many warriors bring their women to pay homage to a great chief of chiefs? And if they did not hunt, where then did the deer and buffalo meat come from?

"Wait until they see you," Stafford continued. "You will enliven their jaded palates, wild woman. Of course, I shall see that you make a splash, my dear. Oh, yes; feathers and beads, skins and furs. You will dazzle them all, I dare say. And once your—ah—hidden talents are known, once again Colonel Sir John Stafford will be welcomed in every manor of the land."

"This England," Tosanna murmured, "is it a far journey?"

"Far enough so the taste of this aristocrat's lost war may not lie sour upon the tongue, so soon after the fall of the gentlemanly Confederacy. Poor Maximilian, a well-meaning blunderer like so many. Still, our side should not have executed the man. That, the crowned heads of Europe will not forget so quickly."

He was speaking more and more of things Tosanna could not understand, so she eased further down the rock and lay more mesquite wood upon the low fire. The golden chain about her waist rattled and she silenced it with her fingers, but too late; he had been reminded of it.

"Exotic," he said. "That's how the lords and ladies will view your little token, my dear—as an interestingly bizarre reminder that slavery is not quite dead. Unofficially, of course. Damn, but I'll wager I have certain horny blue-bloods bidding against each other ere the first ball is over."

Moving to her, Stafford picked up one end of her chain and looped it around his ankle. "So that my future does not depart in the night, though where you would go I cannot imagine. Ah—if you could know how you look, with the firelight touching your hair and kissing your face. Those high, slanting cheekbones, your bottomless eyes and the set of your ripe, rich mouth—you're a bloody raving beauty, Tosanna."

He meant to lie with her again, and she did not mind. She was warm and her belly full, and memories of the fight that morning still lingered in her blood, making it race as she recalled the excitement and the thrill of victory. Now she knew why her tribe's warriors so eagerly sought women when they came from a war trail.

So she met Stafford's lust with her own, thrusting and recoiling, taking him into the fury of her seething depths and holding him prisoner there. Now she was the captor, she was the conqueror, and she battered him with the strength of her pelvis, punished him with the power of her rolling hips.

Hissing words she did not understand into her ear, Stafford dug fingers into her buttocks, and she welcomed the small pain, clenching her teeth into his chest and raking his back. He shook free and cursed her, but his curses dropped into groans, and, when Tosanna arched, cried out and slumped upon her.

Tosanna listened awhile to voices of the night wind, to the far cry of a hunting coyote, listened until his breath subsided. Then she slid from beneath him and urged him unto his back. His shirt was open and breeches cast aside, so she crouched over Stafford and nipped at his chest, sliding her tongue about as she had been taught by Don Joaquin de Arredondo.

While teasing her way across Stafford's rib cage and

slowly down the upper reaches of his belly, Tosanna thought
briefly of Don Joaquin, of his angers and the dark revenge
that lived inside him. Sorrow that lasted too long was a
black owl which ate away the entrails until it reached the
heart. Perhaps he would find his wife still alive, and perhaps find his own death in the search. That would be better than the hungry beak of the black owl.

Twisting beneath her, Stafford caught his breath. She
was accomplished as a dedicated French whore, he thought,
overwhelming one moment and devilishly subtle the next,
her lips and tongue damply moving streams of fire. Worth
every shilling he had paid for her and more, bigod, a mistress fit for a king—if only there was a king upon the
throne.

But since the Widow of Windsor held sway, one of the
lesser nobles would have to do. A duke, perhaps—at the
very least, a disgustingly wealthy tradesman. Stafford caressed Tosanna's flowing black hair and fingered its richness
as he wondered where an unschooled savage had learned
such sensuous tricks. From the sullen Don, perchance? Certainly not in the skin houses of her primitive clan. Males
there were more than apt to mount a woman as one animal mounted another, and Indians he had seen were not
loath to hire out their wives for a bottle of whiskey.

Don Joaquin taught this one well, Stafford thought, as
she brought him power again. Clenching her hair, he
moved with her, rolled and arched, and at last ground to
a spine-melting completion. Warmly drifting then, he lazily
stretched his legs and heard the muted clink of chain.

When she stirred against him, her hands trailing gently
over his spread thighs, Stafford came more alert. There was
naught to keep this comely wench from slitting his throat
and departing for her own lands, except his sense of sur-
vival, honed to a fine edge by many wars large and small.
His instincts told him he should keep a close eye upon this
doxy, lest she revert to form and do him in some dark
and careless night.

So, as the coals embered and they lay wrapped in blankets,
all weapons at his hand or beneath his head, Stafford began
to tell her of wonders to be seen—the frenzy of Vera Cruz
gone riotous in celebration of a great victory; and beyond
that city, one so old and wonder-filled that she could not
imagine its treasures.

And Tosanna listened, her ears pricked beyond the murmured words to any sound of night that might be hostile. But she heard the White Eyes talk of riches, and although her eyes swept the skyline for skulking forms upon nearby low ridges, within her head she saw towering heaps of furs and bright shiny knives, axes; she imagined horse herds grazing—herds vast as the buffalo had once been. Plunder beyond belief, she thought. It would be good if she journeyed to this England, so she could trace the trail firmly in mind and tell the landmarks to her father when she returned to the Comanche. Ado-eeti himself would lead the war party, and he might ask that she ride with the fighting band as guide. Together they would bring much honor to the Kwehar-enuh.

CHAPTER 12

She could not believe there were so many Mexicans. For days, as they rode south, more and more of them appeared. Men and women dug in the earth, and children tended goats and strange, clumsy birds. Small children would run out to trot beside her horse, shouting and laughing. So many children; surely the spirits had blessed this tribe. No band of Comanche was as lucky.

And knowing the Mexicans to be such breeders, Tosanna was still unprepared for her first sight of the city, with its mud tepees crowded tightly upon each and spreading in all directions. From a little rise in the ground, she stared at towering stone temples and high, thick walls that would hold off any attack. She saw a dazzling marketplace heaped with strange foods and riches in blankets, cloth and metals; and she saw a troop of uniformed *soldados* that numbered more than her entire tribe.

Close beside Stafford as their horses picked a way through the swirling throng, Tosanna was assaulted by noise and odors and bright, shouting colors. She was glad when Stafford pulled them up at a mud house with a stick fence around it. She stepped down from her saddle before he tugged a signal on the golden chain. This man she knew; although a White Eyes and therefore her enemy, Stafford was something known in this bewildering turmoil of strangeness and strangers.

"Is this England?" she asked. "You have many slaves."

Stafford grinned at her. He needed a shave, and again

the look of hair on his face repelled her. "No, my lass, this is not England. I daresay most lords and ladies there would happily own as many Mexicans as they could support. Alas, our humane laws prevent this. Lead your horse inside the fence with mine."

When the horses were taken by a big-eyed lad, Stafford led Tosanna into a low-roofed house, holding on to her ever present chain. The smells here were now familiar— chilis and corn and meat. Tosanna realized how hungry she was, but said nothing to the woman who turned from the table.

"*Madre de Dios!*" the woman exclaimed. "Señor—this one, is she *indio?*"

"Pure Comanche," Stafford laughed, "but tamed a bit. Señora Sanchez, we are to be your guests, and I assure you, this girl will not pillage and scalp. See the chain?"

Señora Sanchez was chubby and aproned, her hair was pulled back into a bun, small rings glittered at her ears, and a silver cross hung at her layered throat.

She crossed herself, eyes wide. "It is said that all *gringos* are *loco,* and now I am certain of this. It is madness to hold a Comanche to your chest, for one night she will slit your throat."

Motioning Tosanna to a wooden stool, Stafford sat down also. "Ah, she might enjoy that, but I am a careful man, señora."

"Concerning women, no man is cautious enough," the woman answered, and made another sign in the air.

Worn boot propped close to Tosanna's stool, Stafford said to her, "Where would you go, eh? So many *soldadas* here, all with eyes peeled for unprotected beauties, so many men tired of war and hungers. You would be a feast for them, girl. You could not pass for *la peona,* and certainly not as an aristocrat—which class, by the way, is in high disfavor these ways. Your accent would immediately give you away." Stafford tugged at his bristled face and looked at the *posadera.* "But here we feast, and here we are safe, *es verdad?* For gold is a mighty protector, eh, señora? Your best food, then a hot bath and a bed."

Señora Sanchez bobbed her chains. "So long as you keep that chain upon her—so long as *mis hijos* and their machetes watch over me."

"You will seldom be left alone with her," Stafford said. "She is most valuable to me, and when arrangements are made for a coach, for passage on a ship, why then we will be gone from your primitive hostelry."

Tosanna understood most of the conversation, but gave no sign. It was best they did not know, and again she gave thanks for her gift of tongues. She ate beside Stafford, her chain looped through his belt. The food was good, so many flavors she had become accustomed to at the rancho of Don Joaquin. Chewing, washing down *frijoles* with sparing sips of red wine, Tosanna thought of the Don and his quest. Perhaps he already had his wife home, the expedition financed by the price for Tosanna of the Kwehar-enuh. It might be that he had joined Doña Ynez in death.

He had not been a bad man, only driven by a woman madness she could not grasp. It was good to grieve for a loved one, for this made their passage easier to the spirit land and gave them honor there. But to mourn so long was foolish. Even now, Tosanna's own husband no doubt had another woman in his tepee, and she could understand that. It did not mean he loved her memory less, but that he had to stride among the living.

I am not dead, she said inside her head, and wished wings on the thought, so that it might fly straight to Ado-eeti. I am alive, great warrior, and will yet come to warm your couch, to bear your sons.

Watching the sadness upon her face and reading the yearning in her sloe eyes, Stafford thought, What a raving beauty! Sorrow softens the wildness in her and makes those perfect features tender, but let no man mistake the searing flame that waits within the hidden core of her. He emptied his wine gourd and refilled it, seeing the image of jeweled cups of silver and gold raised in toasts to Tosanna's loveliness, once he got her to England.

Another journey lay ahead of them, but he meant this one to be in style and safety, by coach, and with an armed escort to see them to the ships at Vera Cruz. In all the country, things were still unsettled and volatile. His Juarista pass and letters might not be recognized by peon *soldados* who had learned the taste of blood and vengeance, even if they could read. To them, all gringos were fair game. And there were foreign *pistoleros* who had chosen Maximilian's service and were yet uncaught. Wolves outcast from the pack, they would be ambushing any traveler in hopes of escape money.

When the Sanchez woman brought harsh black tobacco

and brown papers, Stafford rolled himself a *cigarillo*, a practice learned from soldiering with Juarez's ragged forces. Through smoke, he watched Tosanna's face. Only now, after the time they had spent together, could he even guess at the girl's emotions, she was so under control.

But the memory of her in battle against the Yaquis, magnificently fierce and unafraid, was bright within him. Dressed in the height of fashion, her blueblack hair coiffed, scented, and jeweled, Tosanna would be the match of any grand lady of the court. Her demeanor and the controlled, royal look of her would mark her far above the mistresses of dukes and earls who sometimes dared attend soirees when Victoria was absent. Yet the discerning man would search out the meaning of that full, pouting mouth and catch smoldering promise in her dark eyes, more than any well-trained doxy could offer, for it was genuine.

Tosanna waited at the table, hands in her lap, face impassive, and Stafford could not tell if she was impatient. Would it be the right thing to clothe her like all other highborn English ladies? This Last Flower of the Comanches should be placed apart, like a costly diamond mounted in a golden setting especially designed to catch the facets of her light. She should be dressed so as to remind all who viewed her that she was a princess in her own land. Stafford drew upon his *cigarillo* and turned the drinking gourd in his fingers, smiling at the very idea of an imperial household among savage brutes.

Once through the Gulf and across the trackless seas, how many would know that, or care if they did? Stafford's grin stretched as he pictured his Comanche princess in skins—buckskins dyed white, beaded and feathered, high moccasins equally gaudy. Would war paint be too much? A large knife then, prominently displayed—furs against England's foggy chill, but wild-looking.

"Señora!" Stafford called, and when the *posada* woman appeared, he asked where he might find a good seamstress and marketplaces to buy the materials he wished. With many darting glances at Tosanna, Señora Sanchez furnished information, but with a look on her moon face that said Stafford was indeed a madman.

"You are an officer of Benito Juarez, but does El Presidente know you have brought this beast in heat, this *animalucho* into his city? *Por Dios*, señor, if you had not been a guest of my house before, and if you—"

Stafford cut in. "Did I not always show my gratitude with hard coin?"

Sweat beaded the woman's thick neck. "Some things cannot be bought. I had cousins to the north—until *indios* slew them all."

"Death is but a way of life," Stafford quoted. "And has it not been said that El Presidente himself carries *indio* blood, which makes him closer to the people?"

Señora's chins jiggled. "I did not mean—" Her mouth firmed. "Juarez or not, I mean to have this wild *puta* guarded while she remains under my roof."

Making a mock bow, Stafford said, "I sincerely hope so, señora. I will also see that she is watched over—very carefully, you understand. Not only for the safety of your house and sons, but for *her* safety, *comprende?*"

Tosanna heard the change in Stafford's voice, the coldness that crept into it, and remembered the clash with the Yaquis, those bastard sons of skulking Apaches. He had been a true warrior then, his guns firing true, calm in the midst of battle and unafraid. If he ordered this whining woman to obey, it was best she do so.

"And me," Tosanna said. "While you go here and there in this anthill you call a city, am I to be tied like a camp dog?"

He blew smoke at the low ceiling, and beyond the door Tosanna heard the clink and jangle of horse soldiers, the cries of those with fruits and meats to trade for bits of shiny metal: *dinero*—money, gold, silver. She was just now beginning to sense its importance to Mexicans and White Eyes.

Stafford said, "Would you have me free you, Comanche? You are a strong, cunning woman, but here you have no knowledge. Arts that keep you alive in the desert are useless, and you are far from your own kind. Very far, and the way is strewn with enemies, but I have the feeling that you would try to return to your primitive home despite the odds. So you will be chained, yes—and a guard over you day and night. When *I* am not with you, my dear."

And so it was to be, Tosanna found, but not right away. First she helped him bathe, and took her turn luxuriating in hot water and soaping herself. The bathing room here was also their bed place, and nowhere grand as Don Joaquin's hacienda; the tub was shabby and the soap poor, unscented. Still, she enjoyed her bath and stood dripping in the tub to catch her hair in both hands and squeeze water from it.

She felt Stafford's eyes upon her then, but did not turn away. It would be foolish, for the man knew her body well and she was his captive; he could do with her as he wished, for that was the law. So long as she was far from her tribe, so long as he did not torture her, Tosanna did not mind his attentions. In a way, it was good to know that her body could hold such powers over her enemies. A miserable Apache would never allow his soul to be stolen like that. But then, she would have killed an Apache captor long ago, and sung her death chant when the others came for her.

Perhaps the time would come when she would put steel into this *soldado* chief. Only the spirits knew that, and until it was revealed to her, Tosanna would live each day as it was given to her. That too was the way of the tribe, for life was hard in Comancheria, and the Kwehar-enuh must be hard to survive, brave and woman alike. From almost the moment of birth, Comanche babies learned never to cry, learned to accept the biting cold of winter and blistering heat of summer without complaint. And if game became scarce and hunger stalked the tepees during the time of snows, children also ignored flat bellies and sucked harder upon old bones.

When Tosanna began to dry her body with a strip of cloth, Stafford came to her. "Allow me, my dear."

She stood quietly as he rubbed her flesh gently. He looked and smelled better since he had scraped his face with the flat, folding knife. His hands probed her buttocks, cupping and fondling there before trailing up and around her waist to caress her breasts.

"Few men can deny you, Tosanna," he whispered into the nape of her neck and caused tingles to race down her back. "You will drive them insane in England."

Were all White Eyes so weak then? Not this one. But Tosanna already knew that Stafford stood taller than others of his kind, that he was more *hombre* than Mexicans she had seen. But if the rest of his tribe was weak, then she should have little trouble getting away from them. When Stafford nuzzled at her ear, his breath hot, she tried to concentrate upon the long and difficult journey back to her home. She could not.

Turning to him, she dug in her fingers and clashed her

body against his. Now she was adept at meeting mouths and kissed him fervently, tongue flicking, teeth raking. The moves which thrilled this man would stimulate his blood brothers also. Among them, she would find the foolish one who would help her escape, binding him to her with ties of sliding, clenching flesh until he betrayed his people. How Ado-eeti would laugh when she told him; how the elders would roar around the council fire.

Stafford lifted her, carried her to the bed, and placed her writhing body upon it. For a long, shuddering moment, he stared down at her and she saw the unnatural brightness of his pale eyes, the deep breaths he took in an effort to steady himself.

He was with her then, hungry as if it was their first exciting time together, plunging himself into her and penetrating deep, seeking the flaming core of Tosanna. She rocked against him, tried to lift him with the strength of her hips, the power of her arched back and legs. The tom-toming of their bodies was slow, gradually building, increasing tempo until it was a hundred frantic palms beating upon taut skins, until the rhythm blended itself into a single, pulsating thunder that shuddered them together.

Gasping, he lay beside her, broad chest gradually slowing to its normal lift. Stafford's eyes were closed, his face calm. Tosanna watched him for a while, sometimes stretching lazily, as the great hunting cats of the mountains stretched after they had gorged upon a fresh kill. She felt that way, warm and filled, and listened to Stafford's breathing until it was deep and even. Then she rolled carefully from the bed and went to her clothing, to the golden chain that lay coiled atop it.

When she turned with the metal in her hands, Stafford murmured, "Bring it to me."

She hesitated, glancing at the closed door, at him. From beneath the pillow, he brought out a pistol and tossed it casually up and down. Tosanna carried the chain to him.

Stafford said, "To protect you from yourself, dear. Your dress now—that's right, put it on. Now I'll just lock this—"

Again she was his prisoner, his slave, subdued while he dressed in clean clothes and belted his pistol about his waist.

Next morning, she walked her horse stirrup to stirrup with him, golden links of her slavery clinking between them.

"Before we reach the government buildings," Stafford told her, "I will have you stylishly dressed, your hair coiffed. Providing you seem other than Indian, these newly annointed bureaucrats will play the gentleman for a smile of promise, although the role is unfamiliar to them."

She did not ask him why she was being put on display; returning warriors of her own village always showed off their prizes, and there was often bargaining between them and older men who had stayed in camp. Did Stafford mean to sell her to someone else?

When the crowds became thick and busy, swirling around them with noise and color and odors she tried vainly to sort, Stafford pulled up their mounts. Climbing down, Tosanna saw that it was a place entirely for horses, where they could be fed, watered, groomed, and kept safe. It was a good idea, but not one for the Comanche; they moved too often for that. Never would they allow themselves to be crammed into smelly wooden tepees, to be crawled over and gawked at. To see only the same view day upon day—Tosanna could not imagine it.

In her land there were such wide places that the ends could not be seen, and mountains so tall they shadowed the sky, and green grass bright enough to hurt the eyes, and leaping white rivers. There was the shining time of quiet snows and herds of antelope running, black bear and buffalo thundering, and high, high above it all, the slow, watchful turning of great eagles and their blood brothers, the hawks.

"Hold to my arm," Stafford said when they left the place for horses. "The shops are just up this *calle,* this street of the merchants."

Women brushed her poor skirt with hardly a glance, but passing men glanced swifty at her face. They were *soldados* ragged and *soldados* gaily uniformed; they were rancheros in wide, tall hats, and whining beggars—all looked their yearning at her.

Tosanna drew closer to Stafford and away from them all. There were no beggars in her camp, and never would be. What warrior or son of warriors could so humble himself? It was better to starve, or, better yet, to find enemies and charge into them, dying with honor.

The dressmaker was small and gray and moved in quick little spurts, like a squirrel. Wondrous materials made her shop a treasure house—bright bolts of color spread here and piled there, even buckskins and many other shining things Tosanna could not name. They drew her eyes and she tried not to show interest.

"Her measurements," Stafford said after unlocking her chain and finding a chair at the door. "Then a fitting in the white buckskins; the other dresses can follow."

The woman flicked squirrel eyes at him. "And you, señor—will you sit there and watch? It is not proper."

Stafford chuckled. "Her appearance deceives, señora; she is Comanche and must be guarded."

Sucking a quick breath, the woman widened her eyes. "I have heard of such a tribe, far to the north. But why—"

"Just do your work," Stafford said, his smile gone, "and do it swiftly, grandmother."

Pins in her small, puckered mouth, the seamstress moved quickly about Tosanna as she stood uncertainly in her nakedness, tucking, pulling, pinning, and making deft stitches. "Now underclothing," she muttered. "Those I have to hand. Now this *extraño* skin, this animal hide, worn by *pistoleros*. It is not civilized for a woman to wear."

Other dresses were fitted to her, soft and beautiful things that must have been woven by spirits. A tuck here, letting out there, and they clung to her like the skin of a bird. They left her shoulders bare and held her breasts high, as if in offering. Below her knees, the skirts flared out in ruffles, and when Tosanna caught sight of herself in a full-length mirror—one of those strong medicines of the White Eyes wherein they captured the surface of a spring—she almost gasped in shock. A lovely stranger peered back at her, and if the hair had not been familiar, Tosanna might not have recognized herself.

"Except for the hair, which courses down her back like any peon girl's," the seamstress said, cocking her head to one side, "one might think her an *aristocrata*. Of course, now that our beloved *presidente* has taken power, all are equal in Mexico. But the appearance is what you wished, señor?"

"Yes," Stafford said, and brought gold from his purse. "The hairdresser has been alerted?" The saddlebags rested bulky at his feet, never out of reach.

"Only two doors down." The seamstress locked fingers about the coins and pressed them to her flat chest. "Señora Guerra is excellent. She used to do a *contesa,* and two of the French ladies-in-waiting." Remembering, she rolled her eyes upward. "But of course, since our beloved *presidente* came to power, the French have gone."

In the hairdresser's shop, Tosanna wore a simple, but appealing dress beneath the towel which draped her shoulders. The other purchases were folded into a great chest, already a load for two boys Stafford hired. Busy fingers scrubbed out her hair and dried it; Tosanna enjoyed the flower smell left behind by the soap and glanced sometimes at Stafford where he sat sniffing bottles of scent and choosing among them.

Girls chattered about her chair, combing and fluffing. They coiled Tosanna's hair as Señora Guerra watched and snapped commands. Tosanna felt pins lightly against her scalp and eyed the mirror to see a marvelous comb standing high behind her head. With such a comb, she would be the most envied woman of her tribe.

"Excellent," Stafford announced when she was turned to display, "a sight to catch the attention of the most bored whoremaster. My dear, dressed and combed like this, you are a mysterious Spanish lady—in your buckskins, a savage princess."

Fitting Tosanna with proper shoes proved more difficult; her feet were widened by a lifetime of moccasins, and not pampered as those of ladies who had patronized this *zapatería*. But enough footwear was found for her and added to the weight of the chest.

"Walk close beside me," Stafford said when they were again on the crowded, rattling street. He carried the heavy saddlebags slung over his left shoulder, so his right hand might stay free to hover above his pistol butt. "I will not feel safe until these and the chests are aboard ship. Even then, I have hired a friend to watch them."

To the series of bewildering events, Stafford added a closed carriage. Riding inside it terrified Tosanna, although she held her face straight. It was like being inside the maw of a clattering animal, shaken and bounced as the beast ran. She hung to grips beside the seat and wished for the honesty of a saddled horse.

Leaning close to her, Stafford said, "Speak as little as possible, for your Spanish has a guttural ring to it, and your English is worse. No matter; there will be time to teach you properly before we reach England."

Suddenly, looming above the crowded street just beyond

bales and boxes and shapes she did not recognize, was the *ship*. It bobbed slightly, up and down, up and down, so that when Stafford led her up a short plank that also moved, her footing was unsteady and she tried to hold back. She was like a young horse, afraid for her balance.

But Stafford's strong hand gripped her arm and drew her with him. They stepped down then, and her uncertainty increased. Water smells thickened about her; men and women jostled her, murmuring polite pardon.

Stafford allowed her to brace herself at the base of a tall, very tall, tree without low branches. For the first time, she looked beyond the crowd and saw the great water, hidden from her until now by long houses that stored all manner of things.

She could not see across the water!

She clawed for Stafford's arm, panicked for the first time in her life. No river could be so wide! For a dozen shuddering heartbeats, she was shamefully afraid, and felt a scream of mad terror building in her throat.

"You're pale," Stafford said, steadying her, moving her to a doorway. "Is my savage princess frightened?"

She swallowed the scream, but did not answer.

A White Eyes dressed in shortened breeches and a striped shirt came bounding up the ladder before them. He had a quick smile for her and was gone.

"Our quarters are below," Stafford said.

Tosanna locked teeth into her lower lip. "Down there? It smells."

He nudged her and she put one shaky foot upon the ladder. "It will smell much worse before we reach England," he said, "but by then you'll be used to it."

If riding in the coach made her feel like a trapped animal, a rabbit caught in a snare, the belly of this monstrous ship was worse. As she descended deeper into its gullet, Tosanna began to doubt she would ever return to her own people. She was being eaten, and any small seed of her left would be passed into that boundless water.

"Here," Stafford said, and turned them into a tiny room. "When we're ready to sail, I'll take you back on deck."

"No," she said, bitterness filling her mouth. "I—tell me, Englishman—will I see Comancheria again?"

"Probably not," he answered, "but then, you might not want to."

"Then I am already dead, and should sing my death song."

He brought out the golden chain and snapped it to wood of a narrow bed. "Don't do that, my lass. If it's anything like your war cry, you'll scare the very devil."

Not a ship, she thought, but a devil, and it had eaten her.

CHAPTER 13

She wanted to die. Never had any Comanche been so sick without dying, and no medicine man, no spirit talker, could work magic to make her well again. Tosanna was too sick to chant her death song.

Stafford called it a ship, this dreadful thing that rocked and pitched and tore at her belly. She hung onto the side of her narrow bed and sweated, clenching her teeth against salty bitterness that threatened to spew forth. A *ship*, a great tepee with many lashings and uncovered center poles—a devil for torture holding many White Eyes prisoner in its bowels, riding the wind sometimes, at others belching smoke. Its groanings and heavings cursed at her; its terrible odors gagged her.

Nowhere in the history of the Kwehar-enuh was mention of so vast a river that the ship rode. None could see the far bank, and Tosanna was sure they were lost upon cruel, hungry waters, forever lost and afraid.

Yet Stafford walked the decks easily and other men scurried aloft among the lashings and center poles like so many darting squirrels and flitting birds. The ship was several suns out before Tosanna could crawl weakly from her dark and rank room to seek the air and sun. She marveled at White Eyes going about their work, and thought they must carry strong medicine, so as not to fall into the great river and be eaten by monsters. Already she had seen evil fish big as leaping buffalo, and the sight of them put snow into her blood.

Men looked at her as she moved along the deck to where Stafford stood, very careful not to approach the rail. Beyond its flimsy boundary seethed the dangers of leaping waters. After so long, after what seemed many moons in her illness below deck, still land could not be seen and she longed for it.

"Ah, there," Stafford said, taking her elbow. "Fair stands the wind for England, and fair breathes our wild princess. You were ill a long time, Tosanna, but there was naught I could do; *mal de mer* will have its way. Now you will eat and regain flesh you have lost."

She smelled salted air and heavy smoke. "I do not understand fire in the ship's belly, nor where wood is cut for it."

Caressing her shoulder, Stafford said, "Not wood, my dear; a black stone which burns long and hot—*coal*. It's used only when the winds are wrong, but I wager someday steam power will allow Her Majesty's vessels to ignore the vagrancies of wind and wave."

Bracing her feet wide, Tosanna tried to balance against the ship's heaving. "The White Eyes watch me. Must I sleep with them all?"

His hand tightened upon her shoulder. "You are a courtesan, princess, not a common doxy. These sailors have been warned away from you; aye, and the ship's officers also. If any man troubles you—"

"All men trouble me but my own," she said. "I was respected as a wife. I was loved. Since I was taken prisoner, I have no tribe, no standing."

She breathed deeply of salted air and stared across rolling water and small, leaping waves that turned white on top before darting back into their mother, the sea.

"I've missed you," Stafford said. "Damn. I little thought such an old soldier as myself would be restless, alone in his blankets. But yearning I have been. A bit less civilized, and I might cry witchcraft."

She looked up at the great sheets of cloth bellying in the wind, then off to where clouds were falling into the water. Beneath her feet, the deck shifted, and she clung to his arm for support. Was there no end to this great river? How could she find her home again, without a single landmark to point the way?

"Will we never cross this river?" she asked.

And Stafford began her schooling then, explaining seas and travel, but she had a difficult time grasping the con-

cept of such distances. Comanches had no ships to cross
the seas, and horses could not swim so far. Tosanna's
spirit curled within her like a dry leaf, but she would not
allow it to die. Someday she would return this way; some
wonder-filled day she would once more see the lodges of
her people. If she did not believe that, she would die.

The food aboard ship was common but filling, and she
who had thought she could never again swallow a morsel
ate greedily, as does the flat-bellied black bear when he
leaves his winter hole. Stafford did not mind that she spoke
to the ship chief at table, nor to lesser chiefs who worked
magic to keep the ship on course for England. But immediately after meals he took her to the small cabin where he
chanted to her from a thing made of bark and very thin
wood. A book, Stafford said, somehow carrying messages
without picture writing.

She learned much English, almost forgetting Spanish in
the process. She learned to walk just so and to hold a fan
at her chin. In calm weather Stafford taught her to dance,
and this she enjoyed, moving in his arms to rhythmic tunes
he sang. There was little freedom to White Eye dancing,
none of the glad abandon the Kwehar-enuh showed around
their campfires. But there women were seldom allowed
to join in.

Nights when she did not restlessly pace the deck, Tosanna
waited to be motioned into Stafford's bunk, and when she
was with him, mated if not happily then with acceptance.

She was pleased when Stafford said she learned quickly,
and used her gift of tongues often in the learning. Beyond
the English words, her mind did not reach when he told
of wonders in England, of lodges so tall a man could fall
from their tops and be killed, of people many as spring
leaves upon trees, and music. There was a White Eye
aboard the ship called a sailor, who introduced her to
music. He moved a magical bag between his hands, and
strange sounds poured forth—noises that were pleasing
to the ear.

Avid for learning, she stretched her mind to close in
every new fact, so that often Stafford would grunt and
stop talking. At those moments, while the ship groaned and
creaked about them, while the great white robes far above
them snapped and billowed, he would drink from a bottle
and his eyes would go hard. Then he spoke aloud to himself,
of wars and traitors, of bastard lords and lowborn trades-

men who would cheat a soldier. There was bitterness in him, and anger like a hot coal covered with ashes—unseen, but ready to blaze forth when stirred.

And after these times when he sat looking into himself, as a spirit talker does, Stafford would take her roughly and try to punish himself against her body. Tosanna responded with a slow violence she did not feel, but that she knew he expected.

In the days he was often gentle, peering forward past the bows of the racing ship for land he could not see. Then she walked the deck, holding tightly to the railing and ropes, for she would never trust her footing, nor the rolling of this wooden thing no more trustworthy than an unbroken horse.

Sailors tried to speak with her, but she answered only the one who squeezed music with his hands. Sailors tried to touch her when she passed from Stafford's sight, but only one attempted to handle her. That one, when his striped shirt fell apart at the quick kiss of her blade, stumbled back as if he had seen his funeral couch, and she was not bothered again.

The captain of the *New World*—for it seemed the *inglés* named their ships as other tribes named their horses—was of different stuff. His beard was full, his eyes looked into far places, and when he spoke men leaped to his command. He looked upon Tosanna with favor, she knew, but Stafford felt it too.

"Not with him," he warned. "Not with anyone now, lest word run ahead and reach the wrong ears, for what noble would soil himself with a whore who has dallied with commoners? England is not *that* democratic and perhaps shall never be. The master of this vessel has been well paid for our passage and owes his early sailing to me. Do not tempt him, Tosanna; it would mean his death."

So many strange customs to learn, and many of them centering about a man mounting a woman. The *inglés* would kill over a woman, and that was stupid; they could be taught much by the Comanche. If a woman and warrior were drawn to each other, and the woman was wife to another man, blending their bodies was never cause for bloodshed when the husband discovered their meetings.

Of course there was redress; a Comanche could not use another's wife without paying for it—in horses or skins, or whatever fine was decided by tribal council. If the Kwehar-enuh fought over favors of wives, or unmarried girls, or captives, they would have no time for more important things, no time to hunt meat and ride on war parties. The Comanches were sensible men.

When she mentioned this to Stafford, he was in one of his gentler moods, but looked at her with surprise. "You are saying that a woman has no self-respect, no feelings of individuality, of—of *love*, damme! You say that she should not feel soiled when she is raped, that any stranger—" Eyes boring into hers, he paused. "But why not?" Stafford went on. "You are savages, nothing else—only savages to soon be ground into nothingness. In less than a century, even your language will be forgotten—if you possess more than grunts and motions."

Tosanna flared at him. "Savages, are we? Damme—and what does that make you, White Eyes? You bought me; you did not ask me into your bed, but forced me. Is that what you mean by *rape*, damme?"

"Damme, is it?" Stafford's grin made his face lopsided. "Bloody good, miss. I shall have to mind my tongue and polish your language a bit before loosing you among lusting gentry. Yes—rape is taking a woman against her will. Were you not raped by that cheeky Mexican hidalgo?"

Tosanna considered. "There is no such word in the Comanche language. The word for coupling and love and animal mating—it is all the same. Don Joaquin captured me in battle and took only what was his right, though his men faced only children."

"And you felt no shame—or was it you were no maiden, and it did not matter as much?"

When he explained the meaning of maiden, Tosanna told him how Comanche children experienced sex early, almost as soon as they discovered the difference between boys and girls. She described the teaching lodge, where older girls brought in young boys and instructed them.

"Barbaric," Stafford grunted. "Logical in a perverse way, but barbaric. Be certain you do not mention such customs in court, for all England has the idea that American savages are noble redskins, pure and lofty. Keep that image, and we will cause such a stir in London that we won't be able to answer all the invitations."

He laughed. "I can see them now—gouty old Earl Lansdown, limping over to kiss your hand and, at the first opportunity, to whisper in your ear that his affliction does not curtail his randiness in bed. And Sir Edward Baker, sanctimonious and looking askance over his heron's beak; he'll have a hand under your skirts within the hour. Lord Blasingame—ah, he'll discuss lofty affairs of state with you, all the nonce peering down your dress. And others not so obvious, but sniffing about just the same. I will choose carefully for you, my lass."

She listened to sea gently bumping the ship's hull and swayed with its rhythm. "You mean to marry me to some White Eye chief?"

"Marry? Laws no—unless some fool is overly smitten by your wild charms. But I shall expect fair compensation, plus kind words in Her Majesty's ear, an absolvement of my peccadillo against the Emperor of Mexico. Yes, your consort will be most carefully chosen."

"I will return to my people," Tosanna said.

Stafford lifted a tufted brow. "You will wear my chain until a new master acquires you. But return to your primitive existence? I think not; given time, you will not desire it—even if going back were possible."

She repeated her statement. "I will go back."

Slapping a palm against the fastened-down table in the ship's cabin, he said, "You don't realize what I'm doing for you, wench. Plucking you from crawling filth—oh, I have seen how you savages live—from constant danger; women scalps bring as much reward as those of braves. From famine and disease and killing; you stand defiant to tell me you prefer *that* over the comforts of England. You're a bloody fool."

He left her to pace the deck, and for a while she could hear his boots above her head, marking time with the ship speaking in its many quiet tongues. Tosanna sat at her sea chest, fingering the finery Stafford bought, stroking the white leather dress so beaded and feathered and bangled.

The things were beautiful, but so flimsy; they would swiftly turn to rags when tepees were struck and loaded onto travois, or during buffalo cleaning, or scraping skins for drying. No White Eyes dress was meant to last through work done by women of The People. Did White Eye women not work hard? If their *men* labored, then they were too young, too old, or crippled. Perhaps the *inglés* owned many slaves, and many horses, and so even their women did not have to sweat.

Walking in the peculiar rolling motion she had acquired,

Tosanna went to the ladder and climbed it. The ship wasn't pitching violently, so the excitement on deck must have been caused by a far-off storm, or by some terrifying, giant fish about to smash the ship to broken twigs so it could swallow them all. She clung to the rope handrail and lifted her head above the hatchway. Cooler air pawed her face and flung her loose hair about.

"Come here!" Stafford called, and she went to him where he stood by the rail forward, to where sailors crowded laughing and ignored her.

Pointing, Stafford said, "Look there, girl. Just off the bowsprit—England, bigod—land ho for England!"

CHAPTER 14

For the second time in her life, Tosanna felt very small. Never before had she been insignificant, even alone in a soundless, barren stretch of Comancheria, with the desert spread about her like a great, empty blanket. But upon the sea, those lonely, leaping waters so alien to her, in a ship so fragile, she had been lost and afraid.

Now, holding tightly to Stafford's hand as he led her down the gangplank, Tosanna knew another chill, an overwhelming sensation that made her meaningless as a fly crawling a buffalo horn. Because of so long spent aboard the *New World*, her legs refused to obey her, and land seemed to heave beneath her feet.

Everything was huge and noisy here, and even the ship she had come to know was swiftly lost among many others of its kind. All around her, tall houses loomed, one fitted closely to another, lodges so big they reached into forever. And White Eyes—like swarming bees, buzzing, circling, and climbing over each other while horses snorted and gigantic travois rattled across stones laid side by side.

Head whirling, she was lifted into an open carriage. When its pale driver stared at her, she put an uneasy hand upon her knife. Except for the sailors, which she could distinguish by their tarred pigtails and the way they dressed, all the *inglés* appeared washed out and sickly. Weak men, she thought, ailed by disease; they would be easy to defeat—if there were not so impossibly many of them.

"Keep that hidden," Stafford said beside her. "No one

127

carries weapons here." To the driver, he gave an address
and settled back. Tosanna gripped his arm when the vehicle
lurched forward, while above her the great lodges reached
grimed for the sky.

She could not believe *inglés* carried no weapons, even
in their home camp, but every man she saw proved Stafford
right. Maybe they felt safe because their land was surrounded by seas—something else Stafford had told her.
But if they had many ships, did not enemy White Eye tribes
also own them?

Still hanging on to Stafford's muscled arm, she bounced
uncomfortably on the carriage seat and tried not to flinch at
strange and threatening sights. She had been a fool to think
the Comanche could attack this city; Comanches had no
big ships, and she was certain the combined tribes of all
her land could not match the numbers she saw here.

She wondered how they managed to eat, where they
hunted—since she saw no open lands—and where they
kept their horses. A great many horses would be needed
for so many men, even beyond those working beasts throng-
ing the pathways. Bells and shouts and crashes; Tosanna
wanted to cover her ears, wanted to shrink into the seat
and hide. But she was one of The People, and so sat erect
beside the man who had bought her. Her face did not show
the shock she knew, nor that the spirit had almost run out
of her, leaving only a tiny, nagging puddle to remind her
of the Kwehar-enuh.

Why had not the spirit talkers told the tribe of this? Why
did they point out that only *tejanos*, Mexicans, White Eyes,
and Apaches were enemies, and say nothing of this vast
beehive of *inglés*? Perhaps they did not know, for the
medicine of these pale men was very strong. Tosanna
wished hard that she were a warrior, so she might go into
the desert and fast until a vision came to her. But there
was no desert in England, and she was only a woman.

When the box they rode in slowed and found more even
ground, Tosanna said, "The *inglés soldados*—soldiers; does
their chief send them to help *tejanos* or White Eyes in my
country?"

Stafford grunted. "Tejanos *are* White Eyes."

"No," she insisted, "they are different and fight harder.
There were times The People made treaties with White
Eyes, but never *tejanos,* who are only white Apaches."

Stafford pointed. "Out there are men of a dozen nations,

and each nationality belongs to but one country. Does our minister send British tommies to fight American Indians? No, my dear; not enough profit in that, although I wager that Her Majesty is damned-awful sorry she didn't prop up old Max in Mexico. His fall trembled crowned heads around the world, you may be sure."

"Then," Tosanna went on, "would the *inglés* make a treaty with Comanches?"

Cutting his eyes at her, he said, "Oh, so England's might is beginning to impress you? But for naught, lass; to our queen all Americans are still stubborn colonists, and wild Indians—well, mayhap we can interest her in one of them, eh? Damme, even dressed civilized, you are turning heads."

"I do not think much of a tribe that allows itself to be led by a woman."

Stafford laughed. "There are those who agree with you, but many others who stand wide of the Widow at Windsor. There will be lessons for you, my dear—etiquette and the like; not the least will be how to hold your tongue. Damn if I am not disposed to teach you to read and write, but that would be tempting the fates."

Tosanna said, "I read hand language."

"A useless skill here, like skinning a jackrabbit or weaving a rush basket. The only art you need you were born with—that of pleasing men. Here it will stand you in good stead. No savage swain could possibly appreciate you as much as dissolute Englishmen."

She said, "I do not understand all your words."

"I don't expect you to." Stroking a hand across her thigh, he reached up and clinked the golden chain about her waist. "This won't be needed here, since I know you're intelligent enough to know it's useless to run. Policemen will come after you, and if you're lucky they will find you. If not, you'll end in some flyblown crib, taking on every filthy cockney and drunken seaman for a few coppers you'll never see. I don't think you're ready for that, my lass—so I'm your only hope just now. You'll be a good little squaw, but the chain—ah, yes: it might be a special touch, an added fillip."

The carriage stopped before a bustling house that was hilltop high. Brightly dressed men came to carry their sea chests, and Tosanna wondered where all the women were, that men would do such menial labor. Inside she saw them, women wearing the same kind of clothing, skipping about, carrying trays of food, wiping at furniture, and giggling. How silly were women of the *inglés;* none looked strong enough to carry a gutted deer back to camp. And there was not a knife among them.

"Look about you," Stafford said. "Stand erect and cool as you do so. Already they're inspecting you, but covertly. This is an upper-class residential hotel—more than an inn, less than a gentleman's house. You can tell by the lamps there, the chandeliers—crystal they be. And the woods: imported mahogany—"

"The white part," Tosanna asked, "adobe?"

He chuckled. "Plaster and lath; nothing so solid as your hidalgo's home."

"He was not my hidalgo. I was his prisoner, taken in war."

"Ah, yes." Stafford held to her elbow and smiled at this passing man, nodded to another. It seemed he was deliberately lingering in this entrance room, so that many would see them.

Many men and few women, Tosanna thought, all richly dressed. Some men carried little canes she thought were coup sticks until Stafford explained. Some women wore earrings, but none so sparkling as those she'd known at Don Joaquin's.

Nervously, Tosanna waited while Stafford made talk with men behind a wooden barrier, then followed close behind him to climb higher in the big house. Again other men carried their plunder, but not sensibly upon their heads, nor upon a long sapling between them.

"Our rooms," Stafford said with a mock bow and courtly flourish. The *inglés* slaves—for that was what they must be—carried in boxes, raised windows, turned down the massive bed, and scraped before Stafford. He rewarded them with coins, and, when they bowed out, said to her, "It will not be long ere every horny gentleman in the realm will know we stay at the Brickmaker's Arms. Aye, and every jealous lady also, and some not so jealous, but only interested."

He stalked to the window and peered out, loosening his stock. "But you are not to dally with anyone, man or woman, unless you are told to. Understand that. I should not enjoy beating you, but if I must there will be welts raised across your lovely backside."

Upon feet still made uncertain by the voyage, Tosanna

poked curiously about the place. She had seen the like of some things in Don Joaquins's hacienda; some were strange to her. It was odd how *inglés* and Mexicans hid themselves in boxes, away from the sun and wind; how they must be surrounded by objects they could not carry away when the camp moved. Surely there were clean forests *inglés* traveled to when hunting and warring was done. Surely they did not live always in these smells and noise.

Turning, she said quietly to Stafford, "I have been obedient because I must, until I return to my people. Any Apache can tell you that Comanches make bad slaves; they turn on their captors. Death is cleaner than shame."

Peeling off a broadcloth coat that made him look clumsy and uncomfortable, Stafford stared at her. "You're bloody well threatening me."

"I speak truth," Tosanna said. "If you beat me, I will count coup on you while you sleep. It is not honorable, but I am only a woman."

His glare changed to a laugh, a snort. "I trust we do not come to a clash of wills then. I haven't forgotten you standing against the Yaqui, killing and shrieking." He tucked thumbs into his trousertops and laughed again. "Damme—I can just imagine the sickness on certain delicate faces if they'd seen you spilling blood. Bed you then? They couldn't get it up if you lashed their pizzles to candlesticks."

Away from sea breezes, she was warm, and took off the thin coat that reached to her hips. Tosanna pulled a white, ruffled blouse away from sticky skin and blew down it.

Softly, Stafford murmured, "But I have killed Yaqui too—and Mexicans and Frenchmen and men from places you never heard of. I sleep lightly."

"Even the wolf tires," she said.

He shook his head. "Very well. If you obey, I will not beat you. What you do after certain arrangements are made is your business. Hopefully, by then I shall have found where my special talents are appreciated, and will be off again—tallyho!"

Tosanna removed her blouse. Often she had longed for the loose freedom of buckskin instead of these bindings. When she glanced up, Stafford's eyes were upon her breasts. He took a step toward her, his hands lifting. There was a knock at the door.

"Beggin' your pardon, lordship. Baths been drawn like you ordered—one for yourself, another for the lady, with a valet and servin' maid standing by. Right down the hall, sir."

"Very well," Stafford said to the closed door, and Tosanna heard footsteps plod away. "Put on a wrapper, lass, atop your skirts even. Remember this is England, Victoria's England, and appearances must be kept, oh, yes. So long as the trappings of virtue are observed, virtue itself may be diddled. After you, Milady Savage."

In the hallway she said, "I do not need help to bathe."

"Ladies *always* need assistance; common folk do not. You are a princess, remember."

So Tosanna sat in warm water and allowed a fluttering girl to soap her back and wash her long hair. "Coo," the woman said, "but it's wondrous locks ye have, miss. Put up proper, it'd drive men bonkers, ye don't mind my sayin'. I know my man fair rouses himself playin' with my hair, and it nowheres near the softness and heft of yours. Gor, but I'm takin' on so, and your ladyship just off the boat, like."

Tosanna tried to sort each word as it came tumbling out, but some of them fell away before she could judge their meaning. Perhaps this woman was of a different tribe; she did not speak like Stafford.

The maid rinsed away soap and stood by the metal tub holding out a towel large enough to wrap Tosanna in. "Ye come from a far land, milady?"

"Far," Tosanna said.

"And you're—ward to Sir Stafford yon? A fair handsome man, that."

"*Ward?*" Tosanna slipped into the fluffy towel. "I do not understand *ward*. I am his woman. He bought me."

The woman clapped a hand to her mouth. "Gor blimey! *Bought* ye like a blinkin' slave? Oh, no—I see your meanin', indeed I do. But I never thought to hear one of ye—ah, ladies—admit it, to bein' a mistress, like. Coo, but ye be a cool 'un, miss—and honest."

She followed Tosanna down the hall and into the room. "To proper dry your hair, miss," she said seating Tosanna at the dressing table with its captured lake giving back their reflections. No, Tosanna recalled—a mirror, *mirror*. Only a glass and not magic.

Brushing, the maid whispered, "Mistresses now, they don't last like wives, for men can throw 'em over when they tire of us, the ruddy bastards. Beggin' your pardon, mam'. But do ye need a friend, call on Belle Williams. That far land ye be from, it turns out true women, that it does. Nothin' like them saucy wenches what primps around after their *uncles* and acts like servin' girls be dirt under their whorish shoes."

Sitting quietly while the woman brushed her hair, Tosanna heard Stafford enter and watched him in the glass. He passed on into the bedroom, and Belle Williams stepped back to look after him. Rising, Tosanna put one hand lightly upon the woman's and moved the other in the air, making the sign for peace.

She said, "I thank you, Belle Williams. I am far from my people and in need of a friend."

"Laws," Belle breathed, and hurried out.

Stafford sat upon the edge of the bed, rubbing at his ear with a towel. His skin was browned where sun had touched it, and below the neck he was pale as any fish's belly, but hairy. Now she did not mind the hair.

He dropped the towel and spread his knees. She moved between them and put her hands upon his bare shoulders, looking down into his blue eyes. Stafford said, "All our coy women, hiding their desires behind stays and corsets, denying them even in bed—ah, they could learn from you, my desert princess. You have no more love for me than Maximilian's widow, that poor, crazed Carlotta. But you are not loath to show your need for me, a woman's need for a man."

She did not tell him how it pleased her to take the lead, to make the first aggressive moves. Such was accepted when she was only a girl teaching fumbling boys, but once she became wife to Ado-eeti, she must wait for her husband to call her to his couch. With Stafford she could cross that traditional line and make him a shadow less than a man by thrusting her own demands upon him, by not permitting him his own desires, but bending him to hers. Tosanna sank to the floor upon her knees and drew her lips over his chest, her clawed fingers down his muscled thighs.

Teasing, tantalizing, she caressed him to her liking, controlling each gasp that broke from his lips, commanding every arching twist of his body. And when she had tormented him so that he wove his fingers through her hair, Tosanna leaped upon him and bore him back upon the bed.

Hands swift and deft at his trousers, she bared his manhood and attacked it, took him into the clenching, pulling strength of herself to batter his belly and rake his flesh. Groaning, Stafford fought for dominance, but now she was captor and he the slave. He clung to her hips, her wheeling buttocks, and when Stafford quivered in the thunder of his spirits, she continued to take him. In her own sunflashing ecstasies, she cried out again and again, but did not weaken, did not stop until he lay conquered beneath her.

She lifted from him then, exultant in her power. In the spirit world his scalp was lifted high upon her lodgepole. Muttering, Stafford turned onto his side, his furry legs sprawled. She looked down upon him for a long moment, then moved away from the bed to seek coolness at a window. Naked, she stood just inside the protection of a thin white curtain and peered out upon England, at London.

Beyond smaller houses, she could see the river with its palisade of tall ships, and, farther still, the vastness of the sea. Somewhere beyond it lay Comancheria and all she had known, everything she had held dear and prideful.

With a deep breath, Tosanna pulled her eyes from the land she could see only inside her head and stared down at the roadway below, the street. All paths had names here, but she knew none of them yet, and so few strange *inglés* customs. Stafford had said appearances must be kept up, the heavy clothing worn just so, to disguise her woman's body. She must also hide her need for a man, and not show it to him through words or her eyes. Truly, the *inglés* were a tribe of liars.

Noise rattled up from below, and she saw carriages upon the street, saw men shouting market wares without shame of women's work, and women scurrying like so many dark crows. Across the street horses stopped and a coachman leaped to the ground. In his open carriage lolled a woman whose hair turned gold when sun struck it. A man was beside her, tall and lean as a Comanche, but also golden. Tosanna watched him climb down and extend a hand to the woman.

He looked up then, and up, as a quick wind lifted her curtain, and she knew he saw her. Stiffly, hand in the air, he stared until Tosanna remembered she was naked and moved back from the window.

CHAPTER 15

Were it not for the gift of tongues that enabled her to learn quickly all the things Stafford wanted her to know, Tosanna's head might have been touched by spirits, so that she went mad. The noise and smells and staring eyes were cactus thorns catching at her; the chill dampness and ghostly fog were evil things out to capture her soul.

But there was also Belle Williams. The woman was at her elbow often, helping, soothing when all went wrong and the strange words, the stupid customs flew from Tosanna's head like frightened sparrows.

"Not the best lady-in-waiting," Stafford said, "since she's cockney to the core and knows aught of gentle ways. Still, she has attached herself to you and seems faithful. Best I hire her away from the innkeeper, but you will need more than her gutter knowledge so as not to shock the bluebloods."

So Tosanna's only friend became her maid, her helper and guide. The other woman Stafford hired was none of these things, but a prim and corseted tyrant who sniffed through her long nose and peered through glasses held on a stick. Miss Trevelyan looked at Tosanna as if she should be in a cage, or at the least gone over thoroughly for lice.

Miss Trevelyan was to teach Tosanna etiquette, manners to be used among the gentry. She would arrive each day at precisely the same time, nostrils pinched and colorless lips compressed. Time, Tosanna learned, was measured by small machines, not by sun and shadow; it was marked by "seasons," not snows or green grass. These *inglés* were somehow chained to time.

No, Miss Trevelyan said; do not slouch, young woman. Sit up, and use your fork, not the knife. Do not make animal noises when you eat. Oh, Miss Trevelyan said, looking angry, that she should sink to such poverty, when her family had once been wealthy. To think she must teach a wild Indian to pass as a lady, and an Indian living openly in shame.

Tosanna listened and learned, and, when Miss Trevelyan left for the day, mocked her shaking head and pursed lips, imitating the woman's prim distaste until Belle Williams held her belly and laughed.

At first she and Stafford ate meals in their rooms, but later sought the private dining room downstairs. To reach it, they must pass through the common room, as Stafford planned, so that many curious eyes followed Tosanna and excited whispers sprang up in the wake of her retinue.

Stafford saw to it that she was always clad in eye-catching clothing, preferring she be seen often in false buckskins he had sewn by London seamstresses, tightly fitting dresses that molded her body and were hung with feathers, painted with barbaric designs. Even the jewelry he chose for her was bizarre and garish, but Tosanna's proud beauty carried it well. Watching her move grandly through a host of staring tradesmen and not a few lords, Stafford again congratulated himself on such a prize.

His slow, teasing campaign was going well. The lass was rapidly absorbing the language and lessons in manners, and news of her presence, her downright stunning beauty, was already the choice tidbit of city gossip. The powers at Buckingham and Windsor could not long ignore him, persona non grata though he was for the nonce.

He had contacted people at the treasury and made mention of the gift he wanted to make, to Queen and country— a gift of simple gratitude for being an Englishman. The tidy sum he named lifted eyebrows and bent bureaucratic necks, damned if it didn't. It would have been decidedly less costly for him had Victoria not openly declared for Maximilian, although she had sent no help when the old boy's throne was shaky. Dotty chap, refusing to shave his beard and go into disguise when he could have escaped. So the Juaristas shot him on The Hill of Bells.

And because Colonel Sir John Stafford hadn't been dotty

enough to be executed beside Max, because he'd had a hand in the emperor's overthrow, Victoria's displeasure was plain. He would have the devil's own time getting a commission in any army of her allies, and the Widow had political alliances everywhere in the world.

But Tosanna was well on the way to changing all that. Another fortnight or so, and a sly, secondhand invitation would arrive. Sir Stafford and his savage princess would present themselves, informally of course, at some ball or other. And from the background, as if she had but deigned to stop by in passing, would come Victoria.

The onetime child queen had a nose for intrigue and a curiosity big as her stylish bustle; she would be burning to see for herself this reported wild beauty her renegade officer had carried home as spoils of war. A chain about her waist, it was rumored—a golden chain in itself worth an admiral's pay; dressed queer, to be sure, but walks like a ruddy princess—which she is said to be, in her own land.

Stafford grinned as he sat at table with Tosanna. He could picture the envious outrage, her the shocked murmurs that carried like the tide. They were no doubt already lapping at palace walls.

"Sir Stafford," Miss Trevelyan said. "I simply cannot stop her from eating with that abominable knife."

"Tosanna," he said. "The fork, lass. You cut with the knife—and not that skinning knife, mind you—and eat with the fork."

Strong white teeth showing as she took a bite of beef, Tosanna said, "It is quicker with the knife."

"Speed is not the idea," Stafford explained, watching the deft, beguiling movements of her lips. "Eat slowly, enjoy and savor—but act as if you are not hungry."

She raised a darkfeather eyebrow. "Do the English lie about everything?"

Miss Trevelyan choked over her teacup, and Belle Williams stifled a giggle. Stafford said, "When it's convenient, but mostly it's put down as politeness or expedience."

"Laws," said Belle Williams, "but she's learnin' all the wrong things."

Sniffing, Miss Trevelyan said, "As if *you* would know."

"Ladies, ladies," Stafford said, and poured himself a glass of claret. Every move Tosanna made was graceful, he thought, as if she was never unsure of herself, as if she had not been squatting beside a mesquite fire only a short time ago. Her shapely hands, not so brown now that she had been long kept from exposure to the sun, were slim, agile, and strong. And her walk—supple, lithe, and timed to the primitive drumbeats of her heritage. No man with juice in him could tear his eyes away from Milady Savage when she strolled across a room.

He would be loath to lose her. Stafford downed his claret and signaled for brandy. Leaning to light his cigar from candle flame, Stafford caught the dancing reflection in her black eyes and sighed. If he believed in witchcraft, he would think she had practiced some dark art upon him, that she had somehow bound him to her by spells and incantations. But the girl was no rider of brooms, no stirrer of bubbling cauldrons; she was only a Comanche whose diddling was more fiery, more deeply satisfying than he could have ever thought.

He had known women of a dozen nations and crossbreeds of many more, whores and camp followers who knew half the sexual tricks of the world—and ladies who knew the rest. Never had any woman reached him as Tosanna had, down into the heretofore unplumbed depths of his being and along tingling nerve ends he hadn't known existed.

And it was more than enveloping of sweet flesh, more than a containment of flexing muscle, but something else. Stafford didn't want to think spiritual, so he settled for mental, some not yet understood joining of mind to mind that brooked no excuse not natural. It was an interlocking of body and brain that ripped away all false modesty and gave the lie to prudishness. When Tosanna made love, she plunged into the core of a man and loosed raw emotion hidden even from himself.

What the hell was wrong with him? He sat here mooning at his own mistress like a lovestruck farmer. No, not mistress, but whore, servant, slave—bought for hard cash as an investment in his future. All he need do to possess her completely was lead her to bed, no more. Bedding her now would be every whit as gratifying as that first surprising encounter under desert stars. Every bout of lovemaking with Tosanna was fresh and exciting, and there, bigod, lay the difference.

Young and old, perfumed, beribboned wife or hungry youngster all legs and fumbling—it took but little time for Stafford's liaisons to grow cold. What lissom movement, what delighted cry thrilled him yesterday bored him on the morrow, as did coy toss of head and sensual rub of belly, all turning into a dreary sameness.

Not Tosanna, by all the cockeyed gods that watched over warriors—not the Lady Savage. She woke new with the dawning, and through the day ever showed other facets of herself, like a crown jewel turned rainbowing in a caressing shaft of sunlight. At night she was a breathless virgin silvered by the moon, or the naughty-nice princess who haunted the dreams of callow lads—or superbly trained courtesan, or fierce enemy to be overwhelmed, or gentle and submissive. She had the knack of matching his every mood. And that of every other man?

"Damn," Stafford said aloud, causing the other women to jump, but not Tosanna; of course, not Tosanna. "Damn, woman—it would be bloody easy to believe your heathen medicine can work magic."

"Sir Stafford," Miss Trevelyan sniffed, "you must mind your tongue."

And his brain, he thought; the worth and cunning of a man lay between his ears, not in the heart poets were wont to simper about. Red Indians cut out the heart of a bison and cooked it, but they used its brains to soften the hide. His own brains were worth no more, did he allow them to soften over a doxy, and already there were enemies aplenty seeking to cut out his heart—and his lights and liver as well. He'd play the utter fool, giving them another opening by tarrying too long with Milady Savage. His knighthood had always hung by a weak thread, and had he not strengthened it by reputation, the stain of bastardy that had always dogged him would snap that thread.

"Up the stairs," he directed the two women. "Miss Trevelyan, you have instructions to give, and Belle—"

Flowing up from the table, Tosanna made her way into the common room, her appearance stilling the rumble of voices, the clatter of glassware and cutlery. She moved through the silent tables like a monarch bestowing favors through her mere presence, and by the looks on wine-reddened faces, the goggling of greedy eyes, every man jack there would bend his knee to her, did she but command it.

The women, Stafford saw, were something else—gone slit-eyed with envy or cringing in submission—all finding sudden excuse to touch their men's hands or arms in reminder. Of course, no ladies were among them, save with the party just entering and being shown to the private dining room.

There—wasn't that a foreign duchess, Katrina something. or other of Hapsburg? And over there a lady-in-waiting to the royal household; Stafford well recalled the beauty spot upon yon Nancy's haunch. The men he did not know, but the richness of their dress and their casual arrogance announced they were of substance. Although it was early in the evening for supper, the women glittered, and the Hapsburg duchess paused to stare at Tosanna moving past.

Quickly, Stafford fell in behind her, inclined his head slightly to the duchess, and passed a sly wink to Lady Nancy.

"Good lord," the duchess said, bejeweled hand at her ample bosom, "are we being invaded?"

Her escort laughed, but Lady Nancy's did not. Quick and limber as a deer, the man slid into the aisle before Tosanna and bowed. Tosanna halted, showing no sign of surprise or dismay. Behind her, Miss Trevelyan and Belle Williams pulled up sharply to avoid running into her, and Stafford stood awkward after.

"Madame," the stranger said, "Miss, milady—however one dares address such a vision—I cannot allow you to return to the heart of the rose from whence you came—not without blessing your poor subject with your name. But wait! Can it be I have seen you before, outside your native costume?"

The others giggled, the duchess behind a spread fan. She said, "Walker—ah, dear boy; what a jester you are!"

Shouldering near, Stafford said between his teeth, "But without a foolscap. Sir, you importune my ward. You have never laid eyes on her before."

In mock horror, the man skipped back. He was young and medium tall, with no more heft to him than a slender woman, and his long, curly hair was carefully brushed and yellow. Stafford didn't like him, but he might be someone of note.

"Walker Fairbairn, your honor, your worship; I plead ignorance of custom, being late come from the colonies, and—"

A cheeky American, what else? And by the soft mush tongue on him, a Confederate like that defeated band of cavalrymen who had offered their swords to Maximilian, only to lose again. So he was nobody, only hanger-on to the duchess there, who was surveying the scene with coolly detached amusement.

"And damned close to trouble," Stafford said. "Stand aside, boy."

Tapping her fan upon her collarbone, Duchess Katrina Hozenholer said, "Sir Stafford, isn't it—onetime captain of the guards?"

Walker Fairbairn made a sweeping bow that brought his yellow hair close to Tosanna's sleek thigh. "Forgive me, onetime captain; I would not rouse your ire, timid soul that I am."

The duchess laughed again, and Lady Nancy glared. Behind the Hapsburg, a spade-bearded man stood tall and silent, his eyes gimleting Stafford.

"Colonel now," Stafford said.

"Oh? Do peasant armies bestow titles?"

Stafford flushed and caught Tosanna's elbow to steer her ahead. Behind them, the common room had been holding its breath, but let it out with laughter that singed Stafford's ears and hardened his jaw. Ah, they knew he was about, all right; word had spread among the elite that a betrayer was among them and flaunting his pagan mistress.

Practically shoving Tosanna up the steps, he thought how it would have been if that grinning jackanapes had galled him in Mexico. It would have been settled on the spot, and when the gunsmoke cleared, men would think twice before bearding John Stafford.

Damn the old German bitch for bringing out that captain-of-the-guards scandal. As if he could erase the bar sinister laid by rumor to the Stafford coat of arms; as if he could call out his shadowy accusers, now that dueling had been made a common crime. After resigning his commission, hadn't he proved himself time and again on fields of battle that would have terrified his sniveling foes at Buckingham? Ah, the bitches and sons of bitches; on the Continent again, he'd be done with them and their spite, their envy. It was to confound them all that he lifted so many petticoats and made cuckold so many blind and prideful husbands of the peerage.

In their rooms, Miss Trevelyan and Belle Williams mumbled excuses and made themselves scarce. Tosanna walked thoughtfully to the window and looked down to the gaslit street below. She said, "You knew only the women, and they were not your friends. But the man with sunlight hair—he is pretty."

Stafford grunted. "Sunlight hair? Oh, drunken lord of soldier men, save me from the twisted minds of women. He's a fool, but, yes, a *pretty* fool with a woman's eye and a woman's softness."

She turned from the window. "Do you say he is a man who wishes to be a woman in every way? Among the Comanches I have heard of such, but there has not been one in the Antelope band—not in my lifetime." Tosanna frowned. "I do not think that one is a man-woman. I think his softness is a trick, like flowers on cactus, to hide sharp needles."

Splashing French brandy into a glass, Stafford made a face. "Tommyrot! Did you mark his delicate skin, his long hair?"

"Comanche warriors wear their hair long," she said. "It is a powerful sign of mourning to cut it, or great dishonor to lose it to an enemy."

"Scalping, trophy taking made acceptable by mysticism and profitable by buyers. That young buffoon will always keep *his* scalp safely out of harm's way."

"I am not so certain."

He gave himself more brandy. "You do not have to be certain about him; you don't even have to *think* about him. There's too much to learn, too much waiting to be stuffed into your heathen head *below* the scalp. When I put you on display, I want to be damned sure you're presentable. You're to keep your precious Comanche attitude, that special air of mystery, but you will also be civilized enough not to turn gentlemenly stomachs—except cozily against your own."

Standing there with gaslight an aura about her head, Tosanna looked more regal than that damned German duchess, he thought. If ever the two came face to face—once Tosanna was gone from his shaky protection—even Victoria could meet her match. He would like to see those sparks fly, but barring a stroke of ill fortune, by then Colonel Sir John Stafford would be offering his considerable expertise to some foreign prince. Kin, no doubt, he thought sourly, to the late departed Prince Consort. All these inter-married houses were blood to one another in some fashion—

not always lawful—and they dared smear *him* with the name of bastard.

"Take to your lessons," he told Tosanna. "I have business elsewhere."

He didn't, but Stafford never liked to drink alone. There were hostels he knew that catered to military men, to soldiers foreign and adventurers homegrown. He would find his own kind there, men who did not give a tinker's damn about shopworn tales and palace politicians. It would be good to shed his mantle of humbleness and drink with them.

Walker Fairbairn was waiting below stairs for him, and Stafford wondered why the hell. Lady Nancy and the duchess were gone, as was the man with the spade beard.

Fairbairn said, "Colonel Stafford, I would like to buy you a drink." The man wasn't posturing now; his smooth face was quiet.

"Why?" Stafford said.

"I didn't mean to play the fool with you," Fairbairn said. "I wouldn't have, if I'd known who you are."

Leaning an elbow on the stair post, Stafford eyed him. "And who am I? I'm certain the duchess has dragged out all the old stories."

Fairbairn didn't look away. "She named you gambler and soldier of fortune, bastard renegade, and traitor to your own. As an afterthought, Katrina tossed in whoremonger."

Stafford pushed away from the post. "The law won't keep me from pistoling you in the street."

"I imagine not," Fairbairn said. "I repeat her remarks only to let you know I can match every appellation save two. I think my parents were married, and I never had the courage to go soldiering. Perhaps my being a gigolo will cover those omissions."

"I will be damned," Stafford said. "Is this an apology?"

Fairbairn nodded. "I was truly smitten with your ward's beauty, and cannot be sorry for that. But for jesting with a brave and independent man, my deep regrets, sir."

"Accepted." Stafford grinned. "Tosanna might have been right about cactus flowers, bigod."

"Pardon?"

Clapping his shoulder, Stafford said, "Never mind, lad. Will you drink in this gilded snuffbox then?"

"Just once; I have only the price of a round, although

Lady Nancy was kind enough to leave her carriage for my use."

"Being attentive to the ladies doesn't pay well then?"

"At times, at times. But my situation is—well, too involved for explanation here."

Stafford thumbed toward the door. "Then let us put Lady Nancy's carriage to good use. We're off to the Boar and Capstan, where hounds that range the world may drink without a care in company with their own."

"I think I'd like that," Walker Fairbairn said.

CHAPTER 16

Quietly, Tosanna sat for her lessons, repeating words and gestures at Miss Trevelyan's command. But she thought of the man with sunlight hair. His eyes were blue, but not so pale as Stafford's—more like the cornflower in springtime, deeper and richer. Stafford thought him womanish, and perhaps in appearance he was. But she had seen another thing, far below his skin.

Turning to where Belle sat busily stitching, she said, "The pretty man. Can you find his lodge—ah, his house?"

Miss Trevelyan snapped, "Pay attention, girl."

"Reckon I can," Belle said. "Fairbairn's his name? Sounds Scots."

"Girl," Miss Trevelyan said severely, "we are discussing drawing room etiquette. Now to proceed—"

"I think he is of another tribe," Tosanna said.

"Coo, miss; the Scots *are* another tribe, to be sure."

"Tosanna!" Miss Trevelyan said.

"Is Scots far away?" Tosanna asked.

She flinched in the chair when Miss Trevelyan landed a full-armed slap on her bared shoulder. The pain was nothing, but anger that followed the shock of it was everything. The skinning knife flashed as she whipped it from the hiding place beneath her hair, and she lunged at Miss Trevelyan, bearing the other woman back and down. They thumped the floor in a tangle of petticoats.

The teacher's scream was choked off when Tosanna slammed a forearm under her chin. Tosanna's legs blocked the squirming body from rolling, and the first slash of her blade threw lace from a high collar. Then desperate hands were locked around her wrist.

"No—no, milady! No, I tells you!"

Taking a deep breath to clear her head, Tosanna rocked back on her knees and released Miss Trevelyan. She said to her, "Woman, if ever you touch me again, I will open your belly; I will take your worthless hair."

"G-G-God!" Miss Trevelyan gasped. "Please—please don't let her use that knife—oh, oh! Get her off me, for the love of—"

Tosanna rose to her feet and looked at Belle. The maid let go her wrist and Tosanna slid the weapon back into its secret sheath. She said then, "Get up, old woman. You are not hurt."

Shakily, the woman crawled up, hands fluttering at her throat, at stringy hair that had lost its pins. Some color was coming back into her long face, but her lips were still bloodless. "My glasses—where are m-my glasses? If they are broken—oh, I shall tell Sir Stafford when he returns. I most certainly shall tell that his ward attempted to murder me."

"Come on now," Belle said, "Milady just had a fit of temper, like. No need to bother his lordship with it."

"Fit of temper? The—that savage meant to kill me! Sir Stafford should have her locked away."

Tosanna used both hands to smooth her hair. "You will not say anything. Do you know Comanches have noses like wolves? I can track you across London, find and slay you in your bed any dark night."

Miss Trevelyan swallowed. "I—I suppose—"

"Then we continue the lessons. I think we have each learned something this evening."

And when at last the older woman took her portfolio and left the suite, Belle Williams leaned against the door and said, "About that wolf nose—"

"In England small lies are easily believed."

Belle laughed. "And big ones as well. Bloody well right, and the old hag deserved to wet her pantaloons. But I'm thinking you meant to do her in at the first."

"Yes," Tosanna said. "It is not wise to strike one of The People."

"Gorblimey," Belle murmured, "I can see that."

Tosanna went to the window and watched coaches rattle

past in the night, heard laughter, and felt the creeping touch of night mist. Flaring her nostrils, she could catch the far, faint odor of the sea. It was across the street that yellow hair had lifted down a woman from a carriage; it was there he had stood with his eyes pinned to her nude body up here. In the common room below had he recognized her?

"Anything you'll be needin'?"

"No, Belle," Tosanna answered. "And thank you for staying my hand."

"Wasn't anything, milady. I reckon you would of cut more'n lace off her dress, was you a mind to. I'll be off to bed now."

Deep and metallic, the great clock chimed far off, and she counted its strokes. Time, the English claimed, was everything. It ran their lives because they counted it, wrapped it, put it in high towers, and made it a god. For Comanches time was only suns or moons, the time of green and of planting, the time of hunting and war, the time of snows.

Tosanna let the curtain fall and shook her head. She was no fool to think she could walk out across London and find a ship to sail her to Mexico. Even if she got there, how was she to return to Comancheria? She would need horses and supplies, weapons and water; she would need gold.

Gold was everything to the English. Men served and bowed for it, did woman's work for a bit of its sister, called silver. So when Tosanna somehow freed herself here, she would have to carry coins, many coins to pay her passage, to buy protection and necessities.

Fairbairn. Walker Fairbairn. His hair was lighter than gold and gleamed brighter than a handful of polished coins. When he stopped her in the common room, perhaps he had remembered seeing her at the window. Perhaps it had saddened him, for Miss Trevelyan said only bad women— those who rented their bodies to strange men—exposed more skin than was absolutely unavoidable. Tosanna did not understand that law.

She was restless now, held captive too long in these rooms and the one downstairs. She wanted to see more than could be found from her window; already she had memorized every building there, and knew the pattern of passing workmen. Here women worked also, but not the

same as in Comancheria. But in England, men did not
have to hunt or stand ready for the warpath.

Her routine was *boring*—another new word learned from
a much quieter Miss Trevelyan; sausages and eggs in the
common room, and once a horror called kippers. Comanches ate fish and birds only if starving. Only a warning
glance from Stafford had kept her from hurling the plate.

Trying to read was a problem that worried her, and making rabbit scratches on paper another. Her gift of tongues
did not extend to eye and hand.

Belle Williams talked often with her, telling of more
than the Brickmakers Arms, speaking of green fields and
small villages where life was much different. And Stafford,
when he was not out making schemes, sometimes dallied
with her. She heard of other countries, of France and Spain
and Germany—so many tribes of White Eyes that she could
not begin to count them.

Why did she not run away? It was as Stafford had said
when first she set foot upon English soil: she had nowhere
to go.

This night she had need for him, for a man's close body,
but he was not here, and she did not think he would soon
return. She went again to her window upon the world, but
the street was stilling itself. She sighed.

Stafford had not said she was to wait up for him, so she
turned the gaslight down to a small flame and removed her
clothing. Touching her body, fingering breasts and nipples,
stroking her belly and mound with her palms, she knew
this was good. To hide it was to claim the body was ugly,
and this was not so. More and more, she was coming to
believe the English based truth upon what was said, not
upon what their eyes showed them.

When she turned over beneath the blankets, a slim man
with sunlight hair walked her dreams. He rode with her
along the Llano Estacado and through green valleys, along
tall ridges of Comancheria, where wind tasted of freedom
and blew wild as the blood that raced in their hearts. Together they paced the wheeling eagle, laughing into the
flying manes of running horses. Together they swam in the
lake of blue water, and when he kissed her in the English
way, the lake was no bluer, no deeper than his eyes. The
spirits spoke through the caress of his mouth, and all that
was Tosanna trembled.

But she trembled herself awake in the land that was not

hers, in the body that Stafford owned, and Sunhair was left
to the magic mists of night. While Belle Williams bathed
her and combed out her hair, Tosanna learned that Stafford
had stumbled in past dawn and slept on the floor. He was
snoring on the bed now, dirtying the covers with his boots
and smelling like Thames bottom mud.

"And would milady like to take a stroll about, see a few
sights?"

Tilting her head, Tosanna put her cheek against the
fluffy towel which wrapped her. "He did not tell me I
might."

Eyes twinkling, Belle said, "Didn't say you wasn't to,
neither. What's the harm of it, eh? Do you good to take a
turn about in the air, and with the head milord'll have on
him, it's likely to be teatime afore he wakes."

Plainly dressed and bonneted, long hair tucked up primly,
Tosanna felt a rising of excitement as she held Belle's
hand and moved along the bustling, crowded streets. Rabbit warrens must be like this, she thought, with jumpings
this way and that, narrow and confined, touching and
breathing one upon the other. But there was color and noise
not so bad once she was used to it.

Smells bothered her, though; she could distinguish fish
and meat and green things to eat she couldn't name. But
puffs of stagnant air carried odors of urine and offal, stale
beer, and unwashed bodies. It was like a camp pitched in
a narrow valley, with nearby heaps of stripped buffalo bones
gathering flies and carrion birds. The People packed up and
moved then to a new, fresh spot. It seemed these English
never moved away to give the land chance to become itself
again.

There were so many shops whose trade goods were displayed behind glass, and more goods piled high in little
wheeled carts pulled by men, not horses.

" 'Ere, milady," Belle said, catching her arm. "Lor, would
you look at them bonnets all feathers and such? Let's nip
in and you try them on."

"But I have no coins," Tosanna said. "I cannot buy."

"Don't mean nothing atall, milady. You look rich and
ladylike, and them shopkeepers'll fall all over themselves
trying to sell you."

It was the first of many shops where Tosanna learned the
sensuous feel of expensive cloths and laces, where she discovered wondrous bottled scents and sly paints to heighten

a woman's color or hide skin blemishes. She didn't think she
would be comfortable wearing paint. Men of the Kwehar-
enuh used it before going to war and in other special ceremonies; women never touched it.

Winding through other narrow streets, jostled by hurrying men and stiff-backed women, Tosanna was awed by the
great tower where Belle said kings had been held prisoner.
Kings were chiefs, she found, and puzzled over chiefs of
the same band attacking each other. Among The People, if
warriors lost faith in a war chief or council chief, they
simply did not obey him or rode away.

The crowds, the tall buildings and shouting began to
oppress her, so that she only half-listened to Belle's running
description of the town and its people. Although the sun
had come out to warm the day, little of it shone down into
the stall-filled streets, for the upper levels of houses were
built out more than lower ones, darkening the air above.

"Let us go back," she said to Belle, and knew she had to
depend upon the other woman for direction. It was one
thing to find her way through silent mountains and trackless
desert, another to sort out this confusion. Beneath the folds
of her dress, she kept one hand upon the comforting hilt of
her knife.

Stafford was waiting for them, his face dark. "Where
have you been?"

Belle Williams faded toward the other room, and Tosanna said, "Walking, looking; I tried on hats and dresses
and smelled perfumes."

He still wore the soiled shirt of last night, open at the
throat and wrinkled; his hair was tumbled and his eyes
bloodshot. "Guess that's natural enough, but from here on
you travel only when and where I tell you, understand?"

Without answering, Tosanna moved to the table and
took off her bonnet, let down her hair. Collar open, she
pulled cloth away from her breasts.

"Even dressed plainly," Stafford said, "you're a tempta-
tion. I'll wager men sniffed along after you like hounds
trailing a bitch in heat. You give off something—a look,
a scent, I don't know—but something that draws us all."

"I was not bothered," she said, and recalled those who
had spoken to her without answer, ragged men who made
gestures at her and were roundly cursed by Belle. She remembered better dressed men who managed to brush her
thigh or breast in passing. But she spoke truly, for she

had barely noticed them. It was stupid to make approaches in the open and among so many others, where nothing could happen.

Tosanna wondered what she would do if a strange man —say, like Sunhair—whispered in her ear, asking a tryst. Stafford meant to sell her to some high chief, but even afterward, she would still have a mind of her own, and her body might choose a certain man's body it desired.

Now Stafford slouched at the table, wineglass in hand. "The first invitation has come. The German duchess wants to dissect us at her leisure—first at tomorrow's hunt, then during a ball. I had hoped to avoid her, but if we don't appear, she'll poison all London against me again. The bitch has a tongue made of old sword blades, so tell her nothing more than stories of your life as a Comanche."

"Will she buy me?"

He glanced sharply at her. "And hear me, don't mention buying and selling. She's from a different—ah, tribe—and wouldn't understand. Just regale her with fairy tales about being a king's daughter, royalty in your own land."

"My father *is* a chief."

He cocked an eyebrow at her. "Remember, I've seen Indian tribes—ratty, fleabitten beggars, or else wildmen like the Yaquis."

"You have not seen my people. If you had, your hair would hang from my father's lodgepole."

"Always the Lady Savage, eh? So much the better, for most men. What soft and overfed popinjay does not dream of mastering an arrogant bitch?

"I still wonder why we're asked to the hunt; it means we stay the night with her, to rise early. Not all guests at the ball are invited to the hunt." He grimaced. "It also means hunt outfits for us both, but I'll not be dragged through every shop in London."

"Different clothing to hunt?" Tosanna shook her head. "I hope it is stronger than these other dresses; any brush would destroy them at the first crawling—"

Stafford laughed, then sobered and put one hand to his head. "Civilized hunts are not heathen stalks, my dear. They are ridden to the hounds and guided by a hunt master —all very proper and traditional. You *can* ride sidesaddle?"

"I can ride any saddle," she answered.

"Belle," he said, "write down her measurements and I'll buy the costume where I buy my own. Damme; Who would have thought the renegade knight would again hallo over fence and down dale? I wonder if that is not the duchess's plan, to see me tumble arse over teacups? Or *you*, lass. There are walls to be jumped, you know—rails and stone fences."

Tosanna shrugged. "And what weapon shall I have? Do we hunt buffalo or bear, deer or elk? Perhaps the great mountain cat?"

Stafford stifled a groan. "No weapons; we hunt the fox, and usually the hounds kill him. First rider at the scene gets the foxtail as a trophy."

"Fox?" Tosanna frowned. "A fox is so small; it cannot feed more than one man, and its flesh is tough and rancid."

"It's all for pleasure," Stafford said. "Nobody *eats* the bloody creature."

"This I do not understand. Englishmen ride down a small animal for honor? A small Comanche boy with his first bow would not claim coup for such a hunt."

"Nevertheless," Stafford said, rising with a grunt, "be prepared. When I return, be prepared to travel—"

Tosanna left him then and went to bathe, to talk with her only friend, and try to foresee the future. Stafford had changed since coming home; the look of the hawk had left his eyes. He was apt to pace and snarl like a tethered coyote cut off from his pack. But Englishmen were his own kind, she thought—or were they? Perhaps Stafford was an outcast, an animal driven from the pack because he was different. Here he did not seem as dangerous as he was in Mexico, but somehow cowed and sullen. Yet even a camp dog would bite deep if threatened, and Tosanna felt Stafford was licking his teeth.

Yes, Belle Williams told her, no man or woman was bought or sold in England; not for a long time. Not outright, that was, but bodies and souls were traded every day, call it what they would. Hungry women turned whore; hungry men were thieves.

Warm water lapped Tosanna's breasts as she leaned back in the tub. "But there is much food in the markets. After the hunter feeds his own family, does he not share with all the tribe?"

Belle snorted and poured clean water over Tosanna's hair. "Them that's *allowed* to hunt is dukes and earls and the likes. Let a commoner poach on royal lands and he lands in Old Bailey, if he don't get larruped half to death first by the gamekeeper."

"But if there is no true hunting—"

"All the food, you mean? Lor, milady, that's raised by farmers, and mostly they gets only a share of their labor from the landlord."

When Belle explained the ways of farmers, Tosanna dried her hair and thought she would never truly understand the English, nor any tribes of White Eyes like them—planting things like beans and maize, those potatoes men sold on the street, hot from brightly painted carts, and giving most of the crop to those who claimed to own the land. No man owned the earth; it belonged to all, as did the deer and buffalo and wild flowers. If any man claimed all that, he would have to defend it, and no warrior was so great—or so foolish.

She questioned Belle more about the people's hunger, and discovered that, while some grew fat, others starved. It was not right, and no doubt came of a woman being chief of England. Yet were not women more merciful, more tender? Hunger in the tribe was not right, unless hunting was poor and the winter severe, so that flat bellies were the mark of the entire band, not just the weak or old.

"I cannot understand the laws," she said.

And Belle Williams answered, "Coo, milady, and nobody else can, lacking the toffs what wrote 'em for other toffs."

"I am certain Stafford means to sell me," Tosanna said as she lifted from the tub, "and soon. You say this is not done, but he will do it."

"I don't bloody doubt it, milady. A hard man, that 'un. But be there any fashion you can take me with you—"

"You will go," Tosanna promised, for wherever she might travel in the strange land she would need a friend and adviser. If she was sold to a wealthy man, as Stafford planned, her new owner would not object to her having a personal maid.

She wondered what he would be like, this different Englishman. Would he be cruelly demanding; would he have dark tastes that required giving pain? She would not accept this, *could* not accept it. Comanches were not born to be whipped slaves, and even if it meant losing all chance of returning to her homeland, she would strike any man who beat her and run away. And she would strike deep and hard.

Sometimes in the night she and Stafford had talked of such things—of perverted desires and tortures, of men so twisted inside that they could not be satisfied with the good, true pleasures of the body. The Kwehar-enuh had never known such a man, nor the woman who might submit to him. This perversion then was another failing of the White Eyes. They had so many weaknesses; how could they be so numerous and powerful?

According to Stafford, they were master of many lands, and their ships controlled all the wide seas. Nothing seemed able to stay their invasions, their looting of nations which fell to them. Tosanna shuddered to think of them swarming into Comancheria and overrunning deserts, mountains, filthying the streams. They would eat all game and leave the Kwehar-enuh to starve.

The Comanches were fierce and strong, and there was no tribe braver, but a pack of mangy, yelping jackals could pull down a mighty bear. And this pack was many—so many that even the wisest Comanche chief could not count their numbers. And if the *americano,* the *tejano* White Eyes were to join forces with the English, the Mexicans—Tosanna dared not imagine her people as only a fleck of dust flying before the thundering stampede.

Once she did not question that the Comanches could conquer any tribe because of their great hearts and fine horses. Now she knew the White Eyes had more of everything—that, even though their hearts were weak, they could keep coming until a warrior's arm tired of killing and he was slowly beaten down. And horses could not outrun the huge black machines that snorted smoke and fire while carrying a hundred men, two hundred.

This was another reason she must go home, to tell her people of the wonders she had seen, of the limitless power arrayed against them. Perhaps, if the Comanches could make treaties, not raid Mexicans or *tejanos* and allow them free passage through Comancheria, perhaps then the White Eyes would not make a war The People could not possibly win. Her stomach sickened at the thought, for the Comanches lived by war as much as by hunting.

Belle Williams finished putting up her hair, leaving a long, thick mane down Tosanna's back, for Stafford thought loose hair to be more sensuous. It would call attention to her, where all other women were wearing their hair up piled high in curls.

She said, "Don't you fret none, milady. You'll be the prettiest at the ball, though the master makes you wear that heathen getup. Men will fair water at the mouth over you. Sir Stafford must be daft, to let such as you go."

"He has planned it from the first. He is a warrior who must search for wars, else he will turn fat and die; he has no use for a wife. He would not marry *me,* in any case."

Belle sniffed and put down the hairbrush. "More the fool he is then."

Tosanna stood up and went to greet Stafford, took the first step toward a future she could not see, a life that might be peopled with shadows. The man with sunlight hair might not be among them.

CHAPTER 17

The men were in bright red coats and white breeches, their hightop boots polished like so many mirrors of black. Women wore different shades, but all were blacks, grays, and browns; silly little hats dropped ribbons down their backs.

Stafford had bought Tosanna a simply cut black riding dress, its skirt so long she had to bunch its material in one hand in order to walk. He gave her gloves and had Belle pin the dainty hat into her hair.

"This is no ragged Indian charge," he said. "Try to stay balanced in the saddle, and somewhere close to the other riders. If you get lost, the hunt master will return to find you."

She glanced at the white faces watching her, at women making smiles that were not smiles, and saw Englishmen eyeing her with little-disguised interest. Stafford gave her his arm and led her where grooms awaited to help ladies into saddles. A small man bobbed his head at her and handed up a little whip.

She balked when brought to her horse. "Not this gelding," she said. "He is weak behind and has a bad eye. I will take that one—the gray stallion."

"A man's mount," Stafford said, "wearing a man's saddle. The rider doesn't seem to be here yet, but—"

She cut him off. "A good saddle, much like a Comanche's. Those other things—only one stirrup, and the women

156

ride to one side. If you do not wish me to bring dishonor upon you, give me the gray. I will fall off the other saddle."

"Damn, woman, you'll do as you're told, and—"

Tosanna tossed the riding crop to the small and grinning groom. The heavy skirt slowed her a bit, but still she was able to lift one hand to the flat saddle for a grip, raise the other to the gray's croup, and vault to his back.

"Cor," said the groom, and passed her two sets of reins. It was evident that English horses were not well trained; a loop through the mouth of a Comanche horse was enough. She experimented with the clumsy reins and saw that one was meant to set the animal's head a certain way, and that the other set would control its pace. This stallion was taller than any horses she'd ridden, but its chest was deep and the ribs well sprung; a hint of fire showed in his eyes, and his skin fit him well—tight and smooth. He would do well for this ridiculous hunt, and she would need no whip.

"Tosanna," Stafford hissed. "You're riding *astride,* damn-it. No lady does that."

She was well aware of the staring and hushed murmur-ings. "I am a savage, remember?" When she squeezed the stallion lightly with her legs, he moved smartly away from Stafford.

Yelping and milling, the brown and white hounds were held to leashes until a horseman sounded a horn; then they were loosed and went bounding across the short green grass. She sat for a moment, until the other riders, men and wom-en alike, came rushing past. Stafford was the last, waving furiously at her to get started.

No, not last, because she heard quick hoofbeats behind her as she kneed her horse into a gallop. Curiously, at complete ease in the saddle, she glanced to her left as the other mount neared.

Sunhair!

He smiled at her, light and easy in the saddle, his golden hair partly hidden by the funny little black, billed hat.

"Away, Tosanna—away to the music of the hounds!" His horse was white as Llano Estacado snows; Comanches would trade a hundred other horses for one like that, for white was known to be wondrous medicine.

But *only* in horses, she thought, and lifted the gray stallion's head; White Eyes were devils, white-bellied fish and toads and the white-bellied snake Memante—He Who Warns—were bad medicine.

And Sunhair? Tosanna urged her stallion on, and his long legs ate the ground; when they came to a fence, she lifted him at it and leaned to change her weight, making it easier for him to clear the obstacle. It worked as well for the gray as for Comanche horses, and she was tempted to loose a cry of pure delight, for she felt so alive, once more with a strong horse between her legs.

Sunhair rode like a madman, she saw. He flitted in and out of slower horses, laughing as he put his horse full speed at fences and ditches other riders slowed for. He rode almost like a Comanche, she thought, and could not hold back a *yip-yip!* as she raced to catch him.

Just ahead, a black horse stumbled and threw its rider. She swerved around them and took the big gray over a stone wall as if he were a low-flying hawk. *Aiee!* This one had heart to spare, and they went flashing by men who gaped and women who flinched from their nearness. But Sunhair was still ahead, close onto the pack of baying hounds. Somewhere farther on, running for its life and using all its cunning that even The People recognized, was the fox.

She had no interest in such prey, only in gaining upon Sunhair, which she was doing now; stride for thundering stride, the gray was moving up, closing on the white mare Walker Fairbairn rode.

She had not seen Stafford and did not care; two mounts crashed down behind her at a wide stream with crumbling banks, but she did not turn to see if Stafford was there. Sunhair, Sunhair.

Then they were beside the pack and Tosanna caught her first glimpse of the quarry, just a flash of red brown that suddenly swung left into a tangle of young trees. Sunhair swung right, and she followed. Her big gray almost ran into the slowed mare; only Tosanna's quick reflexes saved a collision.

"Why are you—"

Drawing up his horse behind a thicker clump of heavily leafed trees, he said, "Joy is in the chase, not in killing. If the fox goes to ground in a burrow, the hound master will dig it out and throw it to the pack to destroy. Very brave, our English huntsmen."

Her stallion snorted Sunhair's mare, and she lifted a short kick in warning. Tosanna said, "I see no sport in killing animals not meant to be eaten."

Both their horses were lathered, snuffling with widespread nostrils. Tosanna swung down, and so did Walker. Loudly but unseen, the rest of the hunt riders pounded past, beyond the copse and to its left.

"Let them go," he suggested.

"Yes," she said. "I hoped to speak with you this way, when you do not play the fool for the fat woman."

He lifted an eyebrow. "You wound my pride, princess."

"And act no fool for me," she said, "for you are not."

The last of the hunt lumbered by; hounds still belled in the distance. Tosanna stood quietly, staring at him until he turned in some confusion to loosen the mare's girth and loop her reins around a limb. Tosanna moved the stallion further away and did the same, putting him deeper into the brush by habit, hiding him from a casual sighting.

Lifting the cumbersome skirt, she went back to Sunhair and sat cross-legged before him. "You saw me before the common room in the Brickmaker's Arms—at the window, when I looked upon you in the street."

He had taken something from a saddlebag, and knelt before her to display a silver flask and small cups, one within the other, that unscrewed from the top. "Brandy," he said, "and sandwiches of cold beef and cheese. They're really part of the hunt uniform—British tradition and all that, y'know."

She understood that he mocked English speech, but his own softer tones came through. "Only a sip of the brandy," she said, "and nothing to eat."

He filled and passed her a metal cup. "Yes, I saw you in the window, and thought of little else since. Who are you, Tosanna? *What* are you? I drank with your—protector, and he hinted much but actually said little of you. This wild Indian thing, the golden chain he has you wear—"

"Around my waist now," she said, "beneath this shirt. It is his sign of ownership."

Walker gulped his brandy and poured another to quickly follow. "You're no *slave;* slavery is illegal here, and in almost every civilized country. Does Stafford—I mean, has he the right—"

Their knees were almost touching; there was no sound save for a wind softly prowling the trees, but for the far song of a bird. The sun was warm, and made his hair a blaze of gold. Tosanna said, "I do not call you Walker Fairbairn. I call you Sunhair, and you are beautiful."

He went pink. "Men are not beautiful; that's a term reserved for women."

"It should not be," she said, then: "How long can we stay from the hunt before someone comes to seek us?"

"A long while." His eyes were sky blue, blue as a mountain lake, his lashes long and redgold.

"Good," Tosanna said, and stood to free herself of the jacket, the long skirt, and the white pantaloons beneath it. "I will hang this shirt," she said, reaching to a limb, "for it would dirty itself and make sign for all to see."

"My God," Walker breathed, a huskiness in his throat. "You just—you simply bare yourself and stand there so—so—"

"Do you not like me, not desire me?"

"Yes, damn it all—of course. What man wouldn't?"

She spread the skirt, making a cloth of it, making a couch for them upon green grass, a couch open to the sun and sky. "Do you wish help with your clothes?"

"N-no, no, of course not. It's just—you startled me so much—my god, but you are the most beautiful woman I've ever seen."

Tosanna knelt while he struggled from coat, shirt, and breeches, smiling as she saw the swift and gorged rising of his manhood. He was beautiful there also. She lay back and reached her arms to him. With something like a sob, he lowered himself into them.

He did not thrust quickly at her, and she was glad. There was a special sweetness simply in the holding of him, feeling the heated smoothness of his flesh. He was not hairy as other White Eyes, bearing only a fluff of leaf gold on his chest, and flat nipples of pink. Trapping his staff between their bodies, she turned to bite gently at those nipples, and heard him gasp.

Never still but never hurtful, his hands ranged over her body, hips and ribs and breasts; his mouth was hot along her throat and ear. She lifted her face for his kiss and met his tongue with her own, not attacking, but caressing and retreating, her arms about his neck as the hunger in her flamed brighter.

Now their mouths crushed and their teeth clashed. She slid a hand between their bellies and took hold of his staff, rubbing its flared end back and forth across her belly, then up and down over her pulsing mound. Tosanna delighted in the hard throbbing of him in her fingers, and spread for him, arched to fit him into her by hand.

His quick drawn breath sucked her own into his throat. With a single long but easy stroke, Sunhair buried himself in her. Tosanna took him in happily, gladly, grinding very slowly with and upon him, for she wanted this moment to last and last and last.

As if his lovemaking were born solely from her thoughts, Sunhair also moved slowly, hands slipping over her body, cupping her buttocks, lifting his chest just enough so he could pass his heaving chest back and forth across her erect nipples. And he kissed her, his lips honeyed now, his lips gentle and adoring—her eyelids, her cheek, the corner of her mouth, an earlobe, and lingered long at her throat.

There had been no man such as he—not since the spirits shaped the mudball man and breathed fire into the first Comanche. She slowly lifted one leg, and the other, rocking in the slow drumbeating rhythm they were making together.

Crying out suddenly, she flung her arms about his waist —slim as any woman's—and held him desperately tight. Wave after wave of mad happiness shook her, and went quivering to the very depths of Tosanna—her body, her mind, and her spirit.

Her legs fell away from him, but Sunhair continued to move, long, easy impalings that reawakened her. Fluidly, with new desire, she began to match him, lifting to meet him, dropping as he retreated. It was long and very tender, this blending of their bodies, and though she rose again and yet again to the crying-out place, he remained powerful.

She attacked then, not to punish or hurt, but with a fierce determination to bring him also to the pulsing, to ride him and drive him and draw forth the boiling seeds of his innermost being.

When it happened, she moaned with him, writhing and shuddering, speaking his name over and over until there was little strength left to her and she could only whisper. For a long time they lay together upon their sides, and Sunhair murmured beautiful words into her hair and against her skin. If that gray bird, the one that mocked the songs of other birds—if that one could speak, it would be with such words that were also music.

He withdrew from her, and she tried to hold him sweet captive. "We'd better get back," he said. "They'll come looking for us, and I would not want Stafford to see—"

"All right," she said. "But after the ball tonight?"

He helped her rise. "During the ball *and* after, if possible. I have many questions to ask, Tosanna. If they are all answered, perhaps I can speak to Stafford. He's a good sort."

Slipping into pantaloons, donning the shirt, she said, "Stafford—yes. But he is a Dog Soldier, and not to be angered."

"Dog Soldier?"

"Among the Comanche, one who is bravest of the brave. My father, Tet-Sainte, is one. It is the greatest of honors. I have seen Stafford fight, and fought beside him. War is in his blood, as in Comanches. Without a war, he grows sad and angry. I think I am to be part of the trail that sends him where he must be."

She had brushed and shaken out her skirt, and was off to loose and mount her stallion. Reining him from the brush, she walked him to Sunhair, not yet upon his mare's back.

"Has he that much control over you?" he asked. "You said he owns you, that the golden chain—ah, yes, that damned chain. I wish you had flung the thing away."

Little echoes of thrills scampered through her body, and Tosanna knew there would never be another man for her. But her spine went cold as, somewhere in the far, far reaches of her mind, skin drums beat out a name—*Ado-eeti—Ado-eeti—*

Legging the gray, she picked him up into a short canter. Was she traitor to her own people? Had she discarded her husband because he was so far away and changed' now, because she had changed? Did a simple mating with a White Eyes wipe away her before-life, as a child's foot scuffed over stick men drawn in the sand?

Tosanna let out the big gray, one with the flow of him, wind flagging her hair. She did not look behind, for just now she wanted to think of other things, of someone other than Sunhair. How could she, with the taste of him yet upon her mouth, the smell of him not cleared from her nostrils?

When she saw the other horses, Tosanna used the bit gently and the stallion dropped to a long walk. Stafford, she recognized, although he looked wrong in the red jacket and white breeches. She did not know the other men. Wait —as they drew closer she saw the tall, severe man with the black spade beard; he had been with Duchess Katrina in the common room that night. And another man she had never seen, a man gray and old, but holding himself straight and proud. Among The People he would be a council chief, his wise words rich with experience.

"Tosanna!" Stafford said, reining up beside her, his gelding skittish. "Where the bloody hell have you been? I've been damned upset, thinking you lost or worse—maybe thrown and hurt, even killed. You bloody little—"

The gray man held up a hand. "Please contain yourself, Sir Stafford. Your anxiety is understandable, but after all—"

Stafford bit back angry words, and Tosanna glanced at the silent man with black hair around his chin. She did not like his eyes; they were too much like those of the mountain wolf, hungry and watchful.

"Allow me, my dear," said the old man. "I am Gordon Hammers, Duke of Athol, come to assist your—to help Sir Stafford find you." He waited a moment, and, when the bearded man said nothing, introduced him: "And here, Earl of Gatesford, Knox Cokington."

Cokington nodded, those black and sunken eyes unchanging. He showed teeth in a false smile. "My pleasure, miss." His voice rasped and cruelty sat upon deep lines around his near lipless mouth. In a different place and time, she thought, this one would be an Apache chief.

More controlled now, Stafford said, "Where were you? Did you fall?"

Tosanna did not lie. "No—my horse was almost into the dogs, and I turned him the wrong way."

"Did you see that American, that Fairbairn? It seems he is also missing."

She looked back over her shoulder. Sunhair was just now walking his horse from cover of the trees a good distance away. "Yes—he was sitting on the ground, drinking from a flat bottle and eating meat pressed between bread."

Duke Gordon Hammers laughed, and Tosanna liked the sound of it. "Score another for the old Earl of Sandwich."

The earl pointed his heavy riding crop. "Someone over there. The jackanapes probably. I fail to see why Katrina allows him to—"

"Gentlemen," Stafford said. "Shall we ride back together? There's little enough time for my ward to refresh herself and be dressed for the ball."

Bowing, the gray-haired man moved his horse aside so Tosanna could move between them, but Knox Cokington crowded out the old duke, and his stirrup clinked hers. Tosanna looked ahead, looked to Stafford, anywhere but into the black and stony eyes to her left.

She listened for hoofbeats behind them, but no white mare came galloping. Just as well, Tosanna thought; she had to talk first with Stafford.

CHAPTER 18

At first, the patterns were not easy, but as more men asked her to dance, Tosanna began to feel the music and kept its rhythm, whirling lightly with it or doing a slow, prancing sort of walk.

Miss Trevelyan's instructions had done some good, but not much, for what she taught was old like herself. It was better to first watch how other women responded to certain movements, then attempt to imitate them.

There was none of the frenzy of Comanche war dances, no roaring of the blood or thundering of drums and flutes; these English dancers were so prim and proper. Still, Tosanna enjoyed this music that sometimes rippled and tinkled like a springtime freshet, that swooped and soared like the great eagle.

She wished Stafford had not made her wear the white doeskin dress, all feathers and beads and designs never known to any tribe. Silver conchos upon her Apache-style leggings chimed when she pirouetted, and long fringes of thin leather waved from the hem of her skirt and along both arms as well.

All other women were gowned richly, but in somber blacks and grays and browns. Jewelry sparkled upon them, however—diamonds, rubies, and pearls; she knew their names through more of Miss Trevelyan's teachings. They were worth much money, nothing like the baubles traded by Comancheros. And Tosanna's jewelry? Only the golden chain with its small padlock.

When the music was not playing and she sat at Stafford's right hand, Tosanna's eyes searched the crowd for Sunhair, but she did not find him.

Men introduced themselves to her with sweeping bows, men of many ages and shapes, dressed in dark suits over spotless white linens. They asked Stafford's permission to dance with her, and when he gave it, touched her hands and waist as they moved stately to the music.

Outward deportment beyond reproach, they whispered compliments when the dance brought them close, praise for her beauty and hints of meeting in the future—circumspectly, of course. Though Tosanna did not know all the words, she was not uncertain about their overall meanings.

Stafford brought her pale and bubbling wine which dizzied her a little, but no more than this concentrated male admiration which bathed her like warm rain.

Women cut at her with steel-edged glances, their mouths sullen and spread fans slicing the air like so many quick knives. Only Duchess Katrina Hozenholer seemed content with Tosanna's presence at the glittering ball. Now beside the long table spread with colorful, exotic foods, now circling the iced champagne bowl, giving soft commands to the orchestra, the duchess was everywhere. She looked at her other feminine guests, then at Tosanna, and shook with mute laughter.

"The old witch is enjoying every minute of this," Stafford said into Tosanna's ear after a red-faced young man brought her back from the floor upon his arm. "If the Widow of Windsor were to order you executed—myself as well, naturally—every ah—lady in the room would volunteer to pull on our ropes."

Tosanna said, "Why would I be killed? I have harmed no one."

He laughed. "We've both been daggered to death a hundred times over by women's eyes. Ah, now comes one man we have been baiting—the sour but wealthy Earl of Gatesford, called the Stone Earl for his flinty heart. Lean your breast upon his arm, lass; smile and flutter your eyelashes, brush your thigh over his. In short, use the tricks and lures born into every woman."

The tall man with wolfish eyes claimed her for the waltz, but Tosanna did not do the things Stafford ordered. She did not like this Englishman who hid sharp teeth behind a black beard—black as warriors painted their cheek-bones, the color of death.

Before the dance was done, he took her firmly by the arm and led her toward glass doors that opened upon a small porch, pausing only to sweep two stemmed glasses of champagne from a servant's tray.

Taking a breath of night scents, she sipped from her glass and waited. Knox Cokington said, "Your bastard knight displays you like meat at a butcher's stall. Has he put a price upon you?"

"I do not know," Tosanna said.

"Ah—but there *is* a price? He means to sell you outright because you are unique here, a slave and savage. Else you would be a common doxy, a tup'ny whore."

Tosanna drained her glass and balanced it upon an iron railing. "I do not understand all English words, but I look at your heart through your eyes and find it black."

When she turned to go, he caught her wrist and twisted. Tosanna would show him no pain to enjoy; she stood quiet and still.

"I shall buy you, wench," he said, "though it means dealing with your unsavory owner. Then you will be taught respect for your betters. A few strokes of a cat-o'-nine-tails, and you will beg mercy from the whip. If your back should be scarred, thus lessening your value for resale, so be it."

Softly, Tosanna said, "The daughter of Ten Bears was not born to be whipped like a camp dog."

Cokington showed his teeth. "Why not? You are Staf-ford's bitch, led about on a chain." He flicked the golden links that hung about her waist.

"He has never beaten me, and never will."

"You will find me quite different from your renegade master." His fingers closed upon the dangling length of chain, and Tosanna set herself to drive a knee into his crotch, but just over her shoulder a man said: "Ah, I beg pardon, Earl. I think this is—ah—the dance this lady promised me."

Cokington half turned, jerking back his hand. "Yes, Duke, yes. But tell me, sir—are you interested in further company of this—this savage princess?"

Tosanna took the old man's arm. Gordon Hammers said, "I would say, sir, that the subject is personal."

She heard Cokington hiss as the duke pit their backs to

him and moved her gently to the dance floor. Moving to a slow and stately measure, Gordon Hammers said, "I apologize, child. The Earl of Gatesford is not pleasant company, and I thought to spare you."

She turned to the music, catching this man's eye, and that one. She curtsyed in a line of other women, then moved forward to take his thinbone hand. "I thank you, sir."

"It is I who thank you," he said, bowing and once more pacing beside her. "I have not danced in—oh, too long a time. And never with such a lovely child."

The music stopped, and he guided her to Stafford, who leaned upon a wall next to the punch bowl. "Your ward, sir. My gratitude to her and yourself for brightening the life of an old man."

Stafford muttered something, but it was to a departing back. "Eh? The doddering old Duke of Athol becomes rejuvenated at your touch? I hadn't thought of him as a buyer, but—"

"He is gentle and kind," Tosanna said. "The other one with the heart of stone—"

"Cokington and Hammers," Stafford said. "No others as yet? You've danced with enough men here."

"Many have hinted, but few have been direct."

He filled a cup of punch for her and another for himself. "After the Widow arrives—*if* she arrives—there will be more men gathering in the salon to smoke their cigars. Even so, the bidding cannot be obvious, but prices will be understood." Stafford drank half his glass cup of punch. "You know, I think I shall miss you, Milady Savage."

No man approached her for the moment, so that Tosanna had time to really look at the ballroom. Its ceiling was domed, its darkly paneled walls held rich hangings that Stafford called tapestries. The great chandelier was like a captured rainbow, the dance of gas flames within throwing bits of marvelous, bright colors along the walls and over dancers slowly turning upon the marble floor.

Stafford was at the punch again and did not see her put down her cup and glide silently through a window-door onto another small balcony.

The air was cooler here. Tosanna stood listening to the jingle and stamp of coach horses, seeing gate torches that burned the magic air called gas. Horses that pulled the heavy wagons were dull, fat and slow; only the hunters were worthwhile, like the one she rode earlier after the hounds and fox. There had been no kill; the fox had escaped dogs and men, and Tosanna was glad for it.

She breathed in a flower scent and the taste of newly mown grass. Mother Moon was rising, and she would look down from her sky travels, spread light also upon the Kwehar-enuh.

At her elbow he said, "London is always better at night, when high tide freshens the Thames and dark hides the ugliness."

Before she turned her face, Tosanna knew it was Sunhair, come late to the ball. He was dressed not quite as the other men; his coat was brighter, his shirt lacy and ruffled, with a jewel at the throat.

He came to stand beside her at the low railing. "One is forgiven tardiness if he is practically a household member, but I feel my welcome will soon be worn out here. I wish the moon was higher, so I could see it spilling silver across your face and watch its beams stroke your hair."

There was a special way to his words, as if they had been woven to trap the night, or a woman's heart. She liked the sound of them, the slow tender feel of his voice as it seemed to touch her throat and caress her shoulders. She said, "Your speech is not like the English, nor *tejano*—not like Naduah's talk, when she talked as a White Eye."

"Naduah—an interpreter for your tribe?"

"She is a Comanche who was White Eyes before."

"A captive then. Well, my home is captive too. It lies in that part of America ravaged by war, the War Between the States; you've heard of it?"

"Blue Soldiers and Gray Soldiers. Comanches were glad, for a war between White Eyes was good for us. So was the fight between Mexicans; White Eyes and Mexicans both were busy among themselves, and The People could again ride unmolested. Men welcome wars, so there will always be wars."

"Not like that one," Walker Fairbairn said, "pitting brother against brother, father against son—and the bloodiest war in history."

"Then it was a bad war. No Comanche fights his own kind."

He leaned elbows upon the rail, and she noted again that he was only a bit taller than herself and almost as slender, that his every move was graceful as the deer.

"Ah, yes," he said, "the Comanches; I understand they

war with everyone, white and Indians alike. They're said to
be the ultimate in warrior society, to glory in killing. It is
sure to destroy them one day, for the whites will keep
coming, spreading their settlements and diseases. They will
bring guns and more guns, and probably the best thing
they could do for your tribe is to destroy them completely.
Otherwise, when the Comanche are able to fight no more,
they will be forced upon reservations and made into beggars."

"Never!" Tosanna said. "Weak tribes have already been
sent to White Eye reservations, but they leave when food
and presents are not given them as promised by the Great
Father in Washington. But the Kwehar-enuh will never
beg or stop warring; already they ride the old hunting
grounds and raid as they will, because Long Knives and
Yellowlegs and *tejanos* have retreated again. Ours are proper wars."

Sunhair shook his head. "There are no proper wars, only
senseless killings. Those who die in wars don't know if the
fight was good or bad." He sighed and the rising moon
touched his face with pale light. "I didn't want to die in
war, nor did I wish to kill other men, so I came to England."

Tosanna said, "But I have heard the Blue Soldier-Gray
Soldier war is done. You can go home now." She could have
bitten her tongue in half, for she did not wish him to leave
England.

"If I have a home left," he said.

She said, "I shall go home someday."

"Oh? I imagined you enjoy this rich, civilized froth and
pleasure. It must be worlds different from living as a
nomad, always on the run. Do you really wear a dress like
that out on the plains?"

"This is my —protector's creation; no Comanche ever
saw anything like it, but it suits his fancy." Moonlight was
brighter on his face now, shaping the soft mouth, playing
in long, golden hair, kissing his pale eyes. Tosanna went
on: "I do not know some of your words, but The People
do not *run;* they only move to better fighting places."

Turning, he sought her hand, and it seemed natural to
allow her fingers to lie within the warmth of his palm.
Walker said, "Stafford—how did he become your protector?"

She told him, omitting nothing, and told what Stafford

meant for her future; to support his own, he would auction her to the highest bidder.

Walker dropped her hand. "He's putting you on the block like any black, although the English decried slavery for the Confederacy. Why don't you protest, tell the duchess? Word would reach the queen in a trice, and Sir John would be in serious trouble."

A touch of chill was in his voice now, and Tosanna felt it. Wrapping her arms about her chest she said, "And swim back to Comancheria? Stafford has not mistreated me."

He moved a pace from her, as music stopped in the ballroom and the clink of glasses, the ripple of laughter rose higher. "I should expect no less from your kind. Like any house servant bred for lightness, you seem to enjoy your trade. I trust your wares will bring a high price, Milady Savage."

She stared after his back as he swung gracefully into the crowd. Unless she had unwittingly broken some tribal law, she had done nothing to anger him, yet his jaw had been set and his words not kind.

"Tosanna." Stafford came onto the balcony and took her arm. "I've been looking for you. The duchess has a gentleman you must see again; he's already expressed great interest in you."

"Not the one called Walker?"

Stafford snorted. "That popinjay? He's only a pet the duchess keeps on a leash, and what money he brought to England is about done with. Yester eve, he was my drinking companion and I liked him well enough. Until I found he fled here to escape the Civil War. Damn any man who won't do his duty, who is afraid to fight and shows the white feather." Pulling her toward him, he said, "No, the man who lusts for you is the Stone Earl. I would swear his family storehouse yet has treasures from the Crusades. Come and tempt him from up close. If he's taken by you, I shall be able to buy a general's commission in the Franco-Prussian war. But first—"

She heard the familiar rattle. As Stafford arranged the golden chain about her waist, and tested the small lock. "There," Stafford said, "the sign of outright ownership will titillate the old man and have others scratching their codpieces. Bigod, things are moving faster than I expected. I may not have to face the Widow after all. Come, lass, hist your breasts and wiggle your tail for the Stone Earl, and with the devil's luck I'll be off to the wars in a fort-night."

Sunhair's anger had left bitterness in Tosanna's throat, so she did not shake herself, but stood poised and aloof beside Stafford. Duchess Katrina's small eyes glistened as she made formal introductions, and Tosanna looked into the eyes of the man she had seen in the common room of the Brickmaker's Arms, the tall, silent man with a short black beard who had already called her bitch and threatened the whip.

"May I present Sir John Stafford and his ward? Sir John, Tosanna, this is Knox Cokington, Earl of Gatesford."

His voice was flinty as his eyes, and they were hard as Apache obsidian. "I have met Tosanna and heard of Sir Stafford," he said, "and damned little good. But even a rogue may have excellent taste in women."

Tosanna felt Stafford's hand clamp on her arm. "Damn, sir, although dueling is outlawed—"

Cokington continued to stare at Tosanna's dark beauty, his eyes licking at her tip-tilted breasts, at her groin. "I would not face you, Stafford. But neither would I hesitate to set footpads upon you—pay them well."

Trembling against Tosanna, Stafford grated, "Bigod, you may need all the footpads in London to protect your own hide. Come, lass—"

Cokington lifted a splotched hand. Around them, the curious began to gather watchfully. The earl said, "Five thousand sterling, and a colonelcy arranged by me in the army of either side."

Duchess Katrina's pillowed chest rose and fell. "I say —do I hear another bid? How exciting. Come, gentlemen— a bid on the fair body of a wild Indian princess. How much for Milady Savage, as fierce in bed as when she lifted scalps in the American West?"

"Shut up, Katrina," Cokington said. "If Queen Victoria hears your loose mouth, you'll be banished to your gloomy German estates and me to the Tower. But—and *Sir* Stafford will bear me out, I wager—but we are only joking here. I only offer my protection to this homeless child, and gladly recompense this blackguard for his previous expenses. I doubt me anyone will best my offer."

Slowly, dangerously, Stafford said, "Cokington, I may have your liver here and now."

"But you won't. I'm not worth five thousand to you, much less rank with the French or Germans."

Tosanna looked away from them, looked to the iced champagne bowls where Sunhair stood with his glass. Walker Fairbairn seemed interested only in his wine and the older woman clinging to his arm.

Choking back his rage, Stafford said in a strained whisper, "She has a serving maid at twenty pounds a year. When will you—"

"Tomorrow," the Stone Earl said, "delivered to Gatesford. My master-at-arms will pay you—at the tradesman's entrance."

"And my commission with the Germans?"

"Settled soon as my courier can arrive in Prussia. Now"—Cokington rattled the golden chain—"you may take my new bitch back to your kennels for the night."

Duchess Hozenholer laughed, her heavy breasts quaking. Walker Fairbairn came from the circle of onlookers, the older woman still clinging to his arm. "I didn't believe in slavery in my own country, and certainly not here. Whatever the earl offered, I'll go above it but only to set Tosanna free to do as she wills, even if that means returning to her own country."

The duchess laughed louder. "So! My stallion finds another mare. *Sehr gut.* Lady Barrenton, already he proves very expensive to you."

The older woman said, "Walker, my dear—"

"Five thousand pounds," Cokington repeated, "and the cost of a colonelcy in the German army."

In a low and deadly whisper, Stafford said, "I'll kill you for this, Cokington, and I'll change my commission to the French; maybe there will be Hozenholers to kill also."

"Five thousand pounds," Lady Barrenton said. "I cannot afford that, Walker, dear; not so suddenly, that is. I mean, what if you are not—if I don't—"

Tosanna saw Sunhair's lips go pale as a flush mounted his cheeks. He turned quickly, dragging the woman with him. She knew sorrow at his shame. It was not good to be without money in England, or anywhere else. That was a lesson brought home to her more than once. She wanted to run after Sunhair and say it did not matter, but that was not true.

No one had noticed the Duke of Athol; stooped ever so slightly, he moved to put his lips to Stafford's ear. Stafford smiled then, and put out his hand. Gray Gordon Hammers was reluctant to shake it, but he did. Stafford passed him the key and, hand shaking, the duke loosed the lock on Tosanna's golden chain. Backing a step, he drew back his hand and hurled the chain over the heads of the crowd, where it crashed against a wall.

"Look here!" Cokington said. "Damn, but I should be given the opportunity to bid again; in any auction—"

The old duke said, "There is no auction, Gatesford. She is a human being, not farm stock."

"Stafford," Cokington said, "you've gone back on your word. That's to be expected of a bastard knight, I suppose, but—"

The slap rang across the ballroom, loud and meaty. The Earl of Gatesford staggered, and a scarlet handprint leaped forth along his cheek.

"Queen's law or no," Stafford said between his teeth, "I call you coward and liar before this company. Your seconds may call upon mine at the Brickmaker's Arms; the choice of weapons is yours, and the place. I do not give a damn if that place is in the courtyard of Gatesford, for I most certainly shall be there come dawn, and just as certainly kill you."

Putting one hand to his stung cheek, Cokington took another step backward. "Her majesty does not allow duels, and—"

"Affairs of honor," Stafford said, "not duels. Where is *your* honor, coward?"

The duke put a gentle hand upon Stafford's arm. "Enough, Sir Stafford; the Earl has shown his true colors. And the queen—"

From the entry hall, the doorman's voice rang out: "Lords and ladies—the queen's carriage has arrived outside."

"Jesus!" Stafford said. "Duke Hammers, we'll take our leave, with your permission. I'll deliver Tosanna to Athol on the morrow and—"

The crowd was scattering and music sprang up. Gordon Hammers said, "The young lady is free to do as she wishes. May good fortune attend you, my dear."

Stafford pushed along behind the duke. "The money—"

"Delivered to your rooms," Hammers said. "My word that all else will be arranged immediately."

"Thank you," Stafford said, and hurried Tosanna along. In the vestibule, servants moved to find cloaks for them.

The outer doors opened quickly, held back by a pair of large, burly men. A quick and nervous woman trotted inside. Could *this* be England's queen, Tosanna wondered. She did not notice the short, dumpy woman who walked behind dressed all in black.

Stafford immediately bent his knee and bowed low. Tosanna merely stared. The woman in black, much shorter than Tosanna, came to stand before her. "So," she said, "we at last see the talk of all London."

"Your majesty," Stafford murmured, "had I but known you wished——"

"Nonsense," Queen Victoria said, "we perceive you as a rogue and adventurer, Sir Stafford, but we do not name you stupid. Knowing our displeasure at that—that Mexican business, you would never approach Windsor without being summoned."

Tilting her chin, she peered closely at Tosanna. "Ah, yes; a beauteous child. Tell me, child: do you wear such bizarre clothing in your native lands?"

"No," Tosanna said, and at the abruptness of her answer, the two big men moved forward, but Queen Victoria waved them off.

"Interesting," she said. "No doubt a ploy of Sir Stafford's then. Do you know who we are, child?"

"The woman chief," Tosanna said. "They call you queen. I do not know the warriors who guard you."

A quick smile crossed Victoria's jowly face. "Ah, yes; use of the regal 'we' confuses you. What do you wear?"

"Skins like these, but not so gaudy. The buffalo would stampede at sight of these."

Stafford shifted uncomfortably beside Tosanna, but the queen's small retinue waited patiently. Victoria said then, "And did our lordly rogue succeed in repairing his fortunes through you?"

"By your leave," Stafford said.

"We do not give it. Well, child?"

"I—I am to have a new protector."

Victoria sniffed; her small eyes, set deeply behind puffy cheeks, flicked Stafford. "Protector, indeed. We shall be interested in hearing more of this—this farce. Come, child; Katrina's sitting room is just off here, if we remember. No, gentlemen; we shall not require you."

The room was ornate with gilt and chandeliers, crowded with brocade sofas, carved tables and chairs. Victoria moved stiffly to the central couch and sat, spreading her skirts. Taking spectacles from the black purse at her thick waist, she clamped them upon the bridge of her nose.

"That's better; now we can see you properly. Yes, you are lovely, child, and show no awe of us. Why is that? Did not Sir Stafford teach you who we are, *what* we are?"

"He called you the Widow of Windsor, said that your man died, and that you are the most powerful chief, stronger than the Comanches, Mexicans, and other White Eyes banded together. Perhaps this is true, but I do not see how a mere woman could command such warriors."

Victoria coughed and patted at her lips with a snowy lace kerchief. "Mere woman? Child—"

"Women do not command among my people," Tosanna said. "Warriors would never obey them. My father is war chief, but I can never take his place. Women are weak, fit only for camp work and bearing children."

Lifting off her round black hat with veil, Victoria placed it beside her and smoothed at gray hair drawn severely back in a bun. "Words dinned into the ears of female children from their moment of birth—by men. Sit here beside us, child; we will speak of strength and weakness."

Outside, Stafford stalked the vestry, chewing on a cigar and glowering at the sitting room's closed door. Queen Victoria's men-at-arms—for that is what they were, regardless of title—lounged calmly beside it; her lady-in-waiting sat primly upon a straight chair and stared at hands folded in her lap.

Stafford wanted to rail at them, to kick open the door and spit in Victoria's eye, but knew damned well he wouldn't. The old hag could be oh, so proper concerning Tosanna, but she'd said nothing about the gift of gold he'd sent, accepting it as her due. All England was like that—straitlaced and moralistic on the surface, while cavorting and copulating behind closed doors. Bloody bunch of sanctimonious hypocrites.

He'd be glad to be rid of them, and maybe this time come into his own in the Franco-Prussian war. It had been awhile since he'd fought on the Continent, and he'd welcome the taste of powder smoke, a battlefield where a man stood tall as his courage and talents, where breeding and court connections counted for nothing.

What the hell was Victoria doing in there—pumping Tosanna for every detail of her life, drawing out facts about her sale to the duke? If the girl told everything, he'd be in trouble to his armpits, and there was no reason she shouldn't. But somehow Stafford had the feeling she would keep her own counsel; Tosanna was like that, stoic and mysterious.

She was many other things—sleek, fervent gratification, fury and a strange, inner calm when the storm had passed. Tosanna was that high pride no man could ever humble, and a perfect body at once whipcord strong and down feather soft. She was—

Stafford bent to thrust his cigar into a sand vase. Victoria's guards watched him impassively, and he wondered how damned unconcerned they would be looking down the bore of an American Navy Colt or into the maniacal face of a screaming Yaqui. Beefeaters out of their traditional dressy uniform, out of their element anywhere but here.

He was more irritated than his brushes with Cokington and the queen accounted for. He didn't like to think of that smooth, luscious body twisting and responding to another's hands. He was glad it wouldn't be Cokington; there was a streak of cruelty in the man, a viciousness that showed in his cold, penetrating eyes, and cowards had a way of preying upon the weak.

But the Duke's six thousand pounds would make a solid base for Stafford to build on when he got back. He'd need it, for commanding a French regiment wouldn't endear him to Victoria. Victoria was heavily pro-German, because of Prince Albert of Saxe. How had any man, even a threadbare prince, put up with an iron-willed wife, and one so near to distressingly unattractive?

Tosanna, damn it, Tosanna; what was she up to in there? Victoria's official audiences were often shorter than this whimsical satisfying of the royal curiosity. He glanced at the ballroom, where the duchess fidgeted in her eagerness to kiss the royal arse.

Not a woman gliding over that polished floor could compare with Tosanna, and he'd sampled enough of them to know, aristocrat and serving maid alike. She was honest and lustful, no whit ashamed of her fleshly desires, but glorying in them, and making the man she bedded more of a man for being with her. Now she was "free."

The door opened and Stafford came erect. Tosanna's face showed only calmness, and the queen was, as usual, unreadable, but Stafford felt the casual scorn she gave off. Victoria said, "Good night, child. We shall see you again." She gave Tosanna's hand a fleeting pat and turned to Stafford. "Sir, at the moment I can think of no greater fool in the Empire."

CHAPTER 19

Belle Williams finished packing their baggage and retired for the night. Such a heaping of possessions, Tosanna thought, like treasures brought back from a successful raid. But such clothing in camp would be only novelties soon discarded.

Stafford had been generous, but only to put her into a setting to appeal to wealthy lords. It had worked for him, and he would be gone to his war, to take the warpath he so needed. In that this Englishman was much like a Comanche, but an outcast from his own tribe, hiring himself to strangers.

In Comancheria, Apaches and Tonkawas did the same, acting as scouts for *tejanos* and White Eyes to revenge themselves upon all Comanche bands. But Stafford carried no blood grudge; he fought for the joy of it, and the loot.

Behind her he said, "You don't have to go to him. He freed you before the entire company. Odd, that gesture; I mean, the old duke is known as shy and keeping his own counsel. I should imagine he bought your freedom simply to irk Cokington, and I say bravo. Still, there's no need for you to appear at Athol."

She stood at the window. The hour was late and the street empty, save for Stafford's hired coach and its driver asleep curled and blanketed upon the seat. There would be no other carriage paused beneath the gaslight, no gleam of hair touched by the sun, no Walker Fairbairn.

She turned to Stafford. "Where else would I go? Should I

179

return to the ball and auction myself? The hall is bare. Should I find the Stone Earl and offer myself? Maybe he will buy me for the money I must have to go home. He might like beating me for the insult you gave him. He has the eyes of a wolf, that one, and will enjoy tasting blood."

Seated upon the edge of the bed, shirtless and disheveled and turning a brandy glass in his hands, Stafford said, "Damn, woman! I cannot buy you passage, and even if I could, what then? How would you return to your people? Without money, and a good deal of it, you'll be just another Indian squaw for white men to bed. They'll fling a few coppers at you, or take you for naught, and if they discover you are Comanche—"

Tosanna stood before him in her shift, the false doeskin dress thrown across a chair. "Belle Williams said we might whore here in London, save our money and—"

"No, damn it. You're no slattern, no doxy to spread yourself for all manner of men. You will catch the pox, the French disease. All right, damn you; you've made me feel criminal. By all means, hie yourself to the old man; mayhap he'll make a pet of you. Lord knows he's far too aged to do anything else. And better him than the cowardly American. I know you've dallied with him; that story of getting lost at the fox hunt—"

Sitting on the chair, Tosanna faced Stafford. He poured brandy in his glass and questioned her with a lifted brow. She shook her head. "Sunhair is not afraid, only gentle. I think if you had slapped him at the ball, you would be lying dead in the morning."

Stafford gulped brandy. "Now you are a—a—what do you call them: a medicine woman? Seeing the future, and— *Sunhair*. Good lord."

"I am no spirit talker," she said. "I know only what I feel, and my heart tells me he is strong."

Rising, Stafford stamped across the room and found a cigar. He tried to light it at the gaslight, singed his fingers, and cursed. He found a sulphur match and scratched it against the wall. Blowing smoke, he said, "Do you know what your precious American does for a living? He feeds upon rich older women, a he-whore who must jump when they snap their fingers. Think of diddling fat old Katrina— the idea bloody well turns my stomach."

"He is a very good lover," Tosanna said.

Stafford's teeth clenched through the tip of his cigar. He

spat the chewed end and stuck the rest back into his mouth. "Aye, you'd know. And that bloody heathen way of thinking about sex; you'd not be jealous of his other women. But no fear of him returning to you; the ploy he made last night about bidding more than Cokington was only that: a shameless call for attention."

Tosanna said, "I think I will have brandy." She went to the dressing table and found a small glass to fill. It burned her throat, but she would not show that to Stafford.

She said, "Why do we speak of others? Tomorrow you go to war, as you should, as you must. We will see no more of each other."

"True." He pulled at his cigar. "After I deliver you and Belle to the duke's estates, the coachman will hurry me to the docks. Although the Widow's displeasure at sea captains who would travel the Channel to France is well known, England is not at war. And if a frigate's cargo is listed for Genoa, why not a stopover at Calais?"

He looked at the glowing tip of his cigar, then at Tosanna. "I shall miss you, lass. I needed you and you paid off handsomely. The duke offered a thousand pounds more than Cokington, but I think I'd have accepted even a bit less than Cokington's price. A boil that sorely needs lancing, that one. Avoid him, Tosanna; as you say, he may seek revenge upon me through you, and the duke, also. I wish—"

Tosanna waited, but Stafford only took more brandy and bounced cigar ash into a candleholder. Then he said, "It's not been so bad for you. The Spaniard was a man teetering upon the brink of destruction, or madness. And you've learned a new language, seen something of the civilized world. Damn, you have even rubbed shoulders with the Widow of Windsor and come away unscathed. You might have told her the entire story, and she'd have had my arse. Why didn't you?"

"It was not my way. You bought me fairly and did not beat or starve me. Had you done so, I would never have met with the great woman chief, for your throat would be long ago cut."

Laughing, Stafford slapped his knee. "Aye, and I ruddy well knew it. Bigod, the way you stood with me against the Yaqui and saved both our bums with that Comanche screeching—I'd have you as a comrade anytime, woman or no." He stopped smiling and said softly, "As a woman,

I've never known your like, and never will again. Not for six thousand pounds nor twice that."

She said, "My bride price was two hundred horses, a fortune among the Kwehar-enuh. Perhaps my father returned them, for I spent only one night upon the marriage couch."

"Then the Spaniard took you? You never spoke of this before."

"Don Joaquin would never have captured me, but all our warriors were gone upon a raid; he hired Apaches as trailers. It is true their noses are those of dogs, but they set him upon the wrong trail. Another band of Comanches captured his wife, not the Antelope band."

Thoughtfully, Stafford said, "So he made you her substitute. A proud and stiff-necked don, he was. It fair boiled his liver to have to sell you. Is there much chance he found his wife?"

Tosanna shrugged. "Only the spirits know. Perhaps she is dead, or taken to wife; she may be sold or traded to another band. I do not think Don Joaquin will be happy if he finds her. He will regain his honor in the eyes of others, but not in his own heart. He has told me this—that he will not take her to bed again; his spirits and the black robe spirit talkers say she is dirtied now. I do not understand this."

Stafford eyed his glass. "Neither do I, but I'm a rogue."

Tosanna fawned. "If that means to be alone, it is not a good thing."

"Often not, lass, but better this than to bay with the pack *only* when they howl together and never upon my own."

Tosanna said, "Although I am the duke's woman now, and go to him tomorrow, I will be with you tonight."

He looked up. "It was not always unpleasant for you then?"

"You were never cruel, and always a man."

Reaching slowly across, Stafford took Tosanna by her shoulders. "I think the Widow was right when she said there was no greater fool in the Empire."

It was strange, for even as she moved with him in a farewell ritual of lovemaking, Tosanna knew moments when she thought only of Sunhair. She knew he would not like what she was doing, although he lived by being put to stud.

But he did not own her now; no man owned her, and she told Stafford so with the renewed fierceness of her body.

CHAPTER 20

Walker Fairbairn lay comfortably beneath a flowering hedge and looked at the sky, ignoring the throaty *crump!* of shotguns on the other side of the house. Sport shooting, the English called it, but it was butchery without the excuse of hunger. Pheasant, doves, and quail alike driven by beaters into easy range of the nobility's guns—all sleekness and beauty and grace turned suddenly into agonized bloody lumps.

He thought of other things: a softly aquiline face, lips dewy rich and full, night storm eyes hinting of barely contained lightning, and muted thunder throbbing within her. Milady Savage was not easy to forget. Walker rolled over and contemplated a carefully trimmed plot of grass. Tosanna was not like that, shaped by hand, tended and constrained; she brought the feral scent with her, a wildness that might never be tamed.

Had he ever been in love? A few times, Walker thought, and each moment had been aching sweet but fleeting, and thank the fates for that. So many beautiful women yet waited, offering their rare and special flavors.

Sitting up, he inspected the sky, finding it nowhere near lusty and promising as that in Alabama. The blues here were muted, with a look of chill upon them, and clouds were too wispy, a prissy and virginal white. Back home in summer, skies turned sultry, ripe; they were laced with garland scents of honeysuckle and magnolia. And in anger, like a jealous woman, the blueness darkened and snapped

quick, lancing streaks of white fire. Sky rage back home
was epic, tremendous, all violence and cannonading. But
when it passed, the green smell, the flower scents were
stronger.

Someday he would have to go home—if home there remained. Reports after the War Between the States had not
been gentle. The South, as Walker Fairbairn and all the
Fairbairns before him had known it, had been beaten to her
knees, raped and mutilated. Perhaps she would never rise
again.

He'd told them; damn it, he'd made himself highly un-
popular in the telling of it. But the hotbloods didn't want
to hear of great factories and numerical odds, of overwhelming naval, financial, and manufacturing power. They
wanted to hell off through the night, full of good bourbon
astride a blooded horse, yipping defiance and individual superiority to a golden smiling moon.

Guns boomed, and Walker flinched, but it was only the
lord of Clarycastle and his favored guests, scattering raw
meat and feathers. It wasn't cannon, nor the fiery explo-
sions of stately southern homes in their death throes.

A friend up North had kept Walker more or less in-
formed of casualty lists during the early part of the war,
Bull Run and Shiloh and Murfreesboro. But then the reports had stopped, because the friend had stopped too.

"Good Christ, what a waste," Walker murmured. "What
a criminal, senseless waste."

But they had words like honor and duty and loyalty to
throw back at him, even from their unmarked graves—
those laughing, hoorawing boyos. And he could yet see the
stony fix of his father's face, the bitter disappointment in
Jeremy Fairbairn's aging eyes.

Always knowed somethin' was wrong with him, Walker's little brother had said. Him too goddamned dainty to
pop a cap at anything but a water moccasin, and only then
if'n the goddamn varmit was about to bite him.

And his older brother, that calm, sturdy model of manhood: Boy, you got to grow up sometime. You got to quit
lollygaggin' around gals and writin' that moon-eyed poetry
and rear up on your hind legs. This here war is forced on
us, and we *all* got to fight it.

His father had said nothing, only sat hunched in the
old rocker that had been toted on a slave's back clear from
the Carolinas, only stared.

Walker stood up now and brushed his trousers. He'd said all the words he knew, laid himself open wide as a gutted hog to tell them how he felt about killing *anything*, let alone a man. He cited statistics and projections that showed the South could not possibly win the war. They would not listen, and hated him, denied him, cut him off from his heritage because he didn't deserve it.

But his mother came drifting in late that night, a lavender-scented shadow, to bring him gold. Not Fairbairn gold, she'd whispered against his cheek, but saved from her own family. Take it and go, son—oh, my gentle son—and come back when this brutal time is done; it will be different then.

Putting his hand to a soft-white flower upon the hedgerow, Walker thought his mother had been much like it, fragile and short lived. She had been first to go. Then his older brother; then pissant-wild Jackson Fairbairn, all of seventeen years—cousins and uncles and kinfolks close, kinsmen distant. Now the Rebel yell was stilled, and only lonely nightbirds mocked its lost echoes.

Soon Walker Fairbairn, perhaps last of his line, would have to go home, if only to thank his second cousin Sarah for the letters that kept him up to date. There had been a thread of vengeance running through Sarah's letters, a little concealed delight in informing him of each family loss, through the war years and after, somehow laying the blame to him who had run away.

Good God—what would he have accomplished by staying? Another trampled grave, if he was lucky—more likely his bones scattered upon some forgotten battlefield by hungry dogs.

His father was still alive at last word, and Walker didn't want to face that old man, once so fierce and now so alone. But just maybe they could patch it up, start over. It would be difficult without niggers and money, but perhaps something could be salvaged and the plantation set right again. Never the way it had been, for the aristocracy was forever overthrown.

Moving from the hedge and toward the shooting, Walker said, "I just don't have the guts to face Jeremy Fairbairn—not yet."

"Talking to yourself, my young colonist? A bad sign, I would say."

Walker smoothed his face and gave a bright smile to the

duchess. "All poets are a little mad, milady. I merely prove the charge."

Duchess Katrina Hozenholer's smile was a bit strained. "I shall miss your ready wit, Walker—among your other attributes. Since my involvement with that beastly little wench from America seems to have brought on the queen's displeasure—"

"Ah, yes," he said, offering his arm. "Back to gloomy Prussian castles for a while. Don't fret, milady; I expected it."

She squeezed her heavy breast against his arm. "A rare treat, Walker—a—consort who doesn't expect too much. And what of Milady Barrenton?"

The Stone Earl was before them, shotgun in the crook of one arm. "So—the shooting guest appears at last. You have missed much sport, sir."

"I care not for it," Walker said.

Cold-eyed, Knox Cokington looked at him. "Perhaps our colonists never learned the gentleman's sport of shooting."

Although Katrina pressured his arm, Walker said with a smile: "Enough to clutter half the continent with redcoats, milord."

Beyond Cokington somebody muttered, and a lady giggled. Men angled toward them, watching and listening. Walker noted some husbands among them; he knew their wives well. All were Cokington intimates, not put off by his refusal to fight. He searched the crowd's faces for a darker one, gently hawkish, sloe-eyed, and proud; she wasn't there.

"Without the war with France, that outcome would have been different," Cokington said from his square black beard. "But your particular countrymen, rebels against your own government—it seems their fabled shooting eyes were somehow dimmed."

Walker moved through the onlookers to take a shotgun from a gameskeeper. "Hardly a marksman's weapon, but—"

Flipping the gameskeeper's cap spinning into the air, he jerked it upward with the charge from one barrel, then completed its shattering with the other. "I repeat, it's difficult to miss with such a weapon."

Eyes glittering, Cokington stalked forward. "I have some excellent rifles, and a wager waiting."

The duchess signaled no, but Walker shrugged. "If you

also have pistols—say, the U.S. Navy Colt, a .36 caliber, I believe—"

Nodding, Cokington said eagerly, "And the wager?"

"I am destitute, sir. My services, for what they're worth, or—no—my departure from England post haste. That should please you and"— Walker grinned at some husbands—"and several others present. Against my passage home."

"Done, bigod!" Cokington rasped. "Marshall—Marshall Westphal; you are some better with a handgun—"

Walker cut in: "Sir, I do not mean to put you at a disadvantage. You are a rifleman of note, it is said. Therefore, use your weapon of proficiency; I shall match your marks with the Navy Colt."

"Arrogant fool," Cokington said. His smile was certain, fanged. "Again I say done, and bon voyage; do you have to swim."

"Better with your thoughtful gift of first-class passage," Walker said, and brought out a small cigar while waiting for servants to appear with rifle and pistol. As he weighed the Navy Colt's balance, Cokington stroked his English rifle and said, "To your liking, poet?"

"A magnificent pistol, milord—American made."

Cokington snorted and turned. "Charles, Wilson! Set marks where the last flight of quail fell. *If* my—honored opponent does not deem them too far."

"Whatever pleases you," Walker said, and thought of a pecan wood study and fragrant, hickory smoke fire, of guns treated with more devotion than children and slaves.

Damn, his older brother said. Here I am ateachin' you to handle guns, and you flat out born to 'em. Why, little as you are, you got more natural knowhow in your trigger finger than anybody around, and we all *worked* at it most our lives. Hit me that sweetgum leaf; load up and hit me the bump on that cedar log away off yonder. Damn, boy. Won't be long afore you bag your first deer.

No deer, young Walker said.

How-goddamn-come no deer?

'Cause it makes me sick to my stomach to see somethin' die, and *I* ain't studyin' on killin' anything my ownself.

Then you got your head screwed on wrong, but you'll grow out of it.

No, I won't, Walker said.

"I'll take the left target," Cokington said, and sighted his rifle.

Walker saw the white-painted stake jump at about fifty yards; the hit was off center. Casually, lifting and firing the Colt in one smooth motion, he split his target and, for good measure, neatly divided Cokington's.

Trotting forward a few paces, he dropped to one knee and squeezed off a shot at a splintered bit of whitewashed wood, his swiftly following shots skipping it along the turf.

When he strolled back to the firing line, Cokington glared at him. "A trick shooter, a circus performer. You took advantage of me, sir."

"You insisted upon the wager," Walker answered, and the Duchess Hozenholer rescued him before the words grew hotter, drawing him across Clarycastle's tended lawns to the champagne table. Other ladies twittered about him, and a few men who chuckled at Cokington's discomfiture —but only a few.

"Your skill is amazing," Katrina said.

"A talent only," he said, "as some paint or dance—no credit to me."

"Yet you fled your country, called coward by the Confederates. It was not fear then."

"Of a sort," Walker admitted. "The Colonel Staffords of this world enjoy wars and killing. I am afraid of both."

"But not of your skin," Katrina insisted.

"So little worth to that—but I'll wear it long as I can, and not sacrifice my skin for a cause lost before it was tested."

"There is more to you than meets the eye, Walker—or meets the touch. Prussia is not so bad."

"Even in wartime? But I thank you, duchess."

She heaved her breasts. "That affair with the French? Soon done with, I should think. If you do not come with me, what shall you do?"

"Enjoy the trip home, and then—"

"Then?"

He shrugged. "Find other kind and wealthy ladies, write poems; learn to strum the banjo, perhaps."

In a while, Lord Clary waddled nervously to them. "Wondrous shooting, m'boy, wondrous. But salt in Cokington's wounds, hey? Best you not tweak his beard again, even by chance. But you and the duchess are guests of Clarycastle, guests; and if you'd stay—"

"Indeed no, milord," Katrina said. "We would not risk your kind hospitality more. Thank you for the courtesy of your house, and if you will call my carriage—"

Another carriage under ancient live oaks whose branches interlaced overhead to form a swaying, green roof, Walker remembered; the exciting smell of Christmas in clean, chill air, and the team scented it too, hurrying *clip-clop* to reach their stables and extra ears of corn. Grandfather Fairbairn's house was command Mecca to his descendants, come Christmas, and so long as the great Yule log burned in that massive, blackened fireplace, no hand on the place, black or white, was turned to labor.

Chrismus gif, Chrismus gif! Popcorn strung on the chosen tree, lighted by a hundred little candles; a stolen taste of mulled wine, and belly full of usually forbidden sweets. Then drowsy stories by the fireplace, old, oft-told tales of fathers and their fathers, stretching back to Scotland, coming down through wild Indians and always-won wars and haints whose very names made the children shiver deliciously.

It was more than simply putting his back to a war, Walker knew; it was denying every link of those bloodlines and casting himself adrift from all that should matter. Now he could not claim kin to those honored names on worn tombstones, to the rich land that had tickled between his toes and which shrouded his mother.

"You are quiet," the duchess said.

Hames rattled and the coachman clucked before Walker answered. "Do we ever truly leave home?"

"Gott, yes. I would leave those moldy Prussian castles forever, if I could—cold, echoing caverns of man's foolish history. No home to a woman, any woman."

The coach rattled and swayed over cobblestones, and Katrina said, "Where will you spend this final holiday in England? You are welcome to use my apartments here in London when I am gone."

He touched her veined hand. "You've a good heart hidden behind many small cruelties."

The duchess shook her head and chuckled. *"Mien himmel,* but you are a daring boy. Take care, Walker Fairbairn; Knox is a hard man, a vindictive man." She turned to look him in the face. "Or is it an interest in your countrywoman, the lovely savage?"

"Tosanna? She went willingly to him, sold like a common slave, like a wench from the block, eager to please her new master. Though she could have stayed free, she chose otherwise."

"You rise angry to the bait, as a Black Forest trout. What is that little beast doing to you men—*all* of you? She has but to enter a ballroom, and each man there starts to pant, with his tongue hanging out."

Walker pulled back a window curtain and stared out at London, watched it gathering dusk and flinging lights about. "She's a doxy born, that's all. Some women, like the Widow, are meant to rule; others are content as faithful wives—and others not so content. Tosanna came throbbing to her savage cradle born to draw men to her. That's what men sense in her—that, and naught else."

"You speak as if from experience. Or do you overdream, beloved of many women?"

He let the curtain fall and grunted. "Beloved? Used by women, dear duchess, as I use them in turn. Pleasure to us both, a pleasing dalliance and no more—no sticky promises or false tears. Do I boyish dream over one more such wench? Hardly, I think."

"Then stay clear of her," Katrina said. "If you mean to torment Cokington further by flaunting what he cannot have, look to your back of dark nights. Even if you reach your ship to ride his passage money home, walk wide of the rail and bar your cabin door."

"Ah, then," Walker said, "is the Stone Earl's arm so long?"

"Long enough to strangle you half across the world. So —my coachman turns in. You will stay with me a while longer?"

Laying fingers gentle along her doughy cheek, he said, "You're a kind woman, Katrina; you enjoy working sharp claws and are not beyond a quick, hard bite, but a kind woman withal. I will stay until I can gather my few possessions, and do you offer me transport to the docks, I will not refuse."

She laughed. "The same Walker Fairbairn, beloved by many women—no, *bemuser* of many women. But take care, my flighty fellow; a chink is showing in your armor."

Helping her down from the carriage, he pondered her advice and decided to ignore it. It would please him to twit Cokington, and among the Stone Earl's guests were certain ladies he had dallied with before, charming and

lonely wives of England's straitlaced nobility. They would
be glad of the chance to escape stodgy husbands and give
themselves over to honest abandon. If that riled the Earl,
so much the better. But it was time to go home.

Inside Katrina's rooms, she turned to him and said,
"Transport in my own carriage—yes, *mein herr*. And more,
I think—a purse to tide you over until the journey, and
another thing, so I may sleep easier in those miserable
Prussian nights—a U.S. Navy Colt, yes? My men shall find
one for you on the morrow."

Her hands upon his arms, Duchess Katrina Hozenholer
looked him in the eyes. "Mine is a warrior race, *liebchen*.
I see the expert with weapons—upon a wooden target. But
the same uncanny marksman refuses to shoot birds, because
he cannot bear the sight of blood. In the dark mountains of
home, where ghosts of a thousand years lie uneasy upon
their shields, we have learned a great truth. When you must
strike, thrust hard and true. Do not hesitate, do not *think*
—only strike."

Leaning to kiss her cheek, Walker said, "I will try to
remember that, duchess."

And try to forget Tosanna of the Comanches.

CHAPTER 21

They were alone, the sumptuous dinner past, too much wine drunk. Candles danced gay light patterns upon papered walls of the master bedroom, for Gordon Hammers did not like the air-that-burns, and clung to the old ways.

Tosanna wore her best dress; it was pale blue, cool, and dewy as desert sky just past dawn, and held her breasts high, as if with cunning, unseen hands. The whispering material snugged to hips and belly, calling attention to what it concealed. Her hair was always worn down her back, and now it was caught with a simple pin at the nape of her neck. From somewhere Belle Williams had produced a perfume of crushed flowers, and when she lowered her chin, Tosanna could smell it rising from her throat.

"You—you do not mind?" Gordon held a pipe, one finger nervously tamping its bowl.

"No—my own people smoke pipes."

"Yes, of course. Tobacco is originally Indian, isn't it? Ah, Tosanna—if you would prefer not to—" He lighted the pipe from a candle.

She waited and, when he did not explain, said, "I have already bathed for you. I am fresh."

Turning his face away, Gordon said, "I—ah, did not mean that, my dear. What I meant was—well, if you would rather not—" Helplessly, he gestured at the bed. It was large, four posted, with velvet drapes surrounding it, covers turned back to show gleaming white sheets. Gordon

cleared his throat again. "You are under no obligation—
ah—I would not force a lady against her will, so if—if—"

A good man, she thought, old and wise. She moved to
lay her fingers gently across his cheek. "I wish to, Gordon
Hammers. I wish to very much."

Slowly, she undid buttons and hooks: sensuously, she
removed dress and slip, to stand naked and proud before
him. Pipe forgotten in clenched fist, he stared at her without moving. Tosanna glided close and took away the pipe,
placing it in the base of a candleholder. She would have
undressed him also, but Gordon started and turned quickly
around to fumble at his own clothing.

Tosanna frowned. Was this one ashamed? Grayed by
many winters, he had no cause. Old warriors who had
taken many wives should be boastful of their experiences.
While he kept his back to her and made a great to-do of
quenching candles about the room, Tosanna slipped into
bed, delighting in the caress of soft, clean sheets against
her bare skin. They were a thing she had come to like. They
were not as sensuous as new furs, but had a particular slidy
feel she enjoyed.

A single candle flickered at her side of the bed. In near
darkness, she glimpsed Gordon's white body but briefly,
then he was beneath the covers, but not touching her.
Moistening thumb and forefinger, Tosanna pinched out the
candle, although she would have liked to know him in detail.

"Tosanna," he said into the blackness, "I have had no—
no woman for a long time. I am gray, and perhaps—perhaps my years weigh too heavy upon me. I should not
have—damn!—I should not have thrust myself upon a
young and beautiful woman, when I am . . . so . . .
damned . . . *old*."

"It is not bad to be old," she murmured, her lips at his
ear. "It is an honor to have lived long and known much.
One does not mourn growing old; it is a time to celebrate,
a time of leaves painted bright and stars hung close."

"Not autumn," Gordon whispered, "but drear winter
setting chill in the bones and icing the heart; cold, gray
winter, and a man caught in its grip is a fool to think he can
ever smell a draught of springtime again."

Tosanna eased the tip of her tongue into his ear and
Gordon recoiled violently. The movement of his body gave
her a chance to hitch a leg over him and draw him tightly

to her. Not hurrying it, she caressed and stroked this man so afraid his death song might be close. Kissing his throat, she trailed her mouth across his chest, searching from nipple to nipple with small, teasing nips.

When his breath caught ragged in his throat, Tosanna worked on down his rib cage, tantalizing his belly until it writhed and drew taut as hide on a stretcher. His lower groin then, and Gordon Hammers tried to cry out, but any meaning was lost in wordless joy. She grew him just enough, then rolled and drew him with her, pulled him atop her pulsing body and used an expert hand to guide him home.

In case he could not keep his strength, she rolled her hips and worked muscles of her inner self, cupping and ringing him as he moved in and out, squeezing and exciting him. Gordon rode her manfully, burrowing deep, gripping her demanding body close. Her fingers were caught in his hair and her pelvis was sledging his, when he groaned against her panting mouth and loosed himself into her seething depths.

Holding him in position, she continued to arch and heave to him until she had climbed to the top of her own moon-kissed mountain and found its bright-warm silver washing over her.

Against the base of his throat she said, "You are not old." And after he had wine and a cigar, she proved it again to Gordon Hammers. Skillfully, using crafts and wiles taught her by other men, by women of her tribe, Tosanna aroused him again and led him rioting back through the years to exultant youth.

"God—and that's no blasphemy," Gordon breathed, "God—and a prayer. Never has there been a lass like you, to reach so deeply into an old man and make him—no, not young again—make him more than he ever was, young or no."

She lay peacefully beside him, the wealth of her hair spun across his bare chest. Outside in the country dark, crickets fiddled a lively jig and a passing nightbird sang quick solo to silent applause of sleepy flowers. Tosanna moved her tongue through air from an open window, tasting night flavors so different from those of her home. Here something was always greening, a threat of chill even in midsummer, and forever a faint touch of salt to remind her how close lay the sea.

Tosanna tipped her tongue against Gordon's chest with

its silken white hair. She did not mind hair now; it seemed natural on a man's body. Comanches had so little, and none upon their faces, but that was because they pulled it early in their lives. Sometimes, old and revered chiefs allowed hair upon their faces, especially the Kiowa.

Suddenly, lying sated and content beside a kind and gentle man, warm in his bed and within the grateful circle of his arms, she thought of Sunhair. Walker Fairbairn had almost no hair upon his body either. It was slim and smooth as a woman's, tapered and wondrous to the touch. But there was no denying Sunhair was a man—oh, no. He possessed the strength, the power, and size, and—ah, ah, yes—he knew many ways to please a woman. But there were dark places in him, blacknesses heavy as the night now beyond Athol Mansion windows.

He spoke as a bird, words trilling sweetly across his tongue, and the tawny beauty of him was that of the golden hawk or a great eagle riding pathways of the sky. Perhaps he did not know of the dark places, but they were hooked beneath his skin, wormed into his heart, and they were cold, cold as spirit breath stirring in the blackness of an icy mountain cave.

"Tosanna," Gordon said, and repeated her name so softly she knew he sought no answer. Beneath her cheek, his chest rose and fell more slowly. As he slipped into the world of dreams, Tosanna remained quietly with him. Only when he grunted over to one side did she untangle from his body and pull up a coverlet for his shoulders.

Somewhere in this great house, Belle Williams was also sleeping, and no servant of Athol had so much as wrinkled a nose at her.

And the house, its vast and rolling grounds—many ballrooms could be swallowed here. From turret rooms to cellars, it stood tall and wide and was cleaned daily by a busy little army. Its many rooms were mostly closed off, and it was said the duke had not entertained since his family was lost. Therefore the great dining hall, the huge ballroom stood empty and echoing. He had meals carried up from the kitchen and dined in the master suite, always alone.

Until she came, Tosanna thought. It would be good for them both, for her to know security and gentleness, for him to relearn warmth and happiness. She would keep him so, she promised her gods, keep him against the loneliness that pushed him fast toward his burial platform. If his flesh grew cold at night, it would not be for want of her body heat. How surprised he had been when Stafford delivered her and Belle Williams to Athol. Speechless, he let Stafford pump his hand and say polite nothing words.

Before climbing back into the hired coach, Colonel Sir John Stafford bowed and kissed her hand, as if she were a highborn lady of England.

But you are free, Gordon Hammers had said, free. In truth, lass, when I flung away your chain—

And she had said: we have no home; I mean to keep the bargain Stafford made.

If they remained good to each other, she thought now in this first night, might not there be an opportunity—someday, sometime—for her to sail home? In the dark, in softness and hope, Tosanna closed her eyes and held to yet another man who had bought her and freed her. The freeing somehow bound her closer to Gordon Hammers.

Across London, past a dozen fine estates, Walker Fairbairn sipped ale in a public house where the publican had made a few starts at conversation, then left him to his thoughts. In a corner of the bar, drunken tars sang sea chanties, keeping time with tankards upon the bartop. Walker barely heard them.

He still carried a hurt from Lady Barrenton's turndown at the ball. In retrospect, he didn't blame her. She'd taken him on reputation of his sexual prowess, yet unproven to her. On that alone she'd been asked to lay out more than five thousand pounds for a woman he wanted, another woman. It had been the unthinking reaction of a fool, so embarrassing. Staring into his tankard, he again saw himself picking up the golden chain and padlock thrown by the Duke of Athol, symbolizing Tosanna's freedom. No one noticed Walker scooping up the rich metal links, and the thing was worth good money.

Why hadn't he turned it at a pawnshop? Why go with Katrina to Gatesford and the bird shooting? Sir Stafford would not be there, after calling out the Stone Earl. But Walker thought maybe a slim chance—

But no—he'd allowed himself to be angered into a shooting match before Cokington's faithful retinue, and further shamed the man. Watch your back, Katrina warned, and walk wide of the ship's rail. Walker touched the inner pocket of his coat, where a sheaf of five-pound notes nestled, first-class passage home.

Tomorrow, on the full of the tide, the frigate *Sea Sprite* would sail, but he had not yet booked passage on her. Because a few ladies he knew might very well pass him bon voyage presents, if he called upon them for a sweaty finale.

Gesturing at the publican, he asked more ale, and another round of the same for the roistering sailors. Perhaps they were crewmen of the *Sea Sprite,* celebrating a last night ashore. They toasted him loudly, and he smiled at them, glad none came over in mawkish sentimentality.

Why the *hell* hadn't Tosanna and her maid stayed over at the Brickmaker's Arms? He'd gone straight there, only to have a porter tell him Sir Stafford and the ladies settled their account and departed early. Would a rakehell like Stafford give Tosanna passage money to America?

And there had been the sitting room incident with Queen Victoria; one word from Tosanna and the entire slave sale would have exploded, hurling all involved into Bailey Prison, whatever their ranks. The Widow would brook no defying of her moralities, and Tosanna's sale crossed Victoria's personal codes as well as being counter to British law. There were more mysteries within Tosanna than a sane man could count.

Sane? Walker downed his ale in long gulps, placed the tankard atop the bar, and went into the night, the publican's farewell following him. No sooner did one man relinquish her than Tosanna found another man, and richer. So many were eager to share a bed with the pagan princess, including himself.

Sauntering along Fleet Street, tasting the threat of fog and curling his nostril at the mud-flat stink of low tide, Walker heard the slow pealing of Big Ben and was surprised how early the night was. It seemed he had been meandering without purpose for days, not hours.

A chestnut vendor wafted his hot wares beneath Walker's nose. He bought a pennyworth and ate them from a curl of paper as he strolled in no certain direction. Neither too far nor too long, he warned himself; dark and fog brought out footpads, rogues desperate for any small bit of loot—a watch, greatcoat, shoes, anything they might sell. The wad of notes in Walker's pocket turned heavy, and he turned with them, for his cheap hostel near the docks.

Safely there, he brought forth Katrina's final gifts, the

Navy .36 and a slim pouch of gold sovereigns. He silently thanked the duchess with a wry smile, not only for the presents, but for giving him thought for reacquainting himself with certain ladies.

Tosanna had to be at Athol; no fool, she had followed the money. Certainly the ancient duke held no attraction for her. That was it; her former protector gave her nothing, so she betook herself to Athol. To wheedle passage from Gordon Hammers, or further accustom herself to a rich and civilized life? Maybe she was no more eager than he to go home. She would return to wilderness and a savage tribe that would age her beauty in only a few short years. Before she was twenty, she'd be a bent and wrinkled crone.

Over here Tosanna was an oddity, royalty of sorts because cunning Stafford had made her a princess. Her slightly darker skin was no barrier to acceptance, as it would be in Texas, or wherever her heathen tribe wandered—as it most certainly would be in Alabama. Not for him—that prejudice had sloughed off Walker Fairbairn like outgrown skin, beginning when he could read and know what the rest of the world thought of slavery.

Afterward, when he'd started into his teens and bedded the high yellow maid who seemed so willing to initiate him into the mysteries of sex, he wondered if Sheila diddled him because she couldn't deny a white. By the time he fretted over that kind of rape, he'd been with Sheila countless times, and with pure black field hand women. He found them little different from the two white girls he'd rolled in the hay—Elise, the foreman's daughter, and Marcelle Ann Paxman, youngest of the brood at Paxman Plantation.

But if Marcelle Ann's belly had swollen, he'd have perforce married her, but not the others. Sitting on the bed with a cheap, raw brandy searing his throat, he watched the bedside candle dance and frowned at the thought that he might have sired mulatto children. By now they were sold off or freed by Abe Lincoln's Proclamation.

Walker took another drink, swallowed tepid water after it, crushed his cigar into the candleholder, and blew out the candle. Half clothed, he slept restlessly.

His baggage stored beneath the innkeeper's desk to ward off thieves, its guarding well worth the shilling paid, Walker took to the streets in early morning. A cunning forerunner of chill got to him, even in his new, warm greatcoat. He made for a line of hansoms whose drivers huddled around a smoky peat fire built in an old metal barrel. In shabby topcoats, battered tall hats, and cracked boots, they were all of a pattern. When he stood at the first carriage in line, one hurried to him, rubbing one ragged glove against the other.

"The Duke of Athol?" Walker said. "You'd know where he lives?"

The coachman wiped a reddened nose. "To be sure, your honor; Athol lies past the West End. A long haul, but be your worship off to visit a duke, you'll not be thinking of cost—"

Walker chuckled. "I'm not even a poor relation, only a ruddy colonial come to gawk. Damned right I'm counting shillings."

Price settled and half the score paid in advance, Walker bundled into a moth-eaten blanket and thought of Tosanna. Lucky she hadn't been sold South as a slave, though few planters were fools enough to buy an Indian. They didn't make good workers and sickened easily, or ran away. Still, a beauty like Tosanna might have brought a fair price on the block.

There was poetry in London of early morning; cold couplets to be sure, but with a certain beauty to them. He experimented with lines in his head . . . fingerings of air not yet dusted by smoke, cleansed by the rags of last night's fog . . . musical chant of peddlers, iron against cobblestone rhythm of horses' hooves . . .

Putting gloved hand to his eyes, Walker only listened to the city, only smelled of it and knew the washing of it against his face. London had a flavor, a ring, a defiance; it was a crust baked around empty bellies of the poor. It was factory children worked into little old people, coughing black coal dust and spitting starvation.

"Damn!" Walker said and reached inside his coat for a small cigar. He felt better with it clenched in his teeth. For all he knew, his South was worse off. The dark riders had galloped there in force—war, pestilence, famine, and death.

He kept delaying his return there, not wanting to see what was against his memories of what had been. He was afraid to see a grave marker bearing his father's name, the blackened ruin of a great plantation house, its surviving chimneys flung to accuse the sky like soiled legs sprawled by rapists. Maybe he would find nobody who remembered his betrayal.

Maybe he would find nothing.

It would be easier, not facing anyone, especially his father. Being right about the war's inevitable result wouldn't make him any less hated. Why go home then? Why bare his belly for the gutting to come, why bow his head for the raging storm to break over it?

The coach slowed before imposing gateposts and turned between them, wheels grinding softly over fine, raked gravel. Athol, Walker presumed; the pagan princess was bettering herself with every move: from fleabitten squaw to expensive camp follower of a mercenary, and now bed warmer to no less than the Duke of Athol, Gordon Hammers. What next? Would she seek out the Prince of Wales and become semisecret consort to the next regent?

Carefully tended trees overhung the drive, and Walker was reminded of home, of the great, curving drive made white by crushed oyster shells; it led to tall, round pillars along a hospitable porch cooled by canopies of purple wisteria and golden honeysuckle vines. Deep greenblack and creamy white, a hedge of fragrant Cape Jasmine bushes stood parade around the near side of a lush lawn.

Gray and stiff, old Jeston would move from some hidden shade to take the horses, and visitors moved beneath a bower of magnolia trees that held hands overhead and onto the porch, where the master of Fairbairn plantation rose to greet them.

Walker shook his head. He'd get no welcome there; his father might set the hounds on him, or at least order him off the land. The coach rocked to a halt and Walker sat immobile for a while. There could very well be no Fairbairn house; the ancient live oaks could have been cut down for fuel, and the flowers trampled by Yankee boots. The master of the plantation, that hard, tradition-bound man from a long line of hard men who'd fought for their own—he was no doubt dead, if not from Union mini ball or scalawag knife, then from a broken heart.

Why go back, then?

"To know," Walker said, and climbed down from the hansom. "To *know*, damn it—to be certain."

The doorman was cool but polite. "Fairbairn, sir? Please wait in the smoking room until I find whether milady will see you. Instructions, sir, you understand."

"I understand," Walker said, and bit through the end of a cigar. He used a tricky flint and steel lighter found upon a polished desk. No sulphur matches were in sight, and he figured the duke as a traditionalist.

The room was hung with hunting prints and draperies of chase scenes. Another one, Walker thought—another who heroically slaughtered animals in the name of sport. Christ, was he the only man in the world to admit he detested killing?

"Walker Fairbairn," she said from a curtained doorway, and he turned to face her. She was trim and lovely in a black gown that uplifted her breasts and snugged her trim waist, that caressed her hips. He bowed to her.

"I thought—I hoped, to make it up to you. That bitterness of mine at the ball. I'm sorry for that."

She crossed to a tall cabinet and poured brandy into small crystal glasses. Dark eyes looked over the glass she held out to him. "You did not shame me, Sunhair, but yourself."

"But you'll forgive me for—for bidding on you?"

"Is that why you traveled here, for my forgiveness?"

Damn her, he thought; she was so self-possessed and almost regal. Walker breathed deeply and put down his glass to move toward her, but stopped before touching her— just barely. "I couldn't sleep without seeing you in my dreams. My hands keep the memory of your skin, my lips cannot forget the wild heat of your mouth. Tosanna—I traveled here because I had to."

Keeping her brandy glass between them, she probed his eyes and Walker felt he had to keep throwing up barricades, lest this woman get too far into his soul. He wanted her, needed her flesh, the fierce ravenous fitting of her body to his own, but women didn't want to hear that simple truth. They had to have it dressed in pretty words, wanted to believe it was all for undying love.

"I cannot see your heart," she said, "but my dreams have also been troubled by spirits. Yet this bothers me too. My protector is a good man, kind and caring."

"And old," Walker said.

"A good man," Tosanna repeated, "and much alive."

Walker felt his stomach tighten. "Good lord, have you— Milady Savage—turned Victorian? What was all that talk about Comanche sharing and freedom and—"

"I choose," Tosanna said. "And until some medicine can

take you from my blood, I choose to see you. But hear me, Sunhair; Gordon Hammers is not to know and not to be hurt, ever."

Loose now, warm and eager, he made that long step toward her and took her hand. "I will be discreet, milady."

"Yes," she said, "we must."

CHAPTER 22

She could read the strong restlessness in him each time they were together now. It was the same fever that attacked Comanche warriors at the time of the buffalo. They could not sit, could not be themselves on the couch of furs. They paced and stared off at mountains and sharpened arrows and lances; they became short with their wives and young males stayed clear of them.

Until the spirit talker read the omens and told the men they could be off on the great hunt the next dawn. Then they were happy, readying favorite horses, hunters, and carriers; then they laughed and made new songs and were men again.

But Walker Fairbairn did not hunt buffalo or anything else; even the women he sometimes preyed on came to him. He rode well in a casual fashion, but was never in on the kill at a fox hunt and never fired shotguns at birds. Yet she knew there was magic in his shooting, a great medicine given him by the spirits, for no ordinary man could shoot like that. When Walker consented to give a demonstration, it seemed there must be trickery involved, that it was impossible to hit such tiny targets and so rapidly. He could even bounce bullets from a rock, sending them around a tree trunk and into a target he could not even see.

She lay with him in a gardener's cottage, not far from Athol estate. As she turned upon his arm, Walker said, "You're a fantastic rider to watch, Milady Savage. Someday you'll kill a horse and yourself."

Tosanna snuggled her face into his throat. "Horse and rider must first live in order to die well."

"More desert philosophy," Walker said. "You don't like chasing down foxes any more than I do. But we do it. Me, to stay near you and be accepted by the duke's friends; you, because—"

"I enjoy it. I like to watch the women's faces and see anger in their men's eyes. I am always first to the fox, and this pleases the duke, makes him proud."

Walker grunted. "Since he's too old to do his own riding—any kind, I'd say."

"And you would be wrong."

Walker sulked, and she thought how proud she was of Gordon, how far he had come during the past months. No longer a stranger at court, he acted many years younger, said his friends; he was into politics again, interested in his estates. Tosanna knew it was her doing, that she had brought another spring to him, another time of greening.

Moving away from Walker, she said, "I do not like this feeling of wrong."

He stroked her back. "Come on, girl. He isn't your husband."

"That should not bother me either. I am no English-woman, constantly pretending to be pure and sexless, while bedding any man who catches my fancy. I am Tosanna of the Kwehar-enuh, who does not lie, who chooses her lovers without false shame. If I was duchess, it should not make me guilty to make love with you or anyone else."

Walker sighed. "In a strange way, I know what you mean. Gordon Hammers is such a—a thoroughly *nice* man. I know others whisper about us, but he pays no attention. He trusts us, damn it."

"Is that why you are restless, because you feel like a betrayer?"

"No. I don't think so. Maybe."

She sat up and ran hands through her hair. "Or because I do not lie passive for you to rut upon?"

"Damn it, *no!* I'm getting used to that, and you don't always attack like some horny animal—not always."

Tosanna walked to a sideboard. The cottage was small, but its owner kept cheap wine. She poured some for herself. When Walker was like this, doing anything for him only made him worse.

Over her shoulder she asked, "Are you running out of money?"

"That, too." His voice was sullen and the bed creaked when he left it. "But that should be no problem, since the ever truthful, ever independent Milady Savage does not know jealousy. I'll just take up with some of the gentle-women again; lord knows enough of the doddering duke's pristine lady friends have been rolling their eyes at me."

Tosanna carried her wineglass to a narrow window and looked out at the English countryside. Her horse was tethered at the wall there, and Walker's just beyond. Anyone who passed would know what was going on. They would have to be more careful.

She said, "I will not cry; I will not become angry."

"I know that," he snapped, and padded barefoot to help himself to wine. "Sour damned stuff, this. I'll have to buy better swill for our host—providing my next sponsor is generous."

Tosanna said, "I cannot ask him for money to give you."

Walker slapped the sideboard with the flat of his hand. "I know that too! I didn't beg."

Into the little silence that followed she said, "I think your home calls to you."

"If it does, I'm not listening. Not now—not yet. Why are you getting dressed?"

"Because if we love again, it will not be good."

Walker splashed more sour wine into his glass. "It hasn't been all that good lately anyhow."

Sliding into her dress, she looked at him. "You do not have to ride back with me. It would be better."

"Christ," he said, "now it's lessons in cuckoldry from an *Indian*."

"We gave our word Gordon Hammers would not be hurt."

"I remember," he said. "Damn it, I remember."

She rode slowly across damp and chilly fields, smelling burned peat, woodsmoke, that ever present hint of the sea. The sky was gray and a breath of mist kissed cold against her face. Something was wrong with Sunhair, a sickness she could not reach. Long ago he was to have sailed back to America, but he stayed in England.

Tosanna wanted to think it was because of her, his need for her. But Sunhair was unhappy, angry. He had too long denied his father, his tribe, and must someday face them, no matter how long he put it off. She still had difficulty understanding a man who ran away rather than fight for his people, his land.

Walker Fairbairn was strange in several ways: he did magic with a rifle or short gun, but refused to fire on bird or deer or fox. Would he kill animals in order to eat? She thought so.

Would he shoot another man to guard his own life? Again, she thought so.

Reining her horse around a copse of holly, Tosanna allowed it to walk. Although Gordon Hammers pointed out how and why English ladies rode sidesaddle, she refused to try riding that way. It was stupid and dangerous, and probably invented by men afraid that better women riders would shame them on the hunt.

What else troubled Sunhair? Perhaps he was too used to more than one woman, happier with several wives about him. He could not be angry with her for not bringing him money; she had explained her feelings about that. It would not be proper; it would be like a Comanche stealing horses from her husband as presents for her lover. Not even an Apache woman would do that.

Tosanna jogged the horse in Athol's stable yard, and a groom came quickly to take the reins, to offer an arm, although she never asked help alighting from a horse. She did not think Englishwomen were so weak either. It was a fashion of theirs, to make their men believe so.

Holding up her long skirt, riding crop tucked under one arm, she strolled across the garden and into the back of the house. Often she walked through kitchen and laundry and stopped to talk with servants there. It was a happy house and a good land, for the head of the tribe was good.

She peeped into a bubbling pot and stole a nibble of apple tart, then skipped through the formal dining room, whose massive table often seated twenty people. She liked this room and its remembered laughter, the echoes of a thousand candles, warm scents, and happy diners. Tosanna paused in its doorway, one hand laid softly upon old, highly polished wood paneling.

Yes, it was better to eat here, served by quick, deft hands, food that was clean, spiced, and well prepared, food that was not always maize meal, wild beans, and buffalo, or berries, acorn bread, cactus pulp, and deer. Tosanna had learned to like fish and birds—meats Comanches ate only if they were starving; she enjoyed wines and tea, steaming breads, and sugared scones.

Quickly past the library and through a foyer to the stairs, she shrugged away the mantle of guilt that always tried to wrap her when she compared a thing English to Comanche and found the Comanche lacking. The ways of life were different, and one might learn from the other. So many good things the English knew, and so many laws of the Comanche they could use. But this was not her duty, this teaching not her path to follow, for she was only a woman, and as a woman she was duly interested in her man, in Gordon Hammers.

He sat at his desk, candles already going to light his hand as he penned correspondence. Tosanna stood back and looked fondly at him until he felt her presence and turned to peer at her through his spectacles. That was another wondrous invention—medicine glasses that turned old eyes young once more. Many graying Comanche warriors could use them.

She danced over and kissed the top of his head. He held her hand for a long moment. "Did you have a nice ride, Tosanna?"

"A little cold. I must be turning English, and soft."

Gordon Hammers chuckled. "Never you, my dear—though you're exceedingly soft in the proper places."

She touched his cheek and withdrew her hand, removed cloak and hat, mindful that his eyes followed her every motion. He had stopped apologizing to her for being old, and stopped thanking her aloud for her youth and beauty, for the changing over of his life. And only once, in the beginning of them when he was unsure of himself, had this Duke of Athol mentioned passage home to her. Now Tosanna felt he would not say it again for fear she would accept.

Neither could she ask his gold, his permission to leave. Gordon would give both, Tosanna knew, but the giving and her going would kill him. She was bound to this good and fragile man by more than what he had saved her from—whoring in the city streets. Kindness, tenderness, a real dedication to her, perhaps even love: these were cords stronger than buffalo thongs, and tied her to Gordon Hammers beyond her word.

Even Belle Williams understood and accepted that. Belle was happily settling in, not quite one of the household, but not quite a servant either. She still held close to Tosanna, and would allow nobody else to touch bath, hair, or clothing of her friend and mistress. But she held domestics court of sorts in the kitchen, regaling the workers with tales of wicked London.

Passing beyond the book-lined study into their bedroom, she felt no shame at betraying Gordon with Sunhair, no guilt for not telling him where she spent the afternoon. If Gordon had asked her point-blank, she might have answered truthfully, after weighing the consequences; but if Tosanna thought confession of her tryst would hurt him more, she would cheerfully lie. This also was she learning from the White Eyes—that a lie was not always bad. If she tried to show this to the council of wise men, would they believe her?

She looked into the mirror, as always surprised that she had not changed completely, that her eyes were not heavy and old with all the knowledge that had come to her. Overnight the Last Flower of the Kwehar-enuh might very well turn blue-eyed, and her hair go bright as polished gold the English loved so.

Tosanna turned away and unbuttoned her blouse. No, she was Comanche, and would so remain, right through the instant she sang her death song and the spirits called her. It was all very well to accept *part* of the White Eye way of doing things—to take the good and leave the bad; it was foolish to imitate them in all ways, even to clothing.

Here the dresses were not too uncomfortable, despite slavish obedience to changing fashions. But in Comancheria, such long skirts would snag and rip and get in the way of woman's work; they could even be dangerous. Hats, blouses, fancy ruffles, and bows dear to a lady's heart? Frills to be discarded in the first heat of summer. Cruel desert sun called for loose dresses; sand, rock, and cactus demanded tough leather moccasins with leggings, not delicate, fashionable shoes.

And tough hands, Tosanna thought, looking at her own. They were soft now, oiled and scented, powdered for smoothness. Here ladies did no work to roughen them, and wore gloves to hide them from weak sun. In the camps of Tosanna's people there were no great ladies—only wives. True, the wives of chiefs and great warriors might have slaves to do their bidding, but they would work anyhow.

In England, money took the place of many horses.

Money paid others to work, to farm, to slaughter; it hired others to bathe you and comb your hair. It made the difference between riding in a carriage and walking, between a full belly and an empty one. Strength and skill did not count here; what mattered most was cunning in accumulating gold and silver. Or having an ancestor who was.

She pulled the bell tug and moved to her bath, knowing Belle Williams would reach the tub with hot water in minutes. In the other room, Tosanna slipped from her dress and underclothing, touching spots upon them, seeing Sunhair's naked body in her mind, feeling the momory of it running through her blood.

How long since she had thought of her husband like this, dreamed of Ado-eeti with his manhood swollen and ready? Too long. She had difficulty pulling together the details of his face and body. Neither did she arouse herself by thinking of new things to do with Gordon Hammers.

When Belle Williams hurried in with water, Tosanna was ready for the tub, ready for the latest gossip. Relaxing beneath Belle's agile hands, she tried to think of her own wants and not Sunhair's restlessness. What would she do if he left, when he returned to his home? Could she remain as content with Gordon and her position at Athol?

"You saw him again," Belle said. "You always get that look. When is he going back to America?"

"I hope not until I do," Tosanna said, "and that may be a long time."

"When you go, milady'll take me along?"

"If you wish, Belle, but it's very different from here."

Belle lifted a bucket of rinse water and poured it slowly. "Athol's good to me, but that ain't to say it won't fall apart when somethin' happens to the duke. We was that close, miss, *that* close to bein' Ramsgate whores. And thinkin' on it, cleanin' in hostels and such, that ain't much better. America might be a whole new start for me."

Tosanna hesitated. "Comancheria—my part of America—is not civilized, but wild."

"And free?" Belle asked.

"In one way, bound in another."

"But not like England, where my lowly birth holds me back?"

"No," Tosanna answered, "not like that." But she could not tell Belle of the killing and burning, the lightning Comanche raids and Mexican or White Eye pursuit, the sudden inevitability of death. It seemed far away to her now, far and dim as Don Joaquin de Arredondo and his bitter, lonely vengeance. Colonel Sir John Stafford was closer, but he was also tied into that violent and bloody way of life. Tosanna shut her eyes and saw him calmly, efficiently, killing Yaqui Indians in Mexico.

"This Walker Fairbairn," Belle said, "what'll you do about him? A blessed miracle, it is, that the duke ain't found him out."

Tosanna climbed from the tub. "I don't know what to do about him, now or if he leaves. I know only that I am chained to him, and this chain is not golden."

CHAPTER 23

If he couldn't name his soul his own and force a break with Tosanna, then he must make her walk away from him, forever. Walker was in his cups when he figured that out, but it sounded pretty good when he sobered up, and Lady Tracy Glynlyon was just the confederate to see him through the plan.

With Tosanna out of the way, gone permanently to stay with her doddering duke, perhaps he could again concentrate upon earning passage money home. A few generous gifts from certain ladies, and he'd be off, with no more Indian albatross about his neck. He had to believe she was something of a witch. How else to explain all she had done to him?

Back home, he'd laughed at the blacks and their superstitious fear of conjure women. Why was it always a woman and never a man? The Comanches probably had something like them, witches by any other name, dark practitioners knowledgeable of secret drugs and vice poisons to bind a man to them, enslave him forever.

"Wherefore the chants and whence the incantations then?" Walker asked the wall beside his bed. "She does not bay at the moon, nor beat her savage tom-toms—at least, not where I may hear them. No, you fool, she has only somehow infected you, and you must heal yourself, physician."

Because of Tosanna, he had lingered in England far beyond his resources, even beyond his will. He had put off that dread return to Fairbairn Plantation because of her. It was something he'd resisted with all his might, and all assistance grog and other ladies could offer. Yet here he was, like some callow youth, mooning over a magic first love.

Tosanna, Miladay Savage, was certainly no first love—not for him, not for herself. A logical man would say thank you and goodbye, but he lacked the courage. She would have to make the break.

Impatient for it to be done, for the hurt he must do her to be over, Walker strode to the dressing table and uncorked a bottle of brandy. Its golden, shadowed fluid was like Tosanna—beauteous, heady, and powerful enough to numb the mind as well as sate the senses.

"Here's to you, witch woman of the Comanche," he said, lifting a filled glass. "To Milady Savage and the final time around. I shall be rid of you henceforth."

Why the urge to keep pushing, to have her just one more time, and one more after that? Walker had another drink to such stupidity. Hell, he thought, this affair was compounded by the fact that the Duke of Athol was a good man, easily liked, still more easily respected. Jesus! That such a man should take a heathen to his bosom, and walk proudly because of it. Walker had seen that pride, the lifted chin and raised chest, the eye that dared any slur to be cast at the lady Gordon Hammers had upon his arm.

Most husbands well deserved to have horns placed upon their thick heads, else their wives would not be so eager to stray. But the duke, Tosanna—damn! It was so mixed up.

Taking a long swallow of brandy, Walker put down the bottle and splashed cold water over his face, making snorting noises into the washbowl. When he lifted his head to pat dry his face and run a comb through damp hair, she was tapping at the door. Lady Tracy Glynlyon, loveliest, most daring lady of the court. She had all the morals of a vixen in full heat, Walker knew, but she was also a favorite of stuffy Victoria. If the good queen only knew, if Her Majesty could only guess—

"Darling," Tracy bubbled as she swept grandly into the room. "Darling Walker, my sweet colonial—why the hurry-up message, dear? Has something happened to the great lover, to the strongest penis in England—nay, in all the Empire?"

Spinning to show off her new skirts, Tracy tapped the

ivory hilt of a stylish fan against perfect teeth. Wickedly blue, her eyes danced at him. "Say it isn't that wondrous tool, darling."

Walker laughed with her. "Not that, my love. I trust not *ever* that, for where would I be without it?"

"Where indeed?" sighed Tracy as she glided into his arms and pressed the length of her body against his. She was silks and satins, and carried the scent of violets, the taste of wild honey in her mouth.

"Good lord," Walker said. "Just touching you brings it on. You are a remarkable woman, Tracy."

"I know," she said, doffing a tiny hat and loosening the throat of her severe blouse. "I know, darling. And in your own way you are quite remarkable also. Perhaps we are the two greatest lovers in the country. Pity we can't demonstrate that to the court." Tracy's laugh rippled golden through the room. "Can you just imagine our Victoria's bulging eyes popping still more at such a sight?"

Without asking, Walker handed her a glass of brandy, watched her glance around the little room with distaste. She was a studied picture of grace and beauty as she sipped the drink and unbuttoned her blouse further.

He could not help comparing her blonde loveliness with Tosanna's dark beauty. But where Tracy's languid movements were practiced and deft, Tosanna's were natural. Tosanna had been born to grace and rhythm; Tracy had studied, worked at, and gained her place in the sun.

"Well?" Tracy asked.

He went to her and finished unbuttoning her blouse, cupped the freed breasts in both hands, those creamy globes tipped with pink. Walker kissed them both before replying. "It's been a long time, my dear—for me, anyway. Have you had another opportunity to bring another woman into your lovemaking?"

Tracy's cornflower-blue eyes went wide. "La, no! I am not acquainted with another rogue like you. But—" She paused and licked two pearls of brandy from a full lower lip. "But I have often remembered that time with you, and that delectable country lass. Have you found her again, or another as sweet?"

Walker shook his head. "Someone even better. What say you to the scandal of London society?"

Faster, a red darting, Tracy's tongue moved across her lips. "Not the old duke's prized plaything?"

"The same—the heathen mistress."

She smiled, a touch of hunger to her dampened rosebud mouth. "I might have known Walker Fairbairn would not pass such an opportunity to sample the exotic."

"And yourself?"

"Of course I'm available, my dear. I'm here and all atremble."

Moving her to the bed with him, Walker helped Tracy off with her clothing and marveled anew at the lush perfection of her pink marble body. Deftly caressing her, Walker listened for another step upon the stairs. Even as he murmured lines of erotic poetry to the woman writhing beneath his hands, he listened for Tosanna.

Outside the inn, she hesitated, glancing up at the leaded pane window of Walker's rooms. Doubts had been nagging at Tosanna, little black arrowheads not of her own making. The duke never questioned her trips into the city, never asked where she went. It was as if he understood her own thirsts, those he sometimes could not gratify, and tacitly agreed to her slaking of them—so long as she did his name no dishonor in the process. And because she cared for Gordon Hammers so, Tosanna had been very careful in her trysts with Sunhair. It was only Sunhair, and no other man, although many had made suggestions to her.

Beside her, Belle Williams said, "Well, now; I'll be gatherin' myself and off to my own shopping. Shall I meet you here, milady?"

"Three hours," Tosanna answered, "with a carriage, please. I want to be back in time to oversee the duke's dinner."

She slipped in the side door and quickly climbed narrow stairs, her heart lifting as always with anticipation. Sunhair was so good with her, matching the fury of her passion, blending with her sometimes desperate seeking, and being softly, warmly tender when she felt that way. A fine lover, her Sunhair—a marvelous lover. Then why should she feel these sharp little cuts, as if she were doing a great wrong?

She was *not* wrong. The ways of the White Eyes were their own; hers were the traditions of the Comanche; and were not The People far wiser than any other tribe, superior in all fashions?

Firming her mouth, chin held high, she tapped upon Sunhair's door, and pushed back the image of Gordon Hammers. Still, his sad old eyes hung close to her, and

Tosanna could not completely erase them. It would all be simple, if these English followed Kwehar-enuh custom, and the lover, when discovered, paid so many horses to the husband.

But Sunhair had no horses anyway. He was a man who did nothing for a living, who only had money women gave him, or won at cards.

Tosanna knocked at the door again. There were many puzzles within Sunhair. He was a man who could shoot as if the spirits themselves guided his bullets, but his stomach turned at the sight of blood; he spoke with the music of birds, making a song of beautiful words, yet he sang it only in bed with a woman. A Comanche singer would dance proud before the fire, telling his stories for all to hear and appreciate.

He opened the door, his smile bright and welcoming, but Tosanna sensed a flicker in his eyes, those eyes blue as summer sky in early morning and dewy.

"Ah, Tosanna, Milady Savage, come in, darling."

She saw his naked chest and loosened trousers, his bare feet. And as she moved into the room, she saw the woman stretched nude and beautiful upon the bed Tosanna had often shared with Walker Fairbairn.

The woman came to an elbow and shook golden curls back over one smoothly rounded shoulder. "The gossips do you small justice, my dear. You are twice as lovely as they claim—and wear no harpy's wings, no Medusa serpents."

Walker touched Tosanna's shoulder. "This is Lady Tracy Glynlyon, an old and dear friend of mine."

Tracy laughed, a cascade of bells over flashing white teeth. "Not *old*, darling—and very, very dear."

It was strange, Tosanna thought, how White Eyes hair could be bright as sunlight on the head, but darken to reddish copper between the legs. It was thus with both Sunhair and this woman. With interest, Tosanna peered at pink nippled breasts and compared them to her own dark tips. Without a glance at Sunhair, she began to shed her clothing. Lady Tracy Glynlyon's purple eyes followed every movement of Tosanna's hands.

Behind Tosanna, Walker Fairbairn mumbled something, but she paid no attention. He had called her here knowing full well this other woman would be in his bed. If he meant to shock her, he should have known more about Comanche custom. If a warrior died, it was his brother's duty to take in the fallen man's wives. That duty included mounting them, and his performance raised no hubbub in the tepee.

Tosanna dropped her petticoats and stood naked beside the bed, and Lady Tracy softly told her how lovely she was. Then she was on the covers with Sunhair and Tracy, giving herself up to tantalizing caresses of many hands, to mouths that searched and nipped, to sensations more than doubled over and through her like a hotly thundering stream.

She tasted searing lips and moaned between them, lashing back at their tongues with her own, cupping and stroking and feeling as they did. Sometimes she was between them, at other moments beneath, and in a mad spinning atop.

Surrendering, she was the master; dominating, she was yet a slave. Emotions ran wildly through her and them, since they were part of her body and she was a vital connection to theirs. There was a blending, a momentary loss of individual identity to an overwhelming by the whole. It was good.

On her back, sweated and feeling the warmth of the others on each side, Tosanna blinked drowsy at the ceiling. Sunhair had been theirs to share, this golden woman and Tosanna; and in dividing him, they had shared themselves. She felt very close to Tracy now, as if they were blood sisters.

Holding hands, neither of them moved when Walker flung off the bed and stalked to the sideboard to drink deeply from a bottle of brandy. Then Lady Tracy murmured, "A fine idea, love—a marvelous game."

He didn't answer. Tosanna lifted to stare at the back of his head as he drank more from the bottle neck. She wondered what he had expected, why he should be angry now, when their meshing had been so good. Lying back, conscious of Tracy's warm breath fluttering against her throat, knowing the heated woman scent of her, Tosanna closed her eyes. She remembered another inn, with Sunhair cross because she had taken his body instead of always allowing him to ravish her.

Once before she had sensed his displeasure, the crosscurrents stirring beneath the skin of this pretty man. A peep at that swirl of darkness, and she might have walked away from him forever. But after she was brought to Athol, and the desire for him had not worn away, she was ready once more for his call. Even the weight of another man's body upon hers had not been able to rub out the stamp of Walker Fairbairn. He was like the brand *tejanos* placed upon their horses' hips, burned deeply.

It was why she came back to him; turning her back on him before had not healed his brand, but seemed to increase its ache. If she were English, and not honestly passionate as Tracy Glynlyon, she would be hurt by her lover dallying with other women. No icy-faced pretense for her, though all England knew the truth—no prim and proper ignoring of a husband's mistress. Tosanna was Comanche; she could accept.

"Come back to bed, love," Tracy Glynlyon said. "Too much drink dulls the edge of passion, you know. Return to bed and let us continue to please each other."

Walker found a cigar and went through the ritual of lighting it. "Damn," he said. "You women. Black widows all, out to devour a man, to suck the very juices from his body."

Tracy laughed. "In a manner of speaking, my dear. Odd that you'd object."

Tosanna sat up, tucking knees to her breasts. She watched Sunhair pull once more at the brandy and caught his troubled eyes reaching over at her, then shaming away. She did not understand. She had done nothing to harm him, nothing that might anger him, and could not understand this swift reversal of mood. Could Sunhair be like the small lizards of her own desert country, changing colors to hide itself? If so, what did he fear?

When Tracy could not coax him into more love making, she arose and dressed quickly. "It's not always so easy meeting you, Walker. The baron is more suspicious of late, and you know how choleric he is. He wouldn't accept horns without striking back at you."

"I'm trembling," Walker said, and blew a ring of cigar smoke.

"I can see," Tracy said, and turned to Tosanna. "My dear—my lovely, lovely Tosanna—anytime you feel the need to leave your ancient protector and this sullen jack-in-the-bed, please get in touch with me." Her lips were sweet and warm upon Tosanna's mouth, and fleet away.

To Walker she said, "I don't know the reason you sent for me, love, although I'd wager it has little to do with me as a woman. But I'm not angry; I'm happy—because of Tosanna." She blew a kiss. "Until next time, if our luck holds."

When the woman was gone, Tosanna sat quietly for a while. When she began to dress, Walker said, "What does it take, woman?"

Donning her petticoat, she said, "I do not know your meaning. I think I do not know *you*, Sunhair."

"That damned name."

"You wish it changed?"

He blew a furious puff of cigar smoke. "And what do *you* wish, Comanche woman? Do you want to go back to America with me?"

"It would be good," she said, putting on skirt and blouse.

Walker drank brandy and waved his cigar. "And if you stole our passage money from the duke, what then? Do we return to our own country and live happily ever after?"

Sitting on the bed to slip on her shoes, Tosanna said, "I will not steal from Gordon Hammers, nor will I leave him until he tells me. You know that; you always knew it."

He banged one hand against a tabletop. "But you *want* to sail home with me. Why?"

She looked up. "To be with you."

"Good lord, so sweet and simple—to be with me. Nothing else would please you more? No ring and book and forever and ever, amen?"

Tosanna frowned. "You speak in riddles. A ring, a book, and this *amen;* what has this to do with us?"

There was a sound at the door. Walker snatched a robe from a chest and pulled it around him. "Very well, no more riddles. I cannot marry you, Tosanna—not in England, not in America, not now and not ever. You aren't white."

God! Had *he* said that? Not white! All that talk of slaves being human, of black freedom, that unclimbable wall he raised between himself and his family. *Not white.* It sprang so naturally from his lips, so surprisingly from his own mouth: not white. Oh, God, oh, God, that this poisonous asp had lain coiled so long in his heart. Its strike ought to kill him, and maybe had.

Tosanna looked as if the fangs were buried in her throat. Great eyed, back straight, she stared at him, and Walker could read nothing on her face—nothing.

CHAPTER 24

The door was battered apart before Tosanna and Walker had an inkling they were under attack. When the door crashed in, Tosanna found her little knife and held it at her side, thumb along the blade and cutting edge up. Walker only stared, open mouthed.

"Gor," one man said, "if he don't have another one with him."

"Regular stud, says I," another man grunted.

Walker said loudly, "What the hell are you men—"

The third man hit Walker with a staff—not enough to crush his skull, but enough to stagger him back across the rumpled bed. "Manners, coxcomb," that one said. "Mind your manners and be glad the baron would rather kill you himself."

The first man said then, "Ain't this one what belongs to the Duke of Athol?"

"Stud horse," the second man grinned. "Puttin' it to prize fillies belongin' to barons and dukes."

The third man hefted his staff. "Mind your tongues. Baron Glynlyon didn't say nothin' about another woman, so I guess this doxy can go. But *you*, me bucko—"

Tosanna put her back to the wall and one of them saw her knife. Heavy and hairy faced, this one's belly kept time with his laugh. "Look, now; she'd dare us all with a little sticker."

"Tosanna," Walker said from the bed, "this has nothing to do with you. Go home, please."

"Yes," said the third man, the leader, "go home and tell the old duke how the baron's men caught you trifling with a Yankee whoremaster."

She took a step forward, her mouth set, and Walker said sharply, "Tosanna!" She looked at him, at Baron Glynlyon's men, and went out.

"Get dressed, whoremaster," the leader said.

"And if I don't?" Walker asked.

"I'll keep knockin' you down 'til you do. The baron—he wants you to be in a public place when he slaps your face and challenges you."

Walker said, "Dueling's outlawed in England—has been for years."

"Listen to 'im," the first man said. "Tellin' *us* what's English and what ain't."

"Well," said the leader, "there's some lords in Blighty don't hold with that rule, you see. Baron Glynlyon's one of them. Get dressed, Yankee."

They hauled him along a cobbled street, then another, burly men all, with strong hands and cruel mouths. Laughter, hearty and often, told how much they were enjoying this particular chore. Walker staggered when they dragged him up a short flight of graystone steps and into a darkly paneled room. It was bigger than the common rooms of most public inns, and more richly furnished. The leader thrust a hard hand between Walker's shoulders and he staggered again, catching himself at a long sofa.

When he looked around, he saw rows of set faces, grim faces, and recognized a few of them. A whiskery, red-faced man with wide shoulders and waistline to match strode forward.

"Baron Glynlyon, I presume?" Walker said.

There was a fist in the glove that hit him squarely in the mouth and drove him reeling back a step, two steps.

"Seducer," Glynlyon snapped. "Whoremonger, dishonorer of English wives, you've taken your last good woman here. I challenge you to face me on the field of honor."

"Oh, good lord," Walker said. "How childish can you get? All right—you had your lady followed and discovered what you already knew, or at least suspected. Now you want to salve your conscience by punishing somebody. Flog yourself, baron. If you were half a husband, she wouldn't be out playing around."

Which was probably a lie, he thought. Tracy would never be satisfied with one man, or one woman. But the baron probably knew that too.

"You'll fight me," Glynlyon grated, "or, by all that's holy, I'll have you beaten to death and thrown into the Thames with the other garbage."

Walker looked around the room. "You men—I know some of you. I've been a guest in your homes. Are you going to stand for this—this crazy, illegal challenge? Isn't anyone going to call the police?"

"Goddamn coward to boot," Glynlyon said.

"Look," Walker said, "I'll go—I'll leave the country."

From the crowd someone said, "That's what he told the duchess."

"You men," the baron said, motioning to his crew, "rid me of this offal. But not here and now. Take him somewhere and do not bring him back."

"Damn it," Walker said, "if you're stupid enough to fight a duel over a woman, all right. It's pistols then."

Glynlyon snorted. "On Topping Green, at dawn. Does anyone here desire to second this whoremaster?" When nobody answered, he went on: "Then my footmen will be your seconds—and guard, to see you will be here at dawn."

"Not in the club, old boy," a white-haired man said. "Bad taste."

"The old carriage house," Glynlyon ordered, "and keep a close watch on him. Bring him to the Green just before daylight."

Tattered horse blankets kept him warm there, and he got used to the acrid smell of sweat after a while. Sleep was impossible, so he sat and slowly smoked cigars. Wrapped in discarded blankets and seated upon a manure pile so old it was layered by dust and odorless, Walker must have nodded off sometime, because he woke with a start, thinking it would all go away, that he was suffering through a nightmare.

But it was all real, and his guards unbent a bit to offer him hot tea. "For the condemned man," the leader said. "The baron—he's a good shot, and no mercy to him."

"You're accomplices to murder," Walker said, almost scalding his mouth with the dark tea.

"What murder? What duel?"

The others laughed and one said, "And what Yankee? Who'd look for him?"

"Time, I reckon," the leader said, and they took hold of Walker.

Stiffly, he climbed into the curtained coach where they sat tense and watchful with him. Pasty, shadowed faces rocked with the swaying of the carriage, and Walker was reminded of Harpies, or MacBeth's witches. But his was the view from the cauldron, and discomfiting.

He kept expecting something to happen—someone to break the spell, a clear and healing logic to break through the fog's winding sheet, like the sun. But there was no sun, only a sickly light that penetrated gray swirlings. The Inferno, he thought, before the fires were lighted.

"Here he is, your honor," the leader said, and Walker saw a three-man cluster in the fog.

One waded the mists to present him a pistol box lined with red velvet. "Loaded and primed, sir."

"Antiques," Walker watched his hand lift a smooth bore, single shot, from the box.

"They are quite capable," said the baron's second, and about-faced to march back to his cluster.

Walker stood alone. The old pistol had a fair balance, but he didn't dare test its trigger pull. He looked at Glynlyon through fog that was beginning to pull back its coattails. "What are the rules?"

Coatless and without a hat, Baron Glynlyon stood erect, stood tall as his chunky build would allow, pistol fisted and hanging at his knee. He did not answer Walker, but a second did. They would face each other at twenty paces; upon command of the judge (standing with a doctor off to the left, where fog was thicker) to fire, the opponents could loose shots immediately, or hold back for better aim.

"Must I kill him?" Walker asked.

He thought the baron flinched, but couldn't be certain. The second, dressed in funeral black, said, "You—or the baron—may announce yourself satisfied by the drawing of blood. If the opponent agrees, it is over. If not, the duel continues to the death."

Another carriage rumbled through the gray light, horses tossing their heads. It stopped beside a gnarled old oak, and congealed fog dripped upon its roof.

God, Walker thought; I may never see sun play on the green leaves of that oak; I may never see another tree, or the sky, or a woman's soft eyes. Fingers chill upon the butt of his pistol, he wondered if this was how Confederate soldiers felt before battle, seeing every blade of grass as individual lives, feeling each caress of the air, tasting it, trying desperately to savor every moment left to them.

Had they also listened to each tick of a giant clock counting off eternity, and discovered their own heartbeats?

"Take your places," the judge called out, the sound of him loud as cannon shots.

"Ready," roared the judge, and his voice was the trumpet on Judgment Day.

"Fire!"

Walker seemed to be standing in water over his head. His weighted hand and arm struggled through liquid that held him back. Ever so slowly, his pistol muzzle lifted and centered upon Baron Glynlyon's white shirt. Damned fool, wearing white.

As he watched the man's pistol come up, Walker was barely conscious of a thuderclap, and the baron's white shirt spun around. Walker tasted the sharp bite of powder smoke upon his tongue. Lowering his weapon, he stared at Glynlyon upon his knees over there, and walked toward him.

"Sir," a second demanded, "are you satisfied?"

"Yes," Walker answered through numb lips.

"And you, sir?" the man asked Glynlyon.

"God damn it, I have to be!" The baron stared hurt and rage up at Walker. "The bastard put a ball in my right shoulder, and I can't shoot with my left hand. Yes, god damn it—I declare myself satisfied."

Walker nodded and reversed his pistol, presented it butt first. "Then it's done with."

"No," said another voice, and Walker looked at people hurrying from the strange carriage. "No!" one called. "Baron Glynlyon had the bad luck not to kill this transgressor, so *I* demand satisfaction, here and now."

Weak sunlight fought down through the mist, and Walker saw Gordon Hammers, Duke of Athol. He also saw Tosanna, Milady Savage; her face was pale and rigid, the daggering of her black eyes sharp.

The judge, a tall, lean man who should have been an undertaker, cleared his throat. "I do not know, sir. A challenge, acceptance by the other party, formalities; it is too much to ask of this—gentleman to fight two duels in one morning."

Jaw set, face determined, Gordon Hammers said, "He has dishonored my house and my name. I tend to believe the scoundrel will absent himself from England, were I to wait. So I demand he face me upon this field."

"Duke," the judge said, in a low voice, "your age, and this man's gun is incredibly swift and true. Look to the baron there."

"Glynlyon looks to himself; I look after me and mine. Well, scoundrel—will you act the man twice this day?"

"Oh, hell," Walker said, glancing at Tosanna, stiff and quiet in a flowing cape. "Forget it, duke."

"You have made that impossible, sir. Will you fight, or shall I shoot you where you stand?"

Tosanna detached herself from him and came swiftly to Walker. Behind her, Gordon Hammers said: *"Woman!"* but she paid no attention. Up close so that he could breathe the flower smell and woman scent of her, Tosanna whispered: "You cannot, Sunhair. He is old and good, and you must not hurt him."

"He means to shoot me," he said.

She put out a hand, took it back. "He sees badly, and is sure to miss at this distance. If trusting me is not enough, there is this."

Looking down, Walker saw a fiery flash of light in her palm. "A diamond," she said. "White Eyes value it highly. It is yours, if you let him live."

"I don't want to kill him."

"Then don't. Please do not."

"I don't want your damned blood money, either."

She looked over one shoulder. "He worries now and thinks me disloyal. I must go to him. Sunhair—"

He nodded. "I'll fire over his head. But what if he wants to keep shooting it out? Damned if I'll be a target."

This time she touched him, her hand a darting butterfly. "He must make the gesture, for the sake of honor. He will be satisfied with an exchange of shots."

Walker looked over at the circle of men. Glynlyon was propped in a carriage with the doctor. Blood stained the bandage around his shoulder.

"Honor," Walker said.

"It is difficult for you to understand," Tosanna said. "You pledged your word, Sunhair. I thank you for that."

Watching her walk back to her consort, her protector, Walker felt boxed in, trapped. If not for her, he wouldn't be here. He'd staged the scene at the inn to rid himself of her influence. How was he to know she'd happily join an orgy? The Glynlyon duel grew from that meeting, and now Walker Fairbairn was standing upon a chill field as his pistol was being reloaded for a second duel.

In all his life, he had never wanted to kill anything. Life, all life, was too sweet and precious; no man had the right to take it. That he should be here in the early chill of day, posed to kill or take a bullet himself—it was insane. He should have left this hidebound little island when he had the chance—and the money. Again, it was Tosanna who kept him in England.

He walked slowly to their meeting with the judge, to hear the regulations again, to look into the pale and stony face of Gordon Hammers, Duke of Athol. With a shock that stabbed him low in the belly, Walker realized that this man was desperately in love with his mistress, that Tosanna had bewitched him, also. A man so caught up in love and jealousy would do anything to keep her.

Word of Tosanna's *ménage à trois* would spread quickly, and news of the duke fighting for his lady's honor would also flash through the ranks of his peers, effectively stilling malicious gossip. Gordon Hammers would not have to retreat to his castle at Athol; he could continue to pursue his new activity in politics.

Moving slowly back to his position, Walker fought down an urge to stare back over his shoulder. The duke would have no part in promises made between an Indian doxy and a Yankee rogue; he was honorable. He was so dedicated to propriety and tradition and pride that he might try his damnedest to blow off Walker Fairbairn's head.

Walker turned, gripped pistol hung at his knee, his body drawn tight. Twenty paces away, Gordon Hammers spread his boots and waited the judge's commands. Walker couldn't tell whether or not the man was squinting. Very poor eyesight, Tosanna had said. Tosanna said a lot of things.

His movements were mechanical; at the order *fire!*, his fist swept up and out. For an old man, the duke was very quick; Walker barely had time to line his gun sights, to know that split second when he could have stroked the trigger, but held back.

A miniature thunderbolt ruffled his hair, and Walker

flinched from the vicious heat of its passing. No more than an inch, and the ball would have spread his brains.

Betrayal! Tosanna had lied about the duke simply going through the motions, about the old man's near blindness. The Indian bitch meant to see Walker Fairbairn dead.

Standing erect, empty pistol smoking, Gordon Hammers waited honorably for the answering shot that might end his life. Walker took his time sighting in, forefinger taking up the trigger slack. When he fired, he knew exactly where the bullet was going, to the fraction of an inch.

Gordon Hammers clapped a hand to his heart and swayed; then he pitched forward, pistol spilling from his hand.

"No!" Walker yelled. "No, damn it!"

He hadn't shot at the duke. He placed that pistol ball kissing close to Tosanna's cheek; it had come nowhere near Gordon Hammers. Yet the Duke of Athol lay face down on the sward, and an ugly muttering already rose from the watchers.

Dropping his pistol as if the cursed thing seared his fingers, Walker strode toward the fallen man, but the doctor and the duke's seconds reached him first. And Walker threw up his hands so clawing nails would not rip out his eyes, as Tosanna flung herself raging at him.

"You killed him! Yankee bastard, White Eyes son of a bitch—you killed him!"

She was furious and strong; he could barely hold to her wrists, and took an updriving knee upon his hip, instead of the crotch. Walker shook her. "My ball didn't come near him, damn it! You must have felt it brush your hair. I fired close to *you*, not at him. I didn't shoot your precious lover, but he came damned close to dropping me—just as you wanted."

She stopped struggling, her black eyes obsidian. "If I wanted you dead, Sunhair, I would put my knife in your belly. Last Flower needs no substitute to do her killing."

Walker freed her hands and stepped back. "You realize I didn't kill Hammers?"

"Perhaps you did not shoot him," she said, "but you killed him just the same. Why, *why* did you want me to join you and Tracy Glynlyon in a public inn? Why were you so careless?"

He stared back at her. "Why did you come?"

Tosanna looked down at her feet and at her clenched

hands. Softly, she said, "I shall ask myself that a thousand times."

She put her back to him then, and he watched her go kneel beside the duke's still body. Other men drew back and left her alone in her grief. They came toward Walker.

He said, "It was a fight I didn't want. You heard him force me into dueling; I didn't seek a fight with either of them."

Lean and funereal, the judge hovered over Walker. "Your womanizing draws this sort of trouble, and we'll have no more of it. You will be escorted to a ship leaving the country."

"I don't have passage money."

"It'll be paid—in steerage."

Watchful, hating faces ringed him. Walker said, "If I don't agree to leave?"

"You will be trussed and dragged aboard."

Walker looked to Tosanna, cradling the duke's head in her lap. She didn't lift her face to watch him being hauled away.

CHAPTER 25

Half a world away, Walker Fairbairn crossed from ship deck to a stained and splintered dock of massive cypress. He stood aside for a moment, his legs in rebellion at footing that didn't rock under him. While waiting for his balance, his land legs, Walker looked around, trying to relearn the feel and smells of home.

Not exactly home, for New Orleans was more foreign than London, with its exotic odors and disjointed medley of alien tongues. But United States warships rode at anchor on the brown, swirling river, and blue uniforms patrolled the wharves.

A change in uniforms didn't seem to matter to black longshoremen, whose sweat-oiled muscles bunched and roped at their work, naked from the waist up. One line of them, unloading heavy burlap sacks from a steamship, grunted some rhythmic, lonesome chant. Others labored in dripping silence.

Walker saw seamen of a dozen nationalities, just ashore and rollicking off to spend their wages, or others dragging back sick and busted from dens along the river.

Lifting the bag which held all his worldly goods, Walker moved toward Canal Street, noting the paucity of cotton bales along the docks. Normally, they would be piled high as men, mules and a steam engine could wrestle them, bursting little snowballs from their drab, tight corsets. The war, he thought, stepping aside for a pair of surly blue-coats—nobody grew cotton during the fighting, and the

South had lost its most important cash crop. It would take more than these seven years for planters to get on their feet again.

How would they plant, pick, and gin with no slaves? They'd make out, he figured. Men could be hired, probably for less than it took to support slaves from cradle to grave. The freemen—he looked about and saw the signs, the residue of sudden emancipation. Shabby blacks squatted forlorn and hungry against walls, gazing sullenly at their brethren with jobs.

Freedom, Walker thought, but unplanned and too quick. What jobs waited field hands roaming aimlessly in warhurt cities? Where to go, how to eat, no hallelujah promised land of milk and honey—lordy, lordy. It would not be long before they were again slaves, but called by another name.

On across the bustling street, he saw other marks of the war—dispirited white men out at the elbows, crippled veterans hating with hard marble eyes, whether or not a coin dropped into their hats. And lurking at the mouths of dank alleys, some men with the lean and hungry looks of wolves, some with the drooped slink of scavengers poised to pounce or flee.

And fat men, oh, yes—oily, superior Creoles doing brisk business with the latest conqueror of a city that had known and absorbed many before them. Among them strode harsh Yankee traders with no time for strutting and well-barbered men in expensive broadcloth suits, who hired others to hurry for them.

It was easy to distinguish winners from losers, Walker thought; the line that divided them was much wider than the Mason-Dixon. It might stay that way for a long, long time.

There to his right, only shouting distance from the Mississippi, was a railway station, and men swarming like wasps around a shaken nest. On the outskirts of the crowd, Walker switched hands with his bag. He had a five-dollar gold piece, and the diamond. This was no place to exchange the gem Tosanna had dropped into his pocket. A hundred years ago, longer? He thought back over the duel that wasn't a duel, and Tosanna's fury when the old duke dropped dead. He wasn't forgetting his ejection from Merry Olde England either, and recent memories of cramped quarters, the stench of traveling in steerage would long remain with him. Half a crown slipped a crewman bought Walker a sleeping space on deck when the weather was fair; when the sea turned gray and ugly, he was forced below with other miserable, retching people.

Lowering his valise to the slate walkway, he put one boot upon it and slid a hand into his inside coat pocket. The diamond was still there, snug in its nest of torn seam. When he was trundled aboard the grimy merchantman, Walker hadn't known he had the glittering stone. His smile was wry; she would have taken it back, if he hadn't been chased away by the duke's friends.

The single gold piece was his, and the few English coins left him. There'd been no time to search out loans or gifts from ladies. When he found the diamond, Walker was glad the ship was well under way. If he'd been facing Tosanna, he might have thrown it in her face.

And been stupid. The jewel might be a lifesaver, a fresh start. He glanced up the street to where the noted French Quarter began. It would be good to find a solvent banker, swap him the stone, and test a run of luck against the gamblers on Royal Street. It would be even better to cash in the diamond, then spend every penny on food, wine, and women. Both those decisions would also be stupid.

He had to go home. Maybe his father and Fairbairn Plantation needed all the money the jewel could bring. Damn, he hated the thought of going home, but if he didn't, he would carry this tonnage of guilt the rest of his life. Walker got in line behind a little man who had a nervous tic in his left cheek. Without saying more than howdy, he received a rambling lecture on postwar events in New Orleans, accented by numerous cheek twitchings.

The nervous little man cut off his lament after a scathing denunciation—delivered in a hoarse whisper—of General Butler, the Beast of New Orleans, and his occupation troops. Beast Butler posted an edict warning any lady rash enough to insult a Yankee soldier; if any did, they would be treated like "any common woman of the streets."

Walker imagined how that sat with fiery Southern ladies, and wondered why no assassin had reached Butler. The conqueror had gone north three years back, but the stamp of him remained. Perhaps the war had burned out the rebel spirit, or turned weary survivors more logical. But if such methods were standard for the army of occupation, then the South was in for terrible retribution.

Then it was his turn at the iron wicket and the harassed man behind the ticket window. Cocking his head like an old bird inspecting a scarecrow, the man listened, then laughed. "You want to ride the coaches to Alabama? Not less'n you got a pass signed by the president of this here Louisville and Nashville line. Boy, there ain't been more'n a dozen passenger trains out'n here since afore the war."

Walker jerked a thumb over his shoulder. "But all these others—"

The agent used a patched bandana to mop his brow. "Tryin' to get boxcar room. Everybody in the country's got somethin' to ship, seems like." Then he said in a whisper, "Mostly looted furniture and the like; what them damn Yankee soldiers don't grab, the carpetbaggers does."

"Can I ride a boxcar then?" Walker asked.

"Can't buy you no ride from *me*, but there's others not particular, and others ready to knock you in the head for your boots. Might ask around the train yard, or just slip into some car quietlike. Just keep a close watch on them as totes a club."

"Beholden to you," Walker said, and stepped aside from the window, realizing he hadn't used that expression for a long time, maybe all the years he'd been in England. There he'd found himself adopting British ways of speech. Camouflage, trying not to be noticed, to be accepted?

He went through the switching yards and found a freight pointing toward Alabama. A brakeman, marked by cinders and soot, told him Yes, they'd soon be off to Mobile, and he had a place for Walker, was there any money to it. Walker gave him the rest of his English change, and it didn't matter to the brakeman, long as it was silver.

High up on the pile of furniture was a brocade settee, and Walker climbed to it. Across a bit of scraped and open floor, in a pile of boxes and sacks, a man said: "If'n you ain't toting water and victuals, it might be a long haul."

"I'll make out," Walker answered.

"Got some extra," the man said, "if'n you pay for it."

Walker slapped the settee arm. "Damn! Is everybody so greedy here?"

"Believed in Jeff Davis and the flag, once. Four goddamned long years, I believed in 'em. Had me a little ol' house near to Corinth, Mississippi—had a snug house and good wife and two towhead younguns. Come back, I never had nothin'—house got burned and younguns died of the fever; my woman run off with a carpetbagger."

The man paused, and Walker couldn't make out his face in the shadows. From the dark, the man said, "Might of believed in my Maker, too, back afore the war. Onliest thing I put trust in now is hard money."

"Reckon that's about right," Walker said, and curled up on his couch. He could trust his lonesome gold piece and hidden diamond; they were tangible, and all else was not. Already, he was beginning to get Tosanna out of his mind, out of his blood. Her memory was not quite as sharp, no longer as cutting.

Head pillowed upon his bag, he fell asleep sometime after the train pulled out of the station and left New Orleans behind. From what he remembered, Mobile wasn't all that far off, but the train traveled slowly, in jerks and wobbles spaced by long, inexplicable stops. War-torn tracks and roadbeds had been repaired, but only haphazardly, and often the train was pulled onto a spur until crews could repatch the main line.

He awoke thirsty and hungry, with throbbing behind his eyes. Across the car, the other rider was eating. Walker could smell sausage, but damned if he would give five dollars for some. Instead, he found one of his few remaining cigars and scratched a sulphur match to it.

"Smells right fine," the other passenger said.

"Doesn't it? Prime Havana leaf."

"Might trade you meat and bread for one."

Walker blew smoke. "Reckon not."

"You ain't far from Mobile. Heard you tell the brakeman where you're goin'. Get you plenty more cigars in Mobile."

Walker leaned back. "So can you."

"Not hardly," the man said, and now Walker could see his face, pinched and gaunt. "Yankee soljers in Mobile lookin' for me. Have to stay hid a spell."

"Why does the army want you?"

"Never surrendered like Marse Robert said. Busted a provost upside his head and took off. They won't be expectin' me to double back through town. You'd figure with the war over so long—"

Walker rolled smoke inside his mouth. "Where are you going?"

"Somewhere," the man said quietly, "anywhere, I reckon."

Leaning forward, Walker fished an inside pocket for another cigar and tossed it across· the space separating them. "Here."

The freight car rattled and bounced, but its tempo was slower, and Walker looked out a crack in the door.

"Beholden," the man said. "Take some bread and meat."

"I'll only trouble you for a swallow of water. You might need all your food. Looks like we're coming into town, and I'll make out here."

Climbing down from his nest, Walker put the bag between his feet and offered the glowing end of his cigar. The man puffed on his, sunken eyes closed, thin body moving within its cocoon of rags.

"Thankee," he said. "Damn it, man—I wasn't thisaway all my life. Take you some goddamn meat; I'll feel some better."

"Look," Walker said, "we're about to stop. I know, friend; it was the war."

"Folks claim it's over, but it ain't." The man's gapped teeth worried his cigar. "It ain't ever goin' to be over and done with, 'til we're all dead, 'til all us that fought is dead."

Walker lifted his bag and moved to the sliding door. "Maybe not even then."

"You know how it is," the man said. "You been there and fought like me; you seen the elephant, so you know how it is. I'd appreciate it if you was to slide that door back closed after you get down, partner."

On the ground, Walker pulled at the rattling door, shoved it squeaking back into place. A little kindness, and he was claimed a veteran, offered the warmth of a soldierly camaraderie he'd never known. He struggled with a sense of guilt, and the feeling passed. What had the war gotten that man? Home, wife, children gone, himself a fugitive; hurrah, boys, hurrah.

He walked a long way, and on the far edge of town dickered with a jowly carpetbagger and finally accepted a hundred greenback dollars for the diamond. Walker knew it was probably worth ten or twenty times that much, but took the money anyhow. If he waited too long, he might lose his nerve and not ride out of town. Fairbairn Plantation was some eight or nine hours away on a fast, sturdy horse; if he dallied in Mobile, he might never reach it.

He couldn't leave by night, and holed up in the stables where he bought his horse. More swapping with the liveryman clothed him better for travel, and relieved him of his baggage and contents. Turning in the hayloft, Walker figured he was down to the necessities: blankets, coffeepot, and frying pan, two wool shirts and as many pairs of trousers and underdrawers.

Then there was the Navy Colt—a beautiful, well-balanced, .36 caliber handgun that could fire six quick rounds and was easy to reload with brass cartridges. When he stood up, it rode comfortably holstered just below his right hip.

Why had he brought it? Because a Prussian duchess thought to protect him. The liveryman warned of troubles for travelers—scalawags and sullen, hungry Confederate soldiers turned road agents. Mainly, Walker thought, he kept it because it was so beautiful, its lines lovely, polished grips smooth, the metal of it oiled and shiny. It fit his hand just so, and without test-firing it, Walker knew he could group its six rounds tightly into any target.

He slept, and his restless dreams repeated what he'd seen this day—the changes, the South beaten to its knees and not even trying to get up. There was a gritty hoplessness everywhere, in invisible fog that weighted everyone down. He'd expected blind anger, a barely controlled rage, anything but apathy. It was as if the South had lost not only her sons and lands, but her immortal soul.

In his sleep, Walker sweated and turned often, dreading the inevitable meeting with his father. He ached to hold a woman with raven-wing hair, to have her ride knee to knee with him as they cantered shining horses off the highway and onto Fairbairn land. But of course she couldn't; Tosanna wasn't white. Jesus!

The shifting images woke him, and Walker lay back staring at a razor-thin sliver of early sunlight that probed a dusty corner of the loft. Sure, wouldn't an Indian wench be just the present to bring his father? Perfect. If the old man wasn't dead, that would do the trick—his son, already branded traitor, bringing home a woman of color as his bride. Walker sat up and rubbed at his face. He didn't remember dreaming a wedding.

Making up a blanket roll, he climbed down the rickety ladder with it over one shoulder, the Navy Colt snug at his hip. The liveryman shared breakfast with him—sidemeat, cornbread, and acorn and chicory coffee. The man was about forty, already gray and worn at the edges. He ate without lifting his eyes from his plate, chewing slowly.

He said, "I was with ol' Gen'l Hood. Bein' cavalry so long, it helped me get holt of a few stray horses when most of the Yanks went home. Some I stole, and some I traded for. You with the cavalry?"

"No," Walker said.

"Just as well, son. My ass is still one big ol' callus, but I expect the infantry had it worse off, and the artillery not much better."

"I expect," Walker said. "I appreciate this good food, sir, and I better be goin' now."

The liveryman looked up, yellow grains of cornbread on his stubbled chin. "Traded you fair, boy. I ain't studyin' on cheatin' a soljer goin' home. Keep your eyes peeled for road agents, sharp as when you was out on picket."

Walker thanked him again and turned away quickly. In the worn McClellan saddle, he pushed his gelding north. Damn it; everybody hadn't gone into the army. There must have been plenty of men who had better sense, and near the tail end of the war, plenty of rebels had deserted, according to English newspapers. Everywhere he turned, somebody tried to make him feel guilty.

Head down, old wide hat bobbing, he kept the horse moving, knowing the road now. He'd traveled it south and north on horseback, and riding a trap with a pair of spanking thoroughbreds trotting proud before. Pa used to take him to Mobile when he was just a youngun—once to buy slaves, two or three times to load the buggy with Christmas gifts. When did they begin to grow apart? Gradually, steadily, it had happened, until the war made them both see the wide gulf between them.

Walker straightened in his saddle, shifting haunches that would soon ache. It had been a long time since he rode any distance, and his body would pay. His father would see the folly of it all by now. They could get together, decide what was best for Fairbairn land. Surely Pa would see him alive and be grateful they'd clashed over the war's stupidity.

If his father was alive—*if* Jeremy Fairbairn yet stood upon his own hallowed ground. Walker urged his horse into a jog that would save the animal and yet make time. He was anxious now to get home, eager to face the uncertainty he'd dreaded so long. He was a whole man, missing neither arm nor leg; his eyes were not blinded, and no exploding shell deafened his ears.

Walker Fairbairn was whole and alive, and he was going home.

CHAPTER 26

Tosanna moved to the music, almost wooden, going about the curtsies and poses like a puppet. The ballroom was too hot, and she yearned for the dance to be over, ached to be done with this play acting.

But nobody refused a royal invitation that was in reality a command. Still, Tosanna was quickly wearied with pomp and circumstance. She liked Victoria, and even sensed a well of loneliness in the pudgy, aging queen. It was difficult to be alone with her, for matters of state always intruded.

Making a false smile when the music stopped, Tosanna said, yes, she would like refreshment—champagne, if milord pleased. She moved near a tall window and watched Sir Walter Gage maneuvering to the punch bowl. He was tall and fair and attentive. He was also penniless, only the latest of many out-at-the-elbows suitors for Tosanna's hand in marriage.

Smile pasted upon her face, she turned through the opened window into the chill of the garden. Tosanna welcomed the bite of wind and the high, cold torch of the moon only hinted at through gray fog. Around her, many bushes were bare of leaves, and a seawind mourned dirges through naked tree limbs. She put out her tongue to taste the fog, and shivered.

"Here, here," Sir Gage said. "None of this catching your death. Come inside, my dear, do."

In the ballroom again, she looked at his face in profile. He was kind and she might do worse, and marriage might curb other women's jealousy. She was so lucky, Belle Williams had told her—first to be named sole heir to Gordon Hammers's estate, and no blood kin to contest the will, then the possibility of marriage to turn her respectable in the eyes of London gentry. Perfect, Belle Williams said—like you got all England by the pizzle.

Did she? Hurt by the duke's death and hating Walker Fairbairn so, although the doctor said it was not his fault, that Gordon Hammers died of heart failure, Tosanna had known no other man in her bed. She had not wanted any one of a dozen would-be lovers, and still denied them. Englishmen were so easy to deny, now that she had money and estates—now that she was Duchess of Athol in all but name.

"Milord, milady." It was one of the big, watchful men who stood always at Victoria's elbow. "Her excellency desires you meet her in the sitting room."

"Of course," she said, and gave her champagne glass back to her escort. "You will excuse me, Walter?"

She made her curtsy to Victoria and moved forward to take the queen's extended hand. "You have been long away from us," Victoria said.

"I would mourn the duke, your majesty, but it seems I am not allowed."

"We were displeased by the dueling—you know that. And the duke's death leaves a gap in our life. He was a friend to my husband, a dear friend to Prince Albert. We shall miss him dreadfully."

"I, too, your majesty. He was also dear to me."

"Sit here before us," Victoria said. "There. Yes, we believe you did care for Gordon; else we would have abridged his will, or whatever those rascally solicitors call it. But tell us, why have you not accepted any one of the men who seek your hand?"

"I do not care for them, excellency. Not as I cared for the duke, and—"

Victoria's shrewd eyes searched Tosanna's. "And for the rascally American who precipitated the duels."

Tosanna nodded. "I cannot forget him, but I think I do not love him."

"England has been good to you, has it not? Once we named an adventurer a fool because of you."

The queen paused, and Tosanna looked away, stared at

ancient wall tapestries, at dark furniture skillfully crafted, at metal statuettes that would be called magic by medicine men of her tribe, the spirit talkers. They were not magic; nothing here was, but might as well be, so far advanced were they over her own people.

"Well?" Victoria said, with a slight wobble of her powdered jowls.

"Yes, your majesty. England has done well by me. I have learned much here, so much that I am yet stunned by all the knowledge. And I know how much I owe England's queen. I am grateful, excellency."

"Yet you delay marriage that would make you acceptable at celebrations other than our own. Are you not lonely for a man in your bed? We are, but we have no other choice. Our allegiance is to our people, not to our own emotions. But you—"

Daringly, Tosanna said, "Your majesty could have chosen among many men also. I think you were too much in love."

Victoria's short jaws hardened. She lifted a lacy bit of cloth to hide her eyes. "Yes, we are still too much in love, my child." She put away the kerchief and said, "But you claim no such enduring love. We will not command you marry, child. It would be better if you did, but we will not order it. One cannot order the heart. Very well; that is behind us. Now, my child—tell us more of your land and people; tell us of vast deserts and tall mountains and women riding free in the wind, free and wild and with no heavy responsibilities."

Tosanna looked down at her hands. "Comanche women have burdens also, my queen. The life is not easy, not rich." And may have changed much in the four years she had been gone—as White Eyes reckoned time.

She went on to tell Victoria of Comancheria, its beauties and struggles. As she spoke, Tosanna felt a rush of words coming, as memories grew brighter. She could see the eagle visage of her father, Tet-Sainte, sharp against early autumn sky; she saw the tepees and smelled wood smoke, felt the soft caress of a fur couch. Ado-eeti, she thought; oh, Big Tree, where are you now, how are you? His features shimmered and refused to hold still inside her head; she knew only a flashing of his dark eyes, and they seemed to accuse her.

"Yes, child," Victoria said. "Do go on."

There was heavy work of skinning out buffalo, hauling water, gathering firewood, picking mesquite beans, stripping cactus for its pulp and fruit. The men hunted and made raids; women stayed in camp.

"Sometimes," Tosanna continued, "a woman is allowed on a war party—if she is very brave and a fine rider. And sometimes women ride a horse behind their husbands, when the camp is struck or when the tribe is under attack and must escape."

"Attack?" Victoria asked. "Who would attack your tribe?"

"Apaches, White Eyes; mostly it is *tejanos*."

Victoria frowned. "Do you mean Texans? Why separate them from—ah—other White Eyes?"

"They are different," Tosanna answered. "They are much different. *Tejanos* shoot better and fight harder. They do not kill only warriors, but any Comanche they can find, woman or child."

"And your own people," Victoria said gently, "do they not act the same?"

Tosanna said, "Sometimes we take prisoners." She was sorry she had mentioned that, and grateful that Victoria did not pursue it. Neither Comanche nor Apache treated prisoners as the English did, and the queen's tribe would not understand torture. These days Tosanna had trouble justifying it.

"A people can grow," Victoria said. "As we did, as we will continue to do. Once our people were also painted savages; now the sun never sets on the British Empire. But forgive us, child; you cannot know England's history. You have done wonder enough to master our speech."

"I was given the gift of tongues," Tosanna said.

The queen sighed. "Would that we were too. Our German is atrocious, and our French not much better; as for Latin—but we digress. Our wish is that you remain here, and visit us more often. Better yet, if you were to marry suitably, we would like you at court with us. There are woefully few ladies-in-waiting who interest us."

"But your majesty knows I have been mistress to two men and lover to yet another. Tongues will wag."

"Not," said the queen, "where we can hear them."

"You do me great honor, excellency."

"We pamper ourself, for where Milady Savage stays,

something interesting happens. Think on these things, my child, on marriage and our service. You may leave us now; we must carry on affairs of state, even at a gala—and with such dolts, such popinjays."

Tosanna bowed herself away, her head in a whirl. It was true she had been offered a signal honor, especially considering her reputation and the sharp-tongued gossip of women everywhere. She could choose a husband from among many suitors, and stay at the queen's right hand. She could be rich and safe and perhaps bear sons. The great house at Athol was a fine place to raise children.

But she had talked long to the queen this day, spoken of her own land, her own people, and a stirring of the blood was within her. This month, at the beginning of the Time of Snows, the Kwehar-enuh would be in their winter campgrounds, far up into the protective mountains of Comancheria.

The tepees would be warm and snug with many furs, many skins. Enough buffalo and elk meat had been smoked and cached, enough maize and mesquite beans and cactus put away and much firewood gathered. Acorns had been gathered and grass bundled for the horses, tucked into ravine corrals away from the wind. This was the good time, if the tribe had been blessed with good hunting and successful raids. Perhaps there would even be some White Eyes flour and ground corn, some pig meat brought back by a war party. *Ee-yah!* Life was good, and the Kwehar-enuh most blessed.

"Ah, my dear," said Sir Walter Gage. "There you are. I did not realize you had the queen's ear."

"Not truly," Tosanna said. "Not yet." She looked up at Gage. He was taller than Sunhair, and wider, stronger. He could probably crush Sunhair's ribs if they fought.

She said to him, "Why have you never asked about my people, my land? Do you not wonder what my plans are for the future?"

Gage pulled her elbow closer and looked hastily around him. The orchestra was just striking up a lilt, and he steered her to a niche in the wall, his face gone pink. "Why," he said, "I—I supposed you would—would like to erase your unfortunate past. And as for your future, well—if you do me the honor of granting me your hand, I shall do my utmost to keep your properties, ah—*our* properties —secure and profitable."

Tosanna continued to stare him down. "How do you know I will make you a good wife? How do you know I am any good in bed?"

Gage's pink face deepened to red. "I say, my dear—"

"You can't know," Tosanna said, "unless you test me, and I try you."

Again, he swept the room with anxious eyes. "Good lord, Tosanna! You cannot mean, you simply cannot—"

"I can," she said. "I do. Now I intend to return to Athol; do I go alone?"

Gage patted a handkerchief over his face. "If you—but of course I want—good lord."

"You said that, Walter." She put her back to him and walked quickly around dance sets, prancing mechanically, quite properly to music that was mostly strings. What would all these painted and powdered mannequins do to the thundering roll of tom-toms? She would love to leap and stamp among them, shouting Comanche war cries, if only to see their shock and horror.

Walter Gage caught up with her upon Windsor's front steps, as she signaled for her carriage. "Look, Tosanna, I want to go. I mean, I very much need to be with you, ah—to have you, as it were."

The carriage pulled up, the old duke's arms emblazoned upon its door. A footman hurried to drop an iron buggy step and help her in. Gage swallowed hard, then climbed in beside her. "Oh, the gossip will buzz, you know."

"Only about me," Tosanna said, "and I do not mind. Men are expected to leap into assignations—not ladies."

He took her hand as the coach bounced and swayed over cobblestones, but he didn't take her in his arms. Tosanna almost decided to send him away in the same carriage. But he was mumbling compliments and apologies in such obvious eagerness to please, she thought she would wait awhile.

Gage was impressed by Athol's vast baronial sitting room, and almost stumbled into the great fireplace while admiring ancestral paintings which hung darkly disapproving upon the walls.

"Just about w-winter," he said. "Bit of a nip in the air, what? But this jolly fire keeps off the chill."

Removing her cloak, Tosanna draped it across a chair. A wall mirror told her she looked good, brushed hair a black waterfall down her back. The long dress clung to her small waist and front part of her hips, but fell away from her legs in acceptance of Victoria's prim code, which also accounted for its high throat. The clumsy bustle in back was ridiculous, but fashionable. Tosanna felt she was prisoner to buttons, hooks, and bows, but glad she'd rebelled against wearing a choking corset with whalebone stays, much to Belle Williams' dismay.

She turned to the whiskey cabinet, and, without asking, poured Walter Gage half a glass of Scotch, herself only a splash. Walter was in the uniform of all Englishmen—white shirt, strangling tie, dark coat and weskit, dark shoes. He looked drab against her memories of Comanches in war paint, their shields feathered and colorful, their buckskins fringed, weapons clean and shining.

At the thought of Walter upon a warpath, Tosanna smiled. She stood close and offered him his glass of whiskey. "If it's no bother," he said, "I'd like some water; this is a bit much to drink neat, what?"

"There," she pointed, and moved with him, hip brushing his thigh. He flushed again as he drank off the Scotch in a gulp and made choking sounds with water. When Walter put down the glass, his eyes were teary. "Sorry—not—not much of a tippler, I'm afraid."

Tosanna began to unbutton those she could reach. "Yes, I think you *are* afraid. Why should you fear me?"

"Ah," he said, "it's not exactly fear, you know. I mean, it's more like 'discomfited' really. The servants—where are they?"

"Not right here. None in this room, none before the fire upon these soft rugs."

His eyes widened. "Right here? You mean out in the open, like? Before the fire? Your servants—someone might come upon us at any moment. The butler—surely he heard the carriage arrive. I say—"

"You say too much," Tosanna said, and put her back to him, leaned her curves against him. "Unbutton me, please."

Walter's hands were shaky, his fingers clumsy. "Good lord," he said, "your perfume—the heat of you, your hair —can't we go to a bedroom, lock the door?"

Her dress loosened, Tosanna eased away from him and dropped it. Rolling her hips a little, she slowly peeled off her

underclothes. There had been no man since Sunhair, and
the urge was rising strong within her. Other men could be
like Sunhair, as powerful, as tender and loving. She offered
her breasts to Walter Gage, offered her body and all she
was for this throbbing, golden moment.

Still, she had to help him out of his clothing, and he kept
throwing nervous glances at the doors. But his skin was
milky white, and his body hair bronze, and there was no
fierceness to him. Walter was all gentleness and too quick.

He would not speak, and there was tension in his body.
Holding to him, Tosanna continued to stroke and caress
him. In time he might become a passable lover; he would
make a pliant, agreeable husband, and Tosanna would be
acceptable in London society—upon the surface, at least.

She spoke softly to him of the beauties of his body, as
Sunhair had done with her, but she did not own the tongue
of birds. Although Walter's manhood swelled again, she
could not ease the strain of his fear of being discovered,
the shame he felt.

But the fire glow felt good upon her naked skin, and she
knew a soaring freedom, a mastery of herself and the man
she mounted, the pliable man she so easily controlled.
Rolling, thrusting, she took him into her body and trapped
him there. Between her thighs, he was a stallion to be dom-
inated, tamed, ridden like the wind. If he fought her, she
did not know it. He clung to her and she made him writhe;
he lifted against her and she forced him back, twisting and
bucking.

The magic feeling came slowly, not with a maddened
thundering, but a pallid shadow of what could be, should
be.

When she tried to pillow her head on his arm, Walter
Gage slid away to grope after clothing, to hide himself
from any shaming eyes and his own, to hide himself from
her.

Walter cleared his throat, but she did not roll to face
him. Tosanna lay propped upon an elbow, staring into the
fire and listening to its quiet voices. This was the burning
earth called coal, and it spoke softer than its brother, wood.
But it sang some of the old songs of mountain and desert,
the lonely chants of a lonesome land where people did not
swarm like dung heap flies, where there was room to

breathe. It talked of sage and mesquite, and Tosanna's nostrils flared at remembered scents.

Again, Walter cleared his throat. "I—I'm sorry. I apologize for having—having taken advantage of you. It was ungentlemanly, and I offer sincere and humble regrets."

In her own language, Tosanna said to the fire: "Hear me, Fire Spirit; hear this man who is not quite a man, but an Englishman. He has sorrow for coupling with me. Do you mourn as you couple with coal? I think not, Fire Spirit; I think not."

She turned naked to him and Walter Gage averted his eyes. Tosanna came to her feet and strode past him to reclaim her cloak, wrapping it around her. She said, "I will ring for the coachman and send you home."

Now that she was covered, he faced her. "Might as well be hung for a sheep as a lamb, what? I shall spend the night, but not out here. In your bedroom, madam, safe from prying eyes."

"I do not understand this talk of sheep and lambs," Tosanna said. "In my land, great cats walk the night, and tall bears tread any trail they wish, any time they wish. They would feed upon lesser animals."

Walter fumbled with his shirtfront. "Ah, sheep and lambs, yes. Let's see—it means if I commit a crime, a sin, then I might as well be punished for a larger one."

Tosanna looked at him and walked to the bell pull. "I make no sin in the sight of Comanche spirits; I do no crime." She tugged the signal cord.

"I say," Walter said, "I didn't actually mean that you, that I—"

"Perhaps you should wait in the vestibule. The butler will be here any second, and just look at my clothing scattered everywhere."

"Damn, Tosanna, I want—you should not—"

At sounds approaching off the sitting room, Walter turned on his heel and hurried from sight. John, the butler, made a point of not noticing Tosanna's disarray. "Madame?"

"Please instruct Winston to bring round the carriage. Mister Gage is leaving."

"Yes, madame," John said, inclining his balding head. Try as she might, she could catch no condescending flicker, no disapproving blink of his eyes. He had served the Duke of Athol long and well; now his sympathies seemed to be transferring to the duke's chosen heir. Tosanna watched him walk away and knew he and the other servants would be all right, whatever she and Athol's barrister decided.

Because from this night on she would no longer be Milady Savage. She was Tosanna, Last Flower of the Comanche nation, and she was going home.

CHAPTER 27

The house was gone, only blackened stumps of chimneys showing. An old fire had charred nearby magnolia and pecan trees, killing some and crippling others. The yard and garden, that flower garden his mother had been so proud of, was a jungle of weeds standing belly high to Walker's horse. He sat the gelding for a time, sniffing autumn air and catching a faint odor of burning wood.

There were other signs of use, if a man looked closely enough: a narrow footpath beaten through the apple orchard; a vague spiral of gray smoke from a rundown slave cabin; dry branches and lighterd knots piled beside an ax-gnawed stump.

Walker pulled crisp air into his lungs and squeezed the horse forward. He could see where split-rail fences had been torn down and made into black campfire ashes. Troops had bivouacked here, and it didn't matter if they were Blue or Gray; any army left a swath of destruction and death.

Drawing up the horse, Walker hesitated, uncertain whether to ride up to the occupied cabin whole among several blackened shells, or find what he sought in the family cemetery. He opted for the burial ground, conscious of a throbbing in his throat and a dry mouth.

Soldiers hadn't bothered this spot, probably because its fence was cast iron, hammered out by slave blacksmiths themselves long passed on. Dismounting, Walker tied his reins to a sapling and pushed open the rusted, creaking

247

gate. This side of the plot was well remembered—two generations of Fairbairns lay beneath granite stones with inscriptions shallowed by time. Yonder was the new headstone of his mother, and Walker dropped to one knee before it. Hardly daring to look, he pivoted to the place next to it, reserved for his father Jeremy. No stone, no turned earth, and Walker sighed.

A few paces on was a wooden marker, letters burned into it: *Private Jackson Fairbairn, Co. A, 22nd Alabama Infantry, C.S.A. Fallen in service of his country,* and the dates. Walker put a hand to his forehead; so young—the boy was so damned young.

Lifting his head, he looked to see where his older brother was buried; nothing. Cold seeped into Walker's jacket then, as he realized Travis Fairbairn's body never came home. Pa would hate that, he thought; God, how Pa would hate his close kin buried in strange ground—if there'd been enough left of Travis to bury, or if his corpse was ever found.

After laying his hand upon his mother's marker, Walker moved back to his horse, a little more ready to face his Pa. He lifted the reins over the horse's head and walked beside him down the little knoll. It had to be Pa holed up in that slave cabin; while Jeremy Fairbairn drew breath, he'd not be driven off his own land.

Off to the left was a vegetable patch, cornstalks brown and rattling, winter squash and orange pumpkins ready to be picked and stored. Skirting the garden, Walker approached the hut. As he neared it, the plank door swung back on leather hinges and a man stepped out. He was carrying a sword.

"Pa," Walker called out, "it's me—your son."

Jeremy Fairbairn was stooped and weathered, his face ravaged by more than time, etched deeply by bitterness and sorrow. Its wrinkled skin was drawn tight over sharp cheekbones, and the head shook, ever so slightly, wobbled again and again. Walker saw his father wore reading glasses, something he'd never be caught doing outside the library before; one lens showed a hairline crack.

Walker said it again, louder: "It's me, Walker, your son come home."

His father held to the sword hilt, and his voice grated rusty as gate hinges at the cemetery. "I have no son. They're all dead."

"Pa," Walker said, "listen to me. I'm here and alive. I'm Walker Fairbairn, and alive."

The old man stood a little straighter. "You might wear the name, but you're no son of mine."

Walker chewed his lip. "Pa—would it change things any if I was put in the ground out there next to Jackson? Would it help if I fell beside Travis? A hundred *thousand* more Confederates couldn't have won that war. I said it then and shouldn't have to say it now—the war was stupid and lost from the start."

Jeremy Fairbairn rested weight on the sword point. "Honor is never lost, unless it's thrown away."

"Honor? *Honor?*" Walker's teeth grated and he felt like taking his Pa by the shoulders and shaking him hard. "Lord, if you could say that to Jackson and Travis and every other mother's son who died with steel in his belly—what do you think they'd answer? Honor! Good goddamn!"

"Blasphemous pup!" His father lifted and shook the sword at him. "Bad as Yankee carpetbaggers and damnation to both of you."

Walker wanted to cry when the old man slammed back into the cabin. He stood holding his horse with a swelling in his throat and a sickness in his belly, and he wanted to cry for the dead, the destruction, and missed years. Mostly, he wanted to weep for his father.

"Sah? Mist' Walker, sah?"

"Rufus? Old man, how come you're still here; didn't anybody tell you about freedom?"

The old slave shuffled around the cabin, finger to his wrinkled lips. "Hush, Mist' Walker. Where ol' Rufus go be free? This here my home; I be born here and 'spect I die here. Me 'n' yo' Pa—'less'n them 'baggers runs us off. Done run off ever'body else."

Walker's eyes detailed the face he'd known all his life, the white, nappy hair, Rufus's rheumy eyes, deeply crow tracked. He was only a shade more bent than when he'd taught Walker woods lore—and respect for all living things of the forest.

"Carpetbaggers, Rufus? What would they want with Fairbairn Plantation?"

"Sumpin' about taxes started it. But when Marse Jeremy dug up what gold he had left and paid the tax man, yonder them 'baggers comes again. Reckon that's how come he met you at the door with that ol' sword. Ain't had us no guns on the place since I don't know when."

Glancing at the cabin, Walker said, "And Pa means to fight. They'll kill him."

The old black's eyes peered up through bushy white brows. " 'Spects he wants it thataway, standin' on his own land. Does it come off, I bury Marse Jeremy yonder next to Mistess, do they 'low me."

"And you," Walker said. "What about you, old man?"

"Old, thowed-away nigger ain't fit for nothin'. Reckon I sits down and waits. Just as soon be right here than with them other niggers ain't goin' get no forty acres and a mule."

Walker had heard scraps of conversation in New Orleans, whispers in Mobile: Yankee businessmen, like so many jackals darting in to feed on a lion's kill, pounced on the South's prostrate body. They arrived carrying their worldly goods in a valise made of carpet material, and heads full of sharp schemes. They were picking the South's bones before cannon smoke settled. "The law," Walker said.

"Yankee law," Rufus said, then: "Can't see 'em, but I hears 'em acomin', feels 'em in the bottom of my feets."

Walker heard it, too; the drumroll of horses at the lope—three or four riders coming fast but in no particular hurry. He said, "Stay with him, Rufus, and I'm much beholden to you. Try to keep him out of sight."

"I be doin' that," the old man said. "Mist' Walker, you and me, we had us some times in the old days, when you was just a youngun."

"We did that, Rufus—some high old times, and I owe you for them."

He owed the old Bantu for introducing him to Molly Cottontail, Brother Coon, and Uncle Possum and Pappy Terrapin, for steering him safely past Ol' Cottonmouth and water moccasin and sly quicksand. Rufus had pried the forest world wide for him, like opening a big, freshwater mussel, and made him an intimate of animals there, privy to their secrets and beauty. Rufus also taught him to shoot; at least, he'd put the first gun into Walker's hand.

More importantly, Rufus had taught Walker Fairbairn what *not* to shoot.

He said now, "Be particular, Mist' Walker; take care."

When Rufus was out of sight, Walker led his horse to a hitching post that seemed unused since Fort Sumpter was fired on. Tethering the gelding, he moved back in front of the cabin just as four riders cantered into view. He watched them come on, trampling high weeds in his mother's garden, three men easy in the saddle, and one ruining his horse's mouth.

The man up front wore a hard hat and a duster that wasn't keeping dirt off his striped suit and vest. A droopy black mustache hid most of his mouth and some of his chin. To his right was a chunky rider wearing Union cavalry breeches, a civilian shirt, and broad-brimmed hat. His eyes looked out from their dark pits and the hat's shadow, watchful, hardly winking eyes.

Like Ol' Cottonmouth, Walker thought.

Number three snatched his horse to a stop with a snort of surprise. Walker had seen hundreds like him—towheaded, gaunted, and out at the seat of his breeches, shifty eyes of washed-out blue; the spavined, underfed horse and man together wore one label: *white trash.*

The fourth man still wore most of a Confederate uniform, butternut gray badly patched and layered at frayed wrists by grease from forgotten campfires. His scruff of brown-dirt beard looked greasy also; his eyes kept working from side to side, half shuttered behind puffy lids.

Sitting high above him where he stood on the ground, they stared at Walker. He looked them over again, marking their weapons; even Mustache had a Spencer carbine jammed into a saddle case, and the open duster showed a pistol slung up on his hip.

Cottonmouth's Spencer lay ready across his thighs, and his holstered pistol was well oiled and cared for. White Trash and Greasy were armed about the same, but Greasy's handgun was on his left side, butt foremost. He'd have a time reaching it without changing hands with his carbine.

Mustache was the leader of this pack, and showed it, showed a mouthful of gold-capped teeth to Walker. "You, boy. What the hell you doin' on this land?"

Yankee, Walker thought; the words were harsh and clipped.

"Why," he said, "I was born here."

Cottonmouth said, "Uh-uh. Them Fairbairn whelps got killed off. You just standin' in the road, *boy.* You figurin' on livin' anywheres, haul your ass out'n our way."

White Trash had his reins in his right hand, held above the cracked and wired-together butt of a handgun. He kind of whinnied when he talked. "Might be the old scudder's boy what run off, afeared to fight the war."

Greasy said, "That right? You a flat-out coward, boy?"

"It makes no difference one way or the other," Mustache snapped. "This land is condemned for the public good. The Mobile and Ohio railroad right-of-way is going to cut right through here."

Gently, Walker asked, "Through all three thousand acres?"

Mustache threw back his duster and reached into an inner coat pocket. Walker noticed he reached slowly and carefully. Mustache said in his special twang, "Here's the court order; here's a quit claim deed for the old man to sign, and here's five hundred greenback dollars."

"For three thousand acres?" Walker asked.

"Shit," said Cottonmouth from the shadow of his hat brim. "No point wastin' time."

"Stomp on over him," Greasy suggested, and White Trash whinnied.

Behind him, Walker heard the cabin door creak, but didn't turn his head. The others looked past his shoulder—all but Cottonmouth.

Cottonmouth said, "You wearin' a mighty pretty Navy Colt, boy."

From the cabin door Jeremy Fairbairn said, "Hold on there. Nobody else stands up for me."

"Old man," Greasy chuckled, "I'd give you first three licks with that ol' iron, and lay odds you'd come off second to a strong fart."

White Trash threw back his head and hollered. He had no gold in his mouth, only gaps and brown snags. "Goddamn high muckety Fairbairns," he gasped. "Does my soul right good to see 'em 'thout a pot to piss in. Whooie! Damn if'n that ain't a good 'un—second to a strong fart."

Mustache said sharply, "Look here, I'm serving these papers on you all proper and legal, Fairbairn. You go to wavin' that toad sticker around—and that old nigger threatening with a pitchfork—damned if I'll give you even a smell of five hundred U.S. dollars. I'll just have you committed."

"Crazy as a pissant with a hind leg pulled off," Greasy said.

White Trash loosed another snorting laugh. "Leg pulled off. Whooie!"

Walker felt the movement before his ears caught it, a split second before his father lurched forward, lifting the cavalry saber high over his head. Pivoting halfway toward him, Walker saw Rufus a step behind, pitchfork jutted out like a small field of bayonets.

Time slowed itself, thickened the very air until it seemed everyone was moving under water. Time sucked in a deep breath and held it while brightly polishing each individual second before freeing it. Walker saw everything so clear and sharp—a bead of sweat clinging to Mustache's lip—White Trash's mouth trapping the sun and not giving it back—Greasy flinching and bobbling a carbine—Mustache throwing up the hand with papers in it, as if to protect his face—Cottonmouth whipping his Spencer off his lap, its muzzle coming around—

Walker shot him between those unwinking eyes. Cottonmouth's hat flew off and uncovered a bald, white-skinned head. For a long clock tick, he sat his saddle with the Spencer almost lined up with Walker's father. Then he slid off the horse, falling face down, a great hole in the back of his head.

Right, Walker thought, swimming his gun arm through water turned to clear, sticky syrup; he was right about Greasy needing to use one gun or the other and getting tangled in both. He put a .36 caliber ball into Greasy's throat where it joined the collarbone.

He shot White Trash twice, because he didn't make out where the first bullet went into the opened mouth. Then, slow as a music box winding down, he put another shot below Mustache's protective hand and dead-centered the mustache.

Somebody kicked time in the ass and got it started again. Everybody, everything speeded up, turned blurred and cartwheeling as men fell and horses spooked. Sound came crashing back, and Walker wondered why he hadn't heard it before.

"Great God in the mornin'!" Rufus said, pitchfork still aimed.

Walker looked down at the gun in his hand, at a hazed and tangy flavor of smoke. The Navy Colt felt matchstick light, as if he could balance its muzzle on the tip of his forefinger. There was a round left in the cylinder, if he hadn't miscounted—the held-back round, just in case.

Methodically, he began working the lever that kicked out empty brass casings.

"Mist' Walker," Rufus breathed, "I never in God's green earth figured to see nothin' like that. I knowed you hit what you aimed at, but not like no fiery angel athowin' bolts. *Fo'* mens down."

When he had reloaded the Navy from his shell belt and slipped the weapon back into its holster, Walker looked up and met his pa's eyes. The old man had his sword point on a rock, and leaned on the hilt.

Jeremy Fairbairn said, "You were never a coward, then."

"No," Walker said. "I tried to tell you all that. I just didn't want to kill anybody."

"Did a thorough job here," his father said.

"Whilst I knowed him," Rufus mumbled, talking to himself, "he never kilt one blessed thing 'cept snakes, and them onliest when he pure-D had to. Now look. Oh, lord, lord."

It had been so damned easy, Walker thought. He'd felt no emotion, no deep tearing at his guts, no sickness as he felt at a shot bird. He glanced along the line of men he'd shot down, lying crumpled and twisted where their horses had backed off. He still felt nothing. He said, "Rufus, best you take those horses across the river, strip and lose them. Maybe you should keep the trashy gelding there; nobody'll be looking hard for that one, and he's got pretty good lines, if you fatten him up. Acorns, remember? Like the Creek Indians you told me about.

"I'll drag the bodies into a gulley wash and cover them, if you've got a shovel for me. Maybe nobody will come searching."

There was a long time of silence; horses stamped and jingled. A black beetle crawled through a clotted puddle of blood. Jeremy Fairbairn said, "I'm beholden."

Not *son;* his Pa just couldn't bring himself to say that. Not even with his other two sons buried yonder. "No cause," Walker said.

CHAPTER 28

Tosanna put her face to the salt wind and it was good, but didn't blow away all her troubles. The day was fair and crisp, the ocean calm, with only little whitecaps playing in the sun. She pulled deeper into her coat and walked along the deck, her wonder at the sea renewed.

She looked at the bobbing horizon, gave thanks that she had not been deathly ill this time, and tried to think how she would describe the sea to her tribe. The Kwehar-enuh might have trougle grasping the concept of a river so wide it had no end, and its waters so salted that no man could drink from it.

Putting her back to the wind, Tosanna walked toward the stern. She would meet many problems when she returned to her people, and none could be solved here upon the deck of the *Mary Frances*. They were six days out from England, and the steamer was making good time, according to Captain Quint. She sniffed coal smoke from the stack and wrinkled her nose. The sea smelled much better.

Belle Williams—that wise, strong cockney would have little trouble acting as guardian and overseer of Athol House and its lands. Belle's eyes had filled with tears when Tosanna gave her the choice of going to America or remaining behind as legal watchdog of Athol.

"Coo, milady," Belle said, those tears spilling over to channel her cheeks, "it's no fair choice you're giving me. I —I love you so, and it'll for certain make a hole in my life when you leave. But I just c-can't go far from England. And—well, you're offerin' me the chance to act a lady, and to find a man of me own."

"Then stay," Tosanna had answered, taking her friend in her arms. "You can always come visit me, or be here if I return." The *Mary Frances* pitched over a larger wave, and Tosanna steadied herself on the cabin deck rail. Belle Williams come to visit Comancheria? She'd recoil at the sight of "savages" and be totally lost in a camp. Tosanna frowned and braced her feet wider on the ship's deck. *If* her family, her Antelope band, didn't try to kill or capture Belle Williams first.

That startled Tosanna—to know the truth of that—for it was so; all White Eyes were enemies to the Comanches, and enemies were to be attacked. She balanced that against what the English did; in Victoria's court or at balls, she had seen people from many countries, all come to pay homage to the queen. The English fought wars, but when the fighting was done, visitors from other tribes could be at peace in London.

Comancheria was different, Tosanna argued to herself. It was a land and people fighting for its right to go on living. Her people were hemmed in on all sides, and their domain was shrinking. Besides, a Comanche was no true man if he did not blood his knife. It had always been the way of The People and would never change.

Who was she to claim another way might be better? In England a child could starve, or freeze; it could be driven, beaten to work in a dark factory, before it learned how to live in the sun. These things did not happen in Comancheria. Was it because babies were so few and precious? No—all Comanches loved children and so there were never orphans. If a baby's parents were killed, others willingly took their place.

Which then were the savages—Comanche or English?

She left the deck for her cabin, one of only two which carried passengers, for the *Mary Frances* was a steam freighter. Tosanna could have waited on a luxurious passenger ship, but once all business was cleared in London, she was most anxious to go home. Once she'd made up her mind to return, days could not pass quickly enough.

Or was it the nights had turned so lonely?

Tosanna took off her cloak and sat on her bunk. The cabin was tiny, almost like a trap, but roomy enough for her trunks. No, she thought; she would not admit England could never be the same after Sunhair was chased from its shores. The passing of Gordon Hammers had much to do with her restlessness. None of her suitors had Gordon's kindness; none had Sunhair's dark magic, that powerful thing that made Tosanna's flesh tingle whenever she thought of him. And when she *touched* him—

She refused to think of the way their bodies came so fiercely together, as if each was long starved for the other, as if every time was the first wildly exciting meeting. She wouldn't think of that, and got up for a sip of wine to cool her blood.

Instead, she would think of being rich, more wealthy than all her tribe could dream. When she'd gone to her solicitor with instructions to sell, the man rolled his eyes upward and gasped, as if he expected the ceiling to fall and bury them both.

"Do you know what you are asking, madame? Have you any idea how much that may be in pounds sterling?"

"I do. I have had the books gone over by the Crown's solicitors. But Gordon trusted you, and so I am here. Athol House and its grounds are not for sale; all else is."

Mr. Brandywine removed his spectacles with shaking hands. "This will cause a minor stir on the market. The Crown's men, indeed."

"Sell carefully then," Tosanna said, "and wisely, to earn your commission."

Brandywine returned the glasses to his nose. "May I say, madame, you have shown an uncommon understanding of business—and so quickly too. Especially for one who—forgive me, madame—who cannot as yet read."

"I read," she assured him. "I can read prints of a deer and say how long ago he passed by; I read very small green things that lead to water, and folds in the land that also tell me where to dig. I read the sky and clouds and sun for the weather, and omens from the spirits in dog bones and moon shadows. I also read handtalk of the Dakota, Cheyenne, Kiowa, Navaho, and even dog Apache. Can you do those things, Mister Brandywine?"

The lawyer cleared his throat. "Ah, no, madame. Again I beg pardon. Very well, then, I shall proceed upon your orders to dispose of the duke's—ah—*your* holdings. And Athol manor?"

"It is to be left in the care of my dear friend, Belle

Williams, and enough monies banked for her to draw upon for its upkeep and wages until I return to England."

Brandywine started to take off his glasses again, and evidently thought better of it. "And how long will that be?"

"Possibly forever," she answered.

He coughed. "Forever. Yes, madame."

And it was thus that Tosanna came to board the *Mary Frances,* preceded by several trunks. Two held her clothes, and two others much heavier contained all liquid assets from the Duke of Athol's estate. A good portion had been turned into U.S. gold coins, purchased through the Bank of England; there was some American paper money, and a few jewels; then there were the gold and silver bars.

The solicitor had assured Tosanna of Captain Quint's honesty, and that of the British Maritime service as well. That had not stopped her from buying the short guns—one could be hidden in her hand and had two stubby barrels; the other was a weapon that fired six times, fast as she could pull trigger. It was a wondrous pistol indeed, and was called a Navy Colt. With these she would protect her own, if need be.

The ship rolled a bit, and Tosanna put her wine glass back into the shelf that had thin slats of wood across it, a rack so rough seas would not throw out its contents. This, she thought, was what being rich meant; two pistols and Captain Quint's word, and still she must stay alert.

For the money she transported was more than a duchy, more than servants and a fine house and shopkeepers bowing politely. It could be the saving of her people, the Kwehar-enuh. And if they could be convinced of what lay ahead for them, perhaps the whole Comanche nation might see what the spirits had in store. The Kuhtsoo-ekuh, the Yampah-reekuh—the nine tribes that hunted and fought over the Great Plains—all these must be made aware of their ultimate destiny. Change with the new things; adapt, bend as willow trees in the wind: these things The People must do, or perish.

Tosanna looked into her own eyes, mirrored by glass upon the cabin wall, and saw in those reflected depths the loss of any such hope. Comanches were warrior and hunter born. Unless they were shown through blood and fire that they could not win over *americano* White Eyes and hated *tejanos,* they would ride out to raid and battle.

Even after their eyes told them hard and bitter truth,

their hearts would never admit it. From the Llano Estacado in the north to the Rio Grande in the south, The People would fight.

And lose.

The wrench at her heart and pitching of the ship came together; Tosanna went to the porthole and saw rising, choppy waves, a gray and misted wind.

She remembered the rough seas of her other voyage and poured herself another glass of wine to deaden her fears. Her bed was the best place to ride out bad weather, and she took to it, glass and wine bottle close at hand. Another pitch and roll, and iron plates creaked; her trunks thumped each other. Tosanna closed her eyes and told her stomach the storm would soon blow itself out.

Wind howled its fury around the *Mary Frances* and Tosanna imagined the sea spirit angered, churning his waters and flinging great handfuls of surf at the ship and its puny crew. She didn't sort out hammering at her cabin door from hammer blows that thundered the plates at her head, and flinched when she saw a man crouched over her.

He cupped hands to his mouth. "Are you all right?"

She sat up and held to the bunk rails. "Yes."

"The captain sent me to find you and—"

Two of her trunks shifted, bumped, and when the ship did a long, sickening roll, one of them skidded across the deck to slam hard into the steel legs of Tosanna's bunk. The crewman barely had time to throw himself out of the way, and for a quick, stunned moment, she felt the weight of his body upon her, and thought he lay there longer than he had to, that his fumbling of her breast and thigh was deliberate. He smelled of the sea and wet wool, and felt of damp hair.

Smiling, he lifted himself, swung away his legs. "Sorry, miss; didn't mean to bruise you, but the sea—"

His words chopped themselves off with the sharp intake of his breath. "Damn! Look at all the bleedin' treasure!"

Tosanna rolled as the ship did, and heard the dull clanking of gold and silver bars before she found them with her eyes. Their weight had shattered one corner of the trunk, and they were sliding around the cabin floor, kicking gold coins out of their way. Another leap of the ship, and the broken trunk and its spilled treasures skidded to the far wall.

"Son of a bitch," the man breathed at Tosanna's ear, "it's a bloody fortune, a bloody king's ransom."

Tosanna said, "I will clear up, when the storm is past."

With an effort, he pushed himself from the bunk and braced a hand against the wall. His eyes were green with brown flecks in them, his jaws lightly bearded with curly brown, his open mouth wide and toothy. "A man'd sail a dozen lifetimes and never see half that much money."

Tosanna slipped one hand beneath her pillow and closed fingers upon the butt of the pistol. "Thank the captain for me," she said. "I will be all right."

Eyes still bulging and mouth yet agape, he said, "Sure, yes, but if you have any trouble—like putting all that loot back—how about I bring you hammer and nails?"

"I will ask the captain," she said.

He worked his face back into a semblance of calm. Another big wave slewed the ship and rattled bars and coins again. He said then, "You want anything, anything at all, you just call for me, miss. Bucko Johnson, that's me. First Mate, I am; that's next to bein' captain—and sometimes better. Just send any crewman for me, miss."

For once, his eyes left the sliding bars and fastened to Tosanna, penetrating her dress and probing her thighs. "That's for *anything,* miss, like warming your bunk these cold nights."

Seas crashed; the *Mary Frances* groaned and exposed wealth thudded and clinked. Tosanna said, "Get out of here."

Bucko Johnson gave her a mock salute and set his peaked cap more jaunty upon his bushy head. Thick, powerful fingers stroked his beard. "Like you say, miss. But a long sea lies between us and Yank country—and long nights."

He wrestled shut the cabin door and Tosanna took her hand from the pistol, left it beneath her pillow. The ship heaved and lurched, but it seemed the weather was already slacking, once it had made bad medicine to her. Nobody aboard but Captain Quint was supposed to know about her hoard. Now another knew, and Bucko Johnson was a man to be watched.

She now understood the importance of money to White Eyes. Some had no horses and some could not hunt; maize could not be traded with a tribe that had none; and so many had nothing to trade but themselves. On her cabin floor was enough of what Englishmen deemed so precious to buy more horses than she could count, to build more tepees than she had ever seen. In the camp of her people it would be worthless, beyond some initial curiosity. The paper money would be good for starting cookfires, but gold and silver was too soft to fashion into knives and arrowheads. The jewels? Ah, oddly beautiful decorations for subchiefs and some women. Others would still prefer the feathers and beads of old.

She would have to carefully explain money to her people, and use the fortune she brought to demonstrate, to help any way she could. There had been talk in London of ongoing troubles in the American West, but no details and no specifics. Englishmen shrugged off her questions, for it was obvious to them that all America was uncivilized and was sure to remain so.

One white man's war was finished; she knew that much, and also that more and more White Eyes were pushing west, that *tejanos* were becoming bolder. It was certain then that Comanches were fighting and could use her help.

When the sea fell to rolling swells, Tosanna climbed off her bed and began collecting the bars and coins scattered about the cabin. Unloading personal things from one undamaged trunk, she tucked in the treasure, and used the battered chest for clothes. If only she could as easily wipe out Bucko Johnson's knowledge. He had the look of a coyote, that one—hungry and sly. But he also had the chest and shoulders of a bear.

Because of the earlier storm, dinner was served later that evening, and for only the second time since sailing, the ship's other passenger joined Tosanna and Captain Quint at table. Carter Krale had a sharp, pinched face that swung from side to side as he walked looking down. His hair and mustache were reddish, his eyes shifting brown and corner wrinkled, his skin pale and sickly, as if it never felt the sun. He wasn't British like the ship's crew, but American like Sunhair.

"Delicate stomach," he said. "If it wasn't for, *ah*, business, I'd never leave dry land."

Captain Quint's eyebrows were grayed and bushy, the eyes behind them direct as two gun barrels. He said, "And it's an odd business when the son of a rebellion backs a monarchy."

Krale rubbed bony hands and shrugged. "Our rebellion is

better'n a hundred years past, captain. And, *ah,* all England wanted poor old Max to win."

"Not all England."

Tosanna unfolded her napkin and watched the play between them. This Krale was careful and edgy as Pa-tua at sundown, he of the eye-circling war paint that White Eyes called raccoon. He stared at her only when he thought she would not catch him at it.

"No matter," Krale said, "my, *ah,* company must retrench and make up its losses. Who would have thought the, *ah,* monarchies would betray Maximilian in the end? Even the Widow—"

"Queen Victoria," Quint said, "has never been tight with the Frenchies."

"More's the pity," Krale said, breaking a slice of bread into many small pieces, thin fingers quick and sly. "Her people were ready enough to ship guns to old Max—provided I, *ah,* paid cash for them."

Quint tapped a blunt and sea-roughened hand against the cloth. "I'll not discuss the queen or her reasons with you, man, since neither of us knows a damned bit about them." He nodded to Tosanna. "Begging your pardon, miss."

She ate quietly when food was brought, giving the serving boy half a smile. Across the small room was another table, where the rest of the ship's officers ate, Bucko Johnson hulking large among them.

Only half hearing the dry, hissing voice of Krale and Quint's deep, solid talk, she wished again for the friend she left behind in England. Belle Williams had always been at her elbow, full of knowledge and eager to help. Now Tosanna stood alone, facing all the problems to come.

In London, she had tried to study marks on paper they told her was a map. Nothing made sense to her, even when, with much discussion, they pointed out the American West. With help and the weight of royal interest, a landing port had been chosen for her, and information written on papers she kept always with her.

Victoria had been more than kind, although Tosanna sensed the queen wasn't too happy with so much money leaving her country. Over tea in a Buckingham Palace anteroom, Victoria had said she envied Tosanna.

"But you are queen," Tosanna had replied.

Victoria's sharp eyes softened. "No less a woman for it, child. Our entire life has been mapped, overseen, managed, weighed down with duty. If only we had been free as you, if Prince Albert could have run off with us, to some far place where there would be only each other."

She sighed and for an instant seemed to shrink, but the lapse was only momentary; then she stiffened, raised her chin, and was once more Victoria Regina, the most powerful woman in the world. They talked of small things after that, and the queen told Tosanna she was sorry to lose her.

"But we think you are right. Every woman should reach out for freedom and love. Farewell, child; we will always welcome your return."

And the queen's presence followed Tosanna everywhere as she prepared to leave the country, silencing gossiping tongues and turning away frowns. If shocked whispers of the notorious Lady Savage and duels were rife, they didn't reach Tosanna's ears.

Captain Quint rumbled something and Krale's higher, somehow dusty tones answered. Tosanna looked up from her tea, but not at the men. From the time she'd been taken by Don Joaquin de Arredondo, some man had been her protector; from Comancheria into Mexico and across the seas, she'd been guarded, if only for men's selfish interests.

In a fashion, her present sentry was the captain, but once off the ship, she would be totally on her own and still a long, long way from home.

CHAPTER 29

When he rolled their naked bodies into a common grave
and helped Rufus drag a rotting log over the spot, Walker
felt no shock and no sorrow. It had been fated, something
apart from his emotions.

Sweating, about blown from digging, Walker looked at
the old black. "I figure that little field down at the river
bend; good place to hide the horses until any hollering dies
down."

Rufus said, "Don't hardly seem right to be keepin' clothes
with blood on 'em."

"Boots, guns, and whatever they carried in their pockets
or saddlebags; we can use it and they can't. Oh—bury saddles and bridles under old hay, if Pa put any by; sell them
and the horses when you figure it's safe."

"Mist' Walker, you ain't studyin' on leavin' us right off?
Your Pa, he ain't just right in his head. Not clear out'n it,
but kind of too set in his ways."

Walker looked toward the slave cabin. A wisp of smoke
climbed from its sagging clay chimney interlaced outside
with hickory sticks. "He wants it to be like before the war,
but it never will be. Here, three pistols and one long rifle.
I'll keep the Spencer. Good thing two of them were toting
bedrolls. Eeny, meeny, miney, moe; catch a nigger by the
toe."

"Lordy, Mist' Walker," Rufus said, "you ain't playin'
no youngun's game."

Squatting, Walker counted out money; the Yankee had

carried a good bit, but his henchmen only a little. He pushed the biggest pile toward Rufus. "With the horses and tack for trading stock and this genuine United States money, you all should make it for a good spell."

"You all he got left," Rufus said.

"He has nothing left. In his mind he killed me the day I rode off from Fairbairn Plantation and the war. Ma and my brothers died, so I have no right to live."

The old man blinked rheumy eyes. "Might be he just can't say out what he holdin' inside."

Walker stood up. "I can use two sets of saddlebags for my plunder."

"Where you headin', Mist' Walker?"

"Somewhere, anywhere; out west, I reckon."

"Ain't you goin' to say goodbye?"

"Said that when I left home the first time."

Rufus pushed out his chin. "That ain't what I means."

"I know," Walker said. Saddlebags and bedroll in place, Spencer in his stirrup boot, he was ready. He shook hands with the old slave and swung up onto his gelding. "Take care, Rufus; appreciate you taking care of Pa."

"Carin' for my ownself too."

"Yes," Walker said, and put his back to Fairbairn Plantation; soon he would do the same to Alabama. Once across the Tombigbee River, he'd be in Mississippi—home of Jeff Davis and heart of the Confederacy. From there he'd keep his horse pointed west, stopping at civilization only to replenish bacon, beans, cornmeal, and salt.

If he had to slaughter animals to feed himself, so be it. That would be worse than killing humans; damned few animals forced a man into shooting them. Human beings were supposed to think, while lower life forms acted only upon instinct. But how old was an animal before it was driven from the den?

He passed through Coffeeville and was ferried across the Tombigbee. By the time he made his way across Louisiana, he had acquired sturdier boots and buckskins that would last forever, if some Indian didn't put an arrow through them.

And talk of Indians flew thick wherever Walker pulled up to rest and fatten his horse. Kiowas, Apaches, Cheyennes, Arapahoes, and Comanches; near about every tribe raising hell, they said. The tribes had gotten uppity in the

war, when few soldiers could be spared to pacify them.
Now they were raiding every which way, burning, killing,
and taking hair. A good part of the western frontier was
collapsing, and much of the loss could be laid to the
damned Indian Department and Holy Joes who ran the
reservations.

Somewhere in east Texas, he stood at a bar of rough
planks supported by two barrels and shielded by ragged
canvas. The man behind it was heavy in the middle and
wore a network of veins in his nose and cheeks. He said,
"Seein' this, a body wouldn't know I had me a fine place
close to Fort Concho. Damned redskins burned me out.
Lucky to save my hair and I didn't quit runnin' till I pulled
up here."

"Reckon a man could hire out back there?" Walker
asked.

"If'n he ain't got good sense."

For a while, Walker followed the Colorado River, and
past Bastrop, through Austin, the country began to change.
Greenery gave way to vast stretches of open plains where
even the early winter sun hinted how cruel it might be in
the summer.

He rode alertly, instinctively staying off the skyline,
watching the ground for sign. He met a party of travelers
heading east—sullen, angry men; worn and frightened
women; children whose eyes were sunken and old before
their time.

Hell back yonder, they said; bastards scalping and putting whole settlements to the torch. And, no, the goddamned army wasn't doing much about it; the bluecoats
came too late and too few, and when they took off after a
war party, they came dragging back empty-handed.
Damned redskins ran back to the reservations where the
army couldn't go.

Twice, Walker met small bands of cavalry, men saddle-
weary and red-eyed, men who gladly passed along gossip
and looked at him as if he had lost his mind. Yes, a worn-
down lieutenant said, the army hired hunters and trackers
—low pay and high risk.

In no hurry, Walker kept to the river, supplementing his
rations with small trout and catfish as he got the feel of
the country. For some weeks, he saw no human being and
began to learn the great loneliness of high desert. He dis-

covered that danger lurked everywhere; diamond-back rattlers longer than a man's arm and as thick; the black-orange Gila monster; hairy tarantulas that could spring like jackrabbits.

And no less deadly was the land itself, baked dry and merciless away from the life-giving river. It was sentried by saguaro cactus and cholla, with growths he could not name, whose sharp needles were to be avoided. Also lying in wait for the unwary were alkali springs, whose waters meant agony and death.

Walker also learned the country's beauty—sweeps of misty blue escarpments, moonlight turning miles of sand to silver, sunsets that were red and purple glory. And the distances, so vast that they seemed to reach into eternity, making man and horse insignificant specks.

Following crude maps drawn by cavalry officers he met, Walker holed up for a day at the fork where the San Saba joined the Colorado. There was plenty of sign there, a muddied bank, prints of horses shod and unshod, wagon tracks across the ford, burned-out campfires. Since he saw no brass cartridge casings, he figured this place had been safe from Indian raids. Still, when he camped for the night, Walker built his small, smokeless fire back in an arroyo and picketed his horse there.

A cold moon rode high over the mountains when an alien sound woke him in his blankets. He lay still, trying to sort the noise from natural night wind and the far mourning of coyotes. It was faint, a click of stone against a hoof.

Sliding from bed warmth, Walker went low and quick to his horse, to clamp the animal's nose and prevent a whinny. Down at the crossing, he heard guttural talk, the stamp of horses, a low laugh. It seemed a long time before a file of shadow figures drifted off through moonlight.

Walker remained still long after they left. No doubt they were Indians, stopping to water their horses before moving on. No hunting band riding at night, but a war party, and he breathed thanks that his tracks had been mixed with many others.

At dawn, he rode northwest with Spencer carbine across his thighs, his head on a swivel. Thereafter, he kept to hill shadow and riverbottom cane thicket as much as possible, sometimes ground-tying his horse to climb hunched and peer over the next hill.

There were deer in the thickets, quail and rabbits where grass grew, but Walker didn't kill anything until he'd been out of meat for two days and for some reason fish weren't biting. He felt bad when he dropped the young buck, and fretted over the shot's rolling echo. When he cooked a haunch, using dry wood and a fire hole among canebrakes and willows that dispersed the smoke, Walker's stomach almost rebelled.

Grimly, he forced down the meat, needing its strength, and delayed his journey two days while smoking more venison. Determined to kill no more than he was forced to, and to waste damned little, he turned along the south fork of the Colorado, pointing due west for Fort Concho.

Alertness became habit for him, and although his thoughts ranged, Walker was conscious of all around him. The wagon road he now followed cut straight across, catching up to the river whenever it bent. He thought of the home he'd put behind, the father who would never claim him. He had paid any debt to Jeremy Fairbairn when he shot the thieves who tried to rob the old man. He owed nothing in Alabama.

Walker edged his horse up a fold in the ground and halted so he could look over its crest without being seen. Nothing lay ahead but land turning ever more dry and harsh. There had been nothing for him in England either— not since the old Duke of Athol dropped dead and he'd been blamed for it.

Tosanna. She came spinning into his mind, furious as a dust devil that whirled across the desert, snatching up sand and twigs in a mad dance. She was about as unpredictable, too, and no place was ever the same where she had passed. He wondered where she was now, and thought she'd be warming some other lord's bed long since. Milady Savage was no woman to be without a lover, and a rich one.

Rocking with his horse, Walker tried to picture her in this unforgiving land. Her fancy ball gowns would be out of place, and even her everyday dress too bright. He couldn't believe she'd ever roamed these hills and desert, dirty and half naked. Tosanna dressed in latest fashion was beautiful; stripped, she was breathtaking.

He'd never known such perfection in a woman's body,

such cunningly shaped legs, such delightful breasts, and her skin without a blemish, a velvet that itched a man's hands. The fierceness of her flesh, her heated depths—all seemed calculated to beguile a lover. Walker corrected himself: *lovers,* and the lord only knew how many.

When he made camp that night, tucked under mesquite bushes and perfumed sage, Tosanna came to walk his dreams, sprite, mistress, witch. Once he saw her in leg irons, heavy, cruel things used to hold runaway slaves or to ship them in a cavvy. He never saw her in a full, white dress overseeing a lawn party, or just standing quietly at the head of Fairbairn Plantation's winding stairs.

Coming awake just as morning sun began to pink hills to the south, he found the remembered, lingering taste of her in his mouth, honeyed, warm, and exciting. Weapons close at hand, he slid into the narrowing river to wash Tosanna from mind and body, welcoming its penetrating chill. Shivering, he got back into his buckskins and made a quick breakfast.

A day later, he reached Fort Concho, after passing jangling troopers on fresh horses headed south. Guidon flying, equipment gleaming, they looked bright and blue. The young cavalrymen seemed eager, grizzled old soldiers bored. Walker stood his horse off the track until they went by, rolling dust.

The fort sat square against the Colorado River, its hauled-far logs upended upon an adobe base. Up high, below the sharpened points, rifle slits had been cut. The gates were open and a flag fluttered lazy from a pole in the compound. Sentries let Walker pass without a formal challenge, with only a kind of awed curiosity as to how much of the plains he'd crossed alone.

Inside, a row of adobe huts clung to each other for warmth and mutual protection, their stick-and-mud roofs like so many cheap, ill-fitting wigs. The quadrangle was bare and beaten hard by countless boots and horse hooves.

A caisson and cannon sat before headquarters, looking efficient and ready. Something to at least scare hell out of the savages, Walker thought, providing it could be dragged anywhere near them. Hitching his horse to the rack, he nodded to a sentry on a low, wooden porch and approached the adjutant.

The lieutenant evidently took pride in keeping neat,

boots shined and brass polished. He appeared crisp and professional. "Yes," he said, "this part of the army can always use meat hunters and scouts, Mr. Fairbairn. May I ask what uniform you wore?"

"None," Walker answered, watching the tightening of the man's face. "I spent the war and beyond in England."

"I see," said Lieutenant Caruthers. His cropped hair was sandy, his lashes near white. "Your accent—well, many former Confederates are in our ranks now, you see. The men call them galvanized Yankees. Good enough soldiers, I suppose—those who can forget they once held higher ranks."

Walker was introduced to the commanding officer, Major Milton Gordon. He was gray and starvation lean, with quick, birdlike movements; grooves had worn deeply at each side of a thin white mustache. Walker got the feeling Major Gordon was always looking over his shoulder, even when he wasn't. Gordon. The name rang bells of memory, echoed England and Gordon Hammers.

Because he was neither officer nor enlisted man, Walker bunked with neither. He was shown the stables, where three other scouts bedded down in the loft—two Tonkawa Indians and a man introduced as Dobe Davis.

Davis was a short and talky man; Walker was to find this was the way of many who spent the greater part of their lives in enforced silence. When they got a chance to talk, all the saved-up words came tumbling out in an eager freshet.

"Been called Dobe so long I forget why," he said, offering cigarette makings. "Account of I come from Adobe Wells in Oklahoma Territory. You know the Territory? No mind, no mind; it ain't so much and never will be, I reckon."

Walker handed back tobacco and papers and struck a sulphur match with his thumbnail. Against the far wall, the Indians looked on, unmoving, expressionless.

Dobe said, "You don't know the country west of here? No mind; you'll learn quick enough. Main thing is keepin' your hair and helpin' the soljers keep theirs." His eyes were merry, incongruous because an ancient scar divided his left eyebrow and dipped ugly across the cheekbone. Dobe's hair was thin and silver brown; as he rolled a smoke for himself he showed gnarled fingers that had been broken and set badly, but he didn't spill a flake of tobacco.

"These Tonks," he said with a gesture, "is meaner'n snake shit and smell about like it too. You get used to their stink and your own after a spell. The blackest one is Fleabite, and the weasly one answers to Saba, account he claims to've been whelped on the San Saba River. They can track a lizard across dry shale, but they ain't much on facing up to the Comanch 'less they can catch one asleep. Reckon that's account of their tribe is about wiped out by 'em."

Blowing a puff of smoke, Dobe said, "How come you hitched up here, lad? If'n I had my druthers, I'd be squattin' in California shootin' marbles with gold nuggets."

"Might try for California myself," Walker said. "In time."

Dobe grunted. "If'n the Comanch don't stop your pocket watch. They purely raisin' hell hereabouts, and the fort sits just on the edge of their playground. Due west for about a hundred miles you come on another Comanch trace. The army says they been raidin' up and down a piece of map looks kind of like a slice of pie twice't as wide at the bottom—which is the Rio Grande. Got 'em another trace beat down through old Fort Davis and Fort Stockton, north to the Clear Fork reservation. But hellfire—they just as liable to hit three hundred miles either way, outa pure cussedness."

Walker pinched out his cigarette butt to shred paper and tobacco. "And the army?"

"Does the best it can; chases here and yonder like a chicken with its head cut off. Like as not, takes some licks from the Comanch if'n it comes up on a war party, which ain't often."

"How come?"

Dobe scratched at a raggedy beard. "Injuns travels fast and light; they hit and light a shuck. Time the army even knows somethin' happened, they're way to hell and gone, maybe clear up to the Canadian River."

"And nobody follows them that far," Walker guessed.

"Ain't exactly the army's fault; the Great White Father and Injun agents make medicine and hogtie the troopers worse'n the Comanch. Damned reservation Injuns ride out and take hair, then hightail back to the reservation where nobody can get at 'em legal."

Walker glanced at the stolid Tonkawas squatting with

their backs against the wall. Unwinking, they stared back, dressed in shabby, castoff uniform coats, loincloths, and buckskin leggings. They looked dirty and savage and were betrayers of their own kind.

Tonk or Comanche, they were first cousins to Tosanna's people. Walker made a disgusted face.

CHAPTER 30

There had been storms, but they were behind the *Mary Frances* now, making the sea calm and fresh. Tosanna had become closer to the captain, finding new knowledge in their conversations. Quint told of his boyhood and how he'd lived it upon the sea, how he'd traveled the world by water.

His stories made Tosanna realize the vastness of the earth and of its masters, the white men. She grew ever more thoughtful, filing away information for the days she would return to her tribe. They were so few, the Comanches, so few and so weak in comparison. Even if all the tribes she knew—Apache, Kiowa, Cheyenne, and the others—even if they joined into one mighty nation, they would still be only a speck in the white man's eye, only a minor irritant to be destroyed if it became troublesome.

And never would the tribes unite; their suspicions and hatreds of each other reached back thousands of years. Though White Eyes were of many tribes also, they never failed to band together to face Indians. It was almost beyond Tosanna's comprehension. She knew only that she must somehow try to save the Kwehar-enuh from the White Eyes and from themselves.

She saw Bucko Johnson often, because his duties seemed to take him wherever she happened to be. On the fantail, near the bridge, at the captain's table, he was watching her, smiling ragged-toothed and confident, smiling hot-eyed. Tosanna tried to avoid him, but contact with the other passenger was as bad. Carter Krale held forth on fortunes to be made through investments, and she knew that Bucko Johnson had spread word of riches in her cabin.

When Krale kissed her one moonlit evening on deck, she stood patiently, neither struggling nor giving, until he stepped frowning back from her. "Why not me?" he asked. "Every man on board has heard of the, *ah,* notorious Milady Savage. What's the matter—ain't I rich enough to bed you?"

Calmly, hands at her sides, she answered him. "Once I could not choose my lover. Now I can, and do not choose you."

For a moment, she thought he meant to strike her and balanced herself to kick him in the groin. But Krale dropped his hand and glared balefully at her. "Wench, your time will, *ah,* come soon. How far do you think you'll get playing the great lady in Galveston? Quality folks there can tell a fancy baggage right off; they'll know you for a squaw."

"I will not stay there," she said, still calm.

"Clear out to the frontier then—around the Horn to California for that matter—the mark is on you."

"I accept that," she said. "I am proud to be Comanche."

He muttered away then and at mealtimes pointedly ignored her. Captain Quint felt the coolness, she thought, but never mentioned it and continued attentive to her. Bucko continued to trail her with brooding eyes, and as the ship neared its destination, Tosanna spent more time in her cabin, locking it each time she left.

She saw land then, and a lift of excitement rushed through her, a trembly exultation as she anticipated seeing The People. It would be wonderful to speak her own tongue again, to look into the faces of her family and friends. *Hu*—they would be greatly surprised to have her walk among them after so long, and to hear her stories of the *tabay-boh,* the white man.

Did her father still give wise council at the fires and lead the band on successful raids? She stared toward the gray-blue line that meant land, Texas, and a point her eyes could not reach—Comancheria. Tet-Sainte must be there, and would open his heart to his daughter when she returned from the dead.

And Big Tree, her beloved Ado-eeti? Grown older surely, and with wives to serve him and bear him sons, as it should be. Would Ado-eeti be her husband after he heard the black, bad medicine tales she carried?

Captain Quint touched her shoulder and drew her from her dreams. "Landing at first light on the morrow, lass. Tonight we anchor in Galveston bay, and, come sunup, lighters will steer us to the docks." He hesitated, looking down into her upturned face. "I'll miss you, lass. My ship has never known such beauty."

Tiptoe, she kissed his furry cheek and thanked him. Farther down the rail, shadows stirred. When Tosanna turned for her cabin, she saw Bucko Johnson and Krale standing with their heads together. Inside, she sat upon the edge of her bunk and thought over what she must do once the *Mary Frances* docked.

From Captain Quint's information, she knew she must buy horses, equipment, food, and a wagon, that she must join a wagon train heading west, for protection. Wild Indians were running free on the plains, he said, grown arrogant because most American troops had been pulled out to fight the Civil War, and never returned in strength. Though that war was long past, emboldened tribes still rode a bloody, far-ranging warpath.

It was only after he'd passed along all rumors and pertinent information that Quint realized he was talking to a Comanche, and reddened as he clamped teeth around his pipe stem. But Tosanna hadn't minded; she was eager for any news, any suggestions how she might return to her land, her people.

Now she was so close, only a strip of water separating her from the *tejanos* so hated by Comanches. Among them she would have to barter, to hire a driver, and later on risk handling a team of horses by herself, when she decided to drop out of the train and try to find the Kwehar-enuh. Hopefully, she would be able to signal and handtalk any other Comanche bands that might be raiding before they swooped down upon her.

Once deep into Comancheria, she could hide her wagon and contents, cut loose one horse, and saddle the other to ride for home. If she was to meet roving Apaches—well, her medicine had better be strong, and the spirits fight beside her.

Too excited to sleep, Tosanna paced the deck as the ship bobbed at anchor. She tried to count the lights ashore, but soon gave up. A breeze from land brought with it the smells of firewood and excitement, and she clenched the rail, smooth and chill to her hands. She had been long away, had come back from distances no other Comanche could understand, and seen much that her tribe's spirit talkers would not believe.

She felt a light bump through her hands, and peered down alongside the steamer's hull, where a small boat rocked. The wind turned cold, and she wrapped her coat more tightly as she backed from the rail and headed for her cabin. Keying the door, she thought that even this lock, which she accepted almost without notice, would baffle her people and anger them. But then, Comanches did not need locks against each other.

She had just turned up the oil lamp and was half out of her coat when the cabin door slammed back and he hurtled at her. Hands tangled, she staggered under the impact of his body, and the edge of the bunk axed behind her knees. Tosanna was whipped onto her back, breath jolted from her lungs.

When she struggled to sit up, his weight rolled off her, but before she could reach her knife, his heavy hand rang against her cheek and a sun burst behind her eyes.

"Ain't so damned high and mighty now, be you?" Bucko Johnson's eyes glittered and his thick lips curled. "Here I have you, wench."

Tosanna blinked away pain and sat up again. "The captain will have your hide."

Backing to the door, he heeled it shut. "Old Quint's got troubles of his own, I'd say. By now Krale's knocked him in the head and is just waiting 'til the watch goes below. Then he'll be here to give a hand with all that gold."

"No," Tosanna breathed, and lunged from the bed, stabbing backhand at the big man's belly. When she missed, her follow-up swing sliced his uniform coat and ripped a bloody furrow along his skin.

With a yelp of pain and outrage, Bucko chopped a fist down across her forearm. The knife rattled and skipped across the deck.

"Heathen bitch," he snarled. "I been waiting the voyage through for this chance at you. Switchin' your ass and shakin' your tits—well, there's time for me now. Maybe time enough for Krale to take his fill of you, too."

A civilized lady might have screamed and fainted, but Bucko Johnson's blow had brought out the Comanche in

Tosanna. She saved her breath and ran at him, using her head against his ribs. She drove him back, but he was big and quick. One hand tangled in her flowing hair, he whipped her back against the bunk.

"Going to make you beg, you goddamned savage. Going to get in between your legs and ram you so hard and deep that you'll squeal. And after I rip you wide open, Krale can slop it with you, should he want."

Tosanna said, "Then you will take my gold and go ashore in the small boat."

Bucko opened his breeches. "We got two other helpers, we have. Old Quint can put it down as mutiny, or enter in the log that three men jumped ship for the gold fields in America. Either way, we'll be gone and rich."

Holding himself aimed like a stubby spear, he moved at her. She glanced at her knife, fallen beside a trunk, the trunk holding her treasure, her great gift to the Comanche nation.

He said, "Try for it, doxy. I'll break your back and diddle you anyhow. Look what I'm holding; never saw one like it amongst your lords and dukes and such, I'd wager."

She reached down and jerked the dress over her head in a single motion. Towering above her, Bucko fondled himself. Tosanna curled up a leg and rolled her hips to remove underwear.

"You're showin' sense now," he said.

Lacy white drawers were down around one ankle. She reached a slow and careful hand to touch his staff, moving her lower body so she could rid herself of encumbrances.

Cautious at first, he kept one big fist drawn back, but as she stroked him gently, as she teased him, he began to relax. Bucko's grin widened to show his uneven teeth. "Once a whore, always a whore," he said.

That instant, Tosanna twisted and jerked viciously, bracing an upflung foot against his thigh and shoving hard. He staggered and she leaped from the bed naked to dart under his hands and scoop up her knife. Hunched against his pain, Bucko Johnson cursed her. Sliding in and out, she missed his throat and only bloodied the man's cheek. He roared and she went in again, low this time and cutting at his privates.

Awkwardly, he struck at her and fell across the bunk. A lightning slash of her steel opened a long rent in the mattress as Bucko rolled desperately away. He was calling hoarsely for help now, and Tosanna remembered the other crewmen he'd claimed were joining to rob her. Her point drove into his leg, and she skipped back to the center of the cabin.

For a taut, shuddering moment, she was Kwehar-enuh through and through, blood lust boiling within her. *Hu!* This White Eyes had fallen before her, and she meant to finish him off, to take his hair.

But she hesitated, swaying and tensed to spring at him again. There were weapons in one of the trunks, but unless she cut this enemy's throat, she could not reach them. Bucko clenched his leg and hissed at her through clenched teeth. Suddenly she whirled and darted through the doorway to run along the deck.

At the rail, she saw a crewman at a line that reached down into the darkness, that reached to the waiting boat. With a shriek, Tosanna jumped at the man, her shoulder taking him in the ribs. His startled yell echoed her shout of triumph as he went over the side. She chopped twice at the rope and parted it, then raced for the captain's cabin, where she had seen a gun locker, where unsuspecting Captain Quint was beaten down by a ship passenger.

Krale's small pistol exploded as she jerked open the door, and a jagged splinter tore loose beside her head. Tosanna rolled when he fired the second barrel of his derringer. Her knife tore breeches at his kneecap, and when he jumped back, she caught up something heavy and threw it at his head. *Hu!* The spirits were riding with her this night. He took the impact and staggered.

She would have leaped after him, but Quint shouldered her aside and fisted Krale in the middle of his face. The man dropped as if a horse had kicked his legs out from under him. He hit the deck heavily and rolled once. Then only one foot twitched.

Panting, the captain seemed to notice Tosanna's nakedness for the first time. A sweep of his long arm brought a blanket off his bunk and around her shoulders. "There, lass. You should not have—"

"Three others," she snapped. "One in a small boat drifting, another in the water, Bucko Johnson in my cabin, hurt."

His mouth feel open. "By all that's holy, you've done a fine job on these brigands, and I'll finish it. Trying to rob you, were they?" Quint stepped over the prostrate Krale and whistled into a speaking tube. "Bridge, bridge! All hands, bigod—arrest Mister Johnson on sight!"

At the gun locker, he lifted out a shotgun and broke it to check the load. "Lass, can you handle—of course you can. Take this rifle and hold it on this scum when he comes to. I'll take care of Mister Johnson, by all the saints."

In the doorway, he paused. "Did they—did he harm you? If he did, I'll put enough shot in him to sink the bloody bastard to the bottom."

"No," Tosanna said, holding the rifle. "He tried but did not rape me."

Words floated back over Captain Quint's shoulder. "Tried, did he? On my ship!"

On the deck, Carter Krale stirred. Earing back the hammer of the rifle, Tosanna watched him, standing far enough back so he couldn't reach her. Excitement still thundered throughout her blood, and she could understand the frenzy of some warriors who went berserk in combat.

But there was something else—a resentment which seemed to burn to her depths. It wasn't the attempt to take her treasure, although its loss would be catastrophic, but something more—a shadowy displeasure she couldn't bring into the open.

Carter Krale sat up, cupping a hand to his broken face. "I—I'm badly hurt." His voice was muffled. "Let me up, woman. I have to—to seek treatment."

Tosanna kept the rifle centered upon him, her finger curled to its trigger. "You tried to kill me."

He quivered. "Mistake, just a mistake. I thought you were some crewman. At least, allow me to stand at the washbasin."

"No," she said.

"I—we weren't going to harm you. It was just the money, so much gold, Johnson said."

"You lie," Tosanna said. "You would have raped me after he did; he said so."

"No, no, I swear! Johnson, you—" When Krale lowered his hand, she saw his nose was twisted to one side and bloody. He watched the rifle and her hands upon it. When she did not tremble, he looked up into her face. "What difference would that make to *you*, flaunting yourself all over the ship, so proud of being whore to English nobility. And taking your whore's payments back to the damned Indians. What difference if you diddled two more men, since you've spread yourself for so many? It's not like you were pure or white, you slut."

Now she knew her strange emotion. It was outrage, because a man had tried to take her body by force, because he wanted to make her into no more than an animal. She felt anger and disgust and sickness, because Bucko Johnson meant to defile her flesh with his hate, his scorn.

Tosanna's body was her own, not intended for men to maul, to rut upon, to dominate and probe her secret places. The choice was *hers,* if she would take a lover. She would not have one forced upon her.

"Jesus," Carter Krale stuttered, "watch what you're doin' with that g-gun. I didn't mean—I—don't *murder* me."

She paid little attention to him, her head awhirl with that new thought so ailen to a woman of The People. If a woman's body belonged to her, then it could not be owned, even temporarily, by anyone else, White Eye rapist or Comanche husband. And yet what Comanche woman dared set herself above her man?

Krale came to his knees and the rifle muzzle followed, aimed directly at his middle. Maybe the ways of white women had changed some part of her, but the rest of Tosanna was still Comanche and looked out of her eyes.

He did not try to jump her.

CHAPTER 31

Walker was well seasoned now. Dobe Davis saw to that, teaching him desert lore, for the very land here could become an enemy. Many truths of the Alabama woods held their value, and some did not, but Walker was glad he'd spent so much time wandering the forest as a youngster. But back there, no Comanche lay hidden, waiting to kill.

When he hunted meat for Fort Concho, alone or with Dobe, he still felt a twinge of regret when he pulled trigger on buffalo or antelope. He had to hold his mind on other things when he dressed out an animal, so the killing and preparing would not seem like murder to him. At least, it wasn't called sport.

This was a new life, and nothing else lay open to him. He had no other skills, except his uncanny shooting ability. That might get him a job with a carnival back east, alongside moth-eaten animals and freaks of nature.

Sometimes the troops rode out on patrol, or in slow, useless pursuit of some marauding band that had raided to the south or west. Then Walker rode far ahead as scout, or off to an exposed flank. Dobe would be with them too, and the Tonkawas.

"Got to watch them bastards," Dobe advised. "Been more'n once they dropped off to raid a horse herd and alerted the damn Comanch we was comin'. And best you double-check any sign they run up on. They been known to miss tracks that say a big war party went by, but they're hell on little bunches."

Although he worked almost independently as a scout and hunter, Walker came to know several officers and men of Fort Concho's cavalry unit. Major Gordon was typical, old, prewar army. He had been brevet brigadier general in 1865. In the huge cutback of Union forces after Appomatox, he was reduced to his present rank, only one step above where he'd been before the war. He wanted no trouble, no conflict with faraway Washington policies, wrong as those might be. The major was out to pasture on the frontier, awaiting retirement, and the only important thing was the calendar.

Captain Britt Richards was another kind of soldier. Texas born of a staunch unionist family, he had a good, if spotty, war record. Too independent and headstrong, he would never see higher rank if he remained in service.

Over a bottle of redeye whiskey and cigars, he held forth to Walker. Dobe Davis had long since curled up on a pile of hay and gone to sleep.

"It's the damned peace policy in Washington," he said. "Hellfire! They were ignoring us *before* the war, letting Indians run wild from the Canadian to the Rio Grande and beyond. *Quakers.*" Richards took another swallow from the bottle. "Quakers run the reservations, all kindness and light, even when the goddamn Kiowas and Comanches wave bloody scalps in their faces—*blond* scalps, mind you. No soldiers, thank you—and don't chase a war party back to the reservation; that might disturb the poor, misunderstood Comanches." He chewed on his cigar. "Disturbed, my ass. They're laughing like hell at how stupid and cowardly we White Eyes are."

Walker had listened and asked questions. That seemed to surprise and delight the captain. Walker had the feeling that Richards had run out of listeners some time back. What was his solution to the Indian problem?

"One answer is well under way," he replied. "It's the buffalo; hide hunters are destroying the big herds, killing buff by the thousands. A great waste to be sure, such wanton slaughter for hides or tongues—but it's eliminating the Comanche commissary. No buff, no hunters, no meat, no warm robes."

"It's such big country," Walker said. "Surely there's room for Comanche and white, too."

Richards pointed the end of his cigar at him. "That's how they think back in Washington, but it's impossible.

They treat the Indians like government wards, giving them presents and reservations and allotments. Then they turn around and sign peace treaties with them, as if they were separate nations. They're not. One Comanche doesn't give a good goddamn what another Comanche puts his mark to. I know for a fact that two main bands—the Kwehar-enuh and Kutsoo-ehkuh—have never even shown up at peace meetings, and it wouldn't matter if they did. On their way home, they'd probably pull a raid, so the trip wouldn't be a total loss."

Walker sipped raw whiskey and listened to the captain's monologue, for some shred of information might help save his life some day. Richards told how Texas was ignored by easterners who thought the Medicine Lodge treaty took care of everything, that Texans were only disgruntled ex-Confederates interested in stealing Indian lands.

"Infantry regiments on the Rio Grande—infantry! Jesus—like foot soldiers could chase down horseback Comanches. And the Quaker commissioners, so damned godly sure they can make farmers of the tribes. Never—the warrior is insulted by women's work, and won't touch it."

Richards bought himself another swallow of whiskey and relighted his cigar. "Hellfire—what's left of the Lipans, Kickapoos, and Mescaleros raid regularly across the Rio Grande into southwest Texas. The Mexicans can't, or won't stop them."

He stared moodily at the ash on his cigar until Walker said, "What's the answer then? The western frontier can't be held back forever."

"It's happening. A handful of Indians is blocking expansion of the United States and will keep doing it until stopped the only way they understand. The bands must be destroyed—hunted down and destroyed in their winter camps. The reservations can't be used as refuges for raiders, like now. That has to be stopped. The only question is, how many settlers and soldiers get scalped and mutilated, how many young girls and women are raped and tortured first."

He passed the bottle to Walker. "Damn—I rattle on like an empty wagon, but it's my favorite subject. I respect the Comanche way of life, respect them as fighters. But I also know killing them off is the only possible solution."

Walker tilted the bottle. "Seems pretty rough, genocide."

Richards lifted an eyebrow. "And you seem pretty educated, for a scout. It's the only way, because the Comanches

are warriors, nothing else. War is their honor and sub-
sistence. They can't be forced to scratch in the dirt; they'll
die first, and gladly, so long as it's in combat."

"So we must kill them."

Standing up and brushing bits of hay from his breeches,
Richards said, "So you know not to bring in any prisoners.
They're useless for information and take extra men to guard
them. Then, bigod, orders will come down to let them go
or parole them back to the Fort Sill reservation and the
Quaker agent."

When the captain climbed down from the loft, Dobe
Davis sat up. "Left you the whiskey, did he?" He took a
long pull at the bottle. "Too bad he don't run the army,
like. The boy's family got wiped out by injuns while he
was off to war. Reckon that's how come he stayed in, to
get some licks back."

Between meat hunts there was precious little to do
around the fort, and often Walker used the time to learn
handtalk from the Tonk called Saba. The other, Fleabite,
only stared blankly if Walker approached him.

And from Saba, in struggling bits and pieces, he learned
something of the Comanches, ancient blood enemies to
the Tonkawas. The Plains Indians had decimated Saba's
tribe until only a few survived. Those remnants of a once
populous band hired themselves out for revenge and loot.
The Tonk knew his enemies' strengths and weaknesses.

It was a long, hot summer on the plains, spotted by
baked, miserable patrols, but mostly boring days and restless nights. Walker dreamed often, snug in his hayloft
where a woman walked the nights, a slim, dark woman with
hair like spilled midnight.

He said nothing to Dobe of her, because she was Comanche and therefore enemy. And by fall he had yet to see
one of her kinsmen in the flesh. Telegraphs clicked and
couriers brought news, commanded changes. Major Gordon
and his unit rode south to take up positions at Fort Clark
near the Rio Grande. Captain Richards and the scouts were
left behind.

"New regiment coming," Richards said. "Black troopers
and white officers—the Fourth Cavalry."

"*Blacks?*" Walker was stunned.

"Thought you'd better know. Colonel Randall Mackenzie
is commanding, and he's cold and hard. But Grant has

given him a free hand. Now, bigod, the Comanches will catch hell."

"With blacks," Walker muttered. "Freed slaves."

"I'm thinking they'll fight harder, to prove themselves. Under a proper commander like Mackenzie, they soon will."

When they were alone, Dobe said, "You fixin' to quit account of the niggers?"

"You?" Walker said. He had considered quitting, him and his enlightened ways.

Dobe scratched his straggly beard. "Don't make me no never mind, and the Tonks is stayin'. The cap'n talked hisself into soldierin' under Mackenzie, but he's got hisself a reason."

"I've been thinking on California," Walker said; he'd also thought of equality and humans, whatever their color.

"Who ain't? But it's either clear back to Galveston and ship around the Horn—which I ain't got the money for, nohow—or circle around through Mexico, then up into Arizona Territory and acrost. There's a shit pot full of Comanches atwixt here and yonder, and I'd as soon keep what hair I got."

"Careful man might slip through," Walker said.

"Might not, and you don't get no second whack."

"Black troopers."

Dobe grinned. "Injuns call 'em Buffler soljers, account of their woolly hair. And them Tonks ain't what you'd call pure-D white."

"All right," Walker said. "I'll get along."

He found that the black 4th Cavalry might have been raw when it started out, but by the time it reached Fort Concho, the men were tough horse soldiers. Mackenzie looked and acted like a spit-and-polish martinet, but all he cared for was results. His men were dirty and loosely disciplined, but they could ride and shoot.

When they came into the fort, easy in the saddle and travel stained, Walker blinked in surprise, for back in the remuda of extra mounts rolled the supply wagon, and riding its high seat were two civilians, one of them a woman. He continued to stare while they were helped down by a white lieutenant.

Dobe elbowed him. "Close your mouth afore somebody tethers a horse to your tongue."

The sight of a woman, however homely and bedraggled,

set Walker back on his heels. She was a reminder to him that he had no direction to his life. He smiled ruefully; he'd never been much on direction anyway, but he was getting older. Ever since he had left Fairbairn Plantation, he'd let women pay his way. Most men looked down on that kind of life, and some were envious.

Watching the woman being escorted to headquarters, Walker thought she might not be homely at that. Dusty and tired she was, and seemed shaken by more than an arduous journey. The civilian with her clumped along behind, carrying what could only be a Bible.

"Preacher," Dobe grunted. "Just what we needed. Reckon she's his lawful wife?"

A black sergeant swung down from his horse. "You all scouts?"

Walker didn't answer; he just wasn't used to seeing that color in uniform. Dobe said, "Reckon so; ain't there none with your column?"

"Tonks," the man said it spitefully. "They didn't get us to the train 'til it was flat burned out; nobody kickin' except the preacher and his sister. Lucky they got crammed under an upside-down wagon. Might be the colonel means to go after the band that hit 'em, and he'll need scouts."

Walker said, "We'll be here."

And Dobe added, "He'd go chase injuns after a long trail?"

The sergeant's teeth flashed white in his black, dusty face. "Ol' colonel—he don't give a damn about tired or wore out or whichever. Regular ol' piss cutter, the colonel is. Don't give a damn about garrison soljers or pee-rades neither."

"Be a change," Dobe said.

The woman's name was Charity, the preacher Martin Luther Crawford. She was some thirty years old and un- married—not a widow woman, just not ever married. When she was cleaned up, her hair was kind of brown and kind of dull yellow. It was hard to tell, she pulled it back in such a tight bun.

Hard to make out her eyes too; Charity didn't look up much. It seemed like she stared mostly at the tips of her shoes or the Bible, but when Walker did catch her eyes wandering, they were colored greenish brown. She'd got out of the massacre with one other dress besides the one on her straight and narrow back.

Every night Walker saw one dress or the other drying

on a clothesline—cleanliness next to Charity. He only got introduced to her offhand, because white scouts and Tonks rated about the same to Colonel Mackenzie. He figured they ought to be in uniform for five dollars a month and proud to take it. Dobe and Walker opted for their contract twenty dollars.

Mackenzie didn't take to the trail right off, so Martin Luther Crawford got to preach some to them in the stables, Walker and Dobe and their Tonks, with eighteen other Indian scouts thrown in. The hayloft was crowded.

"Don't know where'n hell he scraped up them Tonks," Dobe muttered. "Must for certain be last of the tribe, and ijuts at that."

"Smart enough to slip out when Martin Luther Crawford goes to hell-firin'," Walker said.

"Pull up the loft ladder and they sleep in the corral," Dobe suggested. "If'n we got to set through brimstone and damnation, they got to suffer somehows too."

Fort Concho became a whirlwind of training, but as the sergeant, Abel Greenlee, said, the more than two hundred troopers of the 4th Cavalry didn't polish or parade. They worked out on the plains, riding and shooting, shooting and riding. Former post commander Major Gordon would have been shocked at their appearance, but then Mackenzie would have turned him into the same kind of fighting man or shipped him out.

And while the troopers sweated, Walker found time and excuses to approach Miss Charity Crawford. She was flustered at his present of Swinburne's poems, that slim and dog-eared volume he'd packed from home. But in a day or two, she was eager to discuss them with Walker.

They had been sent to spread the word to the heathens, sent from Missouri, and she still had a gentle distrust of southern cavaliers. But she was also trembly at being paid such attention. When she flushed, she was almost pretty, and Walker paid her compliments just to see the blood rush into her face. There was precious little else he could see of her, swathed in her dragging dresses, high collared and long sleeved.

Captain Richards stood frowning at the loft ladder to talk to Walker about her. "She's a good and simple woman, Fairbairn."

"Yes."

"Well, damn it—what are you intentions, man?"

Walker shrugged. "Intentions? I wouldn't know."

"You're trifling with Miss Charity."

"Not yet—not really."

Richards propped fists on his hips. "I'm warning you—don't."

"She's a woman grown—more than ripe, I'd say—and knows her own mind. Wouldn't you say so, captain?"

"I've had my say." Richards spun and slammed off, boots kicking up spurts of dust across the unused parade ground.

"You got the red ass?" Dobe asked. "Won't do to crowd him too far. Kind of eyeballin' the lady hisself."

"He's a good man," Walker admitted. "Maybe I've been too long hemmed in this fort, and maybe I don't cotton to the belief that every woman is sweet and pure. Cavalry officers notwithstanding."

"Well," Dobe said, "you about to get cured of tepee fever; troop's cinchin' up to move north, all but a few for sick-and-sorry garrison. You 'n' me get to lead off with Saba and Fleabite, and the other Tonks out on the flanks."

"Doesn't give me much time then," Walker said.

Because the post was in an uproar of getting ready for a long trek with no announced destination, Walker found more opportunity to be alone with Charity. Riding with her beyond the stockade, he drew up their horses at a little spring he knew. A few late wild flowers nodded there, unbrowned by frost. They couldn't see the post, and the grass was soft, the spring peaceful; a mockingbird sang in a cottonwood sapling.

When the horses were tied, Charity knelt uncertainly and sipped daintily of cold water. He stood watching her, far from English drawing rooms, farther yet from a plantation ballroom, but the setting didn't matter. He helped her up by an elbow, and when he turned her, she came easily, suddenly into his arms and against him.

Charity's lips were stiff and compressed, but she didn't pull away, and his hands gently stroked her back, her hips. Slowly, her lips parted, softened, and inside her tremulous mouth was spiced with quick, light honey.

"Oh!" she said, and he smothered all else. She was pliant against him, weak and shuddering. Her other wordless murmurs broke gasping against his teeth, and she flinched wildly at the first seeking of his tongue.

But he held her, not roughly, and Charity stopped struggling, if her movement was truly struggle. When he brought her to the yielding grass she was shivering as if she had caught a chill, but her flesh was warm, warm.

He was tender with her, careful and gentle with her, and when she would have fought away in a last moment of righteousness, she was impaled and it was too late. Then she loved him hard, hard, her slim body writhing and heaving, as if she meant to crowd in all the loving she'd missed through her thirty-some-odd virgin years.

Clenching him, imprisoning him fiercely, she cried out softly, and again, and yet again in the throes of unleashed passion. And when the bursting waves had rocked them both together, she lay flat, as if everything was drained from her. Charity's head swung from side to side as she panted, "Lies; they told me lies, lies."

It was a while before she could get up and sort out her clothing, brush her skirt and bodice into respectability. Somehow her hair had fallen loose and she had to repair that also. Face flaming, she did not look around at Walker until he kissed the nape of her neck.

Then she said quietly, "I love you. You don't have to say it back. I just want you to know."

He started to say something, but she sensed it wasn't what she wanted to hear, so she reached up and put her fingers softly against his lips.

CHAPTER 32

Quint had placed his first mate and the passenger in irons. The two ordinary seamen had made good their escape and were now lost in Galveston's crowds.

When he rode ashore with Tosanna in the captain's gig, her baggage was with them, the trunks bound securely now, her money safe for the moment.

"I'll be taking Mister Krale back to England," he said, "for there I'm certain of his fate, Yank or no. He'll be punished alongside Mister Johnson, and thoroughly, I vow. Lass, are you as certain of your safety on this wild frontier?"

Tosanna said, "I'll be heading west soon as I can buy a rig and hire a driver." She watched two oarsmen put their back into moving the gig for shore. Through the salt sea odors, she caught faint scents of land and growing things. She was coming home. Never had she been to this place where she would see so many *tejanos,* but it was her land too. From here she could walk to Comancheria if need be, behind mules carrying her precious freight.

Quint signaled down a trap for hire and saw her trunks loaded. You're a brave and headstrong lass," he said. "May the saints guard your road." To the driver he said, 'The Wentworth Hotel." His strong hand was warm upon her own. "If ever you return, you'll be most welcome aboard the *Mary Frances.*"

"Thank you," she said, and it was like leaving an old friend behind, or a father. She didn't look back at the docks, but ahead to the sprawling, busy city.

Around her trap swirled White Eyes and blacks; no Britons, these, but *tejanos*, deadly enemies to The People. She saw blacks working among them and understood they were no longer slaves, but freedmen like her driver. And twice as the buggy moved slowly through noisy, crowded streets she recognized Indians squatting against buildings, begging. Lipans or Tonkawas, she thought, ruined by white man's whiskey; no Comanche would be seen thus.

The Wentworth Hotel was nothing like English inns, and especially below posh London hostelries. She had to smile at herself, realizing how much she had changed, knowing also that soon she would be in a harsh, unforgiving land, among people who knew no luxuries such as those offered to whites who could pay for them. The Kwehar-enuh would scorn them, even if they knew.

She had her story ready. It was one part Belle Williams and one part Captain Quint. She was Susanna Morgan, a nurse just come from England carrying medical supplies for the frontier in general and Fort Griffin in particular, near the Brazos reservation. Yes, thank you, she did understand the dangers of the road, but she had her sworn duty to uphold. And besides, her brother was there—Major Justin Morgan; did anyone know him?

They did not. Men were curious and helpful; some were curious and predatory, but she put these off with smiles and vague promises. To a doctor who became interested, she pretended great shyness, and pretended she could read labels on additional medical stores he insisted she would need.

Tosanna surprised herself, playacting. To *tejanos* she seemed a bit alien, but dedicated and cool. Inside she was spinning with emotions, some difficult to control when she heard stories of bloody massacres by Indians, when she heard Texans rail against their chiefs and promise even bloodier vengeance. They cursed Washington, their own army, and Indian commissioners; mostly they bitterly damned the Comanches. She managed to hold a serene face, when all her instincts demanded she shriek the truth at them—that all this land belonged to The People and all others trespassed. Of course the tribes fought; it was their due, their way of life. And now they battled for something more: to hold back the flood of *tejanos* who would kill all the buffalo and put the great grasslands to the plow. They were fighting to live.

She had a stroke of luck when she found a teamster with room in his wagon for her and her luggage. He was Ned Barstow, the first black she knew personally. Her white acquaintances were angry when she told them, and insisted it was unthinkable, a lady riding so far with a *nigger,* alone and unprotected. Tosanna listened and nodded and, when she was ready to leave, departed at night with Ned Barstow and his loaded wagon.

Nobody would recognize her easily; she wore buckskins and a slouch hat with her hair up inside it. She wore a Navy Colt at her side, the knife in her boot, and carried a Spencer carbine.

Come daylight, when they were well out from Galveston and autumn winds brought the smell of prairie to them, Ned Barstow said, "Sure don't look like no lady. Look like a buffler hunter, only you too clean."

She glanced at his dark, heavy face, at the sprinkling of gray in his woolly hair. She wasn't afraid of him, nor of the country around them. At the wagon's tailgate, two saddle horses were tethered, canteens slung around the horns, victuals in saddlebags, ready to run.

"Ain't heard of injuns hittin' hereabouts," Ned said, "but I stayed alive this here long by bein' carefullike."

He kept the team moving all through each day, driving until just before dark. The first few nights out, he built fires and Tosanna prepared food. Later on, when they had passed through the small town of Austin, Ned stopped driving earlier and started later in the day, so flames wouldn't be as easily seen.

When they fell in with a wagon train heading for Fort Mason along the Llano River, he suggested she keep out of sight as much as possible. When curious freighters approached, she took to the wagon bed with fever. They not only respected that, but gave the wagon a wide berth.

"Whole lot more folks comin' than goin'," Ned said when they peeled off for Fort McKavett. "Gettin' clost to Comanche Trace, and wish to the good lord we wasn't. Wagon alone like this ain't got a chance."

"Have you ever been attacked?" she asked, eyes sweeping the jumble of ridges around them, searching for some landmark.

"No'm, and ain't fixin' to be, can I help it. I trades some with the Comanch, but I ain't no real Comanchero.

Even if I ain't got much of a scalp, it sure gets uneasy any time I'm clost to any Comanche buck."

She knew the wagon carried mostly foodstuffs and some cloth, blankets and ammunition, but no arms besides what they had. Her few real medical supplies and her trunks rode back there, fair loot for any daring warrior on horseback.

The People had only a faint idea of money, she thought; they were as children about it, but she hoped to change that, show them what arms and food could be bought with gold and silver and green paper.

Maybe she could convince the council to move her band even farther north and break contact with all *tejanos,* all White Eyes. They could deal for trade goods and guns through some Comanchero and continue to live in the old way, the good way, far from white men and their awesome powers.

Tosanna sighed. She knew better. The People followed the buffalo and were fiercely jealous of their domain. They were proud of their skill and fearlessness in war. She might help the Kwehar-enuh in some few things, but much blood would have to flow before they realized the overwhelming strength they faced, before they allowed themselves to be herded onto a reservation.

From Ned Barstow she learned of reservations and the weak men who ran them in the name of the white father. "Lord, lord," he said, snapping the reins along the backs of his mules. "Them pore men means well, I reckon, but that don't help none. Comanch thinks they're scared and buyin' 'em off with presents. Soljers gets after 'em, they go lickety split for the reservation and bluecoats can't touch 'em. For them as *wants* to stay off the warpath, the agents gives shoddy blankets and shorts 'em on rations and such. Ever do get all the Comanch to settle down, they'll just hunker over and die, I guesses."

Tosanna looked at the sky. "Winter is coming, the time of snows. Many Comanches will be high in the Llano Estacado."

"Yes'm, but how'd you know that?"

She covered her slip. "Things my brother told me, wrote me."

She spoke of England to him, and he told her what it was like to be a slave. Ned wasn't bitter about his past and was eager for his new life on the plains. "No better

place to get started. Got me a wife—pretty yellar woman—
and got me two boys by her. Don't usual go down far's
Galveston or San Antone, but with all the injun troubles,
stock's gettin' plumb hard to find any closer. I swony, the
army don't do somethin' about the Comanch, ain't goin'
to *be* no western frontier."

"The—Indians haven't bothered you or your family?"

Ned shook his head. "Had me some fair dealings with
'em, and I reckon they trusts me like I trusts them. Bought
my own wife back from 'em onct. That don't mean some
youngun won't get likkered up and lift my hair just for
fun. Don't have to be redeye neither—just a young buck
out to count coup."

Twice along the road groups of horse soldiers passed
them, dusty and tired-looking men who spared few words
for a black's sutler wagon. One officer did warn Ned that
a war party had been tracked this far and wished them
luck. He took no note of Tosanna.

"Seen this ol' Sharps rifle of mine," Ned grinned, "and
figured certain you a buffler hunter. Them buckskins gettin'
about ripe enough."

Real hide hunters didn't think so, when their four piled-
high wagons came rattling and bumping up to where
Tosanna and Ned were camped by a little spring. That was
her fault; she'd washed her hair and it hung long down
her back, certainly no man's. When she tried to cover it
with her hat, she was a shade late.

"Well, sir," the hunter said, "looka' here what we
come up on out in the middle of nowhere. Got us a nigger
and a white woman—ridin' together, bigod."

He was big bellied and red-faced behind a scruffy beard,
long Sharps buffalo rifle cradled in his arms. The skinners
were all alike, filthy blackened buckskins, lean and whis-
kered, beady eyed. It was hard to tell them apart as they
climbed down and beat dust out of their hats against their
thighs, as if they were going through some kind of ritual.
All stared at her.

"Missy's wagon," Ned said, bobbing his head and twisting
his hat in his hands. "Just drivin' missy's wagon for her,
suh. Usta' be her daddy's nigger and now her'n, suh. Us
totin' potions and such to the soljers, to my missy's brother.
Yall know Major Morgan, suh?"

Big Gut stepped down and looped his horse's reins
through a ring on the wagon gate. Tosanna caught the

sickening odor of green hides, and the four skinners came up to stand in a half-circle and nudge each other.

"Don't know no damn soljer boy," Big Gut said. "Ain't on speakin' terms with no injuns nor niggers either."

"Yes, suh," Ned murmured, twisting his hat. From where she stood, Tosanna could see a dull wink of firelight on the brass and wood butt of the derringer Ned had in the hat. Would it come to that? They were outnumbered and outgunned.

Big Gut said, enjoying his role, "Don't 'pear to be no southern lady to me; 'pears like you just a lil' split-tail got you a nigger stud in the blankets."

Tosanna spoke for the first time. "Let us be and drive on."

"Listen yonder," Big Gut chuckled. "Sounds like fancy baggage, don't she?"

"Missy," Ned said quietly, "ain't no need for you to—"

She silenced him by slowly peeling the buckskin shirt over her head. She heard the concerted gasp when they all stared at her naked breasts, and felt the stir as they leaned at her. All but Ned; he stood where he was, the little belly gun secret in his doffed hat, and there was a sickness in his eyes.

But they were all staring at her exposed breasts and her cascade of hair as she let it fall. Nobody was watching her right hand, and it came up with the Navy Colt. Big Gut was reaching out for her when she shot him. He jerked once, gone goggle-eyed at the pistol in her fist. When he tried to fumble his Sharps around, Tosanna shot him again and slid aside to aim at the skinners.

Ned already had the derringer on them, and Tosanna barely stayed her trigger finger. They were immobile in shock, eyes rolling. Only one carried a rifle in his hand; he dropped it as if the metal seared his fingers.

"Don't shoot!" he gobbled. "Oh, Jesus—don't shoot!"

"You would have taken turns on me," she said through her teeth. "You meant to kill Ned for being black and me for being with him, and then you'd steal our wagon and stock. Why shouldn't I kill you?"

On the ground Big Gut made a funny noise and stopped kicking. She didn't waste a glance on him.

Another skinner kept his hands carefully out from his sides, and that interested her; she couldn't see a weapon. That one said, "Might of been what Bettis there had in mind, but he paid for it. We're spang in the middle of Comanche country, missy, and if'n they heard them shots and seen this here fire, *all* our scalps is about to swing on lodgepoles."

Tosanna said, "I don't know—"

And sharply, Ned said: "Don't!"

The little gun went *pop! pop!,* and the man who'd been talking staggered, the big knife skidding across the fire and banging into the wagon wheel instead of her belly.

Another handgun went off and Tosanna threw a shot in reply. The skinners faded into darkness, dragging the wounded man with them. Red flashes leaped from the night, and Ned jumped to kick apart their cookfire, scattering its coals. "Get down, missy!"

When he rolled under the wagon with her, he packed the hunter's Sharps and the other man's breach-loader. Staked away from the wagon, their mules and saddle horses stamped nervously. Ash and embers smell reached her, and the drifting of gunsmoke. When there was no more shooting right away, Ned poked out a rifle barrel and secured her shirt. She wriggled into it.

He whispered, "Mighty smart, makin' 'em eyeball you thataway. It's certain sure them men didn't mean us no good."

She listened to the night. "They are not leaving. I think they're circling us." On her side, she fed fresh cartridges into the Colt, her eyes trying to pierce the darkness.

"Won't back off account they wants our goods, and blood too."

Beyond their wagon, one hot coal flickered fitfully and went out. The darkness was complete, and only by squinting hard could she make out the bulk of the dead man. She heard a horse snort and thrust out her pistol, but it was only Big Gut's mount sidling up to their saddle horses, loose on his own.

Ned whispered again. "Still four of 'em, and when they gets all around us, we goin' be hard put to stay alive. We move right quick, could be we can reach the horses and light a shuck."

"Everything you own is in this wagon," she murmured. "All I have too. I will not run."

He sighed. " 'Fraid of that. Look yonder to the ridge. Moon's risin' to make us better targets."

No horse shifted its weight; no mule crunched in its feedbag. Ground chill crept in upon them, making Tosanna wish for blankets in the wagon and beyond reach. Eyes constantly moving, she searched the land around them as the moon rose high and full. It was huge and round and yellow, casting long shadows before it, lighting up the countryside.

A Comanche moon!

"Stay quiet," she hissed to Ned Barstow, and snaked from beneath the wagon, bellying where the skinners wouldn't expect her, moving directly for their wagons drawn up in a line. Mules at the first wagon were tired and head-hanging, paying no mind to her as she unhooked trace chains, muffling their sounds as best she could.

Comanche Moon. She pulled herself longways under their wagon, almost choking at the stench of green buffalo hides. A mule in the second bunch made a half-hearted kick at her, but she got her work done. She didn't dare go any farther and run into a skinner. Hunkering down, pistol balanced in her hand, she filled her lungs and let out a long ululating shriek—the war cry of a Comanche warrior.

When she slapped mule rumps, one team broke aside and shouldered the first team as they thundered past, chains rattling and harness dragging. A man yipped a curse, and somebody fired a shot that didn't come near her. Crying out again and again, Tosanna moved back toward her own wagon in the dark, loosing random shots from her Colt.

When she piled in beside Ned, he breathed, "Lord, lord! We atwixt a rock and hard place now for sure. Save one bullet for your ownself, missy; don't let them Comanch take you."

She felt a crazy laugh building up in her throat. All was chaos around them—two teams of mules bucking and whistling off in the night, skinners fighting the other teams and each other for what safety their wagons might offer. Adding to the confusion, they fired blindly in the darkness, stopping only when one wagon started to roll, its driver cursing steadily in a high voice. The remaining wagon clattered after, leaving more panicked shots in its wake.

Only then did Tosanna laugh. Hammering the earth with one fist, she laughed so hard her throat hurt.

"Missy, missy—for the lord's sake! What you doin'?"

"Don't you—don't you *know?* Oh Ned, Ned—I fooled them, scared them into running like children! I—I—cut mules loose and screamed like—like a Comanche, and—and—"

He clamped one callused hand roughly over her mouth. "Hush; hush now and look out yonder in that open patch where the moon's so bright."

She stared. A cluster of men on horseback stood motionless in the clearing, moonlight raining orange and silver upon their bodies, upon horses so well trained that none moved a muscle.

Ned's whisper was thin and hopeless: "See 'em, missy?"

She saw them clearly now.

Comanches!

CHAPTER 33

They'd been so long in the saddle Walker felt nailed to it. Clear across to New Mexico Territory, where they'd picked up supplies, one night trying to get his legs unkinked, then off again. The new colonel meant business and was trying to pin down Comanches before they stored meat for the winter.

Trouble was two hundred troopers and a score of Tonk scouts at Mackenzie's back hadn't found so much as a hunting party that didn't fade swiftly into the hills. Walker credited the man, though; he could be issuing orders from Fort Concho, safe and warm, while the outfit hunted trouble. A hard, cold, and dedicated man, this young officer, innovative and afraid of nothing—be that Indians, public opinion, or his superiors.

And also back at the fort, Charity Crawford waited eagerly. Walker eyed a stony ridge ahead and stepped down from his horse to tether it. Off to his left, Dobe Davis also dismounted. Walker bent low and carefully climbed the hill, thinking that Charity was a mite too eager. She was a woman awakened late in life, and confused. All that giving held in so long; when at last released, it was overwhelming.

He bellied down a good way from the crest, and from the corner of his eyes saw Dobe doing the same. Damn! Here he was with possibly his life depending upon caution and alertness, and he was mulling over Charity's problem.

All right, it was also his problem, and one he'd never before considered.

For that reason he'd been glad enough to get away from Fort Concho and into the field. Already her brother was suspicious, and if that hellfire-and-holler preacher discovered the truth, he'd want Walker drawn and quartered. Bigod, Walker thought, he wouldn't put that past Mackenzie either. The man was a stern disciplinarian. What the hell would be the charge—seducing a thirty-year-old maiden?

He caught movement at a clump of Spanish bayonet and froze until the horned toad puffed its bright sack again. Drawn tight as a Comanche hunting bow, Walker let out breath and edged upward, carefully pushing his buffalo gun along packed earth.

Still, he felt uneasy about Charity; he should have anticipated a strong reaction from her. Because she had surrendered her virginity to him, she thought she was desperately in love. Maybe she was, but more probably the emotion would wear itself out, if given chance.

As his own nagging memory of Milady Savage?

Slowly, an inch at a time, he lifted his hatless head over the crest and caught his breath. There they lay beside the McClellan River, lodges of the Kutsoo-ehkuh Comanches. Beyond the tall tepees and tucked into a narrow valley made for the purpose grazed a horse herd. Walker could see smoke where women were drying meat and a busy coming and going. How many Comanches feeling smug and secure in their winter camp? He could only guess at two hundred or so—more than any man had seen and lived to tell the sight.

When he'd stared at every hilltop and seen no movement of sentry, Walker backed down his ridge and glanced over at Dobe Davis a hundred yards off, lifting one hand in a signal that meant get the hell out.

Tosanna and Charity; Indian and white woman—he had to rid himself of their bother and keep his senses fox keen. Daydreaming would get him hung head down over a fire while imaginative bucks did agonizing things to the rest of his body. It would not matter that he didn't believe in their kind of afterlife, where a mutilated enemy went through eternity as a cripple. They believed.

By the time they'd walked their horses quickly and silently away from that unguarded ridge, Walker and Dobe came together. "Never seen so many damned Comanch," Dobe said. "If'n Mackenzie catches 'em with their tally-whackers hangin' thataway, there just about won't be no tribe. Seen nary a sentry—you?"

Walker shook his head. "It's like we've been playing tag all over Texas, and they made it back to home base where they're safe."

"Home buryin' ground, more'n likely. Just keep awalkin' your horse till we're out'n earshot. Hate like hell to have some huntin' party come up on us unexpected."

Halfway back to the column, they met Saba and Fleabite coming in from the flank. Saba handtalked how they found many, many tracks, and Dobe answered agreement. The Tonkawas' naturally sullen expressions changed and they went nervously wide-eyed. Dobe said something sharp in their own language that turned them for the column.

He said to Walker: "Don't fault 'em much do they get hard to find. Them many Comanch in one pile makes my hair ride uneasy. But we don't want no Tonk slippin' up to steal a horse or two afore that camp gets stampeded. Told 'em if'n they did, I'd stake 'em out on a anthill for the Comanch to find."

While Mackenzie and his officers held powwow at the news, Walker sat his horse and ignored the venomous look Captain Richards sent his way. Charity Crawford was behind that, of course; Richards didn't weigh her as the only white woman he'd seen in a long time, but as someone special and perfect, heaven-sent. He was jealous of every minute Walker spent with her, and Martin Luther Crawford rubbed salt into his unrequited passions.

Walker guessed that Charity's brother didn't want her spoken for by anyone, but if forced to accept a match, Crawford wanted a respectable groom. In Captain Richards he'd also have an ally for his preachments to the savages; cavalry officers served the remote posts where he was driven to bring his word.

He had no intention of marrying Charity Crawford, or any woman. Besides a few pretty words and certain practiced techniques, he had nothing to offer beyond twenty dollars a month and possible quick widowhood. Maybe when and if he reached California, he'd look around, but not before.

Charity was sweet and exciting because her emotions had been bottled up so long, and she gave her body in soft, appealing wonder. She should have been married years back and settled in with husband and children. Walker imagined if her brother hadn't dragged her on his quest, she would be.

When they got back to Fort Concho, Walker meant to tell her gently, and if necessary ride out and leave her to Richards or some other officer. By now, with many hard lessons learned and a little luck, he thought he could make it cross country to California's golden promises. Had he somehow betrayed Charity? He didn't think so; there had been no promises between them, and there was a lot of intelligence behind the false front of her spinsterhood. Charity would understand.

When Mackenzie moved his black troopers out, Walker felt safe riding ahead with Dobe and their special Tonks. The Buffalo Soldiers didn't look parade ground pretty, but they didn't rattle or stray either. The colonel had whipped this regiment into damned good Indian fighters. Unkempt and unmilitary they might be, but they knew how to shoot, ride, and suffer; they had courage to spare. Walker thought this impossible a few months ago, but now he defied any white outfit to put better soldiers into the field.

Watching the hills as they rode slowly toward the hidden valley where one of the major tribes was camped, Walker frowned. If these blacks were good or better at fighting than white men, what was his long-denied prejudice? Unspoken, it had lain dormant within him until brought out by Tosanna. And she had not spoken of marriage; he had. He accepted the Tonks, slept and ate with them. At least, he was learning.

Beside him Dobe Davis stretched out a warning arm, and every horseman behind them stopped. Walker nodded appreciatively; there was no careless clank and rattle of equipment, no horse whinny. The Buffalo Soldiers were damned good, but would he invite one into the parlor?

What damned parlor in what long-gone plantation house? Out here on the plains old notions about life and society got changed. Some black troopers were better off than the son of Fairbairn Plantation. Take Sergeant Abel Greenlee; that onetime Mississippi slave was working toward bringing his family out here, once the Indians were pacified. He hoped to file on a homestead and raise cattle, crossing a starter herd on wild and rangy longhorns that roamed the hills. His black face would light up when he told his plans and bragged on his younguns.

Ah, but there was the rub, as Shakespeare and Walker Fairbairn saw it—pacifying Comanches, Apaches, and such. The tribes didn't give a damn that Greenlee had fought a war just to claim his children his own. There was no way to explain the evils of slavery to a people which enslaved captives taken on raids. They were wont to sell these women and children back to white Indian agents once they'd been passed all around the warriors for repeated rapes and sometimes torture.

Any white planter of the Old South who did that to his slaves was the worst kind of fool. But some did, Walker admitted, and just about every white boy lost his cherry to a black girl who was given no opportunity to say no. That was rape without violence, but no other name could be given it. Jesus, he was rethinking everything in his past. That might mean his future was short.

Walker looked behind and saw the 4th Cavalry quietly spreading as mounted skirmishers at the colonel's signals. He jerked his head at Dobe and the old scout padded over to join him, leading his horse. Saba and Fleabite shifted nervously, fingering their carbines.

"Best we ease out on the flank with the rest of them Tonks," Dobe said. "Might get run over when Mackenzie gives the charge."

Walker said, "Hope he waits until they're just about up the ridge."

"He will," Dobe said. "That young man ain't nobody's fool. He means to kill injuns like they never been kilt afore. If'n you and me and this pair of thieves belly down over yonder ahint them rocks, we ought to find us some targets. The Comanch will come abustin' up that gulley, lookin' for a way out."

In position, Walker sighted down the barrel of his Sharps, the long-range weapon whose heavy ball could down a buffalo bull at better than a thousand yards. Beside him he positioned the Spencer carbine, a quick-firing gun good up close, but inaccurate over a hundred yards. He also checked his Navy Colt and tucked it handy into his belt.

He was about to kill Comanches, Tosanna's people, Milady Savage's kind. Perhaps her blood kin was down there, a sister smoking meat, a brother caring for his horse.

Would it make a difference if by some dark and deadly miracle she were there herself?

Yes, damn it; he admitted that, but he'd possibly feel the same if any man or woman he knew personally was targeted in that peaceful-looking valley. It wasn't just Tosanna, but anyone, Indian, white or black.

The earth shook as the first long line of cavalrymen rode thundering over the ridge and howled down into the valley, firing as they went, raking tepees and fires and drying racks with bullets.

Walker sighted on the gully entrance as the Buffalo Soldiers ripped through the campsite and on into the horse herd. The second line roared down the slope, using handguns and sabers they'd sharpened at their last camp.

Hell exploded among the Comanches. Warriors scurried this way and that, many weaponless, stunned by surprise. Women screamed and children rolled aside from striking hooves. Walker saw sabers rise and fall, and fallen tepees flame up; the rattle of gunfire was steady. His first buck, a wild-eyed man running for his life, bounded up the gulley. The heavy slug cartwheeled him end over end. Dobe's gun went off, then Saba's; Fleabite pumped three shots fast as he could work a Spencer lever. Then all the Tonks were firing, and Walker could no longer distinguish individual shots in the crashing smoke, through Tonkawa war cries and shrieks of hurt horses.

He picked a running man and dropped him, head-shot another warrior who tried to take cover, methodically squeezed off round after round, while the valley's fiery hell lifted up to blanket him. It was easier than killing buffalo.

The Tonks jumped up and careened down the hill, scalping knives waving, yelping like so many wolves closing on prey. Walker stayed down, not using either rifle, surprised their barrels were almost hot enough to blister his hands.

When he and Dobe led their horses down into the bloody vale, the killing was all over. The burning went on at Mackenzie's order: destroy everything. All winter meat was thrown into leaping fires; cornmeal and dried berries, mesquite beans, cactus—everything was fed into ravenous flame. Robes and blankets, hides, utensils and weapons. Until only corpses and prisoners were left, the women literally tearing out their hair and sawing off fingers with rocks. It was their way of mourning.

"I make about fifty dead Comanch," Dobe said, "give or take a scalp or two. Some got away."

"Not many," Walker said, "and we've got all their women and younguns. And most of their horses; what's a Comanche without his horse?"

"Afoot and hungry, I reckon. Mackenzie means to walk them prisoners clean back to Fort Concho. He'll never get the horses back. Comanch will hit that herd, sure as shootin'."

Walker looked across the burning, stinking camp and listened to the women wail. "We didn't get off free; I can make out a score of bluecoats down, but not all dead."

"Wounded and such can ride the supply wagons back, or get tied into their saddles. Be a mighty long trip—for them prisoners too. Wisht the colonel'd do something about them Comanch horses; hoot owl guards could lose their hair."

Walker cradled his rifles. "What else *can* he do but herd them to the fort?"

"Kill 'em," Dobe answered. "Shoot ever'one."

"Jesus," Walker breathed. "That makes me sick."

"Makes Comanch walk."

Shaking his head, Walker said, "*I* couldn't give that order."

Dobe worked a plug of tobacco into his cheek. "Reckon that's how come Mackenzie's a colonel—and the likes of him ain't been too plentiful hereabouts."

Walker put his rifle and carbine in saddle sheaths and held to his horse's reins; the animal blew and trembled, spooked by the fires and blood smell. Walker moved closer to the sad huddle of prisoners. Women eyed him sullenly and looked quickly away. From Dobe's passed-on experience Walker knew the Comanche women expected rough treatment—rape, torture, and killing. It was what they would do in celebration of victory.

He looked into each face, dirtied, tear-streaked, defiant. Of course Milady Savage was not among them; she had left her people far behind, soared far above smoking tepees and stinking buff hides. Tosanna was untouched by blood and suffering, transformed into a "lady" through association and wealth. Tosanna had whored her way out of this hurting rubble.

Turning away, he saw a Tonk scout poke his rifle barrel

into a woman's back, saw the small child clinging to her stained skirts.

"Keep them together," Mackenzie called. "Captain— see to that detail. Lieutenants Smith and Brennan, take charge of the horses. Sergeant Greenlee—mount your men."

Crisp and efficient, the colonel—no nonsense. Do the job and get out. Mackenzie was hard on Indians, horses, and his men, but harder on himself. Part of his left hand was missing and other old wounds still bothered him, but he never showed pain or indecision. He'd been called a monk in boots, interested only in combat missions. He was cold and professional, and if his command didn't exactly adore him, he had the respect and obedience of his troops.

Walker pulled his horse away from the rampaging Tonks. He didn't want to see them mutilating the bodies of their ancient enemies, and the sucking sound of a scalp being torn away always unsettled his stomach.

In England they called Tosanna a princess, claimed her royalty in her own way. Her lovers should see this camp, see where their lady came from, what savage waited beneath her lovely hide.

He rode away from details being called out: horse herd guards, prisoner guards, supply wagons hauling wounded and dead wrapped in blankets. He looked around for Dobe and didn't see the old man.

Sergeant Greenlee said, "Ain't pretty, what we done. Knowin' you're just doin' back don't make it set no easier neither."

"Clearing your grasslands, sergeant," Walker said.

Greenlee took off his cap and lifted his neck bandana to pat his sweaty face. "That's gospel, hard as it sounds. Can't nothin' in God's green world stop folks comin' out here to settle. Railroad's comin', stage lines and freight lines and Conestoga wagons. Someday be cows grazin' here 'stead of buffler."

Walker said, not really knowing why, "And all the Comanches dead or locked up on reservations."

The sergeant put his cap back on and looked at Walker. "Reckon so. Folks can't ranch or farm if'n their stock gets drove off and younguns killed, houses burned. And long as *one* ornery Comanch lives, that's what he's goin' to do. He can't help it; it's just his nature."

Walker said, "As it's ours to take his land; our *manifest destiny*."

"Say what?"

"Never mind—I just can't get the smell of killing off me." He rode stirrup to stirrup with Sergeant Greenlee for a while, horses at a walk. And that also was different, for the trooper was black, so black he would have been called a blue-gum nigger in another place and time. Here he was a man and soldier, respected, a leader.

The Old South and Jeremy Fairbairn would never admit that. But the Old South was dead, and maybe the master of Fairbairn Plantation was dead too. Times changed and men changed with them or were left behind.

Was that what was happening to the Comanches?

"Seen too many troopers, too many plain folks, all boogered up by injuns," Greenlee said. "Hard to figure how come injuns do the way they do, stickin' ax handles and such up a woman's privates, or screwin' girl chillun ain't no more'n babies, or knockin' the brains out'n them same babies. That makes plain, straight-out killin' look good. Time you finds a trooper strung on a wagon wheel head down over a fire or with his eyelids cut off and staked out so he looks into the sun—well, you don't mind the smell of killin' all that much."

Walker swayed lazy in his saddle, the tension oozing from him. "And if we didn't push into their land where they get at us?"

"Hell," Greenlee said, "they'd be just as busy doin' it to other injuns."

"I know," Walker said, "it's their nature."

CHAPTER 34

Tosanna tugged Ned's hand from her mouth. In the moonlit clearing most Comanches sent horses leaping after the fleeing hide wagons, but several horses came walking to the wagon they crouched under.

In a shaken whisper Ned said, "Now us catches it. You 'member what I said about savin' a bullet, missy." He sighted along his gun barrel.

She pushed his rifle down. "No, Ned."

"Can't miss us hidin' here."

"It's all right," she said. "Stay quiet." Tosanna crawled from beneath the wagon.

"You *crazy?*" He caught at her and missed.

A Comanche warrior saw her in moonlight and jerked up his rifle.

"*No!*" she cried in Comanche, "No! I am Tosanna, daughter of Tet-Sainte, wife to Ado-eeti of the Kwehar-enuh."

A startled *hu!* broke from the man as he dropped the gun across his knees. Four others pulled up their mounts and tried to stare Tosanna's face out of the shadows. Carefully, she moved at them, making the peace sign.

"I am Tosanna," she repeated, "gone many summers from my father's tepee but returning now to my people."

"The Kwehar-enuh are far to the north," one warrior said. "We are Kutsoo-ehkuh, making war upon *tejano* buffalo hunters and all White Eyes in the land of The

308

People. I am Paruwakum, and ask how you come here, the woman of a Buffalo Soldier."

Moonlight seemed brighter, the air sharp and clean as Tosanna's hands flowed in hand talk while she spoke. "Bull Elk, I greet you and my brothers, the Kutsoo-ehkuh. That man is no soldier, but a friend, a trader. And I am not his woman. Did I not say I am married to Ado eeti? I have been far away, captive of the *inglés*, a powerful tribe that lives beyond the great waters. Now I am free and returning to my father and the man I married."

Bull Elk swung lithely down from his horse. "Tell the buffalo man to stand up; he will not be harmed."

"Ned," she said, and he came to stand beside her, drawn tight.

"Didn't know you talk Comanch, missy. Is they goin' let us go?"

"Stand quietly," she said in English. "No sudden moves." And back to Comanche which lay sweetly upon her tongue: "A dead White Eyes lies behind the wagon, and long-eared horses have been cut from other wagons, hide wagons. The Kutsoo-ehkuh will sleep warm in the time of snows. I will build my fire again, and ask my brothers to eat."

Off to their right, firing broke out, echoing back along the trail. Bull Elk's head came around and he looked up the trail, as if he had the night eyes of *tene-tua*, the fox. Men mounted behind him stirred, but he cocked his head to listen. A few more shots sounded, then no more.

He said, "We have the other wagons. The dead White Eye here—he is your coup?"

"I shot him," she answered; then, remembering custom for a Comanche woman, said, "His scalp belongs to Bull Elk; I am only a woman."

Grunting, he came closer and stared down into her face. "Your sire was a great war chief; his daughter sprang forth strong from his loins."

He had not used her father's name, and the meaning of that turned the moon cold. Comanches did not speak the name of the dead for years; it was bad medicine. She said, "My father is gone."

Other warriors dismounted now, looking hungrily at Ned's wagon, at Ned himself. Bull Elk said, "The story is told in winter lodges by spirit talkers. He was a *koeet-senko*, one of the ten greatest warriors. When he was made prisoner on the reservation, at council with *americano* long knives, his honor was blackened. They put iron on his wrists and packed him in a wagon. He sang his death song and chewed his wrists beneath a blanket, so the irons would slip off. Then he killed a Long Knife with only his hands, and was killed in turn. *Hu!* That was a fine way for a *koeet-senko* to die."

Tosanna's hands made the sign for honor, and her heart ached. "A fine death," she agreed.

One of the warriors snatched Ned's rifle, and Tosanna whirled on him, glad to be able to pour her hurt into fury: "Dog man! Would you break the word of another Comanche? Give back the rifle, or admit you were whelped by White Eyes, whose word means nothing!"

Bull Elk laughed, and others took it up as the warrior looked sheepish and returned Ned's weapon. "A true daughter of him who died in honor. We will eat with you, Last Flower."

Ned was still so shaken he wasn't much help, which was just as well. This was a woman's chore, and Tosanna did it swiftly, cooking bacon and beans and making a fried cornbread, boiling coffee which she sweetened heavily with molasses. Although there was whiskey in the wagon, she didn't bring it out. It was poison for Comanches. Though they might suspect its presence, they were too polite to ask.

After they had eaten hugely and were drinking up the coffee, Tosanna ate her own meal off to one side. She was grateful for the warming fire that no longer needed to be hidden, for the comfort of her own language after so long. She accepted her father's death in sadness and pride.

But she was glad that fresh scalps had been left on the band's horses and the mules they'd taken. Never people to drive a clumsy wagon, the Comanches had already cut loose harness and loaded the mules with buffalo hides. Around her fire, they passed the weapons gained and trifles taken from the buffalo hunters' bodies.

It angered Tosanna that she should recoil from the taking of enemy hair. That was a warrior's due, and degradation of an enemy in the other life. Comanches prized their own hair highly and never cut it, except in a period of great mourning. Why should she reject any tradition of The People? Despite her travel and years away, she was still Comanche.

Ned sidled next to her as she put more coffee on the fire to brew. "Missy, this here's some kind of miracle. By rights we oughta' been dead, but since you talk their language—"

"I speak it because I am one of them," she said.

"Lord," he said. "Lord, lord. I never guessed."

She sensed him growing distant, fearful now that he knew her blood. "Ned, I am no different. You are my friend and now theirs. If they take me north, I will buy all your goods and ask this war leader to guard you as you leave Comancheria."

She thought about Ned and his trade wagon. Very few traders dared Indian country these days with the tribes taking the warpath. A trustworthy man like Ned, bringing in rifles and ammunition, blankets and food, and all things needed to carry on the fight—that man would be worth a dozen greedy, wily Comancheros. Maybe he could put together a small wagon train and bring it to a secret point.

She touched Ned's shoulder. "We will talk of this later. Now I must speak with Bull Elk."

From him she learned of White Eye disease that decimated the Comanches worse than a hundred years of open warfare—smallpox and measles and dread illnesses of sex organs. Now there was perhaps one warrior in ten left. Any buffalo soldier, *americano, tejano,* or Mexican carried this evil medicine and must be kept from Comanche lands. It was said that even the Indian agents –who were the greatest fools ever born—even they might bring the sickness-that-kills to the reservations.

And Tosanna learned of reservations, where some bands had been pushed by Long Knives, barren lands with few buffalo and elk and deer. There the white father promised to feed them beef, if no Comanche warred on whites. Sometimes the beef and flour came; more often not. Though the *americanos* brought presents and blankets to pay The People to not make war, the blankets were fit only for horses. And because the Long Knives and agents feared Comanches so much, they also paid ransoms for any White Eye or Mexican prisoner.

That was good business, Bull Elk said. Because Long Knives or Buffalo Soldiers had no power on the reservation, war parties rode south and raided, captured as many cowardly *tejano* women and children as possible, and raced back. Then, when they tired of sport with their prisoners, they sold them.

One agent had—if Tosanna could believe this—even

brought in new rifles as presents for warriors who said they needed them for hunting. Bull Elk laughed—hunting *tejanos,* of course. The white agents were very stupid. Comanche war chiefs came to councils and put their marks on a paper saying they would not fight *americanos.* But that meant only *those* chiefs would not make war in exchange for presents. The paper bound no other Comanche who had not put his mark upon it, as Tosanna and all others knew. And naturally *tejanos* were a different tribe—not *americanos.* No Comanche would ever swear not to raid Texans; there was too much spilled blood between them.

Entranced, Tosanna listened, and when Bull Elk stopped talking, she poured him more coffee laced with syrup. "And how goes the war, my brother?"

"Good, good," he said, then frowned into his cup. "There is a Long Knife who is white chief to many Buffalo Soldiers. He brought much sorrow to the Kutsoo-ehkuh. He surprised the camp as we were laying in winter supplies and killed many warriors, carried away all women and children. He also took our horses, but we took them back the next night, stampeding the herd, and even gained some of their horses. But our women and children mourn far away in the white chief's camp. It would be very good to kill this chief, for he is a great fighter."

He drank coffee and stared into the dying fire. Around it lay other Comanches, asleep now. Ned sat back against a wagon wheel, watching. Bull Elk said then, "I think we will have to soon bend our necks to this chief Mackenzie, for only a few Kutsoo-ehkuh warriors live. If we are to get back our wives and sons, we must bring in all our captives to trade."

"Have you captives?" Tosanna asked.

"Only a few; we hoped to take these buffalo hunters, but they fought hard. Perhaps Chief Mackenzie will give us our people if we mark the paper and go to the reservation. It is not a life for Comanches."

Quietly, Tosanna said, "But it is life."

Bull Elk raised his heavy head and looked at her. Firelight reflected sadly in his eyes and bathed his bronzed face. "They come and come, the White Eyes, the *tejanos,* and Buffalo Soldiers. We kill them and kill them, and still they come. If they keep our women and sons, what becomes of the Kutsoo-ehkuh? We will have no lodges, no women upon our couches, no children to teach."

Tosanna said, "That is a sad truth, my brother. And what of the Kwehar-enuh? Have you news of them beyond my father's death?"

Growing bold, Ned eased into the firelight and offered Bull Elk a rolled cigarette. He accepted and Tosanna lighted the end with a glowing stick. Bull Elk said, 'They have signed no paper. Far in the Llano Estacado, they avoid the Buffalo Soldiers and hunt as always. I do not think they raid as much."

"Ado-eeti," Tosanna said.

He shook his head. "I know of no Big Tree. The Kwehar-enuh are led by Quanah; he is called Quanah Parker by *tejanos,* because his mother was once a White Eyes."

"Naduah," Tosanna said. "I know her."

"Yes, Naduah. She bore Nocona two more sons and a girl child. One rode at his father's side, but the other son was young for the warpath. That was before Naduah was taken."

Tosanna gasped. "Taken?"

"And not even by Chief Mackenzie's Buffalo Soldiers; the little camp of Antelopes was very unlucky. Mexicans surprised them when a war party was away. They captured Naduah and her two small children. The Kwehar enuh lost another captive only lately traded for: a Mexican woman."

That moment, Tosanna was a spirit talker, for she was shown the face of a woman seen in a painting at Hacienda de Arredondo, the Doña Ynez. At last Don Joaquin had found his wife.

To test herself, she asked, "The Mexican *jefe*—a man who wears much silver upon his saddle and breeches; a man with sunken eyes, as one who lives with death?"

Bull Elk scratched himself. "If you know, why do you ask?"

"I am sorry. What of Naduah then? Brother, I have been long away and hunger for knowledge of my people."

"A reservation Comanche said Naduah's girl child died and Naduah tried to escape with the boy. She was not lucky. She mourned her child's death as she should—tearing out her hair and slashing her arms and chanting. The *tejanos* who claimed to be her White Eye family put a guard upon her then. She would not eat or drink, and died. *Hu,* a proper wife. The reservation Comanche did not know more of the boy child."

"The Mexican *jefe*'s wife?"

"Carried back across the Rio Grande. I am sleepy now."

Tosanna brought him blankets and spread them close to the fire. She sat nearby until he slept.

"Lord," Ned murmured, "it looks strange to see 'em around our fire."

"I will speak with him tomorrow about trade," she said, and climbed into the wagon to sleep while Ned took his usual bed beneath it.

She didn't sleep right away, but stared out at far-off stars to see her father among them. Inside her head, she could hear his death song—"O Sun, you live forever, but we Koeet-senko must die; O land, you remain forever, but the Koeet-senko must fall . . ."

Ten Bears would have found no better death, and she would carry his image forever in her heart—as she would remember these saddened warriors sleeping at the fire, for they were taking their last warpath.

Biting her lips, Tosanna knew she could have told them of the power they faced, of the sure end that would be theirs—an end that might come in two summers or three, or even longer; the ending would be sure: defeat. She might have told them if she had somehow reached her tribe before now; but would they believe, could they accept?

If she spoke with the tongue of birds, as Sunhair did, they might have heard and become convinced. The Kwehar-enuh always paid attention to beautiful words.

But Sunhair was the enemy. When her first fury at him subsided, when she knew in her heart that he had not caused the death of Gordon Hammers, Tosanna had stopped hating him. She realized that the spirits chose the day for the Duke of Athol to die, with no bullet in him, but proudly. Yet Walker Fairbairn was an enemy, driven from England and now somewhere in this vast, vast land; he was White Eyes and so no friend of hers—no lover.

Restless, she turned in her blankets. Ado-eeti was her man; she was wedded to him. Was he still strong and alive, a subchief to Quanah? She must go to him, to her people, bringing goods and food, bringing her knowledge. That was important—what she knew. It was worth far more than her money, but only if her people would put her knowledge to use. If they could.

Her elation at being with her own kind was tempered by a great sadness, for in them Tosanna saw herself as she used to be, but not as she was now. When she was taken by Don Joaquin de Arredondo's party of Mexicans and mercenary Apaches, she had been a child. Now she was a woman, layered year by year with new experiences, changed by distances unimagined by Comanches, by cultures so different and difficult to understand.

As young Tosanna, she had scorned Mexicans, but Joaquin had not treated her badly, and Carlos Lopez had claimed to love her and would have helped her escape. As a child she had been fed tales of hated White Eyes, but an *inglés* had been kind to her, though he chained and sold her. Colonel Sir John Stafford had not loved her less, but loved gold more.

And what of Gordon Hammers, Belle Williams, and Captain Quint, good Englishmen? And Victoria, a very special woman, besides being Queen of England?

And where did Walker Fairbairn stand, somewhere in a clouded in-between? No man had ever moved her heart like Sunhair; no man ever would.

Because she had been exposed to these men and their cultures, she could see good and bad in all ways of life. Did that mean she could no longer be a loyal Comanche, that proudest of all plains tribes? Tosanna did not know, and that troubled her. The moon went down before she fell into fretful sleep.

In the morning, in Comanche fashion, she tended first to horses and mules, then saw to feeding men. Ned Barstow had somewhat recovered from his scare of the night and was almost friendly with Bull Elk and the others.

While she cooked, she spoke to him of wagon trains and guns, of supplies and bullets. At first he was unwilling to think of turning Comanchero. She talked to him gently, with logic. He would not be alone in dealing guns; others had long been at it. The Comanches—at least, the Kweharenuh—needed a man of truth and honor, a man of dignity to trade with them.

With his help, she dragged the treasure trunk from the wagon and showed Ned what it held. He stared and stared; when she gave him a gold bar and some yellow coins, he would have returned them to her. She convinced him they were advance payment for his next trip, but he must travel the Comanche Trace next time, and go farther north, past this Fort Concho. Word would be passed, and no man of The People would harm him and those with him.

Ned was still shocked by what he'd been hauling in his

wagon, when she conferred with Bull Elk for information. Then she told Ned Barstow where he must bring his goods —to the Brazos River, just outside the reservation there. She would meet him and make other payment. For now she would exchange a wagon of hides and its mules for his wagon. He was to keep the gold.

"You mean to drive it all the way yonder?" he asked.

"I will be safe," she said. "Even if Bull Elk's men leave at Fort Concho, as they say."

When it was settled and they were to part, she embraced Ned and kissed his cheek as the English did with close friends. He choked and turned to hide his woman's tears. She too was sad, but there was a new firmness in her, a new dedication. For better or worse, she was Tosanna, woman of the Comanches. If she must, she would die with her own.

CHAPTER 35

He damned near called her by another woman's name while making love. No woman could stand that without hurt, much less a gentle lady like Charity Crawford. The air was crisp and the ground chilled, but they lay warmed in a buffalo robe, warmed by each other's bodies.

Charity was ever more passionate, dropping the heavy shackles of her upbringing one by one. She was made lighter by the loss of each forbidden delight, turned more free and cheery. Walker had been careful with her, tender with her, leading Charity step by tremulous step through every taboo until the hard shells broke and she could leave them unmourned behind her.

But Tosanna's name lived unbidden upon his tongue, angering him, and when a man was riled, he was not a deft lover. Unless the woman was like Tosanna, who could turn more furious and yet drive her lover to dominate. With Charity there was no such bittersweet battle; she accepted and enjoyed and was more a woman for it.

Even now, with Charity's lean body pulsing hot and quivering against him, Tosanna's ghost lay between them like a knife blade. He stroked Charity's leaf-brown hair and tried to blow Tosanna's specter scent from his nostrils. Where Charity was soap and flowers, Tosanna was musk and feral. He never had to teach Tosanna; through experience, she knew it all. Damn! How could he be jealous of an Indian who made a career of being a mistress to man after man?

317

When he lay with some man's wife, he never felt jealous of the husband. There was no logical explanation for different emotions concerning Tosanna. In fact, there were many solid reasons he should forget her completely. Those reasons could be seen in a crowded barracks—one hundred and thirty Comanche captives. When soap was given those women and children, they smelled it, bit into a bar, and threw it away. Like other imprisoned primates, they squatted on the floor and picked vermin off each other. These primitives had spawned Milady Savage and their mark would forever be upon her.

Charity said, "I'd like to stay here forever with you, my darling, but it grows late and my brother—"

She didn't have to say the rest. Walker knew Martin Luther Crawford had turned suspicious of his sister's long rides with a common scout, little better than the heathens who served with him.

"We'll go," he said, leaving her the warmth of the robes while he climbed back into clothing. They never rode far from the fort, only to this spring and its glade that held so many memories for Charity, but she'd have it no other way. It was bad coming to the same place time after time; they could be easily trailed or, worse, ambushed by some patient Comanche.

She came from beneath the cover almost dressed, her cheeks pink and hair loose. She was a handsome woman, but not a beautiful one; her jaw was a shade long and her mouth narrow. But since they'd been making love, Charity's eyes had turned smoky and made up for any other lack. She'd begun walking with more womanly grace, and not looking at the ground so much. The signs were upon her for any who could read them. Charity was fulfilled and happy.

Her brother wasn't. The regiment's tamed Tonk scouts wouldn't listen to his preachings and he was duty bound to carry them to the misunderstood heathens. The miracle of him and Charity saved from a looted wagon train only proved God had a special use for their lives.

He wanted to go north and contend with Mormon Indian agents for the souls of Comanches on two large reservations there. Colonel Mackenzie would spare him no escort at the moment, for something major was in the wind.

Walker lifted his flop hat respectfully as Martin Luther

Crawford appeared at the stables to help his sister down from her horse. He stabbed hate at Walker with his eyes. "Where have you been, woman? I have needed you; the Lord has needed you and you were—off neglecting your duties. The unfortunate captives are lacking for succor and Christian understanding."

"I'm sorry," Charity said. "I beg pardon."

Stepping down to take the reins of both horses, Walker watched her shrink before her brother, saw her crawling back to some secret place with only a tiny bit of her peeping out.

Crawford said, "And you, sir—I will accept no excuse for riding unchaperoned with my sister and ward."

"I wasn't going to offer one," Walker said.

Face contorted, Crawford took a long step toward him. "Levity, sir, levity? When a good woman's reputation is at stake I will not have it, do you understand? The Lord will not countenance it!"

Walker started to move off with the horses past a couple of grinning black soldiers on stable duty. He said, "The Lord know you and him are partners?"

He shouldn't have pushed it that far. He wouldn't have if he'd known that Captain Richards was moving up on the right behind him. The soldiers laughed and Crawford's face went almost purple, veins standing out at his temples. He shook off Charity's restraining hand. "Blasphemer! Seducer! The wrath shall fall upon you!"

When Crawford caught up a hayfork, the troopers stopped laughing and Charity went suddenly pale, swaying with a hand pressed to her mouth.

"Don't be a worse damned fool," Walker said, dropping the reins. He didn't see Richards and the blow that knocked Walker to his knees surprised him.

His eyes were blurred when Crawford sprang at him with the hayfork, screaming about despoilers and evils and instrument of the devil. Walker rolled and the tines whizzed by his head. Then he saw Captain Richards and the pistol that had slapped him down. Maybe Charity screamed too, but Walker didn't hear.

Once more he seemed to be moving through slow, deep waters so clear that everything was sharpened and stood out better. If only it wasn't so dragging slow. The Navy Colt was in his hand, eared back. The first shot jerked the revolver from Richards's fist. The second shattered the hay-fork handle close to Crawford's grip on it and drove a big splinter into his arm.

Walker fired again from his knees, and twice more, as the sleepy clouds of gunsmoke hung around him. One bullet took off Richards's hat, another ripped his sword and holster belt. One .36 caliber slug snatched at Crawford's high collar, an inch from his throat.

From the stable entrance Dobe Davis said, "Great goddlemighty! And that ain't cussin', preacher. You'n the cap'n just been delivered from the lion's den—by the lion hisself."

Richards stared at his emptied hand; Crawford clutched his forearm where the splinter stood. Charity Crawford let out a soft noise and slid to the ground.

Walker stood up, going through automatic movements in ejecting brass casings and refilling the cylinder of his pistol. Dobe took a step toward Charity, but Walker said: "Captain—you might carry Miss Charity and herd the preacher to the surgeon."

Moving jerkily, Richards scooped up Charity's limp form and started across the quadrangle. Crawford followed, still holding onto his arm, face gone white as dust.

The black troopers walked off quickly. Dobe said, "Noticed that ol' he-lion kept one bite back, in case. Only got off five shots."

"They were coming at me," Walker said. "I didn't kill them. I could have, but I didn't."

"Damned near as bad," Dobe said. "Mackenzie don't hold with his own folks cuttin' down on each other. More'n enough injuns, he figures." He shook his grizzled head. "Knowed you for a good shot, but not no circus trick shooter—nor no gunslick neither."

At the water barrel, Walker dipped himself a drink. A squad of troopers came trotting around the barn, carbines at port—the guard. Its corporal halted the squad and stepped forward. "Davis, Fairbairn—what was that firin'?"

Walker told him. The corporal frowned. "Best you all come with me to the colonel. Your weapons—"

"Not likely," Dobe said, and Walker shook his head.

Hesitating, the corporal said, "Well, then," and swung his men behind them as they walked without hurry to headquarters. The adjutant, a harried young lieutenant, would have remained in the commander's office after hearing the corporal's report. Mackenzie waved him out.

It was the first time Walker had been so close to the colonel, and he was surprised Mackenzie was so young. But hard duty stamped crow's-feet around his pale eyes and lined the corners of his mouth. His hair, a nondescript color, was cropped close to his scalp and he was heavily sun-browned, up to where the line of his campaign hat divided tan from whiteness.

"Captain Richards double-timed here directly from the hospital," he said. "I have his report. Now I will have yours." His voice was flat, unemotional; his eyes did not waver.

Walker said, "Dobe had no hand in it."

Mackenzie said, "As witness then."

Dobe told what he knew, calmly and in detail. Mackenzie looked at Walker. "Many things may get a soldier killed out here—inattention, lack of discipline, lack of training, shortage of ammunition, and a careless or glory-driven commanding officer. To that list I add women. Miss Crawford would seem to have known enough misfortune, would you say?"

Walker nodded and found he'd removed his hat.

"Captain Richards did not spare himself," the colonel went on. "His report is succinct and truthful; he attacked you as Mister Crawford attacked you. You protected yourself with phenomenal shooting and saved their lives—a good thing. If any of you had succeeded in taking a life *here in my garrison,* for whatever cause, I would be forced to hang him. Is that understood?"

Beside Walker, Dobe shifted his feet. Walker said, "I can be clear of the post in ten minutes."

"Like hell," Mackenzie said. "You signed a contract, and I have need of your peculiar talents. Tomorrow I will send the Crawfords north to Fort Sill under escort of twenty Tonkawa scouts, Captain Richards, and six enlisted men."

"Hold on," Dobe Davis said. "That's purt' nigh ever' Tonk you got."

"Saving your two," Mackenzie said. At no time during the discussion had his face changed. "The less known about the coming mission, the better. You four trackers will be enough. See to your mounts and equipment. We march early."

Outside headquarters, Dobe said, "Two more like him and wouldn't *be* no injun troubles. Makes his own medicine and keeps it to hisself. Reckon he means to hit another Comanch camp?"

"Courier came in today, and the colonel's wasting no time. I'd give a pretty to know what those orders are," Walker said.

"Know when Mackenzie lets 'em out, not afore."

Walker saw a narrow shadow waiting at the far corner of the barn. "Best I say my goodbyes."

Dobe grunted. "Best you remember Mackenzie's list too."

Breathlessly she reached for him, but Walker caught her arm and led her away from the barn. Near the stockade fence he stopped and said, "Too many ears back there with all the Tonks getting ready. How do you feel, Charity? I wanted to run to you, rush you to the surgeon, but it was better Richards did that."

Her voice was soft as twilight. "I know, Walker. And I know you spared their lives more for my sake than theirs. I—I just couldn't stand the thought of you being hurt or—or killed. I'm usually far stronger than that. The guns—and so much like the—the wagon train attack—"

"You don't have to apologize," he said, kissing the top of her head in the darkness. For a long time she stood quietly, just a little piece of her body touching him. Walker felt her warmness and smelled flowers and soap.

Charity said then, "Captain Jeffcoat—he's the surgeon—assured me that both his medical and personal ethics prevent him from—from saying anything at all."

Walker put both hands on her erect shoulders, wishing he could make out more than a smudge for her face. He said, "You're pregnant."

Her voice trembled then, almost broke. "I—you—it sounds so raw, said that way. Y-you . . . don't have . . . to . . . say anything . . . else. Ever, ever. You made me no promises, Walker Fairbairn. You said so many beautiful words, but you d-didn't say you loved me—not once."

"I'm saying it now, Charity. I love you." Walker thought he probably did. If he missed the compulsive fierceness of Milady Savage, the hungry coiling of her silky-strong body, if he might never forget her mouth searing and honeyed, that was no matter. This was a good woman, an honest woman, a woman of his own kind, and he was responsible for her, for the child she carried.

"I'll go to Mackenzie and beg off this march. I'll go to Fort Sill with you, and we can be married there by the Mormon agent."

A long sigh brushed his chin like the kiss of butterflies and Charity said, "Thank you, Walker. But if you don't mind, I'd rather spend that long trip talking to my brother, preparing him and—I suppose Henry—Captain Richards too. I'm sure Martin Luther would have me marry Henry, and he *is* a fine man. I can change his mind, make him see you gave him back his life. He has never been a man of violence before, but the wagon train, the Indians—he'll be repentant and I will pray with him."

In the night her soft hand caressed his cheek. "You have your duty too."

Walker held her close and breathed the clean scent of her hair. "I'll take care of you, Charity. I don't know how yet, but I'll take care of you and—our child."

Goodbye, eyes of stormy midnight; farewell, Last Flower of the Comanches.

"I know," Charity murmured, and kissed his mouth, "Oh, I know."

They heard the measured tread of a sentry walking post and separated, moved away from the stockade wall. He kissed her goodbye on the parade ground Colonel Mackenzie had never used, and stood alone for long moments after she faded into the night.

In the barn, he went over the tough, wiry mustang he'd cut out of the remuda. The roan gelding was sound, with no splints or quarter cracks, and had an evil eye. If this was another long search-and-destroy mission, being ornery would help the horse survive.

Marriage. God, marriage. The mustang's teeth popped air where Walker's arm had been an instant ago. He delivered a full-armed swing to the ugly bastard's jaw. The gelding blinked and Walker figured they understood each other now.

Would he understand keeping and caring and cleaving only unto? The new wore off a woman damned quick, unless she was Milady Savage, celebrated whore of England's gentry.

This is what came of trailing after an unmarried woman, a good woman; damn, damn—a *virgin*. A maidenhead was the most overrated commodity in the world, and look who was buying it with the rest of his life.

He left the mustang with grain and hay and legs rubbed down with a turpentine-alcohol mixture he was tempted to drink, and climbed into the loft to go over his weapons. Two lanterns burned up near the roof beams, giving light to Davis and Saba and Fleabite. He looked a question at Dobe and the old scout said, "T'other Tonks cleared out—settin' out yonder prayin' to whatever them bastards believes in. Prayin' they catch scalps and loot without gettin' daylight let through 'em. Purty good prayin', I'd say."

Silently, Walker squatted on his heels, oiling his Colt and running a rag patch through its bore and cylinders. He didn't know exactly how he felt, scared or proud or what the hell.

Dobe said, "Never seen a shoot-out handled just that slick and bloodless, you might say."

Walker looked up. "I never asked to be a gunfighter. Before shooting up those Comanches, and before today, I only faced up to one other bunch. Hell, Dobe—I wasn't even in the war."

Dobe held up his Spencer and looked through the barrel at lantern light. His jaws worked a cud of tobacco around. "That other bunch?"

"Carpetbagger and three hired guns come to push my father off his land. It was all he had left, his land. We had it out, and I didn't know it was so damned easy."

"Killin' ain't easy, son. When you figure that way, purty soon you get to likin' it, cuttin' notches on your pistol butt and the like. And some feller comes along wantin' to hire your gun for more'n you can make in a month of Sundays, punchin' cows, and some other fellers get word how slick you are, and they plain got to test you. Then, whoever you was afore gets left out, and you ain't nothin' but a goddamn *name* and a gun."

Putting his handgun aside, Walker started cleaning the Sharps. Two rifles and ammunition for both was extra weight for his horse to pack, but one was for range and the other for firepower. He said, "What more are we now, Dobe?"

"If'n you don't know that," Dobe said, "then you got no more sense than them muley-headed Tonks yonder."

Walker didn't feel like arguing. He still felt Charity's kiss upon his mouth, the taste and scent of her. Tomorrow she would be gone in one direction, him in another, but part of him would be riding with her, inside her body, feeding and growing.

He had never thought about being a father before.

CHAPTER 36

It was a long way to the Brazos, and Tosanna learned a lot about mules as her wagon labored north. Sometimes Bull Elk or one of the other warriors shared the wagon seat with her, but more often she drove alone. Comanches scorned the slowness of White Eyes vehicles and much preferred the freedom of their horses.

But they came in from the ridges at night, to circle her camp and share her food. If some cavalry patrol spotted the wagon, Tosanna would be better off alone to explain as best she could. She would probably be accepted as white.

Good fortune rode with her, for after many days travel they saw no bluecoats, no armed band of Texans riding a vengeance trail. At her campfire, Bull Elk said this was because The People had struck everlasting fear into their weak hearts, and his men grunted agreement.

She'd forgotten just how proud and arrogant Comanches were. They sneered at a wagon, but when the tribe had anything to move, it went horseback or was dragged clumsy on a two-pole travois. Comanches hadn't gotten around to inventing—or accepting—the wheel as yet.

Tosanna didn't say this to them, of course. She was a mere woman, and her advice would not be heard unless she managed to have the council give her a seat and encourage her to speak. That didn't happen often, but it happened.

She glanced up at the sky as her mules plodded along and, besides the hawk circling high, saw the coming of winter. Although days were still warm, the smell of fall lingered in shadows, and nights were crisp. Her own band would be settling in about now, safe in the far reaches of the Llano Estacado.

Hers would be a tremendous homecoming, a cause for wild rejoicing, for she would be greeted as one who had returned from the dead. She would be praised as good medicine, an omen of luck for tribal ventures; and as daughter to a great former chief, her medicine would be even stronger.

So when she told her story and made her warnings, the Kwehar-enuh would listen. But would they abandon the warpath because she told them of the White Eyes' unlimited power? Tosanna watched the lonely hawk drift behind a hilltop and thought not. The old ways were the only ways; what had been would always be. That was sad and lonelier than high cold wind through the hawk's feathers.

When she made camp beside a water hole that night, as she gathered dry mesquite for her fire, she thought of Sunhair, also gone home. His father's only remaining son, he would be gladly taken back. She couldn't picture the big Fairbairn house, but thought it might be something like hotels in London, or perhaps only a little smaller than Windsor, where she had spoken with a most powerful queen. Neither could Tosanna see an image of Walker Fairbairn as a farmer, even one who hired others to turn the earth for him.

Since she was never to see him again, she put him from her heart and busied herself with supper. Soon Bull Elk rode in and dipped grimed fingers into the pot, laughing and making wet noises as he ate. They had chased a deer for sport that day, he said, and he'd counted coup on it when it reeled desperate and tired, not killing the animal, just touching it, which gave him much honor. Not equal to touching an armed enemy with his hand or coup stick, but honor nevertheless. Even worn out, deer were quick and agile.

She listened to them, these men of another band that were like her own tribe. They were happy as so many English children on an outing and as full of jokes. But they were deadly, changing in an instant to the best, most fearsome horsemen in the world. And a victory campfire would be a site of torture as they sought to humble their captives, or disgrace them in the next life.

The white man didn't understand; he called it savagery, and perhaps it was. But whites were hardly better, shooting down Comanche women and firing tepees with children inside. If White Eyes did not actually torture their captives, they were cruel in other ways. The English forced small children to work long and hard in factories for just enough money to keep them from starving, holding them there to die of lung fever.

And Comanches never held a woman so low that she had to sell her body to any man with the price.

That night Bull Elk asked her to sleep with him. Carefully and politely, she declined. It was her medicine, she explained, to remain without a lover until taken again into her tribe. She did not dare violate her oath until then.

Bull Elk understood and shrugged it off. If he had been English, *tejano,* or Mexican, he might have tried to rape her; a Comanche warrior did not take a Comanche woman against her will. That was unheard of, so others in his small war party only teased Tosanna about her enforced chastity and predicted a sore back for her beloved when she was among the Antelope band once more.

When they reached the extreme northern rim of their territory and turned edgy over signs of Long Knife patrols, Tosanna made a grateful speech and gave many presents. She looked after the Kutsoo-ehkuh riders until they faded from sight, and was lonely again. No hawk, no vulture traveled the cool blue sky as her mules plodded ever toward the Brazos. Tosanna felt better when she saw a remembered outcropping, a line of hills she had known before, and excitement began to bubble within her.

The air tasted better, somehow cleaner and spiced with pine and chaparral. She had been so long away and so long alone that she badly needed the strength and familiarity of her own tribe. Clucking to the mules and flipping the long reins against their stubborn backs, Tosanna urged them to move faster. Waving their long ears, the mules caught a little of her anxiety and lengthened their stride.

She respected mules now. They would never work beyond capacity, like a horse. Neither would they overeat and founder, and if mules were put at some trail they considered too dangerous, nothing short of outright torture could move them. Even then they would nurse a grudge until their driver became careless; then they would do their damndest to take off his head with one swift kick or a sudden snap of big yellow teeth.

Tosanna meant to hold this pair when they brought her home. Some women would want to eat them, but they would be worth more to the tribe alive; with the wagon, they could draw loads of guns and ammunition Ned Barstow would bring to sell.

The sun was tiring and hanging low over the mountains when Tosanna saw a thin spiral of smoke rise to her left, to be answered later by a similar column to her right. She had been seen, and soon Kwehar-enuh scouts would come galloping. Driving the wagon ahead to where upsloping ground turned rocky and without a trail, Tosanna halted the mules and stood tall on the wagon seat to look over a narrow box canyon with brush thick across its mouth. A wagon could be hidden there, its tracks smoothed out and sagebrush moved and replanted.

She climbed back into the wagon and removed her man's clothing, getting into a dress and shaking her hair free. Tosanna replaced her boots, though, and the pistol belt rode her hip; the Spencer rested easy in her hand. And, of course, she kept her skinning knife handy.

Cool wind ruffled her hair as she walked several paces from the wagon to stand out in the open where she could best be seen. Soon her own people would come; soon she'd be where she belonged, no longer alone, an object for pointing fingers and whispered tales.

Then why did she feel this sense of loss? It might be because she was putting so much behind her—new things good, comforting softnesses and exotic tastes, a few men who spoke to her as an equal and respected her as such. And Sunhair—never again would she know the strong-tender clasp of his arms, the feel and flavors of his pale, smooth skin. Through all her life, she would never forget Walker Fairbairn; it would be easier to ignore the sun itself.

Tosanna felt rather than heard them coming and lifted her rifle over her head with both hands. They angled in from two directions, leaping their horses from cover to close on her. Three riders thundered from the near ridge, low over their horses' necks; two darted from Tosanna's right, whooping and shaking rifles.

She knew a wild surge of pride at how well they rode,

man and horse close akin, smooth and quick and daring. Her people, The People, and none other could compare.

When she put down her Spencer and made the peace sign, the riders swerved horses around her, so close that she smelled sweet-sharp animal sweat and was brushed by flying tails.

When they wheeled to face her again, she cried out: "Breaking Man!—Deep Water!—Wrinkled Face!—my friends, oh, my friends! And is that you, Eagle Tail?"

For a confused moment, Tosanna thought they were about to spin away, shaken by sight of a ghost, by the power of their superstitions.

"Masitawtawp!" she called. "Has Clawed Shield grown the heart of a woman?"

He stared hard, then swung off his horse and ran to her, arms spread wide. "Tosanna! Is it true? Have the spirits given you back to us? Tosanna!"

She was roughly against him then, feeling the slabbed muscle beneath Clawed Shield's buckskins, knowing the once familiar smoky odor of man and hides. This was one of her childhood friends, and how she welcomed him now. Clawed Shield—the boy who played jokes and laughed at himself, laughed even at the great bear which almost killed him.

Breaking Man took her away from Clawed Shield, whirling her about in a crazy dance while he chanted an exultant song she'd never heard. They passed her from hand to hand, cavorting, sometimes yipping in high excitement. The Antelope band warriors felt her arms, her legs, fanned gentle fingers over her face and pulled at her clothing, making certain she was real, not some bad medicine specter.

Tosanna was dizzy when they allowed her to settle down. She smiled at each in turn, into snapping black eyes and weather-hardened faces so happy for her. "My brothers," she said, "I thank the spirits for bringing me to you."

"This tepee-that-moves of the White Eyes; how came you by it, and what does it hold?" Breaking Man asked.

Tossana said, "Ado-eeti, my husband—does he live?"

They glanced at each other, and Clawed Shield said, "That one was betrayed by *tejanos;* now his lodge mourns. And your father—"

"I know of Ten Bears," she said, and they frowned at her for calling the name of the dead. Inside Tosanna an emptiness grew, a dry aching, and she realized she had been expecting this, should have known Big Tree was dead, from the first time she could not recall the details of his face.

But Sunhair's image had gotten in the way. Sunhair, one with the blood of those who killed her father and her husband to be. And how many others, lord of the White Eyes? How many others, spirits of the Comanches?

In that sudden change of mood inherent to the Kwehar-enuh, the warriors yammered questions at her and chuckled over many answers. Certainly the wagon should be hidden, and since no one dared ride here but their own band, it would be secure. But Tosanna had to convince them to help bury the money trunk; digging holes was not man's work.

They found room on their horses for presents and food, and Tosanna only looked back once as she rode off on one mule and led the other. Climbing in the forbidding Llano Estacado, her mount picked his way better than Comanche horses, and the other mule gave no trouble. She topped a ridge and looked down, thrilling to the sight of winter camp, tepees spread along the banks of the Brazos River, smoke lifting thinly, children scooting here and there among drying racks.

It made her think of that long-ago day when she'd picked mesquite beans and took a cleansing dip into a spring. They were little more than children then, all those killed around her.

But below lay all the strength of the Kwehar-enuh, where Apaches and Mexicans would never venture. This was the valley stronghold no enemy had ever seen. Here the tribe wintered fat and safe; here spirit talkers and medicine men retold the ancient sagas of blood and glory; here husbands lay with their wives and hoped for sons to be born in the time of the sun. Life was good in winter camp if hunting had also been good, and no belly would go empty, no old one shiver for lack of buffalo robes.

Whooping, the warriors raced downslope, led by Clawed Shield. She followed at a more sedate pace, held back by the mule she led. When she reached the river, the entire Antelope band gathered to greet her. When she returned greetings and hugs, her heart was sad for Ten Bears and Big Tree.

She knew none of the small ones, and had trouble recognizing any younger than herself. But she remembered each respected elder and spoke humbly to them. Of course,

Quanah was not among them; as chief, he would wait in his tepee until she called upon him.

She let excited women tell her of things she already knew—tales of Naduah's bad medicine, of how each time of snows had been, births and deaths and raids.

Since that Mexican raid upon the camp six summers past, no Long Knife or *tejano* had come close to trapping Kwehar-enuh war parties, while losing many scalps of their own. Quanah was truly a great warrior, *hu!*

Tosanna almost kissed him when shown into his lodge. Just in time, she remembered that gesture was almost unknown here—a shame. Instead, she embraced him as an old friend, both to Big Tree and herself .

Taller than her, taller than any in the band, Quanah said, "Welcome, sister; you have been long away from us."

"And far from my brother," she replied, as he honored her by motioning her to be seated. "My travels have been long and difficult, but I bring many good things." She hesitated, then plunged ahead, "And wise advice."

His hair was very long, braided to fall before each shoulder; his chest was wide beneath the fringed shirt. Quanah's eyes were not black, but brown and deep; his face unmarked by battle but early lined with sorrows beyond his years, for he was no old and grizzled chief. With a shock, Tosanna realized this mighty leader of the Comanches was only a few summers older than herself. Leadership had been forced upon him.

"We will speak of wisdom at the council fire," he said. "Now I would hear all that happened to you. Are you hungry? My wives will bring food."

Tosanna shook her head. "My heart overflows and fills the rest of me. Good Scent, Quanah—although it is ill to speak of the dead, will you first tell me of my husband?"

Gravely, he nodded. "Ado-eeti and two other chiefs were arrested at the agency, where he went for presents. The others were Patua-wuni-kai and Kewerts-umi of the Kiowa —Son Searcher and Hungry Man. They were surprised by Long Knives, for never before had the God Speaker, the agent, allowed Long Knives upon the reservation. It was because of a wagon raid where only seven *tejanos* were killed. We did not understand why *americanos* were angry over *tejano* deaths. Besides, no war party raided near the reservation. Still, they were angry, even the God Speaker, who is never angry, only weak."

Seated upon thick buffalo robes, old memories crowded upon Tosanna—the ring of laughter long past; odors of fragrant woods burning, the look of sunlight against the carefully scraped hides of the tepee; Ten Bears and Big Tree; and Naduah, who had been a friend. She said, "And Ado-eeti?"

Quanah looked directly at her. "The Long Knives put a rope about his neck. His wives cut off their hair and slashed their arms. I am sorry; he was a great warrior."

"His wives," Tosanna said.

"Spotted Deer and Red Face; his sons by them have not yet received their medicine names."

She should be proud her lover produced sons to follow him; instead, she knew a pang of jealousy, a sharpness of hurt. Tosanna fought that White Eyes reaction in tortured silence until Quanah spoke again.

"Now," he said, "tell me all you know of White Eyes country, their medicine, good and bad. We war to the death with them now, and if we are to win, I must know more about them."

Drawing a deep breath, Tosanna imparted her first wisdom, "Quanah, we cannot win."

CHAPTER 37

God, he was tired. It went beyond that; he was weary to
the marrow of his bones, so that the very core of him was
numbed. Damned near sixty hours in the saddle; sixty
hours without sleep and on short water rations. Walker
nodded as he rode, jerking awake whenever his horse
stumbled, which was too often. Each time he was certain
the animal was going down, but the wiry mustang was
tougher than he looked.

Miserable damned country, Walker thought—rough
alkali desert and waterless. Forty miles each way was more
than man or beast should have to take. With a slaughter
at one end too. It hadn't been a battle when they hit the
Bolson de Mapimi camps in northern Coahuila. Coahuila,
Mexico, that was, and if Mexican cavalry had caught them,
there would be a hell of a lot less of them now.

Mackenzie had expected a running battle with lancers;
his four hundred riders carried sabers honed to razor edges
in preparation. That snake-mean military bastard was beloved by his black troopers, but that made him no less a
hard-driving, merciless son of a bitch who'd gambled the
lives of his entire command.

Without official orders, Colonel Randal Mackenzie had
invaded Mexico with the U.S. 4th Cavalry.

Walker's head bobbed and he struggled to stay in his
saddle. One group front and one behind, so they'd take
the brunt of any attack, the prisoners rode lashed onto
their horses. They couldn't fall unless the mounts did.

Some had, and had been left for circling buzzards, mercy-shot through the head—horse and captive alike.

And just about all the prisoners were women and children. It bothered Walker at first; later on he was just too beat down to care. What he never would forget was the horses—hundreds of horses of about every description and color, coldly and methodically shot to prevent the Indians from taking them back. The goddamned Lipan, Mescaleros, and Kickapoos had been practically set afoot in the world's most inhospitable country. It was sound military reasoning, more so since Mackenzie had once lost a large horse herd to counterattacking Comanches.

But it made Walker retch, and he didn't give a damn who saw him. He hadn't loosed a single shot at the herd either. Mackenzie could shove that kind of order up his West Point ass. A screaming horse made the worst sound there was, and Walker hoped never to hear it again.

Dobe dropped back from Tonk scouts working ahead of the column. Peering at Walker through bloodshot eyes, he said, "Ain't too far to the river, nohow."

Through cracked lips Walker said, "Do you think that son of a bitch will take us all the way to Canada?"

"Might," Dobe Davis grunted, "did he get word injuns was raidin' from there."

Sure, Walker understood the why and wherefore of Mackenzie's brutally punishing attack on the camps. For years a ragtag band of Kickapoos and Lipans had been using them as bases. They struck across the Rio Grande so often all the southern border lay bleeding, then galloped back to sanctuary. Protest notes from Washington to whatever *generalissimo* was in power did no good. Lately, the Mexican government hadn't even bothered to answer them.

But Jesus—sixty hours on a moving horse, when whole damned regiments of Mexican lancers might be flanking them even now? General Sheridan and General Sherman might have gotten tacit approval from Grant, their old war buddy, but it was Mackenzie far out on a limb. Any official hell raised from Mexico, and Washington would hang Mackenzie out to dry—and possibly his command too. What fat politician gave a damn for black soldiers?

"Buffalo Soldiers," Walker mumbled, correcting himself.

"What?" Dobe said.

"Good soldiers," Walker said. "Worn out, but good men."

"Hell, yes. Way they hit them three camps was a caution. Injuns runnin' hellbound for glory and the troops cuttin' down on 'em like they was choppin' cotton."

Walker fought his eyes open. "Didn't kill more than twenty or so."

"That we *seen;* you know they tote off wounded and dead, if'n they can. Got forty or more hostages though, countin' the younguns."

"Have to count them," Walker muttered. "Might not get their chance to grow up."

Gently, Dobe said, "There was a heap of white younguns along the border, once; ain't none now."

"Shit," Walker said, "I know, I know. I think it was the horses." His eyelids sagged again. What kind of world was it, where animal death affected him more than human? That this was always so, he brushed off.

Tosanna—her name burned behind his gritty eyelids, and he cursed her for it. If he'd never known her beauty, her fierce tenderness, he wouldn't be identifying her with these miserable Indians. He was white and she was Comanche, and never would they blend. The Comanches would never stop raiding, and whites would never stop hunting them down—Mackenzie style.

The method was cruelly effective: hit the villages, take hostage women and children; burn all food and shelter, murder their horses; give no quarter and show no mercy, lest that be interpreted as weakness. Mackenzie had even made use of his infantry, so stupidly sent out by Washington. He packed them in wagons and carried them swiftly to the attack, while cavalry wings spread wide.

And lately the army found an unthinking ally in greedy buffalo hunters; bison were being slaughtered in ever increasing numbers, the once-countless seas of buffalo herds turned into isolated puddles. Before too long, they might be gone altogether, something nobody ever believed could happen. Hell, there were millions of buff, millions. Always had been. But when thousands of animals were killed only for their tongues or hides and the meat left to rot, Comanche food supplies were threatened.

One day the hunting parties would ride out and find not a single red-eyed bull snorting stupid defiance, not a single cow shouldering her calf away from yipping riders. The land would be empty and sad.

Walker saw the lonely plains inside his head, grass

stretching belly high to the horizon with nothing feeding upon it; no tepee would break the flats, no scout would signal from hilltops.

Water splashed Walker's legs and he jerked awake to find his horse stopping for a quick drink. The Rio Grande, shallow and muddy and the most welcome sight he could think of. Legging his mount on, he tried to grin at Dobe. It hurt his mouth.

When the column had crossed, Mackenzie gave the order to dismount and men fell from saddles like the dead. Walker's knees wobbled when he climbed down, but no worse than his horse's. Dully he stared as Tonkawas gathered to pull down captives and torment them.

"Bastards been hatin' Comanches since time was a pup," Dobe commented. "Good cause, too. They won't actual torture nobody—too scared of Mackenzie—and more good cause."

"You'd think they'd just fall out and rest," Walker said, standing by until his horse drank its fill. "I'm about to."

"Look at Mackenzie," Dobe said. "Called up his officers."

"Canada," Walker muttered. "California, maybe."

"Or the front row in hell. This outfit would foller him there."

Mackenzie's voice was strong and clear, and he tried to stand straight against the war wound that never healed right. "Gentlemen, if there should be an official inquiry, I took you into Mexico on my own authority."

Some young lieutenant who'd aged quickly during the long ride said, his voice cracking: "Sir, if I had known that and refused to cross the border of a friendly nation, what then?"

The colonel stared bleakly at the man. "Why," he said, as if there could be no question, "I would have had you shot, sir."

Walker unsaddled and hobbled his horse to graze, and melted to the ground. If he dreamed, he didn't know or remember. Grass against his cheek might have been hair the texture of midnight or autumn brown, filling his nostrils with that musky scent sometimes lost in flowers. When he turned over, he drew starshine over him like a blanket, closing him in with her, and it was good; it was peaceful. There was no need to overcome, only a sweet-soft meshing threaded with moon glow. The face: womanhawk or placid?

"Off your ass and on your horse," Dobe said, toeing him in the ribs. "Come on, gunslick. We got to head north."

Groaning, Walker sat up. Only an inch of flat water remained in his canteen; he drank it and made a face. "What the hell, Dobe."

"The hellio—hellio—shit; that thing with mirrors. They flashed Mackenzie a message."

"Heliograph," Walker said, moving to the river to splash his face and fill the canteen. His mustang had been too weary to wander far in hobbles. It looked reproachfully at him as he spread the blanket and lifted on the saddle. Walker didn't tighten the cinch yet, and put on the feed bag with what corn was left. Orders or no, man and horse were due to eat.

Cookfires were smoking all over the place when Dobe and the pair of Tonkawas squatted to Walker's fire. The diet hadn't changed: fried fatback and cornbread cooked in its grease. There'd been no chance to loot more than a handful of smoked meat before Mackenzie ordered the villages and all supplies torched.

Passing around the skillet, Walker said, "Wish we had some coffee. Anybody feeding the prisoners?"

"Them as'll eat," Dobe answered. "That cotton-headed lieutenant got the job and don't like it. Same one Mackenzie told he'd of got hisself shot did he balk at crossin' the river."

Walker chewed meat. "That heliograph message."

"Didn't get all the clear of it, but I heard the feller say somethin' about Captain Richards."

"Couldn't be important," Walker said, scraping his skillet with a handful of wet river sand, "or Mackenzie'd have us hightailing right away."

"I reckon," Dobe said. His worn and stubbled face seemed to have sagged. But everyone was worn down now—even Saba and Fleabite, who never showed any kind of sign.

When the colonel had "Boots and Saddles" blown, Walker moved out ahead with Dobe and their Tonks, slowly working stiffness from his horse. Although weak, the sun helped warm them, and when they spread into a protective fan for the body of troops following, Walker felt pretty good.

Travel was easier now, and only some Indian gone clean out of his head would dare attack the column. But force of habit and a healthy desire to keep his scalp made Walker stay sharp. He looked over every growth of cholla, anticipated each possible ambush point. For long stretches, the ground was flat and sandy, scattered with cactus. When the terrain changed to long, easy hills, he dismounted and walked to the crests, searching first before' and to both sides. Only when satisfied did he look back to see the long, dark snake of the regiment winding after.

He thought of Charity and wished her back at Fort Concho. It would be nice to ride in and find her waiting, smiling, excited. But Martin Luther Crawford had received one of his direct, personal messages from on high, and like a dutiful sister, Charity followed the family fanatic north to Fort Sill.

Shading his eyes, Walker stared out over diagonal folds in the earth. Sill was one hell of a trip, but what with twenty Tonks, Captain Richards, and six troopers, the wagons ought to be safe enough. Comanche raiding parties were never dumb-eager to strike into plentiful guns; they preferred to hit and run, doing their damage and fading away before resistance could be organized.

Charity would be all right; Charity and her—their— baby. When he saw her again, they'd have to sit down and plan everything out: where they would go, what he'd work at, housing—many details. The first hurdle was easily crossed; they'd be married by the post chaplain at Fort Sill or the reservation agent there. Just about every Indian agent was some kind of preacher.

A little clump of loblolly pines gave off their good green smell, and Walker drank deeply of it. The marrying would be nothing like what would have come off at Fairbairn Plantation. A thousand candles glowing upon velvet and crinoline, music and dancing, snowy linen and sparkling silver, slaves having their own hooraw out back—and his people close: Jeremy, Travis, and Jackson.

Walker pulled up his mustang and sipped water. His father wanted no part of him, and his brothers had fallen. And if he'd known man killing was so everyday, he might have ridden with the Confederacy and changed fate.

Any deviation from the path and there'd be no Tosanna, Milady Savage; no Charity Crawford and her—their— baby. Why had he thought first of Tosanna? The chronology, nothing else, and once he got Charity settled in somewhere, Tosanna would fade from his mind and his blood.

She belonged to that other life, whether dream or nightmare. Charity and his responsibilities were all too real, and as yet he had no inkling how to support them.

He knew only a little about planting, more about horses, and still more about guns. But that much applied to just about every embittered, disenfranchised former Confederate gone west. Walker halted his horse and leaned to study marks in the earth. Maybe he ought to take up preaching, like Martin Luther Crawford. Wouldn't be much money to it, but where else could a man ride scout for the Lord and draw down on any other man who disagreed with him?

Just about anywhere, Walker admitted, provided a fast, accurate gun and callused conscience. Ex-Rebs anywhere out here qualified for that too; and so did bluecoats with years of horseshit and gunpowder behind them and more ahead—if their luck held out.

Hell, Walker wasn't used to studying and fretting over the future. He'd made out just fine by living day to day.

He climbed down to look more closely at sign that had caught his attention. A scuffed deer print, jackrabbit crossing unhurried, and there must be a water hole yonder behind the rise, for all little animal tracks pointed there— gopher, Gila, and desert rat. Maybe a diamond-back made the area his private hunting ground; Walker wasn't sure. Funny, everything seemed to have used the same narrow strip of ground and left the rest smooth. Then he stared hard at the base of some Spanish bayonet and made it out—the partial track of an unshod horse.

Shit! Walker threw himself left and caught his horse a lick with one foot. The mustang snorted and wheeled off just as the bullet *spanged* from a rock. Rolling as more bullets searched the sand around him, Walker came up hard against a tumble of shale. It wasn't much protection, but all that was handy.

There went his horse, toting both his rifles, and here he was with only a handgun. Bellied flat, Walker inched around and chanced a quick look. Where the hell was the Indian, and where the man's horse? Walker pulled in his head and angled around to try the other side of his shelter. He got results there; a handful of shale spewed over him and the echo of the shot bounced around inside his head.

The son of a bitch was yonder behind the little rise, where he could easy remain until rooted out. Walker drew back and studied grains of sand up close, like so many dirty diamonds. Long as the Indian stayed hidden there, Walker wasn't fixing to damned-fool run at him, and if the bastard waited long enough, Dobe and the Tonks would come up on him. The sounds of firing must have reached them by now.

Changing sides of his rock pile again, he peeped, and caught a quick shadow. When he fired, it staggered across the hillock on his side. Walker centered his target again, and the Indian fell over.

Walker waited a spell, but the Indian seemed to be alone. That didn't shake the itchy feeling as he exposed himself and moved carefully to the fallen man. The Indian's eyes glared at him, not yet glazed over. Pistol ready, Walker stepped around and put his boot heel hard on one outflung arm, stooping to grab up the knife, then a repeating rifle a pace away.

Two hits on him, Walker saw; one through the base of the neck, one high up in the belly, just under the ribs. It was a wonder the Comanche was still alive. Since he didn't double over the pain in his belly, Walker reasoned the man's spine was severed, paralyzing him.

Dobe Davis came at a dead run, skidding his horse to a stop that threw rocks and dirt. From each flank came the Tonks, but with more care. Dobe padded to the Indian and prodded him with the barrel of his Sharps.

"Split his gizzard proper," he said. "Looks like a youngun out to make a name for hisself. Funny he's clear down here, less'n they run plumb out'n white folks up north. I make him out an Antelope tribe buck, Kwehar-enuh. By rights he oughta' be settled in for the winter."

The young warrior was doing a good job of not showing pain, though a sheen of face sweat betrayed him. Obsidian black, his eyes hated them all, and through locked teeth he hissed something scornful.

Dobe cocked his shaggy head. "Says for you to finish it; he ain't scared. Way he's watchin' that knife says he's frettin' over his scalp or his pizzle. Loses either one or both, he won't be much of a man in the next life. Them Comanch prizes their hair near as much as their tally-whackers."

Walker glanced at the Tonks squatting close with half-grins on their ugly faces. If he loosed them on the Comanche, he'd be praying to his gods to die quick.

Walker said, "Ask why he's so far south; maybe the colonel would like to know."

At Dobe's prodding, the young warrior spat a string of words sharp as a snakebite. Blood was starting to ooze into his mouth now, spraying red mist as he talked.

Grinning, Dobe said, "Promises to meet you in the promised land and do you up proper, and puttin' blame on his new rifle for not dressin' you out like a head-shot buff this time. Makin' his brag on his chief and a first-class medicine woman. Her magic makes his tribe stronger'n White Eyes and *tejanos* put together. They got new guns and plenty bullets and fast horses, the best in all Comancheria."

Turning his head away, Walker said, "Why not best in the whole world?"

"Hell," Dobe said, and spit tobacco juice. Its brown overlay a thin blotting of blood on the sands. "Hell—Comancheria *is* the whole world to this 'un. Did he travel clean around the earth, he'd still believe that."

The Tonk scouts kept edging closer, laughing and grunting in their own language. Walker said, "I won't take his hair and wouldn't touch his goddamn pizzle. Tell him the Tonks won't either."

Those polished stone eyes flickered and the buck's throat gurgled when he answered. Dobe interpreted: "Makes for a better fight when he meets up with you in the huntin' grounds or wheresoever. Quanah Parker and the medicine woman'll see you get a good send-off from here." Aside, Dobe said, "Figured him right—sassy young Kwehar-enuh."

"Quanah Parker," Walker said. "That half-breed we've been hearing about? We won't hear so much when Mackenzie gets on his trail. Damn, why doesn't this man die and get it over with?"

Dobe scratched his ragged beard. "Not even a Comanch gets in no hurry when that time comes. He's slippin' quick now. Can't hardly make out what he's sayin'—somethin' about flowers, seems like."

A chill raked Walker's spine. "Flowers? Last Flower? Damn you, Comanche—do you mean Tosanna? *Tosanna?* Answer me, you redskin son of a bitch—*Tosanna?*"

Thick and red black, a final pulsing rivered from the warrior's mouth. Unheeding, Walker shook his shoulder, shook him hard and the man's head lolled.

"Didn't catch it clear," Dobe said. "He might of said one more flower, or—"

Staring down as if he could will life back into the Comanche, Walker said through stiff lips, "The last flower—Tosanna. Alive and here and the enemy."

When the Tonks would have taken hair, Dobe shook his head at them. Sullenly, they fell back. Dobe said, "Reckon you ain't been of a mind to say you knowed Quanah Parker's medicine woman personal-like."

Walker stood up and looked off north to where land met sky. "I knew her once, long ago."

Dobe Davis grunted. "Best you don't chew over old times with her. Your shiny yeller hair'd sure stand out on a lodgepole."

CHAPTER 38

A cavalry patrol had passed only a short time before, and even now might double back along the Brazos River. None could predict which direction the Long Knives chief would send his Buffalo Soldiers. The only certainty was that he would keep them ever in the saddle, not allowing The People to hunt properly. And now chill wind spoke warning for the time of snows.

She would be comfortable if Quanah waited here with the party, for she did not care for Older Man as leader. Tenewerka never smiled and complained that the old ways, the ways of his father, were passing, and he blamed Tosanna as medicine woman.

At the council fire, he accepted the idea that she had paid for the supplies and rifles to come, that she would also trade the White Eyes magic metal for other wagons filled with the tribe's needs. But Tenewerka stressed that a wife could have no possessions, since she herself was a possession; therefore all she had belonged by law to her husband, medicine woman or no.

Quanah had thought this over and agreed. Mildly, he pointed out that Tosanna was the only Comanche this black freighter would trade with.

Take the wagon, Older Man had said; kill the freighter who was blood brother to Buffalo Soldiers.

And Quanah had said: And who will bring another wagon when it is again needed?

By then, Tenewerka said proudly, the *tejanos* and White Eyes will be defeated and we will not ask favors.

Tosanna breathed deeply of crisp air flavored with sagebrush. She stood with her horse a proscribed distance behind Older Man and the others. Would Ned Barstow come safely to the meeting place? No Comanche would touch him, because Quanah's orders forbade it. But there might be Lipan stragglers hungry for loot and vengeance. She stared out over the river, remembering what she owed Ned—not only her life, but the understanding and friendship he'd given her. As they'd traveled together, she'd come to not see his blackness or her own coppery color.

She'd had master and lovers, but Ned Barstow was the only man she could count as friend.

Quanah? She wasn't sure. Her new husband was intelligent and thoughtful, but bound by a thousand years of custom. A good and solid man, a magnificent war chief and wise counsel, he was all a Comanche woman might expect on a fur couch. A *Comanche* woman.

Was she so changed now? Had English ways worked beneath her skin and into her heart? No, she thought; she was Last Flower, daughter of Ten Bears. The English had named her savage, and Sunhair made certain she never forgot the difference in their races. Savage she was then, but not primitive, not animal. She was proud of her savagery, her respected position in the tribe, not only as a wife to the greatest leader the Kwehar-enuh had ever known, but for her medicine.

Backing her horse to a higher hillock, she peered across the plain and along the winding Brazos; she saw nothing. Ground-tying the mare, she sat beneath gray-silvered mesquite and wished for buckskin breeches instead of her lightly fringed dress. Pants were better suited to riding, but traditionalists like Older Man did not approve.

As Quanah would not approve of innovations in bed. The husband takes, the woman submits; how it ever had been, how it ever would be. She might look beyond Quanah's tepee for lovers, and make the first approaches. If she was found out, the council would set a horse price to be paid her husband for rental of her body. *Her* body, she thought; not Quanah's. Comanches did not know of whoring, but that kind of flesh selling and English prostitution differed only by name.

That was disloyal. Tosanna felt shadow chill touch her face and throat; she put out her tongue to taste mesquite upon the air. Here the air was free and clean. In London, even in *tejano* Galveston, the wind was a prisoner stained by captivity. Here a woman knew exactly how a man felt; there was no lovemaking followed by guilt or anger. A man was lover or husband, not enemy whenever his body no longer ached for her flesh.

Tosanna told herself she was glad Sunhair would never ride across this plain almost at the foot of the Llano Estacado. Seeing him again would only weaken her more and sap her desire to help her people. She could not turn traitor now. Far better to ride with the Kwehar-enuh into the sunset of their race. It was coming.

Just as it was better to accept Quanah as husband and protector than to be treated like a widow who belonged nowhere and had no one to hunt for her. Leaning back upon her elbows, she thought of the hidden streak of tenderness in Quanah, and of his power. He was no sexual adept like Sunhair, but no man was. Yet he was gratifyingly strong, and if he did not pay enough attention to her needs, mainly concerned with his own—that was the way of The People.

Quanah had not asked her to be a wife; he announced it to the council without consulting her. Since she had no father, no brother, this also was correct. Still, Tosanna might have wished for romance. When she was much younger and had never seen lands beyond Comancheria, when she'd only known lovers from her own tribe, she might have accepted with pride. Now she only accepted.

In a fashion it had been a kind of returning, as she waited in Quanah's tepee when his other wives left her alone. She was excited, but not tremulous upon the couch of furs, and watched the slow burning of the fire, tracing smoke to the open tepee top, where it dimmed stars.

He came to her with his manhood already gorged, and there were a few preliminaries before he spread and mounted her. Deeply he plunged, powerfully he stroked, so that Tosanna heaved beneath his strong body and the buffalo robes, deer hides, wolf and coyote skins, seemed to leap and twist in lives of their own.

She gave herself to his pleasure, grinding with and around him, hammering back at his every sliding penetration. She did not attack him, nor rake his back with nails,

although she did lightly take the skin of his flesh between
her teeth and hang on; she did lift and circle her slim legs
to entrap him between them. And her breath rushed hissing
against his captured flesh when Quanah shuddered and
spurted his seed within her clinging depths.

That first night with Quanah she had carried guilt into
late sleep, because the image of Sunhair intruded; because
she saw his eyes and felt the lean, flowing beauty of him
all over again. That too was disloyal, and since then she'd
struggled to forget Walker Fairbairn.

Her mare stirred, slyly picking at browned bunch grass.
Four other mounts shifted weight under their riders as
Older Man and his warriors saw quickwhite smoke talk rise
in the south. It spoke of a tepee on wheels and a black man.

Older Man said, "He is a fool; he comes alone."

Tosanna stood up. "He is a man of honor and bravery,
not a fool."

Older Man did not turn to look at her. "What does a
woman know of honor—or a Buffalo Soldier?"

"A black man," Tosanna said, louder. "Not a soldier, but
a man who keeps his word to The People."

"His word to a woman," Older Man grunted.

She chewed her lip, biting back anger and frustration.
Tenewerka was stubborn as a buffalo bull—yes, and as
thick headed. At the council fire, he'd been the loudest
detractor of her story, sneering at the tales of unimaginable
numbers of White Eyes and their mechanical miracles.

It was so like the Kwehar-enuh to disbelieve any tribe,
any race could be in any way superior. Were they not the
chosen people, the bravest warriors, the best horsemen
ever to be blessed by the spirits?

Tosanna had continued to speak, and as the long story
unwound, more wise men fell silent and listened closely.
Sometimes she was stopped to answer questions, and that
first long night wore on into dawn. When Quanah led her
to their tepee, she was weary and her throat ached. But
she'd convinced many elders another world existed beyond
their own, and later they named her medicine woman.
Even Kiyou, the tribe's spirit talker, agreed on her special
position.

Lifting braided horsehair reins, Tosanna swung atop her
mare. She could see Ned Barstow's wagon approaching
now, and was anxious to greet him. When she started to

edge past the others, Older Man snarled at her. Rather than having the band turn anger against Ned Barstow, she dropped back again. She would be needed to make talk, to list needs and pay in advance for the next load. Maybe she'd convince her friend to make up a train, in case Long Knives began to search all wagons supposedly heading for the Brazos reservation and Indian agents. That way supplies for her people would be stockpiled.

When the lumbering wagon creaked and rattled near, Tosanna brushed by Older Man and made the peace sign as her mare jogged toward Ned. High on the wagon seat, faded canvas tall and rounded behind him, Ned didn't smile until she was close on him. Then he held out both hands and called her name.

She wanted to hug him, but the warriors would disapprove, so she stepped down and waited for him to climb over the big front wheel. She took his callused hands and looked long into his dark and serious face.

"My good friend," she said in English, "I am so glad to see you again."

She wondered at his difficulty in trying to smile as Ned said, "Me too, missy. 'Times I didn't expect to get here. Whole lots of trouble down south."

Tosanna saw his eyes narrow at the Comanches horseback behind her, and felt tension in his fingers. She dropped his hands and said, "These men are of my own tribe. They will not harm you, and the word of Quanah protects you from other Comanches. If any renegade tried to stop you—"

"No'm," Ned said quickly. "Stopped some folks permanent, but never right out bothered me none." He stared beyond her at Older Man and the others. "Got every lick of what you said, and more to boot, since you give me away too much gold."

He wasn't the Ned she recalled; it was as if he shut his heart from her. "Not too much," she said. "The danger calls for more. Money is of no use to us, only goods in exchange for it. Next time—"

Ned shook his head and looked at the ground. "Don't figure on no next time, missy."

Tosanna threw a quick glance over her shoulder. Older Man's mouth twisted and she said to Ned, "I know you as brave and honest. I know you need to save money for a new life. There must be some other reason you don't want to supply us."

"Yes'm, reckon they is; got two reasons yonder in the wagon." He twisted a battered hat in his hands. "Expect you might have to see 'em to understand."

Knowing that Older Man was watching closely and reading facial expressions, she sent him handtalk to move back. She heard no hoofs; they paid no attention. Frowning, she walked to the wagon gate with Ned, an uneasy chill along her spine.

He climbed to unbolt the tailgate, and when it dropped, he said, "Had to tote 'em along—scared to take time for buryin'. Figure on packin' 'em on to the agency so's their own kind can see to it."

She looked again at her tribesmen, and gave Ned her hand to be lifted onto the tailgate. No warrior would do that, offer a hand. Tosanna saw them then, naked bodies twisted and mutilated, scalped.

Quietly Ned said, "Come acrost they scalps on up the road; reckon weren't enough hair to count, after Comanch lifted 'em. They just chunked 'em away."

"Buffalo Soldiers," Tosanna said. "They ride for the Long Knife chief, Mackenzie."

"They black," Ned said.

"Soldiers," she repeated. "Enemies in Comanche hunting grounds."

"Yes'm," he murmured, "but they still black like me, and lord knows we done had enough tribulation. Both them boys must of been slaves, and time they got to be passable free—well, missy, I just can't be haulin' guns and shells to kill my people with. And I'm sorry as can be, account of I'd do just about anything you want."

She dropped from the wagon and said, "I understand." He said, "Chunked away they scalps after takin' 'em."

"Yes," she said, and motioned to her people to help unload the wagon. A pair of big hide sacks for each of five horses should carry the weight; if not, part of the goods could be hidden. She wanted desperately to say something wise and soothing to Ned, but there were no words that could ever make it the same between them.

Pushing roughly past Ned, Older Man snatched first at the new repeating rifles and brandished one in each big hand as he made a joke about the corpses and promised to stand over the bodies of many more. Crooked Leg and

Rawhide laughed with him; only Coyote frowned, and he was young.

Back on his seat, Ned Barstow smoked his old pipe and waited while they cleared his wagon of lard, beans, corn-meal and fatback, blankets and needles and thread, tobacco; more important were White Eye medicines. Shining new short axes caught her attention, and Ned had even thrown in coffee and sugar, great luxuries to Comanches.

Older Man scorned all but the weapons and ammunition, and Tosanna struggled to load food onto her mare. Sometimes young Coyote helped.

"Make your dog talk with him," Older Man commanded when the wagon bed was bare of all but dead men. "See that he returns with more presents, even in the time of snows. These are good rifles. *Hu!* They will kill many Buffalo Soldiers."

Tosanna said, "He will not come back because his tribal brothers lie in the wagon."

Heeling his loaded horse close to Ned Barstow's nervous mules, Older Man spat at him. *"Hu,* black dog! Quanah, mighty war chief of the Kwehar-enuh orders you to return with more weapons. I order you!"

"He does not understand our talk," Tosanna said.

Ned Barstow lifted his flop hat to her, made a sad little smile, and picked up the lines, clucking to his mules.

Older Man leaned forward and shot him twice very quickly, working the lever of his rifle. Ned doubled against the shock in his belly and fell off the wagon seat. Older Man shot him twice more, this time in the face. The mules jerked and twitched and rattled harness, but did not bolt.

Tosanna's mouth stretched wide, but her throat closed and would not allow the scream of horror and pain. Her teeth ached with the effort, and her entire body quivered like a taut bowstring. Ned Barstow—kind man, brave man, killed for doing as she asked, for bringing her tribe arms and supplies.

Inside her head, the raging shriek whirled around and around while some strange noise mewled between teeth now clenched. Tosanna's legs were dry sticks as she moved from her horse. Her fist clenched white on the haft of her knife. It glittered before her.

"Animal dung! Fish belly! You have the heart of a cowardly Apache, and even those foul *Inde* would piss on you."

Older Man swung around on his horse, smoking rifle searching her out. "She-dog! I will close your mouth—"

"As you killed a friend? Have you the heart to try your knife with me—or can you only kill an unarmed man?"

By the spirits, by all White Eye gods, she hated him to the marrow of his bones. At the corner of her eye lay Ned Barstow, his dark blood soaking the sand. For no cause, for *nothing*.

Dropping from his horse, Older Man said, "I will open your belly and stuff it with his man pouch."

A blurred hand chopped her wrist and Tosanna's knife fell. He clamped her arms hard and held her tight against his body—young Coyote. He said to Older Man, "You would kill the wife of Quanah?"

Crooked Leg and Rawhide muttered. Crouched and ugly and eager, Older Man hissed. "The Buffalo Man would not return to us; therefore he was worthless. This she-dog has insulted me."

"Quanah's new wife has much favor in his eyes," Coyote insisted. "She is also the medicine woman."

Older Man hesitated. "I am not afraid of Quanah."

"And Quanah fears no man," Coyote said.

Rawhide said, "Coyote is wise beyond his years."

"Hu; I grant her life, so that Quanah may beat her with willows and teach her respect." Older Man turned quickly and fired his new rifle twice more. Both mules fell in their harness.

"Fool," Tosanna said. "They might have carried supplies and be eaten later, if hunting is bad. If you only play at being a warrior, shoot yourself in the crotch—if you can find a target there."

Crooked Leg and Rawhide stifled laughter, but Coyote moved between her and Older Man. Nearly choked by anger, Older Man snarled, "Do not burn the tepee-that-moves, but leave it as a lesson to others. Follow me. We return rich with presents."

When Coyote released her, the others were some distance ahead. "Do not anger him further, sister. The trail is long and Older Man's heart is hard. Comanche does not war upon Comanche."

"No," she said bitterly. A small tear channeled her cheek and Coyote turned away to not see it. Tosanna said, "No—we only kill any other we please."

Back to her, he said, "Sister, he was not of The People. That is reason enough to kill him. He would not be used by us, so Older Man was correct."

She waited until his horse was lengths ahead of her. Then Tosanna mourned Ned Barstow; it was the first time she had really cried.

CHAPTER 39

Dobe Davis came snaking back from the ridge on his belly. He touched Walker's elbow and motioned with his head. Walker joined him, eeling along until Dobe felt it safe to stand up.

"Tonks is staked out," Dobe whispered. "Comanch down yonder, right enough, snug for winter."

"See her?" Walker asked, without hope.

"Uh-uh, son; can't tell from this far anyways. Not many movin' around, cold as it is. Snow too beat down to even know if'n the bucks is gone huntin'."

They reached Colonel Mackenzie then, and Dobe made his report: maybe forty tepees; some horses penned up in a brush corral, some grazing in a box canyon. No sentries out, far as he could tell.

"Figure they're safe to home this time of year, and wouldn't no Long Knives dare come up on 'em anyways."

Mackenzie nodded, face tight. "The Tonkawa scouts?"

"Spoilin' to cut down on 'em, but I said I'd lift their hair myself, do they jump the gun."

"Very well," Mackenzie said, and turned to his officers. "You know the tactics and see the terrain. To your troops, gentlemen—quietly. Mister Davis, Mister Fairbairn, you will ride with the scouts as point and right center; control them."

Walker changed hands with his Spencer. "Dobe up ahead and me to the flank, and we didn't see a warrior. Maybe only women and children are down there."

"And maybe not," Mackenzie said, cradling his crippled hand against the biting cold. "I understand your concern, sir; it is also mine. I'm sure you realize that Comanche women fight almost as fiercely as their men. It is not my intention to war upon babes, but destroying base camps, supplies, and taking prisoners is my method of breaking the enemy. Do you agree?"

"What the hell else can I do?" Walker said.

Jogging his horse beside Walker's to where restless Tonkawas waited, Dobe said, "You know he's right, and ain't no cause for Miss Charity to be with this particular bunch. You done all you could to find her. Expect you got to face up to it: she could easy be dead."

"Maybe not, damn it—maybe *not*." Walker divided the air with one hand. "I'll take this half, you that bunch. I'll hold mine back long as I can, then follow in."

Dobe said, "Won't hold 'em long; they're itchin' for this fight."

"This booty, you mean. They sure as hell didn't put up much fight when Comanches hit her wagon. They crawled out of their holes weeks later, the bastards."

Dobe shrugged. "Don't fault 'em for that. Comanch come down on so many rifles, had to be a bigod heap of 'em."

Walker shouldered his big gelding into Tonkawa horses, splitting the scout force and cursing those who didn't move fast. He was about eager as the Tonks to close, but worried. If Charity Crawford was in a tepee down there, her life was balanced upon a knife edge. If her captors didn't slit her throat—which they might do rather than give her up—then bullets from his side might cut her down—her and the child she carried, his child.

He closed his eyes and the vivid scene came back strong: stark and ugly: charred wagon, stench of burned flesh, vultures circling impatiently; bloated mules, contorted bodies among bright cartridge casings.

Six black cavalrymen dead with honor, if that meant a goddamned thing to mutilated corpses; Martin Luther Crawford gone scalped to his martyr's reward; a dozen Tonks belly ripped. Captain Richards must have put up a fierce battle, because the Comanches saved him for special treatment. They lashed him upside down to a wagon wheel and built a slow fire beneath his head.

And no Charity Crawford; she had been taken.

Walker ranged northern Comancheria for weeks, often

with Dobe Davis at his stirrup, and whatever god of luck
that had turned from Charity and her escort, that capricious
deity smiled upon Walker. Although they cut heavy Indian
sign time and again, no war party, no surprised hunting
party came upon them.

Dobe speared through the ache behind Walker's eyes:
"The bugle! Damn you louse-chawed Tonks—hold up!"
Then he threw his horse after yelling scouts.

Walker's group shrieked around and past him, alkali dust
and waving rifles and snorting horses. There was no holding
the Tonkawas when a camp of their ancient enemies lay
open to attack by overwhelming numbers. They slashed
in ahead of the disciplined 4th Cavalry and went plunging
through tepees at a dead run, shooting and hacking anything
that moved.

Lodges went down and fires blazed up—screams and
shots and death cries of gutted horses, thunder clouds of
dust and smoke, mortal red-bright gun lightning. It all
swirled together in hell's own mixture, flinging out dead
things from the living, struggling core.

The hourglass dropped grain by grain for Walker, slowing
all movement as he rode a child's rocking horse into the
fray made more brutal by deliberate ticktocking.

He fired at a buck bent low and saw him slapped by an
invisible hand; he pumped shells into his Spencer and
pumped them out again, guiding his horse with his knees.
Around him Comanches cavorted and leaped and fell
slowly. Once he pulled target because she ran holding a
silent, wide-eyed baby, and a black trooper probably saved
Walker's life. The Buffalo Soldier roared his horse over the
woman as she swept up a rifle from the child's blankets to
fire almost in Walker's face.

Everywhere horses reared and plunged and ran blindly,
trumpeting wild fear at the blood smell, striking out at
everything. Men were no better controlled but more deadly,
their fear shot through with hate and rage. From boiling
smoke, a warrior sprang high at Walker, armed only with
a skinning knife. Walker centered his chest and the Comanche toppled back into the cauldron.

Somehow the Spencer was axed from Walker's hands
and he brought out his Navy Colt, earing back the hammer
in that inch by dragging inch of slow motion that always
mantled him in any kind of fight.

And the alarm inside his head continued to sound a

klaxon of warning. There were so many women, so many
trampled children, such terrible confusion. A pale arm
jutted from a tangle of tepee hides, and Walker swung from
his horse to uncover the woman. It was only dust that paled
her skin, and though her face was crushed, she could
not have been Charity Crawford.

Something pained his shoulder and he turned to block
another blow with an upraised arm. Pistol muzzle against
the buck's belly, he fired twice, then went to one knee and
head-shot a wounded Comanche trying to crawl toward
him.

All individual movement, all sound and taste and feel
mixed into one gigantic ball that rolled over and closed
him in. Walker wasn't conscious of firing and reloading,
nor of faces or shouts. The massive ball rolled ponderously
on, taking him where it would.

Suddenly it was over.

Walker's pistol hung hot against his thigh, and in surprise
he lifted it away. Over against the rock skirts of mountains,
tiny men and horses still raced around, but their sounds
were faint and unimportant. Close by, Tonkawas looted and
scalped.

Troopers moved among the carnage, putting mercy shots
to cavalry mounts and Indian horses alike. It did not
matter that sometimes they also put badly wounded enemy
out of their misery.

Finding his own horse with reins trailing, Walker put his
forehead against its sweated and trembling neck. Horses
weren't at war with each other, but they suffered like their
riders and more. He picked up reins and calmed the shaken
gelding, leading it to creek water purling beyond shattered
and burning tepees.

Something whined and scuttled from a pile of green
hides, more animal than human in its staggering try for
escape. Walker frowned after it, and when a hood slid back,
wheeled with a startled curse.

A white lieutenant shouted and legged his mount to cut
her off, but Walker was already running furiously after.
And when the officer whirled down his saber, Walker
jumped to catch his arm and yank him kicking from the
saddle. She would have darted around him, but Walker
blocked her with his hip and caught at the light hair her
hood had exposed. Hissing, she fought him like a bobcat,
clawing and biting.

"Damn you!" Stunned and raging, the lieutenant reeled toward them. "Damn you, Fairbairn—get the hell out of the way and I'll put a stop to her!"

She was maniacally strong, writhing and heaving, but Walker got her arms pinned to her sides. "You bloodthirsty son of a bitch—can't you see she's white?"

Uniform ripped and stained, his eyes shining with the look of killing some men got, Lieutenant Griffen hesitated, sword arm dropping. "You certain? If you pulled me off my horse for some filthy squaw—"

"Look," Walker panted, "look! Her hair, her face—"

Her face was grimed and streaked, her long hair smeared and tangled, and she spat up at him, teeth snapping like a mad dog. But when he passed his buckskin sleeve across her face, his groin went tight and sick.

"Charity," he said. "Charity, damn it—stop! You're safe now, among friends. It's *me*, girl—Walker; it's Walker."

She grunted something and went still. She stopped fighting, but her eyes were dull and her jaw slack. Charity Crawford didn't recognize him.

Griffen came close. "Even if she's white, you had no call to treat a United States officer like one of your Tonk scouts. When any man lays hand to me—"

Walker said quietly, "If you don't get away from me, I intend to kill you where you stand."

Griffen sucked noisy breath. "You don't dare—"

Looming above them on horseback, neat and military as if reviewing a garrison parade, Colonel Mackenzie said: "Your valor is not in question, Mister Griffen; your logic is. I would say Mister Fairbairn is quite capable of making you a casualty."

"Sir, I didn't know—"

"Now you do," Mackenzie said crisply, and to Walker: "Is she—"

"It's Miss Crawford, all right. She's in some kind of shock."

"Take especial care of her, Mister Fairbairn. We are far from a post doctor."

Without answering, Walker led Charity to the little stream and tried to clean her with a kerchief. Docile, she sat with him, looking off into something he could not see. Her deerskin dress was old and tattered, some Comanche woman's grudging hand-me-down.

Her hair—he wanted to retch; it was greased and

stiffened with buffalo dung and tallow, as many Comanche women did theirs. Charity didn't flinch at his touch, at near icy water. She only stared afar and would not respond to his soft questions.

Maybe she would come back to herself in a doctor's care; she needed medicines and attention to get over horrors she must have suffered since she'd seen her brother gunned down and become a Comanche prisoner.

"Caught up your horse," Dobe Davis said at his back. "Found one for her too. Hold still and I'll pour whiskey on that knife cut in your shoulder."

"She won't talk," Walker said. "She just won't answer me."

"Could be she can't. You check to see she's yet got her tongue? About a hand wider, and some Comanch'd had *you.*"

Charity allowed him to pry open her mouth and peer inside. "Thank God," Walker said.

"Which kind of god," Dobe said, "ours or their'n? Seems like neither come to this party. I'll hand her up and you tie her on."

"She's calm now," Walker said. "No need to rope her."

"Keep her from fallin' off, and—well, I seen me a white woman or so that stayed a long spell with injuns. Some never got right in their heads."

"Charity will be just fine." Her arms felt thin and brittle in Walker's hands. Her belly was flat; it should have been swollen by now. Somewhere along the agonizing road, sometime after her capture and rape, Charity Crawford lost her baby. His throat ached for the right things to say to her, but he couldn't find them.

"I'm taking her to the Sill agency," he said. Mackenzie would be sending a guard detail and its few prisoners there, but Walker couldn't travel that slow.

"Me'n Saba'll ride along," Dobe said. "Comanch got caught real short, but some of 'em'll get un-surprised and try for a lick on their own. Best you have company."

Walker took her horse's lead rope and Charity gave no sign. He said, "You and Saba—what about Fleabite?"

"Ol' Fleabite got hisself kilt. Stopped to lift him some hair and didn't make sure the Comanch was plumb dead. I'll miss that thievin' injun. Me and him go back a long ways."

Fresh scalps dripping red down his horse's foreleg,

beautifully cured buffalo robes strapped high behind the saddle, pockets of his worn-out army coat bulging, Saba the Tonkawa joined them.

"Look at him," Walker said. "Easy as if he was sitting drunk in his own lodge. He doesn't give a damn that Flea-bite is dead."

"Might be you're readin' the wrong sign. I expect Saba run out of damns after Comanch kilt off his whole family, and he ain't had no lodge of his own since; not much tribe neither."

The mountains were still now, any pursuit over. Cavalry-men were gathering, weary and drained. An Indian woman squatted moaning, holding a blank-faced little girl against pendulous breasts. The slowing crackle of fires was loud because there was no other sound. Troopers looked up, then away, as Walker led Charity's horse by them. Only Lieutenant Griffen and two other white officers continued to stare.

They rode a long way in silence, Walker checking Charity often. Since that first desperate fury, she hadn't changed; dully pliant, she looked off into the distance and inward at some dark horror. Walker tried talking gently to her, touch-ing her hand, reminding her of times they spent together and plans once discussed. She didn't respond; only Charity's body was here, the essence of her somewhere else.

Before dark they made camp in a ground fold that would hide a cookfire and offer natural defenses. Walker had to spoon food into her and wipe her mouth. When the fire embered and Charity was blanket wrapped and laid to sleep, Walker saw to his weapons and horse, to resoaking his shoulder bandage with whiskey. Night sky was high and cool, dusted by stars. Saba slept in the arroyo's narrow mouth, and Dobe still hunkered just beyond the dying fire.

Walker sat beside him. "About a thousand years ago," he said, "I ran from war and killing. It didn't make sense then or now, but here I am. There's Charity, what's left of her. She was a kindness to the world, a tenderness; now look."

Dobe pulled at his pipe stem. A coal flared briefly in the ashes and touched his grizzled whiskers with red. He said, "Way I see it, we didn't turn her no favor. If'n she comes to herself, folks'll misery up the rest of her life, account of she let herself get used by injun bucks."

"Damn it," Walker said, "that wasn't her fault."

"White folks figure she should of kilt herself first. Like a plantation lady set on by blacks."

"What the hell does anyone know about a life-or-death choice unless they're forced to make it?"

"Don't make no never mind. They need to *think* they know. Miss Charity now—she couldn't take a knife to her neck, and maybe the Comanch didn't let her. She did the next best and kilt her mind."

Walker nodded and went to lie beside Charity, separate but together and making a protective barrier of his body. Weary clean through, he couldn't sleep right away. Echoes of the fight kept coming back, and something else—a strange sense of relief. Her baby, he thought; he was glad Charity's child would not be born to a crazy woman.

He thought of it as *hers*, where before it had been theirs, even his. Was he glad for her, the baby, or just for himself, relieved of all responsibilities? Walker shied from the thought and went safely back to the fight.

Mackenzie was slowly and surely breaking the Comanche nation, accomplishing more than all western frontier commanders gone before him. By keeping the Indians always on the move, by destroying their supplies and horses, killing and burning in the Comanches' own fashion, he was winning. Deskbound Washington generals sent infantry to fight swift, horsed Comanches. Mackenzie made use of them by transporting them in wagons as secondary troops, but the main job was being done by tough, disciplined Buffalo Soldiers, honed and hardened into a deadly striking force.

Band by band, the Comanches would break themselves upon the 4th Cavalry. The way to the west would be forever opened to hunters and settlers who would alter the face of the land itself. Right or wrong, it would happen, and nothing this side of hell could stop it.

Beside him, Charity whimpered softly in her sleep, and he put a gentling hand upon her. How she must have been hurt, to back into this not seeing, not feeling. Some warrior dragged her from the wrecked wagon and over her brother's body. Maybe he exercised his captor's rights then and there, raping Charity as the others watched. He could have passed her along, each randy Comanche pounding into her flesh. Over and over, her body had been ravished and degraded.

Somewhere along the trail or hauled into camp to be

scorned and beaten by Indian women, Charity escaped by retreating inside her head. She might never come out again.

He suddenly thought of Tosanna, taken by whites and whoring her easy, luxurious way up through English society. Milady Savage had been transplanted into civilization; Charity was ruined by Tosanna's cruel people, possibly her very tribe.

Could Tosanna have been in the destroyed village, her fine, lush body trampled, burned, made one with the carnage? If so, he hadn't found her, and couldn't tell one burned-black woman from another.

She'd damned him because a man died in a stupid duel Walker tried to avoid, a man he did not shoot. If that same gray old Duke had journeyed here to be ambushed along the trail, if he'd been slow-burned like Captain Richards— what would Tosanna have to say about that?

CHAPTER 40

Quanah sat moodily at his tepee fire. With him, Tosanna watched smoke climb up and out the stretched hide opening. For some time now, he had kept his other wives in a separate tent, Red Face, Sees Her Son, and Tail Feather. They did not resent her, but took pride that their husband could afford so many women.

Tosanna looked up when Quanah said, "Again the Long Knives chief has won. The Kutsoo-ehkuh lost many braves, many women and children when Buffalo Soldiers rode into their winter camp."

"And the Kwehar-enuh," Tosanna answered. "Taken in small bites."

"You know the White Eyes. Why do they continue to hunt us down?"

She put her hands together. "Treaties, the Comancheros say—papers signed by chiefs that swear all Comanches will live on reservations."

"I do not put my mark on a treaty, nor did any Kwehar-enuh."

"To White Eyes, one Comanche chief speaks for all."

Quanah sighed. "That is foolish; each Comanche speaks only for himself."

"Long Knives, *tejanos,* and the rest—they do not believe this. If we live on a reservation, they will feed us beef and flour and give presents."

"Like so many coyotes that have forgotten how to hunt, and to fight. We will no longer be The People, if we accept their gifts. We will be only their tame animals, chained to lands they take from us and only partly give back. Are we such fools?"

Tosanna said, *"Tejanos* speak highly of Quanah, calling him Quanah Parker and saying he fights so well through the white blood of his mother."

"Naduah," Quanah murmured. "My mother and small sister were taken by Long Knives who swept down on our camp and surprised us. I tried to buy them back through a *comanchero,* offering many horses. They were held by Naduah's white family, although she begged for return to us, her real people. Small sister died of White Eye illness, and Cynthia Ann Parker—they called her this—was broken by grief and followed her child to the grave."

After a moment, Tosanna said, "I am sorry. Naduah was my friend. My husband, whites do not think as we do. Their laws and customs are different, and they have great power."

His calm, dark eyes fixed on her. "As you have said at the council, medicine woman. As you have told me in many nights. I understand and believe you, although others do not."

"Older Man," she said. "He cost us dearly when he killed my friend."

"He was correct, if the black man would not bring other wagons."

Tosanna bit her lip. "Comanches I knew never lied. Older Man broke the word I had given."

"A woman's word. Not the same."

"There is a woman living across the great, far waters. She sends many soldiers to lands our people cannot imagine, in numbers we cannot count. When Victoria speaks, men and tribes tremble. She is very powerful."

He gave her half a smile. "But she is not Comanche."

She had been gone from her people for a very long time, and only now began to realize some changes in herself. Now she could feel a flick of anger at her husband's criticism. Now she could think him wrong, no matter how great a warrior, how famed a chief.

Tosanna's face must have shown her pique, for Quanah reached to lightly touch her hand. "Last Flower, I know you are wise and your medicine as strong as you are beautiful. When I speak harshly to you, it is as a man, as all men of the Kwehar-enuh. I have thought hard and long upon the magics you have told me, and dreamed with the spirits."

He sat quietly. Cold wind whispered across the tepee, and a nightbird mourned far off. Quanah said, "Perhaps it is my white blood, but the gods have spoken to me, and in sadness. In such sadness no Comanche has ever known. You were right when you said we cannot defeat the White Eyes. Already our Antelope band is the only free tribe left through all of Comancheria, from the Rio Grande to the Brazos and beyond. We are the last true Comanches because we do not crawl to a reservation where others starve if the White Eye great father does not send beef. We do not wash away war paint because Long Knives command it. We are The People."

Tosanna did not stir, enthralled by Quanah's rich voice, by his deep sorrow.

He said, "So I must lead until the final defeat. We must strike the Long Knives hard and swiftly, and ride away. We cannot remain Comanches if we do not gain honor in war, if we do not hunt buffalo and raise our lodges where and when we please, upon land that belongs to the spirits. When these things are past, then we become only dogs. For me it is better to die, but I cannot speak for the children, nor for those yet in their mothers' bellies. I do not have the right."

Tosanna blinked through tears. He knew; he understood, but Quanah's destiny allowed him no choice. Nor could she choose. She had cast her lot with her people, and must also follow her fate.

She said, "Send me to the meeting place to bargain with Comancheros. I will return with guns and ammunition, with food we must have for this time of snows. Do not have Older Man ride with me."

"Once," he said softly, "no man could count the buffalo, for they were many as blades of grass. *Tejano* hunters came to take only skins and tongues, and now the plains are strewn with white bones. Soon the buffalo will be gone, and with them the Comanches. Name those to ride with you, wife; bring food for the children."

Tosanna left after a cold dawn, Crooked Leg, Coyote, and Starfall beside her, leading pack mules. When night came upon them, they had reached the arroyo where her treasure wagon was hidden. There they staked the mules, and come morning Tosanna lifted saddlebags of coins to her mare's back. It had been a cold, fireless camp, for too many Long Knife patrols passed this way. They ate sun-dried buffalo meat and drank icy water. In the hills dark wind carried a promise of snow, and Tosanna settled deeper into her blanket.

"There," Crooked Leg said, pointing with his rifle.

"I see them," Tosanna said. "Do they always ride in packs?"

Coyote said, "No, my sister. This time Quanah sent for many things, and perhaps many were needed to carry it all."

"Perhaps," she answered, "these greedy Mexicans heard of our gold and mean to take it."

Crooked Leg snorted. "They are only *comancheros;* their hearts are weak."

Starfall was an old warrior, going gray and stooped. He had many scars, and traced one across his cheek as he said, "We will guard against them anyhow. Even a rat will sometimes bite."

"I will lead," Crooked Leg said.

"No," Starfall said. "Medicine woman speaks for Quanah, and it is her gold."

"Gold." Crooked Leg spat. "They are such fools about bits of yellow metal."

"It is good they are," Starfall said. "How else are we to get rifles?"

"Take them, of course," Crooked Leg said.

Jogging her mare toward the clump of men waiting at the base of a low hill, Tosanna said, "I count five *comancheros* and ten horses."

"Pack animals," Crooked Leg said.

Starfall touched Coyote and they trotted their horses off to each side, putting distance between them. Now Tosanna could make out the evident Comanchero leader, a man who wore a curly black beard and silver conchos upon his chaps and saddle. Other sombreroed men behind him did not fan out or handle their rifles, and she thought it must be all right. Maybe so many riders came in case of a brush with a Long Knives patrol.

She reined her mare to a stop; Crooked Leg sat his stallion a horse length behind her.

"*Hola,*" said Black Beard. "The Comanches send a woman. Greetings, *chiquita;* are you part payment for these things Quanah Parker must have?"

"I am my husband's tongue," she said. "Have you brought bacon and cornmeal, *tejano* beans, salt?" Beyond the grinning man she saw three patient pack horses, long wrapped shapes that must be rifles, boxes that could contain anything.

"And rifles, pretty girl; bullets to fire through *gringo* heads. You are a fine-looking woman, and we have been long on the trail, dodging *soldados* all the way." Eyes flashing, he snapped his fingers. "Ah, *sí, sí;* you must be her the black freighter spoke of—the same woman that *gringo* hide hunters cursed in the *cantinas*. She of great beauty and much, much gold. Did you bring all your gold, *mujer?*"

Tosanna felt uneasy. "Enough, *señor;* let us count the rifles and see the supplies. Then we will speak of gold."

The man's teeth were white and jagged against swarthy skin; a scar puckered his left eyebrow, twisting it up. His left hand swung in a slow, lazy movement. "There is no need for them to fear, those warriors out there."

"They fear nothing," Tosanna said, a tingle along her spine. "We are Comanches, *hombre.*" She glanced at the pack animals again, three of them.

Only three; two horses had saddles but no riders!

Shouting a warning, Tosanna whipped her blanket at Black Beard's horse. It shied and almost lost its rider. But guns on the hill were already speaking from ambush as a pair of hidden riflemen drove bullets into Starfall and Coyote.

Black Beard shot Crooked Leg with a derringer he'd concealed in his sombrero. Swaying, the warrior caught himself by his horse's mane, lifting his rifle for a shot which snatched a Comanchero from the saddle.

Other pistols flared at Crooked Leg and he hunched against their shock, war cry stopped in his throat. Tosanna tried to spin her horse and fire; the bullet went wild as Black Beard and another man shouldered their horses into her mare. Then they were at her from many directions, and her shoulders slammed the earth with a jolt that drove breath from her lungs and flashed behind her eyes.

She rolled away from plunging hoofs, but her rifle was gone, and when she came up with her knife flashing, they beat at her with quirts and ropes. On her knees again, she stabbed at a booted leg above her head. Reflex stuck a rowel to the horse, and it bucked.

Something hard caught Tosanna along the head, making her blind and numb. Her mouth filled with dirt and she choked. Gasping, she tried to push away the dizzying ground.

When her head cleared, Tosanna jerked at thongs which bound her hands behind. The deerskin dress was ripped down its front and air was chill upon her exposed breasts. She glared hate and defiance at Black Beard, at others who poked hurtful fingers into her body.

A man with a lantern jaw and muddy eyes delighted in twisting her nipples. "Damned if'n this ain't the prettiest squaw I ever seen. Look at them fine tits, Castillo."

Black Beard said, "Later, *compadre*. Now we speak to her of gold, not flesh. Woman, where did this come from?" He hefted her saddlebags.

She spat at him and he slapped her hard. It was difficult to rise with her hands bound. Castillo stroked his beard and showed teeth at her. "Understand, *indio* bitch. I have no interest in keeping you alive. Where did you get this gold?"

"From England, a place the ignorant have never seen, *peon*."

Feet braced now, she only rocked under his succession of open-handed slaps. Tosanna tasted blood when she laughed at Black Beard.

The long-jawed *tejano* said, "Just so long's you don't hurt her pussy none."

Tosanna saw the other faces, staring, grinning, anticipating, sharpshooters come down from their ambush. At least Crooked Leg took an enemy with him. She hoped she might do the same. She said, "Quanah will hunt you to earth for this, *animale*."

Castillo shrugged. "The great Quanah Parker looks to his skin; the Comanches are no longer powerful. I will sell these same supplies many times over. Since your people are so busy running from *gringo* cavalry, there is much time for you to tell us about the money."

Coyote, she thought; only a boy. Valiant old warrior Starfall, cheated of his death song; Crooked Leg, who never doubted the superiority of his tribe—all dead now. Needed guns and vital food lost.

She said, "You should have waited, *perro;* the bone you dogs seek is a night ride away."

"Jesus," said Longjaw, "if'n she ain't lyin', that's too damned far into Comancheria."

Castillo dipped a furry hand into one of Tosanna's saddlebags. "Look, hombre—new minted, most of these coins, never used. And this single bar—"

"Can't keep our hair," another man grunted, "gold ain't no use."

Castillo appealed to the last man. "Juanito, a fortune awaits us and this *puta* holds the key. The Comanches flee, and without guns and food they starve."

"Quanah Parker," a man said. "I don't know."

"A dozen wenches like this one," Castillo said. "A hundred. Women and wine and luxury in Mexico, all the money we can spend."

Longjaw reached out and slid one hand down Tosanna's belly to her crotch. Pulling away would do no good, so she only stared at the stubbled face and muddy eyes. He said, "Good enough for me."

Castillo tugged at his beard. *"Bueno!* You grand riflemen—Perez, Ortiz—the *indio* horses and arms are yours, and later, *mis amigos*—a turn with this wench."

Tosanna said, "I will take you to the wagon."

Castillo showed teeth. "So—of course you will. If you lie, you will be treated as Comanches treat their prisoners. I think cutting off your eyelids and staking you down to look forever into the sun—"

"You will kill me anyhow."

Castillo fondled his derringer before returning the little pistol to its sombrero clip. *"Sí,* but quickly and with mercy once we have the gold. A wagon full, you say?"

Longjaw squeezed and Tosanna stifled a gasp as hard fingers probed her mound. Longjaw said, "Soft and like to boilin'. Any them gunned injuns your man, honey? Won't be nigh as good as him watchin' you get screwed, but you just ain't fixin' to forget his dead face whilst the meat gets throwed to you."

Laughing, Castillo said, "Gently, *compadre;* she would not care to have a *peon* mistreat a *patrona's* ass."

"Better take off my hat," Longjaw retorted. He threw Tosanna to the ground and dropped his breeches. Ugly, throbbing, and distended, his man-thing aimed at her. She closed her eyes.

But Tosanna could not entirely close her mind to his rutting and thrusting. He was cruel but blessedly quick, and her thighs ached when he lifted from between them.

The rest of her dress was torn away; against her buttocks pebbled earth was cold and hard. Someone else mounted her helpless body, rocking and pushing. Tosanna locked her lower lip between her teeth.

Was it the fourth man or the fifth? Stoically, she accepted the pain. But a new, strange part of Tosanna resented each alien hand placed upon her body, each seeking that penetrated her most private places. They brutally kept at her, soiling her flesh, sparing no part of her from insistent probings. Over and over, again and again, their laughter ringing in her ears, the clotting, rancid taste of them forever in her throat, Tosanna lay beneath them.

She was Last Flower, daughter of a Comanche chief, wife to a greater chief; she would let these *mexicano* and *tejano* dogs enjoy no sign of hurt. But that new difference rebelled against such dishonor to her body. Whatever his race, his tribe, no man had the *right* to force himself into her body. She was a woman, a *woman*—not an animal in heat to be bred by the nearest male animal.

Bruised and aching, she lay unmoving when at last they were done with her, knowing pride that they had not broken her. She had not cried aloud, and if she listened to desperate, lonely screams inside her own head, none other would ever know.

CHAPTER 41

A Tonkawa woman servant soaped and bathed Charity Crawford, because the agent's wife—otherwise a good Christian woman—could not stomach the task. Walker paced, unable to sit for long, frustrated at every turn. Maybe he was wrong to lay blame for no solution to Charity's madness, but it seemed medicine could do *something*.

Not to reach the mind, Doctor Julius said; an Indian witch doctor might probably do as much. Surgery could not yet repair mysterious damages inside the head, and potions held no magic.

Pray, agent John Haworth suggested, pray hard that this poor lost sheep be returned to her senses. Amen, chanted Rebecca Haworth; amen, my husband. The woman is unclean in body and mind, she should beg forgiveness.

"For what?" Walker asked the cold and lowering sky. How had Charity sinned, that she should need forgiveness, stay alive? Just that, evidently; the whispers said any decent white woman would choose death over such bestial dishonor.

Of course, the whisperers had never been captive and didn't know that often no choice was given. Nor did they realize how sweet life became to those in imminent danger of losing it.

Walker leaned against a rough-hewn wall and watched some bedraggled Comanches waiting for rations issue. Tired old men and hunched women, the very young—no warriors among them, no strong girls. While these weak components

of a tribal band were fed—however miserably—and clothed
—however shoddy—their kinsmen were raiding settlements
and wagon trains. And torturing innocents like Charity
Crawford.

She had gone so far into herself she couldn't find the
way back. Civilization wanted to fault her for that also. Be
damned if he would allow that, Walker fumed. When
Charity healed, he'd carry her off so she could begin a new
life anywhere she wanted. He owed her that much and more.
Somehow he'd make it work.

When he propped himself against the porch rail, the
agent's wife came out. No part of Rebecca Haworth
looked soft. She was pulled tight over her bones, hair
skinned back in a knot, colorless lips and green eyes only
afterthoughts to her long, sharp nose.

"That woman seems to have forgotten her own language," she said.

"Her name is Charity," Walker said.

"Oh, yes—Charity. It's difficult for one to be charitable
toward a woman like that." Rebecca Haworth drew her
lips and eyebrows together.

"Charity, a woman like *Charity*—which is?"

"You must know my meaning, sir. And it is evident she
must be held under guard, else she will hurt herself or
others."

Pushing off the porch rail, Walker said, "Charity is sick,
not dangerous."

"She means to return to her—to those heathen."

"Then she doesn't know what she's doing."

Rebecca smoothed hair that already looked painted on;
her knife-blade nose aimed at him. "She feels out of place
here. Of course, Mister Haworth will not allow any white
woman to so despoil herself. It is our Christian duty to protect a fallen sister, even from her own errors."

Walker bit back an angry reply and said, "When may I
see her?"

Rebecca Haworth sniffed. "Mister Haworth will decide
that—with Doctor Julius, of course. It's not as if you are
her husband."

"I'm her fiancé," Walker said.

Rebecca Haworth stared off into the distance to some
higher plane. "Well," she said.

Because he could barely keep himself from slapping the
woman, Walker moved away, striding across the hard-

beaten parade ground. No tame Indian so much as glanced at him, and cavalry officers turned from his dour look.

He found Dobe Davis and Saba hunkered behind the stables. "She doin' all right?" Dobe asked.

"So-so; she doesn't talk much, and the agent's wife claims Charity means to run off. I don't think so. She just needs rest and time."

Dobe nodded and changed the subject. "Me'n Saba toured the reservation. Ain't a single Antelope band Comanche on the place, and from what I can make out ain't ever goin' to be, long as that breed is leadin'."

Walker squatted beside the old scout. "What's that mean?"

"Means the Comanch ain't pacified, by a damn sight. Quanah Parker's off in them Llano Estacados till he gets dug out."

"Mackenzie and the Buffalo Soldiers will pry him loose, and then it's done with. I don't think I'll be along this time."

"Miss Charity," Dobe said. "Only fair you stay with her."

Walker smelled horses and tobacco, hay and winter. Saba the Tonkawa sucked noisily upon a pipe and warmed in weak sunlight trapped against the stable wall. Dobe stirred ground between his moccasins with a stick and watched the designs as if they were gateways into memory.

What if Charity never came out of shock, if she remained mindless? It might be better for her, not having to think upon things done to her in the name of war. He would care for her either way, help ease the hurt of the unborn child.

Responsibilities—he'd put his back to them—the War between the States, his father's land, to all the women who mistook his passionate interest for love. This time he couldn't turn away and be true to himself.

Perhaps every man labored under an invisible weight— Dobe Davis, experienced and wise, and never talking about the past; Saba the Tonkawa, living with the specters of his butchered tribe; Colonel Mackenzie, hundreds of lives in his hand and thousands more ahead of his saber.

And Tosanna? Her image irritated him, overlapping Charity's picture. Tosanna couldn't be back with her people. She had no cause to return. She was intelligent and beautiful, sought after by every rich Englishman with a swelling in his breeches. Surely, after tasting the luxuries

and comforts of civilization, Milady Savage would never
come back to slavery, famine, and danger.

But the young Comanche buck—dying, he had spoken of
a great medicine woman, the Last Flower. Maybe the boy
was delirious; maybe Dobe misunderstood. Even if there'
had been no mistake and Tosanna was actually once more
with her tribe, her presence should mean nothing to him.
Especially not now.

Still, he winced at the thought of her in some village the
Buffalo Soldiers would thunder over with roaring guns and
flashing sabers. Those great, dark eyes gone sightless in
death; all that wealth of black hair trampled into the earth;
her enchanted body battered and ripped . . .

And what of Charity's pale and tender flesh, battered
and ripped? Tosanna's people had done that to Charity,
and Walker could picture the bucks laughing and rutting,
one after another brutalizing her. Poor Charity, so long
a virgin, forced into degradation she could not accept and
never forgive.

No more than her own people would pardon her for
living. Damn—at least the Comanches took back one of
their own, though soiled by numerous white men. Walker
wondered out loud about Tosanna's presence with her tribe.

Dobe said, "Mite curious how come you know a Comanch medicine woman, since you ain't been on the plains
afore."

"If it's the same woman, I knew her in England."

Dobe aimed chewed tobacco at his latest dirt design.
"Reckon she's the one. Comanch might change names two,
three times, but there ain't no two Comanch named just
alike—bad medicine. How come a medicine woman took
herself clear to England and back?"

"How come you have an itch to know? An Englishman
fighting on Juarez's side took her or bought her, or some
such. She cut a swath through high society, but mostly in
bed."

"Your bed, too," Dobe said.

When Walker didn't deny it, Saba the Tonkawa got up
and padded away. Dobe said, "Idee of you tucked up to a
Comanch don't set right with ol' Saba."

"Hell, he'd do the same thing. Taking the other side's
women isn't just a Comanche custom."

Dobe nodded. "Sure, but when Saba got done, he'd take
her hair and fix her female parts so no Comanch could use

her in the spirit world. He wouldn't get all het up if some dyin' buck said her name."

"It—it just surprised me," Walker said. "I'll go sit with Charity now, if the old dragon will allow it. I wish I was as certain about sin and innocence."

"She's got her right, just like you and me; just like ol' Saba, even if nobody else can't make head nor tail out'n Tonk spirits."

Walker stood up. "The right honorable Martin Luther Crawford had to force his religion on everybody else? Damn, Dobe; you sound like some kind of preacher yourself."

"Once I was," Dobe said and took himself off, leaving Walker open mouthed.

Dobe Davis a man of the cloth. That was as startling as Colonel Mackenzie selling out to the Indians, or Tosanna turning white. Or Walker Fairbairn growing up.

He left the stable wall to a few flies that had somehow lucked through the frosts and headed for agency headquarters. Stationing soldiers on a post run by peacemakers didn't exactly conform to Quaker notions of propriety, but Mackenzie cared only for his objective: destroy the Comanches. He'd take troops into the devil's bedroom, if that was his duty, and the 4th Cavalry would follow.

And Walker's duty was to Charity Crawford, so he wiped his moccasins and rapped upon the agent's door. Still out of her head, Brother Haworth said, as what decent white woman wouldn't be. Ranting and raving a bit before blessed sleep claimed her; pray for her, sir. Pray for her immortal salvation and perhaps you may visit her tomorrow.

Walker went slowly down wooden steps to baked clay. No word from Haworth about the Comanche prisoners herded into an abandoned sutler shack. But then, to Haworth all Indians were only misinformed children who needed guidance, not force of arms. If Mackenzie didn't get them exchanged for white captives soon, the agent would see the Comanche women and children and old men released.

How did Sister Haworth reconcile that bless-you-my-red-children attitude with her scorn because those same noble innocents had raped Charity? Everybody had a right, Dobe claimed; it seemed right came down harder on some sides than others.

In the hayloft all camps seemed to reserve for scouts, Walker's sleep was troubled by vague shapes and monstrous weights. He woke shaken by dread he could not name, and climbed down the ladder to share a cigar with the night. Blanket around his shoulders, pistol belt loosely at his hips, he leaned against the barn and tried to banish his mood.

Lamps in barracks and office windows told Walker it was still early. He stared at the agent's quarters and wondered about Charity. A dim figure ghosted along the covered veranda and Walker cupped the cigar ember in his hand, shielding its light. Sister Haworth off to the "necessary" in secret to hide her mortal needs? Her pale shape winked out and he drew upon his smoke.

A sentry's challenge snapped the night, backed by hand slap on a gun butt. Comanches? Walker pinched out the cigar spark and buried it by a boot scuff.

A rifle went off amid hoarse shouts and running boots. All the fort came awake in confusion. Walker trotted for the agent's house, Colt in hand, but no warrior skulked there, so he veered toward the old sutler's shack.

In its black shadow, a rush of desperate, silent figures poured over him, and Walker hacked at one with his pistol before he realized the shapes were women and children— Comanche prisoners scattering free.

Someone had loosed them, so Walker angled across the running river of Indians in search of the bold raider. Another gun flashed briefly and somebody screamed. The gate guard must have gone down, for the tall gate rattled wide upon massive iron hinges.

A man loped into Walker, and when he cursed, Walker recognized Lieutenant Griffen's voice. "Fairbairn here—for god's sake, order the sentries to cease fire. They're killing women and children."

"Out of my way, damn you! I'm officer of the day." And Griffen was gone. So were most of the Comanches.

A sea of bobbing lanterns swelled and eddied, and it took Colonel Mackenzie himself to bring some sort of order to turmoil. His clear, decisive voice sliced through the hubbub and men obeyed.

Shortly after, Walker discovered Charity missing.

"I just don't know," Brother Haworth said. "One minute she was safely abed, then—"

Hidden chin to shoetop by a flannel nightgown and a wrap of the same drab material, Rebecca Haworth said nothing, but stared disapproval.

Sweeping a lantern from a soldier's hand, Walker started

a search of the agency. He looked into every corner, beneath each building and in every cranny large enough to hide a cat, but Charity was nowhere on the grounds. Helplessly, Walker stared into darkness beyond the palisades. She was somewhere out there, either taken by the Comanches or drifting with them, confused and frightened.

"Play hell comin' up on 'em in the night," Dobe Davis said, "and come daylight, they'll be from here to yonder. Reckon Miss Charity'll be easier to find though."

Walker said, "If they haven't strangled her."

"That too," Dobe said as they stood together in the headquarters building.

Mackenzie stalked in, hatless and shirtless but giving the impression he was in full dress uniform. "Officer of the day, your report."

Griffen was flustered. "Sir, we recaptured three and shot nine others."

"Caught three old men too stove up to run," Dobe whispered.

When Mackenzie fixed cold eyes upon the lieutenant, Griffen stuttered, "S-sir—it was im-impossible to suppose a woman, a *white* woman, would distract my—the—sentry and release those savages. If she wasn't crazy as a bedbug—"

Walker slid forward and caught Griffen's arm. "Charity? Are you talking about Charity Crawford? Are you holding her?"

Griffen shook off his hand. "Colonel Mackenzie—"

Softly, Walker said, "If I don't get a straight answer, I mean to kill you here and now."

Mackenzie said, "Mister Fairbairn."

And Griffen sneered. "With all of us armed? I can't credit you with—"

Sharply, Mackenzie said, "Mister Griffen, answer Mister Fairbairn."

Face red, Griffen said, "Very well, *Mister* Fairbairn; your inamorata hasn't been caught yet, but I am certain my patrols will bring her in. If she and her Comanche friends resist arrest—well, that would be better all around. Stark mad or just an Indian lover, it's evident the woman would be better off dead."

"Sorry, colonel," Walker said, and the familiar killing slowness was upon him as his pistol crawled into his hand.

He dragged Griffen along the head with it, and the lieutenant seemed to take forever in falling.

"You," Walker said to the adjutant, to Sergeant Abel Greenlee, and the orderly.

"Not me," Greenlee said, and the adjutant didn't move a muscle. The orderly stared. Mackenzie said, "You were provoked, Mister Fairbairn, but I cannot countenance gun play in my unit. The paymaster will see you off in the morning."

Time picked up its pace once more, and Walker said: "Respect for you kept me from killing him. He won't be lucky next time, or any trooper who so much as *points* at Miss Charity."

Unafraid, Mackenzie said, "My orders are that she be returned alive."

"Thanks," Walker said, "but I'll see to that myself, and I won't wait until morning to do it."

CHAPTER 42

Tosanna ached all over. She was bruised and bitten and clawed, but her deepest hurt was lodged in her heart. It was like an arrowhead driven between her ribs and called humiliation and she could not let them see it. Any sign less than courage and she would bring dishonor to the Kweharenuh and shame to all The People.

And she felt great shame for herself, a soiling that ground into her flesh and dirtied her blood—in that she was not Comanche, but White Eye, and it was difficult to know when the changing took place. But she now understood why *tejanos* and Mexicans and White Eyes were so maddened when their women were degraded. It was a great truth to share with Quanah, if she lived.

One Comanchero had taken more than his turn with her body, drawn back again and again by the grunts and moans of others mounting her. At last, sated and grinning through his dark brush, he squatted beside Tosanna and tested the rawhide binding her wrists. He looped another tie to her ankles, pulling them together.

"Won't have to spread your legs for a spell," he said. "Damned if'n you ain't got the hottest, tightest box I ever knowed, even with all them randy bastards puttin' it to you."

"I can be much better with only one man," she said through swollen lips.

He rolled her nipples between forefingers and thumbs.

378

"Now you wouldn't want me to do 'em out'n their rightful share?"

Tosanna whispered, "And share the rest of the gold also?"

He put a hand over her mouth. "The rest? Bitch, if you lie—"

When he took away his hand, she murmured, "As much more as you already took."

The man glanced over at Black Beard and others around the cookfire. "Where you got it?"

"A night's ride."

He moved hands from her breasts to her throat. "How come you tellin' *me*?"

"So you will not kill me," she said. "I will not be left here alive."

The hands fell away. "Pretty smart, but how you figure slippin' away from that bunch?"

"The horses; walk out a way with two, scare off the rest. They will think you crazy for leaving your share of the gold."

He kept stroking her thighs. "You just mean to toll me off where them damned injuns can get at me."

"My tribe is a full two-day ride. There is so much yellow metal only half that distance; and jewels that shine in the sun."

"Where the hell injuns get hold of diamonds and the like?"

Tosanna rolled her pelvis so that his palm slid to her wet mound. "From where the loot was already taken. England. Think, *hombre*—to be wealthy, to have me to yourself. When you tire of me, let me go."

"Yeah," he muttered, "yeah." She felt his fingers search into her. "Sure now—turn you loose and light a shuck. Not Mexico, account of they'll look for me there."

"Somewhere else," Tosanna said, "anywhere you wish, because you are so rich."

"New Orleans," he breathed, "San Francisco."

"London," Tosanna said.

"Yeah, clear to England and who's to stop me. They'll kiss my ass account of the money."

"All yours, *señor;* everything just for you."

"Damn right; nobody tellin' me what to do all the time. Just me and all that goddamn money, them pretty diamonds."

Tosanna held her breath and begged good fortune from the spirits. She remained very still when his knife sliced between her ankles, then sat up. Mouth to her ear, he said, "Keepin' your hands tied; you can ride thataway."

Around the fire men laughed and made jokes about the squaw and why the *tejano* couldn't get enough of her, about how they meant to spend Indian gold. Waiting crouched in darkness, Tosanna listened hard for any sound that might bring Comancheros to their feet. Her lover-rapist was talking well and raised no alarm.

Her inner thighs felt raw, and she despised the stickiness there. More than this shame at being used was her guilt at failure. Quanah and the tribe depended upon her for food and weapons, for ammunition they must have to remain free. She had failed them and the dead warriors whose bodies lay stiffening in the night.

The *tejano* would have made a good hunter; he returned to her by a wide circle, desert sand muffling horses walking. By then she had half-chewed through her wrist thongs. He led both saddled horses and her, and when she stumbled, pulled her erect by her hair.

He hissed, "Stuck pistol shells in a hollow branch and laid it clost to the fire. When them things go to poppin', they'll figure injuns is all over 'em. Cut horses loose from the picket line, so they'll spook time the shells go off."

Tosanna caressed him with her voice. "You are very wise."

"Ain't nothin' but slick," he replied, then snapped, "Hit the saddle!" as ammunition exploded in the fire.

He kept the lead rope taut between his saddle horn and hers as they raced blindly through the dark. Twice her horse almost went down, and his fell hard, but he never let go the rope, rolling to his feet and urging his mount back up.

Behind them shots split the night and men yelled in shock. Tosanna urged her horse on, clinging to the horn with bound wrists. Guns popped as Comancheros fought phantoms, and her captor dropped their horses into a trot. When they slowed to a rapid, flatfooted walk, the camp was only an echo behind them.

Tosanna's savaged groin ached and she felt each jolt of the horse in her breasts. If she only had her knife—but it had been taken from her and she was still a prisoner. Beside her he said, "Point the way, woman. Don't make no mistakes or get sassy, account of I done left my part of them gold bars ahint, and if'n you're markin' me for a fool, I'd as lief shoot you and be done with it."

"This way," she answered softly, lining up a bright star and a mountain peak. If the stars were really Comanche spirit lights, she hoped for their kindness. Her captor was cunning and suspicious, not as lust and greed minded as she hoped.

She breathed easier when no pursuit came thundering after, and bobbed in and out of catnaps, swaying in the saddle. Tosanna was grateful for the gray light of cold dawn. Not far from the secret canyon and its depleted treasure, she thought; she certainly did not intend giving up the few remaining coins and the jewels.

Would Quanah have sent out a small war party? Not yet, she thought, but there might be lone scouts prowling the hills. She could not risk waiting on them; she must take the risks herself. Pulling up her horse at the canyon mouth, she pointed hands that yet seemed bound and the *tejano* made out the wagon hidden by brush.

"Damned if'n it ain't here," he said. "Light down, injun, and stay right close or I'll jerk your hair off. Might be a gun in yonder."

Pocked face stubbled with gray-brown hairs, shifty eyes here and there in quick estimation, he looked no better than when he had covered her with his sour, sweated body. Some of his juices might yet be trapped inside her debased flesh.

No weapon, no pistol or sharp knife, and now he looped the lead rope about her neck and tugged it painfully tight. "In case you mean to turn rabbit, and if'n there ain't no diamonds and gold waitin'—why, you'll be awishin' you was still back yonder where Blackie and them ol' boys would kill you quicklike. That's account of me keepin' you alive a long spell, and you beggin' and carryin' on all the time."

Meekly, she bowed her head and accepted the noose. Tosanna's mind darted like a ground squirrel; there was no weapon in the wagon. She would have to find something else, but what?

Holding to her rope, he climbed into the wagon. When he found the iron box and its contents, the man whistled in awe. "Whole pisspot full! Didn't lie none, did you, squaw? This here's worth more'n all you damned Comanch put together."

The rope went slack and Tosanna bent slowly. The cactus was deeply rooted and she set her teeth against the needled pain of its spines. Twisting, feeling a hundred sharp, agonizing stabs, she dragged the plant from the sandy soil to hold it by the roots.

Tears nearly blinded her, but when he backed over the wagon tailgate grasping the iron box, she saw his face clearly enough. Tosanna swung the cactus with all her strength. It slashed the man across his eyes and mouth. His scream was full of pain and horror.

She jerked free of the rope and ducked around the wagon as the cactus stuck to his face and he continued to scream, even as he pawed at the torture blinding him. He shook cactus loose and fired his pistol wildly.

One random shot ripped a splinter from the wagon seat. Below it, Tosanna worked to loosen a singletree near the tongue, muffling harness links in her good hand. He heard something anyway, and speared bullets close to her knees. The tapered length of wood came free and she drifted around the wagon.

The *tejano* was reloading by feel, cursing steadily; blood and something else leaked down his contorted face. Tosanna could see bits of green hanging to his eyes, see long brown spines fixed in his face and through his eyelids.

The same kind of needles worked deeper into her right hand as she picked up the rock. A gasp nearly escaped her when Tosanna heaved the rock past him. He fired at the sound, half turning from her. She stepped in and hit him with the metal-bound length of wood, hit him again behind the head when he went to his knees.

He folded over, pistol arm outflung. She waited a long moment and, when he didn't move, eased around and dropped the singletree, exchanging it for the gun.

For a while Tosanna watched him breathe wet sand against his tongue; two needles had pierced it through. If she followed tribal custom, she would spread-eagle this man, staking him down so he would live for days in agony and think upon what he had done to her. He would remember the dead Comanches while he fought his bindings and his eyes swelled shut, his tongue turned black.

But the other Comancheros might trail them this far, if they had the stomach for coming so close to the Kweharenuh camp. They would release him by a pistol shot. He twitched and Tosanna knew she could not leave this man to suffer so.

Earing back the pistol's hammer, she shot him cleanly through the head. She would have done the same to a crippled horse.

For those who might discover this *tejano,* she left a sign: a single gold piece braced between his teeth, so it would be known he died of greed.

Now she could carry the coins and jewels in one saddlebag, but Tosanna led the other horse anyhow. A watersoaked bandana around her swelling hand, she pointed her horse for the hills and home. Her medicine had been bad, for herself and the Antelope band, and the time of snows would come down hard upon her people.

She rode steadily, stopping only once at a spring to water the horses and work at embedded cactus spines with her teeth. Tosanna drank water but ate nothing from the saddlebags. She kept the rifle across her lap and the pistol in her belt. Although she had gone long without sleeping, cold winds and pain in her hand kept her awake and alert.

When Quanah himself rode out to meet her, Tosanna passed him the lead rope and slumped. She was weary. Saying nothing, he led the way into camp, and men who watched them come began to slash their hair and women wailed in mourning, for she rode alone.

Far off, at the edge of the Llano Estacado, Walker Fairbairn rode slowly, checking every foot of ground for sign. It was difficult, since one trail often cut another and he couldn't sort out Charity's from the rest.

Now he figured he might. Where other sign began to arrow straight for the tangled ridges ahead, one set of tracks wandered, uncertain of direction. That would be Charity, he thought, and jogged his horse beside scuff marks in the sand.

From his left came the flat crack of a rifle, and another; soldiers coming upon fleeing prisoners who tried to stand and fight. Fight, hell; more like rabbits standing to wolves —old men, women, and children against Griffen's cavalry troop.

Not his worry, but Charity was. What distorted reasoning led her to free Comanche prisoners and run with them? They were kin to the warriors who had raped and driven her mad. Maybe in her twisted thinking she was liberating herself.

More rifle fire came from ahead. Griffen's patrol wasn't only shooting at resisters; they were butchering Indians in a blood orgy. It was easier to kill them than herd them back. The son of a bitch; Walker should have gunned him and be damned. Concentrating upon Charity's track, he had to slow or lose them, and when close-up shots rang out just over a rise, Walker went to earth. Then he heard troopers shout and remounted to flag his hat high in the air and ride in the open. Since Griffen's men were throwing down on anything that moved, he didn't want to catch a bullet by mistake.

Troopers turned his way but relaxed when he yelled and waved his hat. Nearer, he saw the lieutenant himself among them as Griffen lowered a smoking carbine and bragged that he got them both, bigod; how was that for shooting? When Sergeant Abel Greenlee saw Walker, he held out empty hands palm up and shook his head.

"Well, now," Griffen said, "seems like the great scout hasn't done near the job we have."

Lifting in his stirrups, Walker shaded his eyes with his hat brim and stared out across a brushy flat where two horses were beginning to graze, their saddles empty. "Thought the Comanches were afoot."

"Stole a few horses," Griffen said smugly.

"That paint horse looks familiar," Walker said, and loped his mount onto the flat. A cold warning snaked up his spine when he definitely recognized the paint as Saba's. Damn— not the Tonk scout shot down by a trigger-happy bastard.

And who else?

Stiff-legged, Walker swung off his horse and reached to turn over a body. It was Saba, come so long and far only to die from an ally's bullet. Walker's gut tightened when he made out a tangle of blanket in the mesquite. Dear God, no—it couldn't be.

But it was, her face smoothed of trouble and eyes gone gentle in death—Charity Crawford. Walker knelt to close those eyes and cross her hands upon her breasts. It seemed to take him forever, and when the troopers rode up, the sound of horses' hooves were spaced and deliberate drumbeats.

One by one, Walker heaved the words up at Griffen: "You killed Saba for bringing her in. You killed her too."

Griffen squeezed his carbine. "I never knew—an acci-
dent—they were coming at us together—"

"You didn't make certain; you didn't even check."

Griffen glanced around at his blank-faced men. "I took
proper military measures. They shouldn't have come at us
without warning from the direction of the enemy."

"Enemy," Walker said.

"It's not like they were important. One filthy Indian more
or less, and as for her—crazy woman, traitor, Comanche
lover—she's better off dead."

"Abel Greenlee," Walker said, "best you all back off."

"Wait now," Greenlee said. "You know the colonel—"

"Anybody stands with this stupid, murdering son of a
bitch takes his chance," Walker said.

"Jesus," the black sergeant said.

Griffen's face was mottled with rage as he brought
his carbine around.

Walker shot him twice in the heart and knocked him off
the horse.

The soldiers didn't move, and Walker said, "Yes or no?"

Abel Greenlee sat very still and his troopers copied him.
He said, "Ain't nobody loved that man, but he a U.S. officer. Ol' colonel, I expect he mighty mad when us goes back
'thout fightin' you. That how it be though. Lord, lord."

"Miss Charity and Saba—"

"Us take care of 'em proper."

"Tell Dobe not to track me."

Carefully, Abel Greenlee pushed back his campaign hat.
"Don't reckon he be willin' nohow. Man, you can't go back
and let ol' colonel hang you; nothin' ahead but them mountains and Quanah Parker. Horse soljers one side, Comanch
the other, your tail in a crack spang in the middle. Me,
now—I be takin' my chance with the colonel."

Backing off, Walker holstered his pistol but kept his hand
on the butt. Easy and watchful, he lifted to his saddle and
walked the horse off without looking again at the bodies;
he couldn't.

When he reached the foothills of the Llano Estacado, he
pointed west to circle them. Sergeant Greenlee was right;
any cavalry patrol for hundreds of miles would soon be on
the lookout for him; if telegraph wires were cut, heliograph
mirrors would flash the news quicker than Comanche smoke
signals. If he managed to make it through Comancheria and

beat the army, he stood a chance of reaching California and disappearing there.

Just now he didn't much give a damn one way or the other. It seemed he poisoned everyone he touched, put the mark of death on them, and he was sick of killing. Once out of here he would leave blood and death to soldiers and Comanches.

To Griffen's kind and Tosanna's tribe.

CHAPTER 43

One by one, Quanah bit cactus spines from her hand. Her jaws ached from holding in pain and misted eyes betrayed her, but Tosanna made no sound.

"Only a few small-knives left," Quanah said. "You were brave to grasp the cactus."

Tosanna said, "There was no other way. I am ashamed, my chief; my medicine was bad, and warriors fell."

"Even the bravest may be trapped by ambush. Comancheros no longer fear to cheat us, for they think we will soon be gone."

Sighing with relief, Tosanna submerged her hand in a clay pot of heated water. "Will we?"

Quanah looked into her eyes. "When you first returned, you said we cannot win against the White Eyes. This is so, for every man's hand is against us—*mexicano, tejano*, the Apache, and lowly Tonkawa, Long Knife, Buffalo Soldier. My heart knows sorrow because of this."

She put her good hand upon his forearm and battle scars there. "Then we must surrender."

"Not until the spirits turn their faces from us—not until we have eaten the last horse and fired the last ammunition. Only then will the Kwehar-enuh lay down their arms."

"Many will die," Tosanna murmured.

"They die as The People, proud and unafraid, the fortunate ones. When we bow our necks upon the reservation, the Comanche nation itself will be dead."

Blanket around his shoulders, Quanah smoked his pipe

387

of clay and reed, his face sad. Tosanna said, "If we do not take their wives and children, if our warriors do not mount their women, White Eyes and *tejanos* may not pursue as far or fight as fiercely."

He stared at her. "But that has always been the way, even among the Apache and Tonkawa. It is so with the Kiowa."

"Not with whites, my chief." She had to use the English word: "*Rape* enrages them."

Quanah sucked smoke and said, "And you."

"And me. I am not as before. Now a man who rapes me steals a part of my soul and shames me before the spirits."

He nodded and drew upon his pipe. "This is strange, but I will think upon it. Your stay among *inglés* has changed you and made you wise."

"It is said that Quanah's white blood makes him wise also. I do not believe this, for I found little wisdom among them." But much hate, Tosanna thought, and scorn for any not exactly like them. Sunhair refused her because she was Comanche—a stupid thing, when their bodies cried out for each other. But he belonged in that other world, and her reality was here in the twilight of her people.

"I yet have gold and jewels," she said.

"We cannot eat them," Quanah said.

"If I took the wagon—"

"You would have to drive alone and unprotected, one Comanche woman where warriors failed."

"Still, I can try."

He shook his head and tapped ash from the pipe against the heel of his hand. "And lose. I need your knowledge of White Eyes."

"You are my chief," she said, and wondered why she did not call him husband.

They moved next morning, loaded horses dragging travois through shallow wet snow, climbing higher into the mountains to more easily defended camps. That afternoon, after tepees went up and needed fires were started, two mules were butchered and boys set snares for any small animal.

Here the cold bit at them and winds were sharp edged, but smoke rose almost unseen against snowy gray spires of rock. Hunters ranged far and took great care to cover their tracks, but returned with only one tough old buffalo bull. Deer were scarce this high up, and rabbits wary. A wakened bear clawed a hunter, who dragged back to camp and died.

Bundled women picked certain leaves and stripped tree bark to boil with bones. Camp dogs vanished and the horse herd was depleted. Hunger stalked The People and cold continued to attack.

"We must go down," Quanah said to Tosanna. "When we cook fish bones and quarrel over the carcass of a bird, the Kwehar-enuh are desperate."

"Buffalo Soldiers still patrol," she reminded him. "This time of snows, they do not stay warm in their camps as before."

"It is their chief," Quanah said. He had long been without tobacco, and lipped his pipe stem from habit. "This Mackenzie is strong and always seeks a fight. When he comes upon a Comanche camp, he burns all and kills all—even the horses. Yet we must go down the Llano Estacado."

Two infants died on the way down, and their mothers sorrowed and slashed their arms, for the dead had been man children. But the valley Quanah chose was rich with moss and dry grasses beneath the snow, and horses prospered. Upon them hunters and fighters went out again.

Quanah led them against a patrol of Buffalo Soldiers. He struck hard and swiftly, and rode away with a supply mule while they counted their dead.

This was Quanah's way and wise, for he would not meet Long Knives in a head-on battle. His riders circled bluecoat columns and nipped at them, pinching off a man here, a horse there. All through the winter the Kwehar-enuh counted coup and lost but few braves.

But each fallen warrior was a catastrophe, a loss not made up, for all other bands shivered and begged against starvation on reservations. And Mackenzie's determined troopers plodded steadily after Quanah, never giving rest, allowing no time for hunting, so bellies of The People were always flat.

Quanah no longer took captives, nor did his men mutilate and torture, for time was precious and better used. No white women were raped or otherwise brutalized. When *tejanos* learned of this, fewer took the field against the Antelope band, but the black riders never slackened pursuit. They came down upon Quanah's camp and methodically destroyed tepees, blankets hastily dropped, meat being smoked, and all Comanches who did not get away. With

Quanah, Tosanna watched heartsick from a ridgetop as most of their horse herd was shot down.

"The time grows close," Quanah said. His face had thinned and there were deep lines about his mouth. Old and tired, his sunken eyes were sad. "Perhaps we can remain at war until the next time of snows, but then—"

"Never could they defeat Quanah in battle," she said. "And if they did not slaughter the buffalo until there are no more, if the iron horse did not bring ever more soldiers—"

"Ah," he said, "and if the Kwehar-enuh did not capture my mother, I would not be born Comanche. That was the will of the spirits, and so is our defeat. Soon I will send a warrior to Mackenzie and ask truce. You will be needed for talk between us."

"Quanah," she said, "the gold and jewels—"

"I have thought on them, wife. White Eyes overly prize them, so they will help the tribe, buy cows to replace our buffalo. If the path of the Comanche is closed, now shall they walk the road of the white man, and not become beggars."

"Be careful," Tosanna said. "There are many thieves among them. Trust no man's word and do not pay until proper goods are delivered."

He looked down at the empty bowl of his pipe. "You will remain as medicine woman, and advise us."

"Yes," she said, thinking he should never doubt that.

Late clouds scudded across the sky as Walker Fairbairn pushed his horse through foothills of the Comanche winter grounds. Spring rains had dusted the desert with new bright green and brought forth flowers to briefly show celebrant colors before summer sun browned them. Now they gave generously of perfume, spicing the washed air.

He was staying to the hills because he would be more easily seen on the plains and, in another day, would have to chance a dash as he peeled away from the Llano Estacado and headed due west. So far he hadn't cut Comanche sign, but he remembered the advice of Dobe Davis: When you ain't seein' Comanch, they're watchin' you.

He missed Dobe already—his first true friend, his only friend and mentor. He had learned much from the old scout, not only desert lore to save his life, but also a slow and easy philosophy that took each day as it came and laid mistakes only to the maker.

A rare spring glinted ahead, clear, sweet water that would dry up only weeks from now. It was tucked into a gully carpeted by new grass good for his horse. Walker stepped down and hobbled the horse, loosened the cinch, and slipped off the bridle. Refilling two canteens, he settled back and divided his thin ration of jerky and pone, saving half for tomorrow, when he might have to divide it again. He couldn't hunt; firing a shot anywhere near here was risky, for the Comanche would surely be ranging down from their cold heights.

Walker tried to think on them, to figure what their hunters might do, whether Quanah Parker would continue to run or send forth more lightning raids. But the image of Charity Crawford crowded in and he couldn't banish her forever. It was something he had to live with. Being sorry couldn't bring her back. Gunning Lieutenant Griffen didn't either, but made Walker feel he was doing *something*. And if ever a man needed killing, it was Griffen.

Everybody killed—everyone died, and none of it made sense. Once he'd run from that basic truth, but it was like running on a giant roulette wheel—the same stupid thing always came up: color it red for blood, black for death.

And what color was bigotry, what delicate shades cloaked fear and hate? Tosanna's color was golden brown, and what was so damned superior about pinkish white? Shoot a black cavalryman, a Comanche, a white officer, and all their blood ran scarlet.

Now was a hell of a time to accept that concept. He wished—oh, he wished many things: that he had never denied Tosanna, that he'd never left home, or left England, or loved Charity, or killed a man.

He was drowsy and between clouds; the sun was warming; mingled scents of horse sweat and crushed grass were pleasant. Walker told himself not to nod off; soon he must move on.

Maybe the horse alerted him, maybe his own senses—but a moment too late. Starting up from the ground, pistol half drawn, Walker tried to roll away from a smash to the head. The blow downed him, and the next exploded through his brain and turned it black.

When he came to, he was sick. Roped belly down across his horse, his belly heaved from the painful, swaying bob of his head and he threw up. Incongruously, he thought first of the food he'd just wasted, and next of his life.

Twisting a bit, he could just make out the broad back of a Comanche leading the horse. Walker had to flop back and stare at blurring ground, and that didn't help his queasiness, so he closed his eyes. That was only a little better. Damn, he'd played the fool and let an Indian slip up on him, and it was a pure marvel that the redskin hadn't finished the job and taken his scalp.

Why was he being hauled back? Word had spread that Quanah Parker stopped taking prisoners long ago. The Comanches must have something special in mind for him—like long, exquisite torture. Walker fought the rope until he retched again and gave up. His head felt like a great, bruised melon and blood had dried on his cheek.

Consciousness came and went, light and dark, pain and sweet blankness, and always that nauseating rolling. Walker thought his tongue swelled and was choking him; he tried to force it down and struggled for air. When the Comanche loosed the rope and let him fall to earth, Walker welcomed the thump.

He lay staring closely at a clump of grass and heard voices, the overlapping sounds of an excited camp. When he slowly straightened his legs and rolled onto his side, his arms ached behind his back. Walker could see moccasins and deerskin leggings. Somebody kicked him in the chest; he grunted and curled against the pain.

Someone else yelled harshly, and hands dragged him along the ground like a deer carcass. The gutting would come, he thought; it would surely come.

Rough hands propped him against a lance driven into the earth. His hat long lost, Walker tried to clear his face of fallen hair by rolling his head. That was a mistake; he choked back sickness. If he hadn't lived like much of a man, he could do his damnedest to die like one.

Hard and guttural, the Comanche language broke around him as warriors argued. Walker thought they were discussing the most painful way to torture him and tried to focus on some act that would make them kill him quickly.

Then a man squatted before him and held his head up by the hair. He said something in border Spanish, but Walker could catch only a few words. He blinked at the big gaunt Comanche and the man changed to rusty, accented English.

"I am Quanah. You are Yellow Head, scout for Mackenzie."

Thick-lipped, Walker said, "Yes." These Comanches evidently had good military intelligence. He wouldn't have believed it, but who would imagine this man and his ragged band could defy all a crack cavalry regiment could throw at them?

"I speak with you," Quanah said, and made a motion. A chill knife blade kissed Walker's wrists as his hands were freed. A surly, heavy-shouldered warrior flung the knife to quiver in the ground beside Walker's leg. He picked it up and cut rope from his ankles. The wide man must be his captor, and for a stretched-tight moment, Walker considered going for him with the knife. It would bring swift, clean death.

But if Quanah wanted to parley there must be a reason, and some kind of hope. Walker stuck the blade back into the earth and tried to rise. It took several tries and no Comanche stooped to help. Once on his feet, he was still groggy and off balance, staggering like a drunkard while Indian women laughed and pelted him with dirt and stones.

His legs were stronger when Quanah reached a tepee off from the rest, and when Walker stopped, he braced them and cleared hair from his eyes. He winced at the cut bump on his left temple; the back of his head hurt more.

"Here," Quanah said, and would have motioned Walker inside, but the tepee flap swung back and she ducked out.

Walker's knees went weak again. "My god," he said. "Tosanna!"

CHAPTER 44

She caught at tepee skins for balance. Dirtied and bloody though he was, she knew immediately it was Sunhair. His golden hair and sky-blue eyes, the soft curve of his mouth almost like a woman's—*Sunhair!*

Her tongue would not work and she only stared until Quanah said, "Wife, this White Eye speaks your name."

"Y-yes," she murmured. "I-I knew him once, in the far land of England." Walker Fairbairn should have aged, wrinkled, gone heavy at the middle, for it seemed lifetimes past when she had seen him. But he had not. The slim body that had lain against hers ever since, if only in dreams —it was the same. Only when she looked closely she saw the eyes were different; they had known pain not of the body.

"He is no guest," Quanah said, "but Yellow Head, a scout for Mackenzie who leads Tonkawas against The People."

Inadvertently, she said, "Sunhair."

Quanah glanced sharply at her. "So, Sunhair."

Walker swayed and her hands came up to help him, but dropped back to her sides. As if he had not noticed, Quanah motioned, and she drew back so Walker could enter the tepee. Without asking, she followed. Again Quanah looked at her and his face softened.

"Water then," he said. "Allow him drink and wash."

She felt Sunhair's eyes, sadder and wiser, follow her quick moves, and her hands shook when she gave him a water gourd. She was being a fool, for nothing escaped Quanah, but the shock of seeing Sunhair unnerved her and she could not think straight.

Oh, how she wanted to bathe his head and clean the hair she had so often kissed. How she needed to hold him close and tell him all would be well. She dared not, and outside in the camp warriors muttered. Only Quanah's power held them from killing this man, and he could change at any moment.

Crouching back upon the sparse and worn fur couch, she was fascinated with Walker's hands, the way they moved over his face; never had water seemed so like jewels, falling liquid from his slim fingers.

"Sunhair," Quanah said, the name strange in his mouth, "my wife will speak your language better than I, but it is Quanah who makes the words. You understand?"

Without being told, Tosanna slid forward on her knees, her traitor fingers trying to smooth her hair, to cool her warmed cheeks. She interpreted, her voice weak and uncertain but gaining strength.

Quanah said, looking into Walker's face: "Mackenzie has almost won, but it has not been his doing alone. White hunters killed the buffalo, so there is no meat to feed us. Once there were so many buffalo that no man could count them. I have seen them flow past a camp like a mighty river for days on end. Now they are gone. My hunters return with tales of bones far as the eye can carry, and wasted meat where only vultures eat.

"My heart is sad. Children die and few are born. Women cut off fingers and warriors shear their hair. There is no glory for the young and only the telling of dreams for the few old men left."

Tosanna spoke her husband's words into English for her lover. Sunhair nodded and his fingers searched his shirt to bring forth a crumpled cigar. Breaking it, he offered half to Quanah. It was a fine gesture, she thought, one Quanah would appreciate. She was right; his lips twitched as he accepted tobacco and stuffed his pipe.

Tosanna's practiced fingers flicked an ashen ember from the sleeping fire and dropped it onto her husband's pipe. She watched Sunhair bend to light his piece of cigar; he did not flinch at heat close against his hurt face. That was also good. Her heart ached at the thought of that beauty seared by a torch or glowing knife blade.

Quanah said, "I will talk with Chief Mackenzie."

For the first time since he'd said her name, Sunhair spoke. "I cannot bring your words to Colonel Mackenzie. His soldiers seek me, for I have killed one of them, a sub-chief."

"Ah," Quanah said, and quickly Tosanna broke in: "Long Knives honor a white flag, no matter what man carries it."

"Not always," he said.

"Mackenzie wants to end the war; when the Kweharenuh go to the reservation, it is ended."

"Yes," Quanah said, "it is forever ended."

"Use this man, my chief. His hair and the white cloth—"

She dropped her eyes when Quanah said, "You have known this Sunhair well, I think. But he cannot live by my word alone; Great Son captured him."

"Ado-tua will accept your wish."

"If I ask. This man is a renegade who killed one of his own. Also, this man called Yellow Head has killed many of us."

Tosanna said, "As we killed his people. There must be a finish to it."

"Once I would deny this," Quanah said. "Now it is so, and shadows walk all Comancheria."

"I thank you, my chief." She told Sunhair with her eyes that he would live, and her lips trembled.

Quanah said, "For many sleeps, you have not called me husband. You have been dutiful and worthy, and much help, but I think this man always lived in your heart."

She kept her eyes down and did not answer. Quanah stood up, drawing a worn blanket about himself. "I sleep in the tepee of my other wives. When my warriors bring news of Mackenzie, this man will carry the flag and my words."

The tepee flap rose and fell; Quanah was gone and tears came to Tosanna's eyes. Was there ever such a warrior, such a man? It was fitting he should be the last great Comanche war chief.

Sunhair said, "There's a presence about him, a lordliness no peer in England can match."

She let out a long breath. "You are safe for now. But you must carry a truce to Mackenzie and say that Quanah will talk. He will surrender, but they must allow him to keep his dignity."

Walker drank her in through every pore of his body. Here in her own environment Tosanna was more beautiful than ever, a true princess with none of the glitter of Milady Savage about her. He wanted to tell her this, to pour forth all that had been dammed up in him for so long. But though he knew one part of her so well, this was another woman, and perhaps he did not know himself.

So he said, "Quanah Parker's picking a good time to quit. Mackenzie should be coming up .with the Fourth Cavalry and wagon infantry—about six hundred men. Colonel Miles is ahorse toward the Arkansas River, and two more columns underway along the Red and out of New Mexico, and six companies of Texas Rangers to patrol any exposed flank."

"Always *tejanos*," she said with a curl of lips he longed to kiss. Her hair glistened and there was magic in the pulse of her throat. Watching it eased his own aches and bruises.

"This time there were no treaties, only submission. Every tribe will be pursued and harried—Kiowa, Arapaho, Cheyenne, and especially Comanche. This time they cannot leave the old, the women and children safe behind; those will die on the trail."

Tosanna said, "We already die; Quanah surrenders because of this."

"If it's not a trick."

"Quanah never lies; that is left to White Eyes."

"I didn't lie to you," he said. Nor to Charity Crawford and himself? There were lies of omission, of self-deception.

"You did not have to," Tosanna said. "I wanted to believe more than you offered."

"You blamed me for the duke's death."

"I know now his spirits called him. Then I hated us for bringing him early to his time."

Entranced by the play of her lips, the velvet blackness of her eyes, on another level Walker was nagged by guilt. Had he brought Charity early to her death? If he hadn't made love to her, would the wagon and escort have safely passed the Comanche ambush?

"I have often been a fool," he said. "I hope to be wiser —with your help."

"My help, Sunhair? I am only a woman, a savage Comanche."

Walker looked away; it was difficult to think clearly

while this woman filled his eyes. "I can't right all wrongs,
but I'll try not to make the same mistakes."

Like judging the stature of a man by color. In any company Sergeant Abel Greenlee would stand tall, and Buffalo
Soldiers were perhaps the best cavalry in the world, except
for Comanches. And was white valor superior to Comanche? Old Fleabite, Saba—so many brave men on both
sides. Yes, and brave women too. In this inevitable, insane
war, numbers and weapons and supply counted more than
courage, and that was sad.

Tosanna stared at him and found sorrows, a thoughtful-
ness he had not shown before. She brought a water gourd
and a precious bit of cloth. Cleansing his face and hair of
dried blood, she shivered at the heat and closeness of him.
How she wanted him, how she needed him.

He said, "Quanah Parker is your man now."

She rinsed and wrung out the rag, then salved his wounds
with such herbs as she had left. "Eat," she said, "if you can
stomach what we have. The Kwehar-enuh lost nearly all
their horses to Buffalo Soldiers. Unable to hunt, we have
lasted the winter by eating what might be found—nuts,
grubs, mice. This night we will feast upon your horse."

"I'm not hungry," he said.

"We are always hungry," Tosanna said. "Yes, Sunhair, I
am Quanah's wife, and would have been if I had the choice.
Does this bother you also—that I have lain with a savage?
Proud Sunhair, so certain his *man's* way is best."

"Is Quanah any different?"

"He walks his own trail, as you and I must."

He said, "Why did you return to—to this? After riches
and comfort in England? I was forced to come back, but
you—"

"I returned to help my people, to once more be Comanche."

"Did you help, are you fully Comanche?"

Tosanna added a handful of bark to the flickering fire.
"Perhaps I only prolonged suffering, but here I am not
scorned for the numbers or colors of men I have slept with.
I am no longer pure Comanche; now I am shamed by every
man who raped me, and there have been many. I know
The People cannot fight on, that the whites are many as
leaves on the trees, but my heart, my blood, tells me to
stand and die a Comanche; it will be better than living as
the white man's dog."

For a while Sunhair was silent, and Tosanna refused to touch him again. Then he said, "I am a man come late to manhood, Tosanna, named renegade for gunning a man who killed a woman who once carried my child. He might have thought she was Indian, but she's just as dead."

She listened, hearing of a white woman driven mad by rape and pain. Sunhair's woman, she thought, and mother to his son, but for Comanches. But his own kind had murdered her, as her people shot Ned Barstow. It did not matter which side killed most or set brighter fires. It was all blind agony, and must stop.

He said then, "I'm grateful you saved my life."

"Your own soldiers may take it. If the price of surrender includes giving you over, Quanah will not hesitate."

She thought his smile was sad. He said, "Then I will have lived this much longer, and I have seen you again."

"Against all we have spoken, is that important?"

"Nations may war and fall and, learning nothing, war again, but the truth of love will last."

Leaning over knotted hands pressed into her body, Tosanna said, "You say *love* to me, Sunhair? You do not owe me this in exchange for your life."

"I owe you for all things warm and tender, if I am to know them. Whatever happens between our people, for good or bad, I wanted you to hear this."

Tosanna bit her lip so hard she thought it would bleed, and her mouth went dry as summer desert. "I—I am glad."

Then the cold, hard thing she had carried hidden for so long broke within her, and she reached out to him. She reached for this boy-man with the tongue of birds who had once refused to hurt small animals and had joyed in women without commitment or responsibility. And when she touched him, what he had since become dissolved—wary scout, swift, heartless killer, friend to none and a danger to all.

He became an older, much wiser Sunhair. She loved him. She had always loved him, but now there was reason.

Although he was hurt and she was worn lean by hunger and defeat, Tosanna drew him to her, and they lay upon the tepee couch as if this were their marriage night, as if they were turned young and unafraid and knowing their bodies for the first time.

He was beautiful; he was gentle as no man had been before, and smoothed away the shame other men had done her. She tasted the spices of his mouth upon her tongue, and her mound joyously received him, oiling and enfolding him.

Theirs was the rhythm of stars, of forever springtime, and the bloodbeat of eternal life celebrating itself. Calm and steady, yet aching and hungry, she blended her body with his and felt him giving her the newness of his soul.

No tepee enclosed them and no sounds of war reached their ears where they traveled together, one with earth and sky and their mother, the wind. She took them higher than man and woman had ever reached, and as soaring butterflies they broke themselves against the face of God.

CHAPTER 45

Tosanna's hand warmed him against harsh reality beyond the tepee flap. Out there waited hunters and prey, the eaters and those to be eaten. Inside there was love.

"Quanah Parker's couch, his wife," he said.

She held him a little tighter. "Last night he left me with you. He will not speak against what we have done."

If Quanah Parker changed his mind, and threw him to the starved-mean, frustrated warriors for torture, Walker would understand. If the war chief didn't, there were still Colonel Mackenzie and thousands of alert troopers crisscrossing the Great Plains throughout what once was Comancheria. Behind Mackenzie swung a hangman's rope sized to Walker's neck.

Lifting Tosanna's hand, he presented it to his cheek, his lips. In silence and peace she comforted him, but he released her hand. It would not do to drag her down with him. In time she could leave the reservation where the last Comanches would be driven and take up her life again.

"The white woman," she murmured, and haltingly Walker told her of Charity Crawford. The story was a purging, and when it was done he did not blame himself so much. Charity would never be forgotten, nor the child she had never known, but she would not weigh as heavily upon him.

For as long as he had, Walker thought. Any time now, Quanah Parker's warriors would spy a cavalry column. Skulking afoot because all their horses had been shot, they would still find Long Knives before they themselves were seen.

Then he would raise a white flag and walk forward to speak for Quanah Parker and be arrested for killing Lieutenant Griffen. That the murdering swine sorely needed killing wouldn't matter; the law had been broken and eye-for-an-eye payment was demanded.

As this last surviving band of Comanches must submit to white man's law and no longer defend ancestral lands. Their transgression was monumental: they had delayed westward expansion and progress and greed. For this there could be no forgiveness.

Tosanna said, "I will speak for Quanah instead. You hide, and when the chance comes, run."

"He didn't ask you," Walker said. "The soldiers may not listen to a woman—even the medicine woman of the Comanches. They won't come in as fast when they see my hair."

"But they mean to punish you, kill you." She put her hand upon his arm and this time he didn't shake it off. All they had was now, when eternity would not be enough. For bringing him to this realization, he owed Quanah Parker—not for his life, but for a greater treasure, love.

He said, "I've hidden from myself too much already, and run before the wind—any wind. I have been a child, and it's time to become a man."

Tosanna took away her hand. "Do you think women see men through the same eyes? Though Kwehar-enuh women praise warriors, in their hearts they want live husbands, not heroic dead. I will ask Quanah to speak for him."

She was so beautiful, so fiery, and had a strength to her no other could match. Tosanna deserved strength in return, and Walker would have told her so, but for Quanah Parker ducking into the tepee.

Looking closely at Tosanna, Quanah Parker smiled, then turned a serious face to Walker. "Buffalo Soldiers come."

Through Tosanna Walker said, "Better the Fourth Cavalry than new soldiers who do not know and respect the Comanches."

Quanah said, "There is little difference when you are trapped between the bear and the wolf."

Nodding, Walker said, "There will be no peace terms, as with other tribes, no presents. Now you must choose between surrender or war to the death."

The great chief looked down, and Tosanna's mouth quivered. Then Quanah said, "This I know, and we would make war if there was a way. The children cry with empty bellies; old men lie down and never get up; warriors are weak and very tired; we have lost our horses. Now we must walk the path of the White Eyes, wherever it leads."

Tosanna's eyes misted, but she refused to shame her chief by crying. She said softly, "I would take this man's place when the Long Knives come."

"And leave his side?" Quanah asked.

"Only to let him live."

His eyes looked into hers, and through them to her heart and soul. For an instant, she thought he was going to caress her, but this was not the way of the Comanche.

His voice was gentle as he said, "You are strong and brave, Tosanna. When you were named, the spirits must have been watching, for now you are truly the last flower of the Kwehar-enuh. You deserve to live free as you were born. Although your heart has changed, you returned to our people, bringing wealth and knowledge and yourself."

"My chief, I—"

"No," Quanah said gently. "I say neither you nor Yellow Head may speak for Quanah, war chief of the Comanches. I will meet the Buffalo Soldiers myself."

Tosanna pressed the back of her hand to her mouth. "But they—they might fire on you."

"Then it is the will of the spirits," he said.

"Wait," Tosanna said. "Here is the bag of gold and jewels we could not exchange for guns and food. Take it, Quanah; hold it close and learn how the White Eyes worship wealth. Then trade wisely and well, and no man will ever spit on the Kwehar-enuh and name them dogs who beg."

He sat cross-legged on the ground as a sentry shouted outside the tepee. He said then, "Take enough for yourself and this man. I will remember your words and buy life for our people. But you must also live, and this man you love."

A tear escaped her eye and slid down Tosanna's cheek. "You are the greatest of chiefs, the greatest of men."

Now Quanah surprised her. He took her hand. "Go now, Last Flower. Behind the tepee, Older Man waits with two horses—the only horses we have left. Take them and ride to the north or toward the setting sun."

"But you—you *must* meet your enemies horseback. To walk before them—"

"Pride cannot feed an empty belly; time and the law changes." He dropped her hand and squared his shoulders as he stood erect.

Walker Fairbairn said, "What is it, Tosanna? Why is he—"

"Come with me," she said. "Quanah, last war chief of the Comanches, makes us presents of our lives, yours and mine. Quickly, Sunhair—do not shame him by refusing."

"Damn it—"

She pushed him outside where Quanah walked tall and proud to gather the remnants of his once mighty tribe. Quanah did not look back, and somehow Tosanna knew he never would, that this man among men would yet control his own destiny.

Older Man held their horses. Giving reins to Tosanna, he said, "I obey him in all things but one." Drawn to bone and sinew, the stubborn warrior stared at her and murmured, "You were right, woman. Quanah is right, but it is too late for change. I do not carry all the Kwehar-enuh upon my back, as he must. I am responsible only for myself."

"Farewell," Tosanna said. "May the spirits be kind to you."

She led the way around a ridge and up a narrow draw to where low trees gave them shelter. Faintly, she heard the singing, and Walker said, "What's that? What's he doing?"

"That is Older Man's death song," she answered. "When he finishes, he will fall upon his knife. May he go without pain."

"And Quanah Parker?"

She looked down upon the camp and saw the white flag lifted, saw her people walk to meet oncoming black cavalry. "He still leads," Tosanna said. "It is more difficult than dying."

Walker said, "I should—"

"Live out time he gave us," she said, and turned her horse down through the brush.

He looked down the slope a moment longer, then moved his mount to follow. Slipping through the military ring that would soon get word of the surrender, they would find peace in Canada or California. The place didn't matter, so long as they were together.

Watching her slim figure rock with the horse's slow

rhythm, Walker knew it was not too late to put their lives together again.

When they had put miles between themselves and the destruction of the Comanche nation, he moved his horse up beside hers. For a long way they rode quietly, almost stirrup to stirrup.

He tried to know her loss and share it. He had been long without a family, living tightly within the cramped confines of himself. It was good to share with another human being, even sorrow. Leaning near, Walker Fairbairn took her hand.

Tosanna drew a deep and settling breath. There was a sour odor to defeat, and when hope died it left only a fading bitterness to lie brassy upon the tongue.

But there were other smells, for it was springtime. Nostrils flared, she drank of green births and new grass and exultant buddings. Winter did not bring eternal death, only sleep.

When the time of snows passed, as it always did, the land reaffirmed itself. A warrior fell; a child was born. For each death song, there came a new hymn to life.

As Quanah said, she was in truth the Last Flower of the Comanches. But no more would she have to stand alone and lonely.

When Sunhair took her hand, she clung tightly to his, and smiled.

EPILOGUE

Last Comanche chief to surrender, thirty-year-old Quanah led his ragged, starving Kwehar-enuh onto the Fort Sill, Oklahoma, reservation. Other Indian leaders had been hanged, shot, or jailed for long terms, deported to Florida.

But Quanah had never parleyed with whites, never put his mark on treaty paper, and was born to a white mother. He had gained the respect of his enemies.

No other leader made the transition to "civilized" life so well. Though he spoke little English, he was soon valuable help to the Indian agent and spokesman for all Comanches and Kiowas on the reservation. Yet he was no "tame injun," and walked as proudly in defeat as in triumph.

The buffalo were gone, never to return, but huge long-horn herds were being headed for Kansas railheads. The shortest route lay through the reservation, and Quanah arranged for one dollar a head toll. This helped his people start their own herds.

Later he made a fortune for himself and his tribe leasing grazing lands to powerful Texas ranchers. He became a major stockholder in a railroad, lived in a twelve room "Comanche White House," and had a town named for him. Along the way he was elected deputy sheriff of Lawton, Oklahoma, and appointed criminal judge for the reservation, where he blended Comanche tradition and White Eyes law to everyone's satisfaction.

Ever struggling to protect and enrich his people, Quanah traveled often to Washington and met Presidents during his long legal battle to hold reservation lands together. He shared hunts and mutual respect with Theodore Roosevelt. Now he spoke and wrote English, sometimes with a certain poetry, and often showed wry humor—as when the High Commissioner of Indian Affairs ordered Quanah to choose but one wife from eight he married and send all others away. Quanah shrugged and said: *"You* tell them to go."

Surely, some part of his white blood called to him, for when he knew barely enough words to ask the way, and was armed only with a letter from the Indian agent at Fort Sill, Quanah set out to search for his mother's family. The trail was difficult, and beset with danger for him; many *tejano* memories were long and unforgiving.

He found his mother's kin in East Texas and slept in the bed once hers. The rest of his life he carried with him a tintype of Cynthia Ann Parker and his baby sister. Later, with government permission and financing, they were reburied in a little corner of once mighty Comancheria, where Quanah Parker—he took his surname proudly now —was to lie beside them.

Although he admitted "the Jesus Road is good," he never became Christian, although his son, White Parker, had become a Methodist minister. When he lay dying of pneumonia, he wore the full dress of a Comanche war chief, his last moments not attended by priest or preacher, but a spirit talker.

The spirit talker stood over him, making the hand motions that symbolized the flight of an eagle, a great chief's journey to the Comanche afterworld.

There beside the graves of his mother and sister, a monument stands: *Resting here until day breaks and darkness disappears, is Quanah Parker, last chief of the Comanches. Died Feb. 21, 1911, age 64 years.*

The reservation is now a nuclear artillery range, and perhaps the old war chief likes the sounds of guns. Sometimes, just sometimes, in a chill sky, a bright moon rises and a half-wild mustang stops to graze. It is the time of the Comanche moon.

Then, say those who yet carry blood of the Kweharenuh, the earth trembles.

41